1 MONTH OF
FREE
READING

at

www.ForgottenBooks.com

By purchasing this book you are eligible for one month membership to ForgottenBooks.com, giving you unlimited access to our entire collection of over 700,000 titles via our web site and mobile apps.

To claim your free month visit:
www.forgottenbooks.com/free789857

ISBN 978-0-483-18810-5
PIBN 10789857

FIRE AND FLAME.

FROM THE GERMAN OF

LEVIN SCHÜCKING.

TRANSLATED BY

EVA M. JOHNSON.

NEW YORK:

D. APPLETON AND COMPANY,

549 AND 551 BROADWAY.

1876.

FIRE AND FLAME.

------→—◆—→—←------

CHAPTER 1.

IN REDUCED CIRCUMSTANCES.

In the year 1851 gossip in the good old town of H., in Lower Saxony, was busy with the affairs of a family that had lately moved into the place—a family belonging to the country nobility, and formerly possessed of considerable property in the vicinity, but now very much reduced. In the course of a century, one estate after another had been sold, until at length the last was gone, and the family had moved into town—with what remained to them after the debts were paid. There, instead of mourning over their lost greatness, they seemed bent on indemnifying themselves for the forced seclusion and Asiatic *ennui* of the country life of a household in straitened circumstances.

The family consisted of three persons—Herr von Melroth, and his two daughters, Matilda, twenty-three, and Elsie, twenty-one years old, neither of them engaged, but both—so gossip declared—very much inclined to enter into an engagement. Such an inclination would, indeed, have seemed no more than natural, since the life the von Melroths were leading must soon dissipate what was left of their property, and the girls could be provided for in no other way than by marriage. And the life they led seemed, indeed, senseless enough to the gossips. They kept open house for a few young people from some of the best ourgher families, with which Herr von Melroth had formerly been acquainted. These young people spent their evenings at Herr von Melroth's whenever they pleased, with conversation, music, and social games; sometimes they had little concerts, and sometimes, when the company was a little larger than usual, they danced. And all of this with a very simple and frugal style of housekeeping!

In this quiet, uncommercial town, rents, like all other prices, were low; and Herr von Melroth, who on this account had taken up his residence in H., which was not far from Asthof, his former estate, had not needed to deny himself the luxury of a very convenient and spacious dwelling. The house he occupied had, indeed, a somewhat dismal and sunless appearance, for it faced the north; but it was a fine old patrician house. The court was quite small, and the back part of the building high; in winter its fantastic roof kept the sun from the rest of the house nearly all day. The sunlight could be seen only as it shone through the windows of this part, which contained a great banqueting-hall, occupying the entire first floor; and as this hall had on each side a row of high, uncurtained windows, the view from the front part of the house at sunset was always pleasant, and sometimes magical, when the sunlight broke through the windows on the opposite side, throwing its clear splendor or its purple glow into the antique room, lighting up some parts of it strangely, and transforming the whole into a fantastic realm. Still more peculiar was the effect when the full moon shone in from the farther side, its pale light resting on the ancient cupboards, mouldings, and furniture, and giving to the great room a weird and ghostly air; and, indeed, tradition affirmed that it was not quite canny in the old hall.

One evening in the winter of 1850–51, there was assembled in Herr von Melroth's parlor a little company of people who might called the regular guests of the house. These were an elderly gentleman, a young lady, and three young gentlemen. The most elegant-looking of the latter was tall and slender, with very prepossessing features, a remarkably fine forehead and delicate lips, around which hovered a slight expression of cynical disdain, and shrewd, fiery eyes. If this young man were really, as he said and hoped, to enter upon a diplomatic career, through the help of a rich cousin, after he should have passed the assessor's examination, then, according to the evidence of physiognomy, he must have found his appropriate calling. The second was a fine looking officer, a relative of the future diplomatist, though his name was just plain Schott, while his younger cousin was distinguished by the aristocratic *von*— Ferdinand von Schott. A physiognomist could say nothing against his face, for, with his somewhat coarse, bronzed, and thoroughly good-humored features, he looked as if he had been predestined to be a soldier, and as if he would develop, in the course of time, into a mere fighting automaton. The third was a very tall, slender, blonde young man, in a gray habit, suggesting the calling of a forester. In connection with this, his face was somewhat puzzling; for, with his great, liquid blue eyes, his fair curling hair and rather pale complexion, he looked much more like a poet, a musician, or some other art student, than like a forester or hunter. With his delicate face and the quiet grace of his movements, suggesting an indolent rather than an active nature, he could not possibly have been made to battle with the elements or take the lives of God's harmless creatures.

The young lady we have mentioned was tall and handsome, very energetic in her movements, and somewhat loud-voiced; she seemed to have arrived at that uncertain age when many young ladies develop a tendency to make their presence more emphatic, and to give to their utterances a peculiar loud jollity. The elderly gentleman was a pensioned judge, who had been a student-friend of Herr von Melroth, and often dropped in of an evening to play Boston with him. Herr von Melroth was very grateful to him for coming; for he was often not a little bored among the young people, to whom Captain Schott also joined himself, though he was near middle age. It was particularly tiresome to Herr von Melroth when they were engaged with music or with games, which gave him no chance to indulge his propensity for telling anecdotes and making harmless jokes; he was not the man to make for himself the opportunity for indulging his inclination; he was a good-humored soul, who had always allowed himself to be mastered, first by his wife, then by his increasing business difficulties, and now by his two daughters—or, rather, by one daughter; for the older, Matilda, had much of his quiet, yielding disposition, while Elsie, the younger, ruled her, their father, and the entire household.

How could she but rule the house, whose star she was? Elsie was wonderfully beautiful and brilliant, few as had been the opportunities for intellectual culture at their country home. Whence this proud, imperial blood came, this high, self-conscious nature with its brilliant gifts, in this last shoot of the von Melroth race—a race that had lived along through the centuries in peaceful mediocrity—heaven only knows!

Elsie von Melroth was tall and slender; the perfect development of her form was shown to advantage by the proud grace of her bearing, which, however, was not lacking in maidenliness; her head with its abundant black hair was carried proudly; her features were delicate, the forehead low, the nose straight and finely-cut, and the eyes of a peculiar charm. They were large and dark, and shaded by long, silky lashes; at times, when they were fully opened, their ordinary quiet and dreamy expression was exchanged for a sudden fire, that revealed a remarkably passionate nature. They were a little too round, those eyes, a little too far apart; but if any one who felt their charm thought of this as a defect, he could not but regard her face with its delicate and slightly roseate tint and its perfect oval, as a whole of extraordinary beauty.

And since, together with her beauty, Fräulein Elsie was gifted with a most keen and ready understanding, it was but natural that she should be the centre of her circle, that she should rule it, and receive universal homage. Her sister Matilda was much less beautiful; her spirit was very little like that of "Flame," as Elsie was called at the house, Herr von Schott having first given her the title. Matilda's nature resembled rather a quiet, peaceful lake, where moved the nymphs of good and pious thoughts; whether the lake was also deep, who could tell? Captain Schott, at least, seemed to think so, for he directed his attentions, which Elsie had treated with somewhat brusque disdain, to Matilda, who received them with a certain quiet, almost *naïve* readiness, as if it were a matter of course that a young lady should accept the attentions shown her with equal courteous warmth, and show herself grateful for them. She was lighter than Elsie, her hair quite light brown, her eyes blue, her complexion lighter and rosier; if her handsome sister had not thrown her into the shade, she would have been considered very pretty; but the difference between them was too great for justice to be done Matilda when her sister was present.

Elsie's acknowledged suitor was the future diplomatist, Ferdinand von Schott, though even he was not treated much better by her than his cousin, Captain Schott, had been at his first advances. However, Ferdinand seemed too deeply in love to be frightened away by such treatment. Emil Drausfeld, the mild forester, followed her every movement with his enthusiastic eyes; but this quiet youth could not be regarded as a suitor, on account of his being entirely without prospects. Still, it was he whom Elsie seemed to prefer to all others—that is, she treated him like a child, scolded and criticised him, gave him errands to do, and in return supplied him with the largest

piece of cake while her sister was serving the other guests with tea. He seemed, however, to hold his place in the circle chiefly by right of his musical talent. He played the flute and the violin, often accompanying Elsie's performances at the piano, which gave evidence of a high order of talent, though, like her other gifts, it had received but little culture during their residence in the country.

The musical performances had been almost entirely given up for a few days, for the little company was occupied with other, more important business. They were excited over the preparations for a great and bold undertaking; they were about to establish an amateur theatre, or, rather, had already established one; for the stage was as good as finished in the great hall, and the little comedy with which they were to open the theatre, and which was to be followed in the course of the winter by half-a-dozen others, was in process of preparation. The performers were gathered about a round table, before a sofa, in one corner, while the two older gentlemen were at their card-table in another. Ferdinand von Schott, who took the place of manager, was hearing Matilda rehearse her part. She seemed to be very much in need of training, for he frequently interrupted her with the exclamations, "Louder!" "More force!" or, "More fire, more fire!" repeating the passage himself, with a passionate power of voice, that was the more effective as he knew how to modulate it so perfectly as to give the impression of most complete control. His declamation was so striking that his cousin, the captain, remarked, when Matilda had finished:

"You have much more fire than I gave you credit for, Ferdinand; a future diplomatist, like you, should not be such a pent-up volcano."

"Ah!" said Ferdinand, laughing, "it was not for nothing they gave me the nickname of 'Fire' at the University. But you will admit that I have learned to control it, Alexander."

"Oh, yes, when it is a question of controlling the emotions of Fräulein Tannenheim, the beautiful character that Fräulein

Matilda has to represent, you do very well, as we have just seen. Whether you could do the same with your own—that is quite another question."

"With my own, too. Just ask Fräulein Elsie whether I do not control the volcano admirably, when she does everything to excite it to a terrible eruption."

"I?" asked Fräulein Elsie, as if at a loss to understand.

"Yes, you, fräulein, with the air of innocence. Do you not often abuse me in a way to put a lamb into a passion?"

Elsie shrugged her shoulders, and the captain said:

"And so you suppress your fire? That is very foolish, for if Fräulein Elsie is 'Flame,' then you can only succeed by showing that you are a kindred element."

"Yes, indeed; fire and flame belong together!" exclaimed Fräulein Theresa Holbrecht, the friend of the sisters, with a loud laugh.

"Do you think so?" asked Elsie. "I think kindred elements repel each other; only opposites are mutually attractive."

"That would go hard with the fire, little Flame," said Theresa, smiling.

"In spite of all, he sees his hopes fast turning into water," said Ferdinand, with a sigh. "What is to be done then?"

"Nothing, but to quench both fire and flame with this peaceable liquid," who, in the meantime, had been pouring out tea, and was now passing it around.

"Right," said the captain; "Fräulein Matilda is always the peacemaker, the mediator. Let us quench all the strife of fire and flame with this."

"Only not the flame itself," remarked Emil Dransfeld; "or what would a poor moth like me do, when deprived of the sweet privilege of circling around it and burning his wings at it?"

They laughed, as usual, at Emil's remarks, which were generally aimed at himself, with a characteristic irony, and then the two old gentlemen, who had laid aside their cards to take a cup of tea with the rest, came up and seated themselves with the young people, and Melroth said:

"I think one good thing, at least, will be accomplished by your undertaking in the great hall back there. Such a thoroughly frivolous, sinful, worldly amusement as an amateur theatre, must have as terrifying an effect on the spirits that haunt it as holy water does on the devil. Probably they will hereafter shun the room you are going to desecrate with your nocturnal amusements—which, by the way, are rather childish pleasures—and hunt up some other theatre for their performances."

"And do you call that accomplishing good?" said Ferdinand. "I think that would be depriving this fine old patrician house of one of its chief charms. What can make it more attractive and interesting than a haunted room?"

"It is a charm that, at all events, is growing rare enough," said the judge. "In my youth, we had any number of such houses in the city. In fact, there were but few—that is, real old family houses—in which something mysterious had not occurred, the key to which could be found only in the realm of the supernatural. Now, the spirits seem to have been gradually drawing together, like a tribe of Indians driven from their hunting-grounds, until finally there is no place left to them but your hall——"

"They are doomed to extinction," interrupted the captain, "if that expression can be applied to people already dead. But I believe that you, the present inhabitants of the house, have not seen or heard anything of them?"

"Oh, but we have," said Matilda, eagerly. "A few weeks ago, in looking from my chamber, which opens upon the court, I saw all the windows of the hall illuminated with a strange blue light, and shadows moving across the panes, like human forms. I told you about it the next morning, Elsie."

Elsie merely nodded, looking as if the matter did not interest her much, and passed the sugar-bowl to Emil Drausfeld.

"The bluish light was probably that of the moon, and the shadows were thrown very naturally by light clouds passing over it."

"Oh, no, no," said Matilda, clinging to her assertion. "It was not so at all. Clouds would have hidden the moon, and so have withdrawn all the light in the room; but the light remained, and the shadows were those of men; I am not mistaken; they were, in reality, very mysterious forms."

"How can any one be so superstitious, Fräulein Matilda?" said the captain.

Matilda became suddenly silent, either because she was offended at the rebuke, or because she did not want to annoy the captain. Emil Drausfeld, however, took up the conversation, and said:

"Instead of doubting Fräulein Matilda's testimony, we ought to ask the judge, who, as the oldest native of the city among us, must know something of the affair, to tell us the story of the haunted room, for the visitations of the spirits are always connected with some tragic story of their mortal existence."

"That is true," said Herr von Melroth. "So, tell us, judge, the history of our hall."

"The history of the hall?" said the old gentleman, curtly. "You are asking a great deal! Who knows all that has happened in an old building that has stood for centuries? Who could give an account of it? I would not even undertake to give a truthful and complete history of any lady's little modern boudoir! The most remarkable and interesting things that happen in the world never get into history——"

"Many things," interrupted Ferdinand, smiling, "that escape the serious Mother Clio fail to evade the gossipy Aunt Tradition."

"That is true," answered the old gentleman, "and what tradition says of your hall is, that, during the Seven Years'. War, a handsome officer was in winter quarters here, and won the heart of the daughter of the family, which was one of the oldest of the city; and that in the spring, when he was about to march away with the others, there arose great lamentation and mourning, and the girl passionately demanded—you see there were 'Flames' even then—that the officer should leave his comrades, resign his office, and remain as her husband. The young man would not consent, either because his ambition was greater than his love, or because he didn't like the idea of

taking up his residence for life in our quiet town—where perhaps even then the flies fell off the walls for very *ennui,* as they are said to do now in warm summer afternoons —or possibly the reason he gave to the incredulous girl was the true one—that he could not think of procuring his discharge now, at the beginning of a new campaign; at any rate, he tried to comfort her with the promise that he would return and take her to his home as soon as peace was declared. This rather questionable comfort did not satisfy our 'Flame;' she held to her first demand. During the evening and night before they were to march away, the officers of the regiment were assembled in your hall, to take their farewell drink, which they seem to have done very thoroughly and exhaustively. At midnight, the passionate girl burst into the hall, into the midst of the drunken officers, and stormily demanded of the colonel that he should give her lover his discharge, and forbid him to march away with the rest. She talked to the wine-heated soldiers like Clärchen, in Göethe's "Egmont," to the citizens of Brussels. They listened, at first, with puzzled surprise; then with laughter and jeers. Surrounded by these wild fellows, ridiculed, enraged, and wholly beside herself, she seized a knife from the table in her excitement, and, before any one could arrest her, she thrust it into her lover's heart, with the words, 'I will find a way to keep you from marching off!'

"The unhappy young man fell, and the girl escaped from the officers who crowded around her, down the stairs leading to the alley at the rear of the house; the men followed, in wild chase, down the streets, across the market-place, over the court of the old castle, till there, at the end of the court, where the old weir dams back the waters of the Luter, she vanished from their eyes."

"Oh!" cried Elsie, who had been listening intently, her great eyes fastened upon the narrator, "she threw herself into the water!"

"Yes. The corpse of the officer and that of the drowned girl lay in the hall the next day in their coffins; and they were buried together in the Stephanie Cemetery. This is the story as I heard it in my youth; a story of the Seven Years' War, they said then; but before that war it was told as an incident of the Thirty Years' War, and before that as one of the Smalcaldic, or some other. In reality, there were no troops wintered in our town during the Seven Years' War. In order to determine the time, it would be necessary to have some one acquainted with the costumes of different periods on hand, to examine the dress of the officers when they are at their banquet again, by the bluish light that Fräulein Matilda says she saw."

" Do they hold banquets there, then?" asked Ferdinand.

" So it is said."

" There is nothing very extraordinary about the story," said the captain. " It is easy to believe that it happened just so."

" The only extraordinary thing about it," said Elsie, " is, that the girl should not allow herself to be deceived, and take it as gently and quietly as girls usually do——"

" And so destroy herself entirely," said Ferdinand.

" Yes; but not until she had revenged herself and punished the faithless lover, who perished with her."

" Elsie is right," cried Fräulein Theresa Holbrecht; " it would be a good warning to fickle men if more girls would show them that they are not afraid to take extreme measures to guard their rights."

Elsie shrugged her shoulders, disdainfully.

" Oh!" said she, " the best thing would be to show them that it was a matter of indifference whether such a man stayed or went! I wouldn't throw away a word to keep him!"

" That is a view of the matter à la Fräulein Elsie," exclaimed Ferdinand. " Wholly unmoved by the tragedy of the story—just hear what her wicked pride has to say of it!"

" Are you surprised at that? You have often said I had no feeling."

" Feeling? Oh, yes; but much more pride and malice; they are ready to spring up at any moment and get the better of your feelings. Sympathy with you is the left hand, and malice the right. You know we take everything at first by the right hand."

" Because the right has grown stronger by practice. Why is it that men give the women more occasion to exercise their malice than their sympathy?"

" Oh!" laughed the captain; " that is something new! A man does not address himself to the malice of the girls, but to their kindness only."

" And by abusing the kindness he awakens the malice."

" Consequently," said Ferdinand, " I, on the other hand, address myself to the malice of Fräulein Elsie, in order to awaken her kindness."

" Oh! you needn't hope for that," said Elsie, pouting.

" Very well, then; I will not hope for it— what's the difference? But love is a warfare, and it is well to have a clear understanding beforehand. So let us continue to use the weapons we have been fighting with."

" I should think," said Emil Dransfeld, dryly, " that it belonged more properly in my department. Love seems to me to be a chase——"

" In which the girls are your prey, my dear sir," said Elsie, more mockingly than usual.

" Then it is more honorable to be the captive of an honest warrior than the prey of a hunter," said the captain, looking tenderly at Matilda, who blushed a little.

" Oh, you do not know what you are saying," said Ferdinand. " It is not a question of captives for you, my dear Alexander, or of prey for you, Drausfeld—do not deceive yourselves. We are the conquered in the battle, and often fall in it."

" Why do you begin the battle, then?" said Elsie.

" That is our nature. We are the weaker sex," answered Ferdinand, " and allow ourselves to be drawn into the conflict: Drausfeld expressed it correctly; we are all poor moths, and the flame attracts us by its brilliancy and destroys us!"

Elsie looked at him thoughtfully for a while and then said:

"Would it be a misfortune to be destroyed by a great and splendid flame?"

The judge, to whom this conversation was not very fascinating, rose to finish his game with Herr von Melroth; the young people returned to their rehearsal, until the little clock on the mantle struck ten, and the guests prepared to depart.

Ferdinand and Emil Dransfeld took the same direction. They went along together, the sound of their steps echoing back from the gables of the old black and red houses that looked into the deserted and silent streets. They talked only in monosyllables, till Ferdinand said:

"Did you notice, Emil, how excited Fräulein Elsie was by the judge's story? Didn't that make you a little anxious?"

"Me? Why?" said Emil.

"Oh, now, you will not deny that you are her favorite. It must be your gentleness and meekness that have enchanted her."

"Oh, you are jesting. I am only a sort of page for her, her *souffre-douleur*, her model boy, who is rewarded by kindnesses for not boring her with declarations of love. She wants the rest of you to take me as an example, and be as modest——"

"I am not sure whether it is so, dear friend. At any rate, Elsie said at last that she wouldn't waste a word to keep a departing lover. That must be pleasant for you, for the hour for going must very soon strike for you. You will soon have to take your examination, and will do better than you did the first time. Then you will be appointed to some distant, romantic, but quiet old forest lodge, to which you can no more expect our proud lady to follow you than the soldier of the Seven Years' War could take his high-spirited sweetheart to the camp and field. You have no money, and Elsie has none!"

Emil laughed, but not without a certain sadness, which did not escape Ferdinand's notice.

"You talk to me like a fatherly mentor," said he. "If a little jealousy is lurking behind the fatherly solicitude, I will set you

at rest by confessing my deep consciousness of my unworthiness to sue for the hand of Fräulein Elsie. It is true, I am a poor devil, intended by nature to go through life as a poor musician, but prevented by my parents in their solicitude for my future from attaining even to that. For, as they thought fiddle-playing and flute-blowing a very poor occupation for the son of an auditor adorned with the red eagle of the fourth class, they compelled me to adopt a "burgher" calling. I chose the occupation of forester, and failed in my first examination."

"I know, I know," interrupted Ferdinand. "Those are unpleasant accidents of which it can too often be said, ' *hodie mihi, cras tibi.*' Who knows whether it will go any better with me in the assessors' examination, for which I am preparing? I should be sorry, Drausfeld, if my fatherly warning, as you call it, had hurt you. It was not prompted by jealously exactly—only a little anger and vexation."

"Anger! At what?"

"You see how I am always at swords' points with Fräulein Elsie; and often I am angry at everything, and especially at you in your character of a meek Fridolin, as if that would not help to spoil such an arrogant creature, to make her still more haughty, and lead her to imagine that all men ought to take pattern by your——"

"Soft-headedness? Is that what you were going to say, Schott?"

Ferdinand grumbled something angrily, and Emil continued:

"I will not lay it up against you. Such a hopeless attempt as the one you are engaged in would make any one ill-humored."

"Hopeless? And why hopeless? I do not think so by any means. I love Elsie passionately, and, in the end, love conquers in spite of everything. Hopeless? Really, if I were to acknowledge that to myself, I should put a ball through my head in despair!"

"Oh!" exclaimed Emil, as if frightened. "Then, to be sure, it was not for nothing that they called you Fire at the university. But then——"

"What were you going to say, Emil?"

asked Ferdinand, eagerly. "Now that we have begun these confidences, speak out plainly what you mean by that 'then.'"

"Then you are to be pitied. That is all I can say."

"Are you so sure that I shall never succeed!"

"I am," answered Emil. "If you will take my advice, you will drive this passion from your heart. It is hopeless!"

He said this with a sigh, with a peculiarly earnest and almost melancholy emphasis, as if it were himself who must tear a deeply-rooted passion from his heart.

Ferdinand gave a forced laugh. "How tragically you speak! Do you mean to tell me that Elsie is in love with some one else, and is that sigh for your own defeat? For, really, you cannot mean that your own quiet devotion has so won upon our 'Flame' that others must despair. Tell me, have you found out that Elsie is secretly in love with some one whom I do not know?"

"Do not ask," answered Emil, quietly. "I cannot tell you anything more about it."

"There is no need of it," said Ferdinand. "If you think I cannot conquer this proud beauty, because I do not court her sentimentally, because I am constantly carrying on a petty warfare with her, you are mistaken. Such a proud nature, where the feelings do not predominate, such an aggressive spirit, which knows instinctively that the best kind of defensive warfare is offensive, wants to be fought with, conquered, subjugated. She does not want to see a man at her feet; she must respect, look up to, fear him. A little superficial liking can be won from her girlish vanity by devotion and flattery, but she can be permanently conquered only by conflict, which will at last subjugate her, or lead through hate to love!"

"What a psychologist you are!" answered Emil, shaking his head. "You seem to think girls can be divided into two classes, like hunting-dogs—one class to be trained by kindness, the other by force."

Ferdinand laughed. "That is a comparison for which you, as forester, must be responsible; I didn't make it. But here our paths diverge, most judicious Emil. Pleasant dreams to you, faithful, warning Eckart!"

"Good night," said Emil; and they separated to reach their rooms by different routes.

When Ferdinand had arrived at his, the landlady brought him a light, and gave him at the same time a large, old-fashioned key.

"The carpenter," she said, "has been here to tell you that he has done the work you last ordered at the theatre, and to return the key of Melroth's Hall. Here it is."

Ferdinand put the key into his pocket. It belonged to a little door that led from a narrow back street into Melroth's large hall, where the theatre, in which the amateur performances were to take place, had been arranged, according to Ferdinand's directions.

CHAPTER II.

AMBITIOUS DREAMS.

As the little stage in the hall was ready, the first rehearsal could now be held there. It took place very soon, and went off extremely well—at least to the entire satisfaction of the performers. Every one felt fully repaid for the trouble—if not by the success of the play, at least by the pleasure coming in by the way—the little comic episodes, and the excitement. As regards the performance, Ferdinand von Schott, who was a sharp critic and a strict manager, found much to blame. Emil spoke too indolently, his manner was too negligent and slovenly. Fräulein Theresa Holbrecht was too angular and violent in her movements, and could not be reasoned out of the notion that in declamation all the adjectives should have a peculiar pathetic emphasis, and the nouns should be slurred over as much less important affairs. But the captain, who had to direct the declarations of love in his part to Fräulein Matilda, played well and with feeling, much better than had been ex.

pected: and Matilda developed a talent for accepting them with very simple and natural grace. Elsie, whose suitor in the play was Ferdinand, escaped criticism entirely. He contented himself with looking at her, accompanying all her movements with his eyes and keeping silence. It seemed that he found nothing in her to criticise; what she did and said probably formed his standard of correctness.

After the rehearsal, it was the universal opinion that the performers deserved some special reward for it; and, therefore, Herr von Melroth was obliged to consent to shorten his afternoon nap, and accompany the young people after dinner to Mount Michael's, a beautiful place of resort, a quarter of a league from the city gate. It was a bright, sunny day; the winter had been unusually mild, and now the days had grown much longer, and the first indications of spring were beginning to appear. In the hedges, which were enlivened by the chirping and twitting of the sparrows, the branches of hazel and willow were beginning to bud, and the young grass was spreading its green carpet over the fields. In the parlor of the coffee-house which overlooked the picturesque old town with its many towers, and the windings of the river, the hours pass over the merry company much more rapidly than they thought necessary or kind in those careless, swift-dancing nymphs; if they must dance, why could they not assume for such occasions a leisurely and dignified minuet? Why not, for the sake of young people with such an incredible amount to say, and in company with a papa whose friend, the judge, comes regularly at six o'clock for a game of Boston, and must not be allowed to make a journey for nothing?

"Play dominos with papa," whispered Elsie to Emil Drausfeld, as Herr von Melroth looked at his watch for the first time; and Emil Drausfeld offered himself up with touching resignation.

But the conversation was not so lively after that. It was evident that Emil's dry, humorous comments were a necessary part of it. Elsie, in particular, took much less interest, and was much more quiet than usual. Ferdinand noticed it, and he, too, grew less talkative; why should he talk when Elsie would not listen? Should he exert himself to entertain Fräulein Theresa? Or disturb Matilda and his cousin, Alexander, in their conversation, which was growing more and more exclusive?

Herr von Melroth looked at his watch the second time, and no one now had any objections to starting for home as he suggested. They began to look for their hats and wraps. Elsie was the first to be ready, and while the others were busy with their preparations, she stepped through a glass door upon the balcony in front of the parlor. Ferdinand, who had noticed her eyes resting thoughtfully upon him several times during the last hour, followed her into the balcony, slightly excited and agitated. She was leaning on the balustrade, her eyes turned toward the setting sun, which seemed to be sinking into an abyss between two neighboring hills beyond the town. Elsie took no notice of his approach; her eyes rested fixedly on the same point.

"Your thoughts are travelling on a path not unknown to mine," said Ferdinand, after a pause.

"Indeed!" she answered, raising her head, haughtily; "what do you know about the travels of my thoughts?"

"Will you deny that they were travelling through that chasm yonder, along the road that leads to Asthof?"

"It is possible," answered Elsie, blushing slightly. "I have spent many happy days on our place there, and it is natural that I should think of them when the sun draws my eyes in that direction. But I should like to know what attracts your thoughts there, Herr von Schott?"

"If you want to know, I will tell you, Elsie. They say that the faithless steward, who is now in possession of the estate, had much to do with getting your father's affairs into such a condition that he was obliged to sell it——"

"My father thinks so, and cannot be convinced to the contrary," interrupted Elsie, with unusual warmth; "but I do not believe it. It is false—I am sure it is false!"

"It may be. What I was about to say is

this: my favorite air-castle is the fancy that some day, when I am rich enough, I can buy Asthof, so that——"

"So that you may have the satisfaction of being master in the house from whence we, the rightful heirs, have been driven out and sent into the world with nothing. Fie! What a malicious spirit of revenge!"

Ferdinand colored at this unexpected explanation of his words.

"Revenge? What, in heaven's name, could I have to revenge? But since you know my intentions so well," he added, angrily, "I need not explain them any farther."

She turned to go. "Come," said she, "I heard the others pass out."

When they stepped from the door of the coffee-house, they saw Herr von Melroth, Theresa, and Emil, some distance in advance, and the captain following with Matilda, to whom he had given his arm, probably on account of the steepness of the path. Ferdinand, who saw that he had been foolish to get angry at Elsie's words, as they were evidently thrown out only to ward off a declaration she saw to be coming, offered his arm, which she took, without hesitation.

"You expect," she said, "to be a diplomatist; and the desire to possess a large estate does not accord very well with that idea."

"I think the desire to have some settled habitation is very natural for a man who has never had a home and a family circle to go to. My father was a soldier, and with the many removals to which an officer is subject, he could never make a permanent home anywhere. He married late, and I lost him when I was quite young. Since then, my cousin, Johann Heinrich, the banker, whom you probably know by sight, has provided for me. When he was a young man and needed help, my father assisted him, and took him for a time to live with us. Cousin Johann Heinrich has never forgotten that, and revenges himself on my father's son. So I have never wanted for anything. I have been able to study whatever and wherever I wanted to; but, you see, a domestic hearth, a pleasant home, such as an old bachelor as my cousin could not give to a young man."

"Have you not a sister?" asked Elsie.

"Yes, a dear, good sister, Adele, of whom I have seen too little; she lives with an aunt in L. on the Elbe. But let me go on. You can see how it would be one of the dearest wishes of my heart, after all my wanderings, past and to come, to have at last a settled home, which may serve as a sort of gathering-place for our rather vagabond Scottish (*schottisch*) clan, and where I, when at rest, may meditate like a philosopher on what is permanent and enduring amid all the varying phenomena of life—on the absolute, to speak even now like a philosopher."

Elsie, who had been listening sympathetically, nodded and said, "Yes that is natural; and I have nothing to say against your granting yourself the little luxury and buying Asthof."

"I beg your pardon, Fräulein Elsie, but we haven't got to Asthof yet. You must allow me, as a philosopher, to discuss the preliminaries thoroughly, before I come to that. To proceed with the little speech that I had the honor of making to you, I would ask first: what is the absolute, among the varying phenomena of life; the enduring, the one thing permanent? what is it? Answer me."

"Who? I?"

"Yes, you; for every girl has the answer in her heart. It is the great philosophic axiom with which every woman is born, the ideal after which she constructs her real world. So answer, Elsie; what is the one thing permanent?"

"Oh, nonsense!" replied Elsie, with a haughty toss of the head.

"No, not nonsense, Elsie, but love—though, indeed, the two may seem to be a little mixed, and never can be entirely separated! But enough of philosophy; 'I have had enough of this dry tone,' as Mephistopheles says. As I have said, it is love. And since I love you, as I have repeatedly told you in the most sensible, touching, and intelligible way, past all measure, and almost to madness, it is naturally one of the deepest desires of my soul to be able to take you as mistress to the home where your cradle stood, under the feudal roof of your noble ancestors. So now, we have arrived at Asthof by a logical course of thought; my speech is at an end and you have the floor. Do not use your privilege too cruelly, Elsie, I beg of you—will you?"

"Oh," answered Elsie, "you are a frivolous man, Herr von Schott. How can you talk to me like that? What if I were foolish enough to believe you, to let you 'put nonsense into my head,' as they say, though it would be better to say into the heart? How unhappy it would make me! The thought is terrible. You want to be a diplomatist. For what reason? Do you think that nature has given you so much cunning and skill, that it would be a source of incalculable injury to the political interests of Europe if you should fail to adopt that profession?"

"By no means," answered Ferdinand, smiling. "But you have started well; go on, I beg of you."

"Answer me first, you future Talleyrand, what is it that sends you among the men that make use of language only to conceal their thoughts? Do you really think you share in their talent?"

"A little. I have learned foreign languages easily, and can, therefore, keep silence in several, and conceal my thoughts in several. Isn't that a good deal to begin with? And then I have a horror of spending my life as a petty justice in some little, forlorn, out-of-the-way nest. I have higher aspirations. I want to learn the ways of the great world, to live in it, to be carried on with the current of the time and its events. I am an idealist, as you must know; and as an idealist, I long for the heights of life, to be surrounded by the richest and noblest forms of life, among the privileged classes who live in splendor and luxury, with ever-changing excitements and——"

"You must, indeed, be an idealist, if you have such an idea as that of the world in which a diplomatist lives. My idea is entirely different; I imagine diplomatists to be a peculiarly repulsive race, whose greatest delight is to persecute men who have fallen into misfortune through their love of country and of liberty, to act the sheriff toward poor political refugees in foreign lands——"

"Oh!" cried Ferdinand, in surprise. "You—every inch an aristocrat—have you such sympathies? I should not have expected that."

"Perhaps not; I have them, nevertheless. But that is not the question. I only wanted to show you how inconsiderate you are. When you have lived in your ideal world two, three, four years, you will have become so accustomed to the brilliant creatures in the circles where you will move, the cultured ladies, the beautiful countesses and princesses, that you will think of poor Elsie Melroth, the wild country-girl, only with a pitying smile. If I should listen to your words now you might, perhaps, from a sense of duty, send me a gracious, half-cordial letter about once in three months. And then I could sit here in H. and think longingly of the faithless one afar off, who would send me at Christmas a program of the dance that some ambassador's beautiful daughter had placed in his button-hole at the court ball. Do you think I would like such a *rôle*? Do you think I should do well in the character of *Dido Abandonata*?"

"Oh, you are abominable," answered Ferdinand, deeply hurt, conscious as he was of the sincerity of his feelings. "It doesn't speak very well for your character that you have no faculty for understanding the true language of the heart, even when it expresses itself playfully. My nature is firm and constant. When I once love, I must love forever, even to the last breath of my life——"

"I see, Herr von Schott, that you do not put too low an estimate on your character," said Elsie, her lips quivering with emotion. "And if your nature is so tenacious and constant, as you say, you must take extreme care not to set your affections in the wrong place."

"You are angry with me; but that has very often happened before, and I have survived it. But I am most deeply conscious and most thoroughly convinced that we are homogeneous natures, that we belong together, like fire and flame, and that I shall some day succeed in bringing you to the same consciousness."

"And what would you have accomplished then?" said Elsie, sighing deeply, her tone changed to one of intense sadness.

"Then," he exclaimed, in perplexity, "I should have accomplished everything that I want to and must accomplish, if I am not to make an utter failure."

She shook her head sadly and quickened her steps.

"Let us not fall so far behind the others," she said. "Come, Matilda and your cousin Alexander are clear out of sight."

She did not speak another syllable until they had overtaken Maltilda and her companion. Ferdinand, though he had been hurt and humiliated by her blunt words, did not interpret them unfavorably. He believed that he had moved and excited her feelings, and that her haughty answers were only an attempt to hide her emotion. In regard to Elsie, he had the proud confidence of final victory, the feeling that she was destined for him by nature and fate; yes, even that she was already his, and that it was only her pride that prolonged the struggle—that she was acting just as he himself would have done, if he had been a girl and she his suitor. To gain her love seemed so necessary to his life, such an indispensable condition for his existence, that he could no more bear to think of final failure than a man can bear to dwell upon the thought of his death or any other horrible possibility.

When they separated at the door of Melroth's house it was with the exclamation from both sides, "*Auf Wiedersehen* to-morrow evening!" for it had been agreed that they should meet the next evening for a general rehearsal.

But shortly before noon the next day Ferdinand received a note signed by Matilda Melroth, begging him to postpone the rehearsal a few days, and not to come that evening, as her sister Elsie was suffering from a headache, and would, therefore, not be able to enter into her part with spirit enough to satisfy the demands of so strict a manager and her own.

"The headache cannot be very severe," said Ferdinand to himself, somewhat ill-humoredly, for he had looked forward with pleasure to the evening; "or else she could not have dictated this well-written note to her sister, as evidently she did. It is one of the caprices of the princess!"

And then came the thought that his conversation with her the evening before, and the impression it had left upon her might not have been without influence on this caprice; and there was nothing in the idea to wound his self-love.

CHAPTER III.

A BETROTHAL.

The second day after the excursion, Ferdinand sat in his room, which, by the way, exhibited none of the disorder of a bachelor's abode. It is characteristic of strong and intelligent men, with clear minds, to feel the need of strict order around them; and it is usually only the weakly good-natured, who, with a praiseworthy indulgence toward others, unite a fatal one toward themselves, and endure a chaos around them, which is considered a mark of genius, while it is simply one of stupidity.

Ferdinand was strong, too, in the ability to control and concentrate his thoughts. He was, therefore, not thinking of Elsie; he thought of her only when he was not engaged in his work or his studies; at this moment the latter claimed his entire attention. He was poring over a thick manual of international law, and was absorbed in the complicated subject of the rights and duties of neutrals, when there was a hasty knock at the door, and his cousin, the captain, entered.

"You, Alexander!" he said, in surprise, "at this hour, which is usually devoted to your fatherly duties for your company; have you given them a holiday?"

"Not them, but myself. Yet it is for no child's play, but for that serious game where a man stakes his all, even his soul, on a single card!"

"What? not with the devil?"

"Not with the devil exactly, but with something that he sometimes rules—that is to say, with fate. But the one card is the queen-of-hearts; in a word, my dear cousin, I am engaged."

"Engaged? Seriously? To Fräulein Matilda?"

"To Fräulein Matilda Melroth."

"Well, no one can escape his destiny. Joy to you, brave cousin of Northumberland! And how do you feel after this bold deed?"

"I seem to myself," answered the captain, "like the air after a thunder-shower. When once the storm has broken out and the lightning is over, the air is clearer, milder and cooler."

"What a confession! You must have felt yourself intoxicated with happiness."

"Yes; and, so far, I am perfectly happy. Perhaps if she had rejected me, I should have thought I must shoot myself dead. Now, when it is not the case, I wonder at happiness being so quiet a thing."

"Yes," said Ferdinand, smiling, "that is a fact in the meteorology of human life. The thermometer—that is, in our temperate zone—rises to the thirtieth degree of heat, but falls only to the twentieth degree of cold. In the emotional world, it is the reverse. Joy never rises so far above zero as grief can fall below it."

"That may be so. But let us return to the fact that will, I hope, bring us into the pleasanter relation of brothers-in-law. I believe you can now follow my example——"

"If you are no happier, as you say, there is no great inducement, Cousin Alexander."

"No happier? You take me too literally. My happiness is still too new; I do not, as yet, fully realize it. I am like a swimmer who has just plunged boldly into the water; at the first moment he is bewildered; the pleasure and the warmth come afterward."

"It is certain that Matilda would not feel any more warmly toward you if she knew that you were swimming around in so cool an element."

"Matilda is very reasonable and very considerate. She will understand that one cannot be fully self-conscious in a new po-

sition, and needs a little time to realize where he is."

"I think," said Ferdinand, "that few girls would keep their promises of marriage if they could hear the conversation in which their future husbands announce their happiness to their friends, with the comments made, and the irony that is often only half-concealed in their congratulations."

"Yes, but then it is not so ill-meant, and the girls would be wrong to take it seriously. One often hides his feelings before his good friends, who are too frequently fellows to whom it would not do to express one's emotions. Beside, their ironical congratulations often conceal some envy. Isn't that a little the case with you, dear cousin?"

"Envy? I? At your winning Matilda?"

"I know you do not envy me for winning Matilda; I mean, you envy me for winning her so soon."

"Perhaps. But, to be frank, I should prefer a conquest with greater difficulties."

"Oh!" laughed the captain. "Then you cannot complain of Fräulein Elsie. She gives you a lively chase enough!"

"That is true. You are right. She is a wise child, and knows what she is worth."

"Very true," was the answer. "But let us return. Day before yesterday, when I accompanied Matilda home from Mount Michael's, I made my declaration, and yesterday I spoke with her father and received his consent. Herr von Melroth asked me to tell you that he should expect us both to dinner to-day, to a little family party. The affairs usually connected with an engagement are to be considered, and Melroth wants you to be there."

"With pleasure. Will our cousin, the banker, be there?"

"My uncle, Johann Heinrich? No; I am going from here to him, to give him due notice of what has taken place. But he is not invited. We are to be entirely to ourselves. Then, we shall have the advantage of being able to take this same good Johann Heinrich, and the necessary funds he is to help us with, as the chief subject of our discussions."

"Yes, indeed. Our good cousin will again have the happiness of realizing how useful and necessary he is to all his dear relatives."

The captain smiled, rose, and extended his hand to his cousin.

"Do not forget the hour—two o'clock," he said, and went to introduce himself to his uncle in his new character.

Ferdinand's thought were now so thoroughly drawn in another direction, that he closed his book and walked up and down through his room.

Notwithstanding all his confidence and assurance of success, his love for Elsie was too great and deep to allow him to escape moments of despondency, and to consider his cousin's easy success without some envy. He told himself again and again that he could not win Elsie in the ordinary way of sentimental devotion and adoration; that he must impress her with his talent and energy; that her feelings were proportionately too weak to attract her toward a man who had nothing but love to offer; that she wanted to be mastered; that, like every woman of strong feeling, she must also fear the man she loved. And he did not shrink from such a strife, as he often said, defiantly and confidently. But, notwithstanding all this, there were hours when he would have preferred to follow the broad highway, and act like other lovers, commending himself by bouquets and sonnets, and touching the heart of the beloved one by sighs, and blushing, stammering declarations. This would have been more in accordance with his deepest feeling and with the nature of love itself: and his own method, by strife and war of words, interrupted by times of studied coolness and estrangement, often made him suffer acutely.

The time at length came for him to dress for the dinner to which he had been invited by his happy cousin. When he arrived, he found the master of the house alone. Elsie seemed to be busy with her toilet, and the captain and Matilda had not yet returned from a walk they had taken together.

"You must walk arm-in-arm on our promenade, the cathedral square, for a quarter of an hour before dinner," said Herr von Melroth, laughing; "that is the established way of proclaiming an engagement in this town."

Aside from this remark, Herr von Melroth's tone, in speaking of the matter, was very serious and solemn, as if it were not altogether calculated to give unmixed joy to his fatherly heart. He had given his consent because he had been attacked so impetuously—although, and in spite of, and notwithstanding—Ferdinand hardly listened to the reasons for the objections which Herr von Melroth, as he explained at length, might have made to the marriage, as a careful and provident father; Ferdinand was looking, with beating heart, toward the door by which he expected Elsie to enter. She came at last, and it gave him a pang to see how charming she looked, how conquering and queenly. He felt that the prospects for success in the plan he had chosen to win her were to-day very poor; that with this proud beauty he should be forced, like any common mortal in love, to descend to entreaties, and lay the weapons of his warfare at her feet. She was dressed in a silver-gray dress, very simply made, with a lace bertha round her shoulders; a single dark-red camellia glowed in her rich dark hair. That which to-day gave her a peculiar charm was the quiet, gentle, thoughtful expression of her features, that were wont to look out into the world with so much self-conscious repose; Ferdinand had never before seen her with this thoughtful and subdued expression. In tendering his congratulations, he offered his hand, and felt that hers was icy cold. Her sister's engagement, he thought, must have had upon her a peculiarly strong and, singularly enough, depressing effect. The question suggested itself, whether she had, after all, been in love with the captain, and this was the secret in Emil Drausfeld's possession when he had warned him? But no, that was impossible; he would have discovered that long ago! The groundlessness of the supposition was soon shown by the unconstrained and perfectly natural manner of Elsie's reception of the captain, when at length he arrived with his companion. Matilda looked out from her hat and fur collar with a very blooming face, flushed by happiness and the cool, fresh air. She seemed to be really happy, though she spoke a little louder than usual, and her laugh sounded somewhat affected, as if she felt under obligations to appear happy, which never suggests itself to those who are really so. Perhaps, thought Ferdinand, she is happy rather at the prospect of being a bride than that of having our good Alexander for a bridegroom, as may be the case with many brides.

Emil Drausfeld and Fräulein Theresa, the friend of the sisters, were also at dinner, so that the company was large enough to allow Ferdinand, whose seat was next to Elsie's, to talk to her without making the conversation general. After Herr von Melroth had proposed the toast, and had steered his eloquence safely through the waters of his emotion, until, at length, he ran into port, amid great applause, Ferdinand said, half aloud, to Elsie:

"We are about to enter into a sort of relationship, Fräulein Elsie, and that imposes upon us new duties toward each other."

"Duties? What duties?" she answered, abstractedly.

"Well, first, the duty of concord and mutual forbearance."

"I thought I had always practiced the latter admirably."

"By no means, proud Fräulein Flamme; you have shown so little forbearance toward my timid and modest advances that we have always lived in discord."

"You should have made your advances to some one who would have been more grateful."

"Nature would not allow it. The fire struggles upward to the flame, it has no other mission in the world. The flame does, indeed, consume; but that is also its trade, Fräulein Elsie. It does no good to struggle against it; we must submit. I will, therefore, give up the conflict and consent to be consumed, if you will grant me peace. Let us drink to that!"

Elsie lifted her glass negligently and touched his with it.

"Peace," she said, in the same abstracted tone she had used throughout the conversa-

tion, "peace! Can peace be had by merely speaking the word and touching glasses?"

"And by the will to keep it: why not?"

"Oh, yes; you are a diplomatist. It is your business to convince the world, when you have made peace, that all strife is at an end."

"Do you mean to say that there is no real peace between us? It can be had only upon conditions, can it?"

"Certainly; on the conditions the victor prescribes."

"Prescribe them, then; for you see, from all I have said, that I have no objections to declaring myself fully conquered."

"You would find my conditions very hard," said Elsie, with a faint smile. "The first would be that you cease to long for your ideal diplomatic world——"

"Agreed. My longings are only for you. So I am to give up being a diplomatist, and instead be—what?"

"That is a matter of indifference to me—only something that you can attend to anywhere, so that you will not be bound to any particular place."

"It would be difficult to find such an one. I should have to be an artist, or something like that, and I have no talent for anything of the kind. And supposing I had some little talent, for instance, that of our friend Emil, and could play the flute as he does, the life of such a wandering musician would be a dismal sort of career. And then?"

"Then you would have to follow me without any will of your own, without any remonstrance, wherever I might want to go —to-day to the Cape of Good Hope, and to-morrow to Greenland, if that should be my fancy."

"But tell me, I beg of you, what should I do in Greenland? Play the flute for the polar bears?"

"Obey me, obey me unconditionally, like a faithful, submissive servant; you would be obliged to do everything I commanded, even carry *billets-doux* to an Esquimaux prince for me if I should happen to fall in love with one."

"Oh!" laughed Ferdinand. "That is too much. And for all that I should have—

nothing but peace? Then I prefer war—war without all its horrors—and the right to seize the *billets-doux* of the Esquimaux or any other prince, and murder and annihilate him! But, tell me, how can any one be so very fond of ruling?"

"I should not require it from love of power, but only as a wise precaution; it so often happens that men treat a heart they have gained the mastery of as children do their playthings—throw it away when they get tired of it. Is it not wise, then, to take precautions, and arrange it so as to rule and reserve to one's self the privilege of throwing away?"

"Fräulein Elsie, how you talk! That is dreadful! What hatred you show toward men! But, after all, there is some comfort for me in it. Heretofore I have thought you hated only me; now I see that I only have the misfortune to be included under a general condemnation. But have you instilled the same principles into your sister? If you have, I pity my poor, unconscious cousin."

"Oh, no," answered Elsie. "She is not capable of adopting such good principles. She will be a very humble, submissive wife to her lord and master."

Elsie now turned to answer a question of Fräulein Theresa, who sat on the other side of her, and Ferdinand had an opportunity to reflect on the enigma presented by this young girl in her sharp and almost angry declaration of such unmaidenly principles. Would a young girl speak so without some definite personal experience? Would she speak so from the head only? Must it not be from a deeply wounded heart? Who knows? he thought; perhaps she has read some unnatural, cynical novel that has put such things into her head. Perhaps, when she lived in the country, she had some little romantic love affair with some rustic swain in the neighborhood, who proved faithless; therefore is not dangerous to me, though Elsie would feel it strongly and deeply, and it is hard to efface such an impression, and though Emil, with his owlish croaking, gave——

Ferdinand's thoughts were here interrupted by another toast, and he did not have an opportunity to resume the conversation with Elsie, for they soon rose from the table. The company went into another room to take coffee, and Ferdinand found himself engaged in a conversation with Fräulein Theresa, who had been made very voluble by the champagne, and who, as Ferdinand remarked to himself, seemed to have grown a little malicious with it also; for she made all sorts of biting and derisive remarks about the family whose guest she was, great as was the want of tact in making them to the cousin of a man just about to connect himself with the family. Ferdinand concluded that Fräulein Theresa herself had not been without designs on his cousin, and that there was a little *dépit amoureux* at the bottom of her remarks; he thought he had detected the same thing before. In the meantime Elsie was talking in a low tone with Emil Drausfeld; Herr von Melroth was sitting in an arm-chair in the corner, looking thoughtfully at the blue clouds that rose from his cigar—much more solemnly and seriously, Fräulein Theresa had remarked, than he had watched the blue smoke in which his farms and meadows had gone up.

At length he rose with a sigh, and, laying his hand upon the captain's shoulder, disturbed the cosy *tête-à-tête* in which he and Matilda were absorbed. The captain rose and nodded to Ferdinand, who followed them into a small cabinet, Herr von Melroth closing the door behind him.

"We must now introduce a little business into our conversation," he said, motioning the cousins to take seats, and placing himself in a sofa-corner; "the picture of the future that my two dear children—you, my dear captain, and my Matilda—are painting with the brilliant colors of love must have a golden, even though only a narrow frame, and that is what we must talk about now."

"Very well, then; let us talk of the frame," said Ferdinand, smiling.

"Which at first might be made of modest oak-wood if the gold is lacking," said the captain. "You know, my dear papa-in-law, that I have no property, and, according to the intimations you gave me last evening when I asked you for Matilda——"

"And which, in the tempest of your feelings, you scarcely seemed to hear," interrupted Herr von Melroth; "I have none either—that is to say, no considerable amount which I could use freely for the benefit of my children. For I must tell you—you, too, Herr von Schott—I should like to have you understand how matters stand; I must tell you that after the sale of my estate of Asthof to that infamous swindler, Bousart, I had only about twenty thousand thalers at my disposal. With the interest of that amount I could not, of course, supply my own needs and the wants of my daughters—that you can see—and I, therefore, expended the greater part of it for an annuity which yields me much more than the ordinary interest; and, therefore, the sum itself is no longer at my disposal——"

"And the interest ceases at your death," interrupted Ferdinand.

"With my death, certainly," answered Herr von Melroth, avoiding a little shyly the eyes of the young man, in which he might perhaps have read the thought that this was no very fatherly way of providing for the future of his daughters, and continued: "Thus, you see, my dear captain, that Matilda cannot bring you the capital you need to gain the consent of your humble servant; and the subject of our discussion must be how we shall raise or make it eight thousand thalers, it should be for one in your position."

Captain Schott cleared his throat a few times before he answered, keeping his eyes on the carpet:

"That is, indeed, a little stone of stumbling! We Schotts have very little, whether we write our names Schott or von Schott, like my dear cousin here——"

"With a single exception," interrupted Ferdinand. "And as regards the question before us, it happens very fortunately for you, my dear Alexander, that he writes his name Schott, and not von Schott, and is, therefore, more nearly related to you than to me, and will not be inexorable in regard to this affair."

"That," said Herr von Melroth, "is the established and widely-known banker, Johann Heinrich Schott."

"Johann Heinrich Schott," said Ferdinand.

"What is your exact relationship to the worthy counsellor and banker?" asked Herr von Melroth.

"He is simply my father's brother," answered the captain.

"And my grandfather's grandson," said Ferdinand.

"Your grandfather's grandson? I do not see into that. You must explain."

"Then I must begin with my grandfather," answered Ferdinand. "My grandfather was steward and manager of a cloister domain. His oldest son succeeded him in that position. That son had two sons, the oldest of whom became a soldier, rose to the rank of major, and was the father of my dear cousin, Alexander. The younger, named Johann Heinrich, became a banker, which was very practical, and grew very rich, which was very praiseworthy in him, but up to this time has not been tempted by the domestic bliss of his older brother to renounce his bachelor life."

"And you, Herr von Schott, where does your line begin in this Scottish clan?"

"With the younger, much younger son of my grandfather, the steward. This son, who had the honor to be my father, was a soldier, also, rose to the rank of lieutenant-colonel, and gained a title of nobility. He married late, and you see before you the heir to his title and fortunes."

"So," said Herr von Melroth, "you are really the uncle, *à la mode de Bretagne*, of our captain."

"Who will assure you," answered Ferdinand, "that I have always taken care to act in a manner becoming this relation, and never have failed to give my nephew good advice and good precepts when he has come to me for them."

"And on that," answered the captain, smiling, "I base my confidence that you will not confine your favors to good advice, but will show your paternal interest by deeds."

"Oh, I can guess what you mean. You called on your uncle, the banker——"

"I called on him, and found it easy to gain his consent to my union with Fräulein

Matilda von Melroth"—that he had been obliged to use all his eloquence with his practical uncle to gain it, he would not, of course, betray in the presence of Herr von Melroth—"but in regard to this financial arrangement, I could not, of course, say a word."

"And so," said Ferdinand, "I am to be put forward to break the ice; the ice in Johann Heinrich's countenance when this proposal is made to him, I can see before me now."

"And just because I, too, see it so vividly before me, am I convinced that only the warmth of your eloquence can melt it," said the captain.

"But I think the warmth of your love could do greater wonders than the warmth of my eloquence."

"No, no, Ferdinand; you have the great advantage of being his favorite, almost his adopted child, and he has the most flattering views of your acuteness and your judgment. And so if you tell him of Matilda's good qualities, and how happy I shall be with her, it will have a great deal more weight with him than anything I can say. Of course I cannot, as a witness in my own case, make as much impression on him as some one more disinterested. So let me persuade you to undertake this mission."

"The mission of saying to him: ' Dear cousin, it is expected of your generosity that you will give your nephew the sum of eight thousand thalers, which he may invest, and use the interest for his future domestic necessities.' It is not altogether pleasant, this mission."

"But are you not the diplomatist of the clan?"

Ferdinand stroked his blonde moustache, and assumed an air of reflection. His cousin was not always in the humor to be approached on such a subject, and he was himself too dependent on him financially to feel entirely free to go to him with such a request. But he reflected that the very fact of his being entrusted with so important a commission, and his success in it would make an impression on Elsie, and he said:

"Very well, then; by way of practice for my future calling, I will accept the mission.

It must succeed, for as cousin Johann Heinrich is the only one who can help you, I do not see on what pretext he can slip out of it. And in order that the native hue of resolution may not be ' sicklied o'er with the pale cast of thought,' I will go at once. The warmth of my eloquence, as you have the goodness to express it, will, I am sure, be increased by the enthusiasm with which we have been inspired by this beautiful day, and the libations we have brought to the gods that preside over marriage." With this he arose; his cousin brought his hat from the hall, that he might not have to explain his early departure to the company, and he started for the banker's office.

CHAPTER IV.

COUSIN JOHANN HEINRICH.

It was deep twilight when Ferdinand stepped into the yard of the great gabled building in the market-place, in which was his cousin's banking-house and where he lived. At the left, on the ground-floor, were the business rooms; on the right, a small ante-room, and behind it the private office of the banker. When Ferdinand entered this room, the tall, thin, pale man, who bore a strong family resemblance to his handsome young cousin, was just lighting the gas above his great writing-desk.

"That's right, my dear cousin," said Ferdinand. "Let there be light; I have come for a little battle with you, and it will be well for us to look each other in the face."

"For a battle? Indeed, I did not know I had given you any occasion for hostilities, cousin Ferdinand. But have a chair, if your warlike mood will allow you to sit down quietly. Perhaps, too, you will not disdain to accept a cigar, notwithstanding your thirst for the fray. You will find some there on the stand. I confess I am not much inclined to strife with you rash young people, after laboring as I did with Alexander this morning, to keep him from taking an insane step—and all in vain."

"Ah! we are approaching the subject," answered Ferdinand, taking a cigar and seating himself. "From an insane step did you say? Alexander could not have made a better choice. Matilda Melroth is a thoroughly good, sensible, domestic, well-bred, cultivated, and, moreover, pretty girl, and of a good family."

"Is she?" said the banker, in a somewhat sharp, positive, and imperious voice. "Have you finished with your adjectives, or have you more in stock? No? Well, then, that may be all true. However, as regards the good family, she is the daughter of a broken-down country gentleman, who will not leave her a dollar; the affectionate father has invested all his property in a life-annuity—in a life-annuity, when he has two children; did you ever hear of such a thing?"

"So you know of that?"

"Such things get about among business men."

"It is unfortunately true; and as Matilda has no property, Alexander must thank Heaven that he——"

"Has none either?"

"No: that he has a good, generous uncle, who is like a father to him, and being blessed with worldly goods, is always ready——"

"So?" interrupted the banker; "do you know of any such uncle? So far as I know, Alexander has but one uncle, and he is a sensible business man, whose generosity does not go so far as to make him give his hard-earned money to encourage foolish marriages."

"Oh, Cousin Johann Heinrich, do not make yourself out less liberal than you are. You are a splendid business-man, as everybody in the city knows ; it is no small matter to begin with so little as you did, and go up to half a million!"

"Say rather a whole million!" interrupted the banker, laughing aloud.

"And for all that," continued Ferdinand, without answering the interruption, "you have always been noble and generous toward us poor relations, and have always had an open hand for us. Have you not furnished me with the means for pursuing my studies, and promised to help me until I can obtain a lucrative place as secretary of legation or the like? How is it possible, now that you can leave Alexander in the lurch—now, when the happiness of his whole life depends upon it—that you will refuse him the eight thousand thalers that he must raise in order to be married——"

"Eight thousand thalers!" exclaimed the banker, as if frightened. "I believe you are a lunatic—eight thousand thalers!"

"You are not to give it, only entrust it to Alexander, so that he may draw the interest until he is a major——"

Johann Heinrich Schott shrugged his shoulders with an air of great contempt.

"How can reasonable people get such preposterous notions?" he said

"I think the notion was natural enough to occur to even unreasonable people. You are the only one who can help him."

"And suppose I will not help him?"

"Then Alexander's marriage will have to be given up. The poor fellow would be wretched. I believe he would resign his commission and go off——"

"Oh, nonsense ! he will get reconciled to it. He will give up the whole affair, and remain a bachelor, as I have. Then some day he will thank me, with tears in his eyes, for keeping him from doing a stupid thing. That is all."

"How cross you are about it, cousin ! Now do you think I don't know why you give such ill-natured answers?"

"No; why, then, if you can read my motives so well? Perhaps because I am secretly desperate about my bachelor state, and envy keeps me from helping Alexander to the domestic happiness I have missed myself. Is that the reason?"

"No, not that; but because you are angry at your own good-nature, which, as you very well know, will out with the promise—before I have finished this cigar—that you will be the generous savior of your nephew——"

Johann Heinrich Schott laughed scornfully, and was just about to answer, when he was interrupted. A servant came in and announced that there was a stranger in the large counting-room, who insisted on seeing the head of the firm. Herr Schott ordered the man to show him in, and Ferdinand withdrew to the back part of the room, where he seated himself in the corner of a sofa and was almost invisible in the shadow of the green shades over the gas-jets above the writing-desk.

The stranger, who soon after entered the room, was a young man of remarkable appearance. He was tall and well-formed, with a head too young yet to be called lion-like, although the broad, powerful forehead and his abundant tawny hair and beard, suggested the comparison; though there was nothing, indeed, in the bold and well-opened blue eyes to remind one of the blinking, half-closed orbs of a lion. He was dressed like a country gentleman, in quite elegant, but loose and easy-fitting garments: a red tie was knotted loosely around his neck, and partially hidden under his broad, turned-down shirt-collar.

He appeared slightly excited; his voice was loud, and yet sounded a little uncertain, as he said to the banker, after a slight, scarcely perceptible bow:

"I come to you, sir, after having a debate with your clerk; your book-keeper or cashier refuses to take this American bond, and I need the money; I must, therefore, beg of you to do this favor for me, as yours is the only considerable banking-house in the place. The paper is perfectly safe, and I cannot understand why I have been refused in so simple a request."

Johann Heinrich Schott threw a sharp glance at the stranger, and seemed to be satisfied with his manly form and his frank face. It was probably only his haughty tone that drew from the banker the sharp reply:

"If we refuse it, sir, we have our reasons; let us see your security."

The stranger had already handed him the paper; the banker unfolded it, and ran his eye over it. It was a thousand-dollar bond of a North American railroad company. He then took from his desk a report in which he found a favorable notice of the company, and then began to turn over the leaves of the smallest and thinnest of the large volumes that stood on the secretary.

"We can take the paper from you," he said, "but cannot at once reckon the exact value; that is probably the reason my clerk refused you. We cannot follow closely the fluctuations in the relative values of gold and paper; we shall have to send it to our correspondent in London, and see——"

"And I must wait for that?" cried the stranger, indignantly. "I need the money at once. I beg of you, take the value of the paper as it is given in your latest report, and compute by that. You will not lose anything, for paper is rising now, and gold is falling."

"And what if we should pay you too little?" said Johann Heinrich Schott, shrugging his shoulders.

"My God!" cried the stranger, quite beside himself at the suggestion of so many difficulties; "that will hurt no one but me; what can it matter to you?"

The banker shook his head, looked again into the reddened face of the stranger, and then took a slip of paper and began to reckon; at length he named a sum to which the other eagerly agreed.

Herr Schott took another paper, in order to write a formal statement, and said:

"I must ask for your name."

"Is that necessary? Well, no matter. My name is George Demmin."

The banker took down the name, and went on with his work. At length he handed the stranger the paper, made out, as it seemed, with unnecessary care, with the words:

"Have the goodness to show this to my cashier."

The stranger took the paper with a nod and an "I thank you," and went.

Ferdinand came forward to the light. "I believe, cousin," said he, "your clerk was wiser than you, this time. What if the paper were stolen?"

"We must not be so suspicious, cousin," answered the banker. "We must not be so ready to believe the worst of our neighbor; that does not speak well for one's own character. Beside, I looked in my book containing the numbers of stolen papers, and this is not among them. If it is stolen, it has not yet been made public."

"So, then, in spite of your noble freedom from suspicion, you took the precaution to look in the book," said Ferdinand, laughing.

"Only as a formality. The man was no swindler; that you could tell from his face. If he had been, he would not have appeared so impatient."

In the meantime, Ferdinand had cast a glance at the paper as it lay upon the desk. He looked for a moment at the colored print, and the pretty vignettes and stamps; then, just as his eyes were turning away, they were arrested by a name written with ink, in quite small letters, but distinctly, on the upper edge at the back. "Philip Bonsart," he read, and then exclaimed:

"Oh, ho, cousin, we have made an interesting acquaintance without knowing it. The stranger was Philip Bonsart. I saw by his face that his real name was not George Demmin. He threw it at you with such a mocking air. Evidently he had forgotten that he had written his real name up here on the edge of the paper."

"Philip Bonsart!" said the banker; "that wild fellow that was known as the ringleader among the insurgents in '49, and had to fly, and then appeared again in the Baden revolution—the democrat, and communist, and demagogue? Do you really believe it was he?"

"I am convinced of it; it certainly was that 'Mirabeau of the Lüneburg Heath.' I have never seen him, but the descriptions I have heard of him agree exactly with this man's appearance. At any rate, I can easily find out; I have only to describe him to the Melroths; they must know him."

"The Melroths? Why?"

"He is from their old estate. He is the son of the former steward and present proprietor. Herr von Melroth, who is generally a good-natured old fellow, once fell into a confidential mood, and told me, angrily, how this Bonsart had deceived and cheated him, till at length he was able to buy the estate, and sit in the hereditary dwelling of Herr von Melroth's ancestors, like a rascally, impertinent Davison in the castles of the Avenels."

"Ah," said the banker, "that is the morbid idea of every weakling who has lost his property by his own carelessness and stupidity. They have always been cheated by their stewards or agents."

"That may be," answered Ferdinand; "I do not know. I only know that Herr von Melroth cherishes the deepest hatred toward his former steward and present successor; and if one may judge of the tree by the apple, he may have reason for it. Philip Bonsart! I must tell the Melroths at once of this remarkable meeting. Where can he come from, and why does he venture to be seen here? So far as I know, the warrant for his arrest has never been withdrawn."

"He must have fled to America, and he seems to have had some good-fortune there; otherwise he would not have had this thousand-dollar bond to sell. Perhaps his communistic views have been somewhat changed. How he ventures to allow himself to be seen here is, indeed, hard to understand; I doubt whether it was really he, after all."

"I can very soon find out by describing him to the Melroths," said Ferdinand, taking his hat, as if to go; "but," he added, turning back to the banker, "I cannot go back there without carrying to them the result of my mission to you. So, may I not, Johann Heinrich, great cousin, most brilliant representative of our Scottish clan, rock of our confidence, and inexhaustible fountain of generosity for all us poor relations, brave, noble, ever-constant benefactor, model of an unselfish, lofty, noble mind, finding its only pleasure in lavishing favors upon others——"

"Well," he said, suddenly interrupting the stream of his own eloquence, and speaking in a changed voice, "does not your native modesty compel you at last to cut short this panegyric, this high-flown eulogium, with the words, 'Yes, yes, yes; only stop, only be silent; I will give Alexander the sum he needs——'"

"Then I should be the first," laughed the banker, "to pay eight thousand thalers for the privilege of not hearing his. own praises."

"Shall I, then, take the opposite course,

and make you out so fearfully bad that you will buy my silence with the promise——"

"Heavens!" said the distressed banker, "the affair is certainly not so pressing but that we can take a little time to reflect whether some other way may not be found ——"

"Can money be made by reflection? If it were, how wise and thoughtful the faces of all mortals would grow! But, Johann Heinrich, you know very well that wisdom and thoughtfulness are not the means for getting money. Therefore, make up your mind; you will not get rid of me until you do, and you see by the clock there that it is time for you to go to your club."

Johann Heinrich Schott passed his hand several times over the back of his head, muttered something between his teeth, and said, at length, drawing his tawny brows together, wrathfully:

"The cup, indeed, will not pass from me. But I will give the promise to Alexander himself, so that for my money I may at least have the pleasure of telling him again what a stupid thing he is doing. Tell him to come himself."

"With pleasure, cousin; he shall come, and you shall see how ungrudgingly he will grant you the pleasure of telling him the truth roundly. Other people try to gild the bitter pills they give. You are nobler; you give your golden gifts only a little embittered, like green-shelled walnuts with sweet kernels. That is true philanthropy, and I thank you from the bottom of my heart."

The banker did not seem to think any formal answer called for. He hastily pressed the hand Ferdinand offered, and began to close his desk and prepare to go.

Ferdinand was now anxious to get back to Herr von Melroth's; he, therefore, took his leave hastily, and was very soon in the street, now quite dark.

———

CHAPTER V.

IN THE OLD HALL.

It had been a bright morning. In the afternoon the sky grew cloudy, but without threatening immediate rain; Ferdinand was, therefore, surprised when he found that a light, drizzling rain was falling; he did not at first take much notice of it, but it soon began to make itself felt on his elegant dinner-suit, which was protected only by a light overcoat. He had no umbrella, and, therefore, quickened his steps in the direction of Melroth's house. From a wise economy, the gas-lamps were not lighted, since the almanac promised moonlight, and hence the walking over the wretched pavements was doubly unpleasant.

Not very far from his destination he came to a narrow and dark alley, leading to the right from the street he was passing through. It was the one that led to the rear of Herr von Melroth's house. Ferdinand felt in the side-pocket of his overcoat and found there the key his landlady had given to him two evenings before, and which had been left by the carpenter employed to make arrangements for the theatre. With this he could open the door from the alley, and then pass through to the front part of the house. It would make his walk considerably shorter, and though it must be very dark on the stairs and in the hall, still the place was so well-known to him that he would rather grope his way through than make the circuit necessary to reach the front part of the house, especially as the rain was growing heavier.

He walked rapidly through the alley, and soon reached the door of the old building which extended directly across the end of the alley. Over the door was a deep projecting canopy. He was just about to draw the great old key from his breast-pocket, when he observed, with surprise, that one side of this door was slowly and carefully opened, and a figure stepped out, shutting the door carefully behind it, and then turned, as if to make sure that the bolt had entered the lock.

Ferdinand had stopped, so that the sound

of his footsteps might not draw the attention of this figure to himself before he had had time to recognize it. Now, as it descended the steps, and observed him, it stopped close to him, and he said, in a low tone:

"Who are you? Why, I really believe it is you, my gallant friend Emil! But where the dickens are you coming from? You walk as noiselessly as a cat!"

"You, Herr von Schott?" answered Emil Drausfeld, drawing a long breath and stammering a little—he was evidently confused by this sudden, unexpected meeting; "it is I. And you, where are you going?"

"I was going through the hall to save a few steps in the rain," answered Ferdinand.

"I took this way, too," said Emil, very quickly, "to shorten my walk a little."

"You? But your way does not bring you to this side, it takes you in the opposite direction."

"Does it?" said Emil, half inaudibly, "You see I must have taken a little too much at dinner, so that I am slightly confused. Come, take me home. You will be doing a benevolent work."

"No, my good friend, you show altogether too much cunning in inventing a pretext for your strange appearance here, to allow me to feel any anxiety about your finding your way home. Go on with Heaven's protection. I am wet enough already."

"Where are you going, then? Back to Melroth's?" said Emil, grasping his arm hastily. "You are no longer expected there. The company is all broken up; Herr von Melroth has gone to the club, and your cousin has started for home, and the ladies have retired to their own rooms. Come, let us hurry, and get out of this rain and under shelter."

With this Emil hurried on and drew Ferdinand with him.

Ferdinand tried to remember whether it had not been agreed that they should await his return from the banker's at Herr von Melroth's. Possibly they had not. He might only have taken it for granted.

"Have you, then, a key to the old hall?" asked Emil, after a pause.

"I happen to have with me the key that was given to the carpenter who did the work for the theatre. He returned it to me," answered Ferdinand.

Emil walked on so rapidly that Ferdinand could hardly keep up with him, and had scarcely a chance to reflect on the strange circumstance that his friend had left the house by that route, and that he had been so evidently confused at meeting him. But by degrees the strangeness of the circumstance came over him, and he resolved to get rid of Emil, and find out whether he had told the truth in regard to the breaking up of the company at Herr von Melroth's.

He stopped at the next cross street, and said, "From here you must find your way alone, friend Emil; the rain is getting unendurable. I will take shelter with an acquaintance that lives in this street."

"Well, then, good night!"

Ferdinand passed a short distance down the street, and then turned and went back. The sound of Emil's steps had died away in the distance. Ferdinand's suspicions were awakened, and his thoughts took him back to the old hall. Was Emil in reality Elsie's favorite, and had she led him out by that way, so that their tender leave-taking might be undisturbed? But, in that case, why should Emil have been so anxious to prevent him from going through the old hall? The best way to avoid a mistaken inference was to return to his former project, and enter the house by the way he had proposed; perhaps he should find Elsie still there, or something else that would explain Emil's distress about his design.

He, therefore, retraced his steps at the risk of getting wet through, though the rain had abated, and was now a fine drizzling mist. When he arrived at the door of the old hall, and looked up, everything was black, the outlines of the high windows could scarcely be distinguished. Ferdinand saw that he would hardly be able to make any great discoveries in this darkness; but he had started on the way and so went on, notwithstanding the risk of stumbling, or striking his head against some obstruction in the dark passages. The key, which had been often used of late, opened the door without noise; the old winding staircase behind it was made of sandstone steps and gave back no sound from his footfalls. He had nearly reached the narrow arched door that led from the staircase into the hall; it must have been half open or merely swung together, for at the last turn of the stairs he distinctly heard a hasty whispering of voices in the hall, a suppressed but lively conversation.

He stopped, in surprise, and held his breath; it was impossible to understand anything, impossible even to recognize the voices. He must venture to go a little farther. He ascended the last steps with noiseless care; then, looking through the half-open door, he could see nothing but the nearest of the deep window-recesses, which was distinguished by a gray shimmer from the rest of the wall. He drew a few long breaths and then stretched his head forward to hear as much as possible of the conversation of two persons, whose outlines he at length perceived dimly, far within the hall.

They were in front of another window farther from the door, through which also a faint gray light glimmered from without. One was a man, leaning against the wall, the other a woman, who seemed to be sitting near him on a foot-stool. Ferdinand soon discovered that she was sitting in a kind of step, fastened to the wall below the window seat. The man stood near her, leaning against the wall; his back was turned to Ferdinand.

It was impossible to understand what they said, and Ferdinand dared not venture nearer; he could catch only now and then a word of their eager whispers; but he soon distinguished the voices. One was Elsie's. The man's voice seemed to him at first, and then familiar, as if he had heard it very recently—and then—then he knew to whom it belonged—it was the same voice he had heard scarcely an hour ago at his cousin, the banker's, the voice of the fugitive, the traitor, the communist!

Ferdinand grew alternately hot and cold. His heart seemed to stand still—he could have uttered a cry of rage and have rushed upon this man in his fury!

Elsie in a secret conversation with this man, this Philip Bonsart! And in this hall at night! Sitting at his feet, and—as Ferdinand thought he detected, though he was not quite sure—with her arm raised and his hand held tenderly in her own!

It was a terrible experience to Ferdinand, that of these few minutes. In his excitement, his pain at what seemed to him like fiendish treason against his love, he breathed so heavily that they must have heard him, if they had not been so thoroughly absorbed in what they were saying; and at this moment it would not have made much difference to him if he had been discovered —if he could have been brought to a hostile encounter with his fortunate rival; if he could have had the chance to strike him dead! The thought that such an encounter might have been more serious in its results to him, than to the robust young man whose tall and powerful form was dimly outlined before him, did not once occur to him. But gradually he became conscious of his disgraceful position as a listener—a listener, while at the same time it was quite impossible for him to understand anything; he heard only a few words which Elsie spoke in a more excited and louder voice, but which gave him no idea—"Asthof"—the name of Herr von Melroth's former estate; "Chaplain Heimdal"—a name entirely unknown to Ferdinand, and then "Matilda's company; there is no objection to that now." Where Matilda should accompany or be accompanied, Ferdinand could not discover; in the answer the young man gave, he could distinguish only the words "Hamburg" and "The Thusuelda."

Ferdinand could endure his position no longer. With the desperation in his heart, it was impossible for him to stand there any longer still and breathless. He was just about to turn and withdraw noiselessly, when his attention was again arrested, and he peered with redoubled interest into the darkness; he thought he saw Elsie withdraw her hand from that of the man before her, and hide her face in both her hands, and he thought he heard a low sobbing. It was strange. The conversation of the two seemed to have been of a quiet nature— why should she have been so suddenly overcome by violent sorrow? It could not, however, have been very surprising to the man before her; he stood silent for a short time, then bent down and kissed her forehead; after that he stood erect again and seemed to be waiting quietly for her to regain her composure.

Ferdinand had had enough. He began to retreat quietly, and succeeded, with the greatest caution, in reaching the door behind him. His exit was noticed no more than his entrance had been. He glided down the stairs, cautiously opened and shut the outside door, and was in the alley again.

He stood still for a while, to recover from the stunning effect of what he had seen, and regain his self-control—to ask himself, too, whether anything was to be done. As if anything could be done! As if everything were not forever at an end for him; as if he could not now tell himself what a vain, ridiculous fool he had been with his confidence; his vain assurance in believing he could gain Elsie by his infallible method, while she—and the thought drove him to desperation—she had not been feigning the contempt she manifested for his attentions; it was no maidenly reserve, no mere form assumed for a time by girlish pride; it had been serious earnest, because her heart was full of this man who had long possessed it! It was enough to drive him to desperation— the deep humiliation, and the sudden hopelessness!

He could not entirely comprehend it, not realize it—this irremediable hopelessness. Ferdinand's love for Elsie had in reality been only the love of a self-conscious, vain young man, filling only half the heart, and leaving room for a hundred other interests and ambitious plans. But now, under the smart of this sudden revelation, it seemed to him as if, with the loss of Elsie, the ground was drawn away from under his feet; as if existence were no longer possible for him; as if the best relief would be that of the unhappy girl who had rushed from that fatal hall to her death in the waters of the river. He had a sudden understanding of such passion—he, too, could have committed murder in his wrath, in this terrible storm that was laying waste his whole existence.

He wandered about the streets in his torturing excitement. The rain had ceased, and the wind was driving black clouds across the pale face of the moon; the old houses with their projecting gables were looking with a sullen and hostile expression into the streets they darkened; the grotesque old carving on their façades and the quaint projecting gargoyles looked down, dark and phantom-like, on the few passersby, like a wild race of kobolds.

But few houses were lighted. In H. the streets were deserted at an early hour; but few shopkeepers found it profitable to light their show-windows in the evening. The dwellings had the deserted air seen almost everywhere at night. Whole façades were completely dark—a window lighted only here and there through the length of an entire block. It would seem that men feel the want of very little light—as if God had made the sun quite unnecessarily large —they could have got along with a much more modest outlay; less intellectual light, too, would have served them quite as well; they find no use for the greater part of it.

So Ferdinand wandered aimlessly through these dead, deserted streets, until his thoughts turned from his own sufferings to his cousin, whose interests had been so suddenly thrown into the background—his cousin Alexander, who must be awaiting him in the greatest suspense, and who, it occurred to him, was, after himself, most deeply concerned in what he had just discovered—most deeply and most painfully.

As an officer, it could by no means be a matter of indifference to him that the sister of his bride should stand in so intimate a relation to such a notorious demagogue and traitor. Ferdinand, therefore, resolved to seek him and impart to him his discovery. But on the way he was obliged to pass the house where Emil Dransfeld lived. He noticed a light behind Emil's windows, and was suddenly seized with a desire for an explanation of Elsie's relation to this Bonsart; forgetting the suspense of his waiting cousin, he turned to go up to Emil's room, and compel him to explain the whole affair, since he seemed to be initiated as their confidant and assistant.

He found Emil in a modest little study, which was in the greatest disorder. There was very little to remind one of Emil's future occupation: a pair of antlers fastened on the wall, to serve as a hat-rack, was all that seemed connected with a forester's calling, excepting the green Tyrolese hat, adorned with a chamois-hair and a black cock's feather, which lay upon an open music-book on an old piano. The piano was open; a flute lay in an open case on a round table in front of an old hair-cloth sofa, under a dismal, smoky lamp. Emil did not seem in the mood for his favorite occupation; he had been walking slowly back and forth in his narrow room, his head dropped, and his face expressing the deepest melancholy; there was something about the tall, slender, and bent form to remind one of a weeping-willow.

As Ferdinand stepped in, after a hasty knock, Emil's face expressed no surprise— only a mild sort of inquiry, as if he were just awakened from a dream.

"Emil," said Ferdinand, throwing his hat on the table and himself on the hair-cloth sofa, "I have come to say to you that you are a false, deceitful friend: yes, you, in spite of that pious, patient expression of yours."

"I a false friend?" asked Emil, quietly, and not in the least startled out of his apathetic mood; "why do you say that?"

"Because you lied to me shamefully, to keep me from going into the old hall at Melroth's; because, when you uttered your diplomatic warnings, you gave only dark and unintelligible hints, when you could have told me the whole truth."

"Could have told you the truth? What truth could I have told you?"

"The whole truth; can't you understand? The whole truth that I have come now to demand. You are playing a fine *rôle*, Emil, to be the confidant of a man like this Philip Bonsart; to be used by him as a sentinel to guard his tryst with Elsie! Was it for this that you were received with so much friendliness at Melroth's house? How will you answer for it to her father when he hears of it? And he shall hear of it, I promise you,

unless you give at once a complete explanation!"

Emil looked perplexed while his visitor's wrath was being heaped upon him.

After a pause, he answered: "Moderate your fire a little, Herr von Schott. If Herr von Melroth has a right to call me to account, it does not follow that you have. I do not understand what you mean; I do not understand you at all."

"You do not understand me? The deuce you don't; I am not talking forester science. I want you to explain how Elsie von Melroth and this cursed communist have come together; how the thoughtless creature can so throw herself away, can meet him in that dark hall, and how you can be a party to it, and stand there as a sentinel!"

During Ferdinand's violent speech, Emil had stood in the middle of the room, looking at him with great eyes. At its close, he turned and drew a handful of cigars from the drawer of a little table, and, placing them before Ferdinand, said, with perfect composure:

"Take one. It will quiet you. I will light one, too, and then we can talk. What do you say to a little grog? I have something here to make it with. We are both in wet clothes. Yours perhaps may be dried by the fire of your indignation, but mine are not. I am of a lymphatic temperament, you know. I am chilly."

With this he opened a cupboard and brought out some sugar, a bottle, and a couple of glasses. A teapot, containing hot water, stood in a niche in the stove.

"If you had not come," he said, "I should have forgotten, in my abstraction, that my landlady had brought me the water. Is it hot enough now? If not, I will ring for some more. What do you think? I think it will do."

"Yes, it's plenty hot enough for what you want of it; you are making your grog to get time to reflect what story you had better tell me," answered Ferdidand, wrathfully, who had been following with his eyes Emil's quiet, phlegmatic movements.

"No," answered Emil, coolly, "there you are mistaken. I really want the grog, to prevent my taking cold, and you cannot make any objection if that seems more important to me than answering your stormy questions. Have some."

Emil emptied half of his glass, and sat down quietly beside Ferdinand on the sofa; then lighted his cigar, and smoked in silence for a few moments.

"You see, my dear Schott," he began, "you must not be surprised at my taking your excitement so coolly. Every one has his turn, and when one has got through his own trouble he naturally looks coolly at another who is just floundering in his. When one shipwrecked man has got safe to shore he looks with perfect equanimity at another close behind him who is still struggling with the waves. Don't you think so? I think that is natural to human selfishness."

"That is to say?"

"That is to say that it is the unalterable fate of all of us here to fall in love with Elsie Melroth—your cousin, you, I, and *tutti quanti!* Your cousin has been the wisest of any of us; he did not wait for the hopelessness of his case to be unmistakably proved to him, but transferred his affections to Matilda. But I clung to my foolish dreams until a terrible awakening came, and it seemed to me as if all the waves had gone over me. That was when Elsie came to me and said, with charming frankness:

"'Herr Drausfeld, you are my friend, are you not, my true, firm friend?'

"'Certainly, Fräulein Elsie,' I answered, enthusiastically: 'certainly; you know I am.'

"'And if I should ask you, you would not refuse me a great favor, for which I can never repay you?'

"'I would die for you,' I answered, and I am sure my whole face must have beamed at this promising beginning of our conversation.'

"'I rely upon you,' answered Elsie. 'I trust you fully. You need not die for me, but you must swear to die rather than betray my secret. Will you swear it?'

"'I swear it.

"'I thank you, Herr Drausfeld, for being so very, very good to me—as good as a brother. I have never had a brother, but I am sure one could not be better to me than you

are. So it will not be hard for me to be frank with you. Hear, Emil; I am engaged, have been for years. But nobody must know it, nobody. I am engaged to Philip Bonsart. We grew up together at Asthof. My father hates Philip's father as his worst enemy. He thinks Herr Bonsart deceived him, and cheated him out of his estate. And, then, Philip is so enthusiastic, so free-thinking and high-spirited, such an untamable fellow when once his enthusiasm is awakened. Hence, as you must have heard, he got into the worst kind of trouble, into the revolt and the revolution, and then he had to fly; and now he has come back from America, where he has found a very good position: he is so active and so determined when once he has begun a thing to carry it through. He has already secured an excellent place, and has the surest prospect of becoming very, very rich. So he has come back, and now we will be married.'"

"Married!" exclaimed Ferdinand, almost crushed by the story.

"Yes, married; so Elsie said, as quietly as if it were the most indifferent word a young girl can speak—very much as a child would say, 'Now we will dress our dolls.' 'Married?' I exclaimed, so startled that I had to catch my breath; but she answered, 'Yes, of course, married, now that Philip has a situation and a home to take a wife to. He has come back for that. He is now at Asthof. The chaplain there is to marry us, but it is to be kept entirely secret. For, in the first place, my father must not know anything about it. When we get to America we will try to reconcile him to what we have done, and I am sure we shall succeed. But now he must not know anything about it. And, then, no one, no one at all must know that Philip Bonsart is here. He is a fugitive and is persecuted by the courts, and if he should be caught it would be terrible. So it must be kept a perfect secret; Chaplain Heimdel, at Asthof, who is a friend of Philip's, will marry us in the chapel at Asthof at night. Philip is sure that he will. He will give him a hundred thalers for the poor of the congregation if he does it. So that is all arranged. But, now, I must see Philip beforehand, to make some arrangements with him, and for that he will have to come here. He has some other business in the city also. Now, where can he stay while he is in the place, and who can bring him to me? There are many people in the city who know him, so that he can venture to come only with the utmost precaution, and he cannot ask the way to our house and come there. He might run against my father. I can talk with him in our old hall; no one will disturb us there. And you, Emil, you must help us. You will, will you not? You are so good—I trust you so—I do not know what I would not confide to you. We must have some friend, too, some witness at our marriage. I have thought I should like to ask you, but that can be arranged hereafter. For the present I would like to have you take Philip to your room, perhaps only for one, or, at the most, two nights. You will do that, will you not, for my sake? And you must be silent as the grave about it to every one, every one! And then you must bring Philip to the old hall through the alley in the rear; the carpenter has the key now, but there must be another; I will get that for you, and'—well that is about what Fräulein Elsie said, and I promised everything; and now you know what you wanted to. How I felt at the frank recital of this lovely romance would be of little interest to you. Perhaps something as you feel now at making the discovery—Heaven knows where and how—that for you, too, love's labor is lost—the discovery that came to me from Elsie's honest and trusting confession. Perhaps not much less desperate and not less strongly tempted to suicide! But what is the use of falling into such desperation? 'Lost love, lost life' is an old story. But it is well for us that we see at once how hopelessly lost it is, that we are spared the long agony of vibrating between hope and despair. For that seems to be the case with you as well as with me. How did you find out? Did you go back to the old hall and witness the *rendezvous* to which I took the American? Or did Fräulein Elsie at last admit you to her touching confidence?"

"No, she did not; I saw their meeting. So, then, you yielded to everything. that

Elsie asked. You took in this Philip Bonsart, and led him to the house?"

"Certainly; how could I do otherwise? Would you have acted differently? I did not exactly take him in—you need not be afraid that he may come in here at any minute—I found lodgings for him in a neighboring house, at a mechanic's, who had some unoccupied rooms. The oath I made to Elsie to be silent as the grave about the whole affair I have broken in regard to you. But I saw that you had already discovered it, and so I have told you all."

Emil Dransfeld lighted his cigar again and emptied his glass.

Ferdinand sat moody and absorbed, his arms resting on the table, and his eyes fixed on a knotty place in the top of it. The glass Emil had placed before him, he had pushed away, untouched.

"I wish, Drausfeld," he said, at length, "you had been more frank at the time you warned me so mysteriously. I could then have warned my cousin against an alliance with the family. I think now I must put the question to him, whether he can or will become the brother in-law of such a notorious demagogue."

Emil threw a suspicious glance at him.

"So," he said, "you think less of your own disappointment than of the injury to your cousin's prospects? To speak candidly, Schott, that seems to me not a very noble trait of character in you. It looks to me as if your ultimate purpose were to use your cousin, who now almost belongs to the family, to betray the affair to the old gentleman, and he, you think, will interfere and separate them before it is too late. Do not dream of such a thing! If you should make use of what you have seen accidentally, and what I have told you, it would be ungentlemanly and base. But it would also be useless, and you would gain nothing whatever by it. You would not raise yourself in Elsie's estimation, and as for separating her from her Philip, there is not the slightest prospect of it!"

Ferdinand sat and stared a while at the spot on the table. Emil threw aside his cigar, sprang up, and renewed his walk back and forth through the room.

"Let us console ourselves," he said, at length, "and take the affair philosophically. It may be harder for you, as it is perhaps the first blank you have drawn from the lottery of fate—at least since you have been grown up. Those little blanks which we now and then receive when we have staked our very best, even our whole hearts, are more familiar to me. And so I know better how to console myself. I repeat to myself what great men who understood women have said, as, for instance, ' Give a woman your heart, and she will give you sorrow and smart.' 'A woman is never worth what a man suffers for her.' This Elsie is a firebrand, and a wild fellow like this American is just the man for her; over there she can set the woods on fire without doing much damage; for our modest hearths such a wild flame would be a little too much. God give her all happiness in her new home !"

"And you," said Ferdinand, bitterly, "you talk like that, after you have professed to love her ? Well, it is not to be wondered at in such a meek soul—one that could consent to be used as their *postillon d'amour*, as their sentinel, as their marriage witness, and even—perhaps you will give her away, too ? No," he cried, springing up in anger and stamping his foot, "away with your sorry comfort. My only consolation would be in strangling this fellow, this Bonsart, before her eyes."

Crossing his arms over his chest, he stood silent for a while; then suddenly took his hat and said:

"I must be alone. I will take the night to think over what is to be done. To-morrow——"

"What is to be done, Schott?" cried Emil, seizing him by the arm and holding him back. "To settle that, I think you have no need of solitude, or of any great amount of time. You can do just nothing. If anything could be done in such a case, then it wouldn't be such a cursed, maddening position to be placed in ! Give up all idea of doing anything. There are but two results possible: either you will make yourself ridiculous as a despised lover, or you will draw on yourself the reproach of having acted ignobly and basely."

Ferdinand looked at him as if he had not understood his words.

"That may be," he answered, in a strange and absent tone, then turned and walked quickly out. Emil took up the lamp and hurried to the door to light him down the stairs; but he was already nearly out of the building.

CHAPTER VI.

A BURGLARY.

Nothing to be done ! To do nothing, to acquiesce silently in the decision that nothing could be done, that Elsie was irrecoverably lost, to look squarely in the face the fact that she had long ago given her love to this Philip Bonsart, and would soon be his wife—it was a terrible cup that destiny pressed to Ferdinand's passionate lips. And yet it was not merely the cold-blooded advice of his friend, it was also the conclusion that Ferdinand, himself, could not escape after a night of sleepless struggle against the iron force of the unalterable.

On the next day he avoided all his acquaintances. He did not see his cousin, Alexander, or go to Herr von Melroth's. He sent his cousin a few written words in the morning, telling him of the banker's promise. He would not see Elsie again—but to betray her secret, even to his cousin, he no longer thought of it. Emil was right. It would have been base and unknightly. He could not reproach Elsie in the least. She had not coquetted with him, or with any one. She had not given him any hope; the hopes he had made for himself had been those of an over-confident fool; in all his passionate excitement he was just enough to confess that to himself.

On the second day he spent the morning at his rooms, as he had the whole of the preceding day. He was expecting a call from his cousin, who, he thought, would probably come to-day, to thank him for what he had done. He was more firmly resolved to betray nothing to his cousin than he had been the day before; and yet he half unconsciously feared the first meeting; he feared himself; he doubted his own self-control in case his cousin should speak of Elsie.

About ten o'clock there was a knock at the door. He cried " Come in," and looked up, expecting to see the captain enter. But it was not he; it was the barber.

" Do I come at the right time, Herr von Schott?" he said.

Ferdinand nodded and gave himself up to the man's care. But he had scarcely begun operations, when he cried out :—

" Well, what do you think of it, Herr von Schott, of this bold burglary ?"

" Burglary ? What burglary ?"

" Don't you know that yet, Herr von Schott? of the recent burglary at your cousin's——"

" The captain's ?"

" The captain's ? Oh, no !" said the barber, smiling; " they do not so often undertake such things at the houses of officers. I mean the banker, Schott."

" The banker ? Has there been a burglary there ?"

" Yes, last night. The thieves got into the court, and forced off one of the window-shutters of the room where the money is kept; but they could do nothing with the iron bars over the window."

" But the clerk always sleeps there, I believe."

" Yes, but not last night. Your cousin had given him permission to stay at home with his sick wife."

" Ah ! and the theives knew it?"

" It seems so; but it did not help them much. They succeeded in getting into your cousin's ante-room, and from there into his back room. They took a paper of considerable value, so it is said, and that is all they found."

" That is strange," said Ferdinand; " a paper they found in the writing-desk in my cousin's room ?"

" So I heard only a moment ago; it is all over town, and it is said the police have their suspicions."

" What kind of a police would they be if they had no suspicions?" said Ferdinand, smiling and thoughtful. " Have you finished, Herr Markoetter ?"

" Yes, in a moment," answered Herr Markoetter, moving his long hands briskly, as he gave the finishing touches.

When the process was ended, and Herr Markoetter had flown to other fortunate customers to whom he could tell the news, Ferdinand hastily finished his toilet and hurried to his cousin's. There was no trace outside of the attempt that had been made; everything was as quiet as usual; the clerks were sitting at their desks and writing; the messenger only ran past Ferdinand with a face more flushed than usual, carrying his bills of exchange and bags of money; and as Ferdinand entered his cousin's office, he met a policeman who seemed to have just finished an interview with the banker.

" I have come for a visit of condolence," said Ferdinand. " I have just heard, cousin, that you had a robbery here last night."

" Yes," answered Johann Heinrich, " and it was committed with most remarkable boldness ! Fortunately, the thieves accomplished only a part of their design. They did not succeed in opening the safe, but they opened this writing-desk with a picklock, and took out a valuable paper—why, you were here when I bought it from that American, day before yesterday—that is the paper they stole. I neglected giving it to the cashier, but, in my confusion, I locked it up here. In reality, you are to blame for it, you alone, or, rather, that stupid love-story of yours."

" Oh, you are jesting !"

" Jesting ? Would you jest if you had just lost one thousand dollars ? It would be just like you, though. But I am not jesting. You had confused me with your demand for money for Alexander, and it was that that excited me, and made me so absent-minded and careless. You see what you have done."

" Oh," answered Ferdinand, smiling, " my conscience is perfectly clear. You are not the man to lose your presence of mind over a matter of eight thousand thalers; on the contrary——"

"You don't believe me? I tell you it is so. But I will make no reproaches. A banker should not allow himself to be confused. I have been punished for it, and will take the punishment with composure. And if the police cannot recover my thousand dollars for me—and I have little hope that they will—then I will put it down, uncomplainingly, in my account of losses. The poor man that broke in at my window may have a cousin who is in need of a settlement. And as he has none of your persuasive eloquence, but instead of it, audacity and pick-locks, he took that way of applying to the good-natured Johann Heinrich Schott. Why should we make a great ado about that? Every one must help himself the best way he can."

"I see the affair has made you very sarcastic. But I think you give up your thousand dollars for lost very hastily."

"Do you think the police can recover it for me? Commissary Groebler, who has just left me, says that two very dangerous tramps, just discharged from the penitentiary at W., passed through here yesterday, giving out at the hotel that they were on their way home. He has already taken steps to have them arrested. This lively Herr Groebler, by the way, seems to me a phœnix of a police officer."

"Does their way of breaking in indicate professional thieves?" asked Ferdinand. "How did they operate? They first broke the window shutters of the room where the safe is kept?"

"Yes; they climbed over the wall between the garden and the court, which would not be difficult for any one with a little acrobatic skill; it was more difficult to get off the shutter without making noise enough to awaken either me or my servant in the first story, or the housekeeper and kitchen girl, who sleep in the front part of the second story. But, then, they were probably not very pleasantly surprised by something like what landscape gardeners call a 'ha, ha'—by the strong iron bars over the window. They, therefore, turned their attention to another window opening on the court, the one leading into the back room, and there they had better success.

3

They removed the shutter, broke a pane of glass, and so reached the catch. They could then get into this room very easily, and had no great difficulty in opening my writing-desk, judging by the slight traces they have left. When my servant came in this morning to make the fire, he found the writing-desk standing open, as well as the door between these two rooms, and one side of the window looking into the court."

"And there was no indication that your nocturnal visitors had made the attempt to get from here into the business rooms, and from there to the room where the safes are, as probably they could have reached it more easily by that route than through the bars of the window?"

"No indication. After making their *coup de main*, the thieves withdrew like peaceable, sensible people."

"Did not that surprise you?"

"Surprise me? It only surprised me that they knew how to choose a night when the clerk who generally sleeps there had received permission to stay at home—his wife is very sick. And yet I have unbounded confidence in the honesty of this man, to whom I have to entrust thousands every day. It is impossible that he could have been concerned in it."

"There might have been other people employed about the building and acquainted with the clerk or his family, who could have known of it soon enough to mention it indiscreetly, so that the fact could be made use of. But are you sure that it was intentionally made use of? I am inclined to believe that it was by mere chance that the burglary took place in the absence of your clerk."

"Indeed, and what makes you think so? It seems that the combinations of your wisdom have already led you to a definite suspicion. Speak, then, without any more diplomatic preliminaries."

Ferdinand shook his head.

"To a suspicion? No. I said so only because it is an old observation that 'chance' has a demoniac nature, and knows how to arrange things so that what happens is the very thing that just at this day and just at this hour ought not to have happened! I have no suspicion; it only came into my head that possibly the American might have remembered afterward that he had written his name on the paper, and have thought that it would endanger the safety of his sojourn here, and that possibly he might have recovered his paper in a true Yankee go-a-head manner. But that is foolishness——"

"Ah, you thought that would explain why no farther attempt was made to break into the other rooms? The thieves must have been simply driven away by some noise; this Herr Bonsart may be a bold traitor and revolutionist: he is not a thief!"

"No; it was folly to think of such a thing. You are right. I had seen the improbability before you spoke. Beside, he would have supposed that if his name were noticed on the paper, and the authorities set on his track, it would probably have occurred yesterday, so that would be too late. So——"

At this moment, the conversation was interrupted by a hasty knock, and the police-officer stepped into the room again.

"Excuse me, Herr Schott," he said, "there is one thing I neglected. I have sent the necessary telegrams, but now it is best to advertise the stolen bond in the newspapers, as a warning against buying it, and, if you choose, to offer a small reward for its recovery."

"It might be well to do so, Herr Groebler," answered the banker. "I will write you a description of the paper. Unfortunately, as I had not put it into the safe, it was not entered regularly in the books—in consequence of my attention being somewhat distracted—and, therefore, I cannot give the number. But there was one peculiar mark upon it—the name, Philip Bonsart."

"Philip Bonsart!" exclaimed the police-officer.

"Philip Bonsart," repeated the banker. "The name was written on the edge at the back, and my cousin here is firmly convinced that it was that gentleman himself who was here day before yesterday and sold me the bond."

While the banker was speaking, Herr Groebler's eyes glided slowly from him to Ferdinand, and it was singular the complete change that came over his eyes in this short journey from the one to the other. Those deep-set eyes had rested on the banker with a weary and expressionless gaze, like that of a sleepy dog; but now, as they turned upon Ferdinand, they glowed like the eyes of a bird of prey. Herr Groebler's long, narrow, yellow face was subject to such transitions. To one it said, "You need not be disturbed or frightened, whatever reasons we may have had for meddling with your affairs, we have nothing to do with them at present; we will attend to you hereafter." To another, it said with those glowing eyes, "Now we have you fast; now we shall bring all your fearful sins to the clear light of day!"

But this language of the policeman's eyes was entirely without effect on Ferdinand. With wrinkled brows, he seemed to be studying Herr Groebler's physiognomy. It was as if he were observing, with extreme anxiety, the effect of the name, Philip Bonsart, on the police-commissary. He remained quiet in the sofa-corner he had taken, leaving his cousin to answer, when Herr Groebler exclaimed, in a suppressed voice, as though suddenly distressed for want of breath:—

"You believe that this Philip Bonsart is here in the city—here? You believe that? Philip Bonsart?"

"According to what my cousin says, it must have been he himself," answered Johann Heinrich.

"I think," observed Ferdinand, smiling slightly, "you are very foolish, cousin, to bring this dangerous man into the game. You have only to look at Herr Groebler to see that at this moment he is very little concerned as to where your thousand dollars have gone to, but very much as to where he can lay his hand on the traitor; the police do not take such game every day!"

"Unfortunately, Herr von Schott," answered Herr Groebler, "the police are used to being on the track of more than one kind of game at a time, and they are prepared for it! Will you tell me whatever you know that may be of service to me in securing this dangerous man?"

"Dangerous? He is dangerous to you, to be sure, since, if he escapes you, he may cheat you out of an order or a promotion!"

"1 beg of you," said Herr Groebler, without noticing this remark, "to tell me everything about him that may help us to find him—his appearance, his dress, his statements about himself—where he came from, what had brought him here, and why he needed such a large amount of ready money. He must, of course, have given a false name? It was day before yesterday that he was here. At what hour?"

While speaking, Herr Groebler had taken out his large note-book to make memoranda of the answers.

"It was day before yesterday," said the banker, "that he was here, between five and six o'clock—nearer six, was it not, Ferdinand?"

"You must know better than I, cousin," answered Ferdinand. "You had better give your attention, Herr Groebler, to my cousin's statements, for, as for me, you must know that I had just come from a little dinner in honor of a betrothal, and was, therefore, in a condition that weakens the ability of most people for sharp observation. You understand that, Herr Groebler."

"Your eloquence, at least, was not weakened," said Johann Heinrich, smiling bitterly.

"But," said Ferdinand, "the tongue and the eyes are quite different things."

"At six o'clock, then," said Herr Groebler, "and what name did he give? you asked his name?"

The banker answered, and gave farther details, of all of which the officer made copious notes. When he put questions on points as to which the banker was not quite sure, he turned to Ferdinand, who gave, without concealment, what information he could regarding the special point in question.

But that was all he did to facilitate the work of the police. He did his duty toward the officer, but kept silence when Herr Groebler did not question him. Sitting in his sofa corner, observing, with contracted brows, the slight signs of excitement which the commissary could not quite conceal under the cold exterior of his official dignity, he thought how happy he could make this man by telling him even a small part of what he knew about Philip Bonsart, and the object of his visit; how many useless efforts, how many journeys, how many examinations of landlords, how many long watches at dépôts, how many telegraphic despatches he could spare these people, if he should speak. But he would not speak. No, he would not. He would have liked to speak, and would have given much if he could—if he could have brought sudden ruin on the man he hated above everything else on earth, and so have made him harmless to himself forever. He did not forbear for Elsie's sake. The tenderness, the sentimental self-denial that would have held him back from anything that might have made Elsie unhappy, was not in him. His love for her was too much that of a selfish man who desires to win, to conquer, to possess, and that of a vain man, to whom it could never occur to doubt that he could fully replace the love he might deprive her of. No, it was not for Elsie's sake that he forbore, but for his own sake. He would have despised himself as a dog, if he could have betrayed his rival. In the first moment, when Emil Drausfeld made those bitter revelations, then, perhaps, his pain and his rage might have driven him to sieze, blindly, the most effective weapon for destroying his fortunate rival. But to-day it was otherwise. He had regained his self-control, and if not composure of feeling, at least enough clearness of mind to make it impossible for his passion to drive him to a base action.

And did he not, too, revenge himself on Elsie, now when he quietly defended her, held over her the shield of his silence?

So Philip Bonsart remained unbetrayed by him, although he did not hesitate to tell the truth when the officer addressed questions directly to him, for confirmation of his cousin's recollections of the man's appearance and dress. When the commissary had withdrawn with hasty steps, he left his cousin and went out to the wall of the old city fortifications, now planted with lindens, and used as a promenade, though it was but little frequented. There he could be alone with his thoughts, and had leisure to reflect on the destiny that awaited

Elsie with such a man, pursued here as a criminal, and for whom, on the other side of the ocean, there would be abundant adventure and shifting fates; it could not be otherwise with such a character as Philip Bonsart's must be, having a magnetic attraction toward adventure, and unfitted for a quiet, peaceful life, such as a woman craves. But perhaps it was her choice; perhaps her longings were all for a new world, full of change and adventure. Perhaps if all that could await her, her entire future could have been shown to her in a magic glass, even this might not have frightened her from following the man she had chosen. It was too late now to separate them!

But not too late to watch over her. The more Ferdinand thought of her and her future, the more anxious did he grow about her fate, and uneasy about the consequences, for her as well as for Bonsart, of the fact of his presence in the neighborhood being known to the police. Here, in the city, indeed, they might seek him in vain; he had gone; but would not Herr Groebler at once extend his search to Philip's home, to Asthof, and might not that sly and shrewd detective succeed in laying hands upon him there? Was it not necessary to send him a warning? At first he shrank, in his wrath, from doing so much for his rival. But gradually he grew to regard it as a duty toward Elsie. He felt that he should despise himself if, from base jealousy, he should neglect it. The blow would be too cruel, it would drive her nature of "flame" to the verge of insanity, if her lover were to be snatched from her at the very moment of their union, to be thrown into a dungeon! It would not be necessary that he should personally warn Philip; he could take Emil Drausfeld into his confidence, and give the warning through him. This he resolved to do.

He looked Emil up, and told him everything that had occurred.

Emil was frightened. "This Groebler is a dangerous bloodhound, and we can rest assured that he will be in Asthof long before evening! I must send Philip Bonsart a warning to-day; to-morrow it may be too late. But how?"

"Best perhaps through Elsie. She must have found a way of keeping up communication with him."

"Elsie has gone," answered Emil. "Yesterday morning she started, as she told them at home, to visit a friend in B., two hours's journey from Asthof. Philip is to go there for her and bring her to Asthof."

"Gone! Then she has really gone to be married to him!"

"Did you doubt her resolution?"

Ferdinand was silent a while, and then said, shrugging his shoulders:

"You are my witness that I have done what I could. I have placed the matter in your hands. It is for you to devise means for warding off the misfortune from these people!"

Emil stood thinking. "The safest way," he said, at length, "is for me to go as soon as possible to Asthof. It is a long way. If I go at once, I shall be there sooner than Herr Groebler."

"Without doubt," said Ferdinand, who felt rebuked at Emil's zeal.

Emil began to make his preparations hastily; Ferdinand gave him his hand, turned, and went away in silence.

When he was alone in his room, the reaction came in full force—the reaction that, with a character like his, must always follow an impulse to self-sacrifice, to conquest of its own passions. He reproached himself for his foolish generosity; he condemned Elsie's reckless, mad action; he cursed this Philip Bonsart, and still more himself, with his unhappy love for this girl, whom he called unworthy of it, and yet whom he could not tear from his heart. He was overcome by a sorrow and desperation that seemed to him remediless; he told himself that he should never be able to conquer it, that it would paralyze all his powers, would poison the sweets of life, and make him forever wretched. Resting his head upon his hand, he said to himself, with a bitter smile, "You are now one of those rare psychological phenomena, an unfortunate in love; and all that remains for you to do is to study the pathology of the disease."

After thinking and dreaming for a long time, he raised himself.

"No," he said, "to make an utter failure on account of such a woman, to die of a broken heart, that is not the fate the gods have reserved for you. For that you are still too good, too strong, too decided, too truly fire! I will go away from here, away from the atmosphere of this city, where the enchantment first came upon me. I will go to Berlin, and urge them to give me an early examination. Then I shall be obliged to busy myself with other things, and such a necessity is the best means for driving away regret. And I will see and hear nothing more of the people here; I will not hear her name; I should have to go, after a few days, to make Father Melroth a visit of condolence, when he has found out and it has got abroad that his daughter has escaped with an adventurer. None of that! I will pack up and be away. Let them wonder, the Melroths, Alexander, Emil Drausfeld, all of them, at my sudden disappearance; the discussions I should have with Alexander, when he hears of the affair, would alone be enough to drive me away. I will take leave only of my good cousin, Johann Heinrich; he can bid the others good-bye for me."

In his hasty way, he began at once to carry out his decision. He sent for his servant and ordered all his bills paid, packed up his effects, went to his cousin, the banker, on whom he was dependent, to give him his reasons for taking the step, explaining it by his desire to get on in his profession; and in the evening he was in the night-train for Berlin.

Berlin! The great city with all its feverish life took him up and roared, and whirled, and thundered around him, and yet he was more alone than in quiet H. He dreamed of Elsie and devoted himself as much as he could to his studies, without hearing a word from the old provincial town. The first news from there, which came after a long delay, was a short business letter from the banker, to whom he had sent notice of his arrival and his address in Berlin. Johann Heinrich wrote in a postscript that Herr Groebler had succeeded in catch-ing the two suspected tramps, that the bond had been found in their possession, and that they would be tried at the next assizes. Alexander, he added, wished to be remembered; he had been promoted and transferred, and on that account would hasten his marriage. That was all the news in Johann Heinrich's letter.

A week afterward, a letter came from Alexander. He informed Ferdinand of his promotion, and his wedding which was to take place the next week, and to which he begged Ferdinand to come. This letter, too, had a postscript. It ran:—"Poor Emil Drausfeld! As his written work for his second examination was found wanting, and he is now spoiled for the career of a forester proper, his relatives have procured him a miserable place as under-forester in an out-of-the-way place, and are now urging him to go there, to devote himself to his flute and his disappointment!"

Singularly enough, the letter contained not a word about Elsie!

Ferdinand thought over and over about this remarkable silence, and could find no explanation of it; when he wrote to his cousin, declining the invitation, he could not refrain from adding, "And the house of Melroth? You did not tell me a syllable, either of the father or of Elsie."

About ten days afterward, Ferdinand received a printed notice of his cousin's marriage. With the brevity of a bridegroom too much occupied to write letters, Alexander had added the words: "We are going to the Rhine, for our wedding journey. Father Melroth is in excellent health, and sends his regards to you. Elsie? Do not ask after her. The sooner you get her out of your mind, the better. Yours,

ALEXANDER."

Ferdinand stared gloomily at these lines for a long time, as if he must succeed in reading from them what Elsie had passed through since he saw her. At last he crushed the paper and threw it into the stove, saying—

"Well, it is done, she is on the other side the ocean, and lost forever! May her memory perish as this paper perishes in the flames."

The fire in the little stove devoured the slip of paper, but the fiercer fire within him could not fulfil his wish and destroy for him the memory of Elsie.

CHAPTER VII.

FORGOTTEN.

The events just related are now stories of long-vanished days. Many years have passed since then, seventeen, perhaps eighteen. Men since then have died, friends have separated, vows have been broken, alliances have been made between people who then had never seen each other, and have again been dissolved; ambitious men have grown old and tame, modest and quiet men have come into places where they assert themselves haughtily and imperiously. If we should go again into our old city, we should find it a little older and grayer; there would seem to be more fissures in the ancient houses, greater quiet in the streets; if we should ask after our old acquaintances there, we should find that many had been sleeping for years under the green turf, the dress that nature weaves for us all at last, and from which no changes in the fashions, whatever other wonders they can do, can avail to save us. If we should ask after the banker Johann Heinrich Schott, we should hear:—He died a few years ago, quite suddenly, of an apoplectic stroke, after suffering for a long time from a liver-complaint, which made him so cross in his last years, that he did not seem to be the same man. And father Melroth? He, also, died several years ago—how many—who knows now? Of what? That, too, is forgotten. And his daughters? Long, long gone from this region. One, the oldest, married an officer, a Captain Schott; directly after they were married, they went east, to Prussia or Pomerania, "back there in the geography;" there he, too, is said to have died, Captain Schott, soon after his marriage—or perhaps a year after—or two, it is not known precisely. Nothing more has been heard from them. Such people come, and we see them and associate with them; they take their place among us, a large or a small one, as the case may be, and then their business calls them to another place, and they move out, and the stream of life fills up the gap they left, and they are lost sight of, forgotten!

These are the answers we should receive, should we return to that old city where the preceding events of our story took place, and inquire for those concerned in them. We must look among quite different scenes for those in whom we are specially interested.

The first is a man, now in his full vigor, whom we find taking a tedious journey on a miserable day, in a wild, desolate, forsaken region. The great, boundless plain, sprinkled with sand-dunes, looking like dams half-built and then abandoned, was covered with a light, wet snow, which balled together under the feet, and here and there stood in little watery pools in slight depressions of the ground, but seemed too indolent to yield at once to the warmth of the oncoming thaw. What did it matter though the snow should remain a week longer in this desolate, uninhabited place? The little, roundish heaps of turf scattered here and there through the hollows and along narrow ditches, in which the sunken ice was covered with brownish-yellow water, did not trouble themselves as to whether the snow staid on their round heads or not. A heavy gray fog extended over the whole region, shutting in the otherwise wide prospect, and giving only here and there a shimmering view of the outlines of the dark pinewoods, which lay to the right and left. Two men were passing through this desert on horseback. One was in the uniform of a forester, over which he wore an old dark-gray cloak; he was seated on a bony horse, with extended neck, drooping head, and weary eyes. With him, on an animal not much better, was a man apparently from a very different sphere of life; he wore a closely-buttoned, heavy gray overcoat, and fine boots, reaching to the knee. He was tall, and his face had that type of distinction given by clear and rather sharply-cut features, and a head rather oval than round; the chin, which was a little too strongly developed, was hidden in a long, light beard; had it not been, one would have been struck with the expression of energy in it, especially in connection with the eyes, which, though half-closed, had a sharp and aggressive expression. It might have been the wearisome expanse of snow around that kept the eyes half-closed; he opened them wide only now and then, when he raised his eyeglass to look at something in the distance. He sat in the saddle like a practiced rider, and his bearing had something of a military air. This was Ferdinand von Schott. After both had been silent for some time, he resumed the conversation.

"But over there, at the right, I see something glimmering that looks like a church tower," he said, in a remarkably sonorous and pleasant voice; "there, at the dark edge of those woods."

"You are right," answered the forester. "It is the church-tower of Ehleru. We have now a league and a half to ride."

"A league and a half yet! And I think we have already come three leagues. Three leagues, you said, we had to ride?"

"Three leagues; and here, at the point where the church-tower of Ehleru becomes visible, we have passed over one-half the distance."

"It is a fearful place, and I am afraid it doesn't look much better when this horrible winding-sheet of snow is off."

"Not much, but a little," said the forester. "Then you can at least see the sandy roads which cross it, and now and then a living creature, to afford some little diversion; you can hear the plovers cry, and see the storks and herons, and now and then a fox, sneaking among the sand-heaps. There are but few rabbits; they cannot find the right kind of food; and the partridges only come here in harvest, when they are scared away from the fields. But now, at this season, no living creature could thrive here, except the hooded crow, like that just crossing our path on beyond there, unless it were brought from Siberia and domesti-

cated here. A little more to the left, sir; our road leads to the dark woods at the left there."

"Our road?" said Ferdinand, shrugging his shoulders. "I'll be hanged if I can see any trace of a road or any track there!"

"It is not necessary," answered the forester. "The roads run over the heath as if they had their own way entirely, and troubled themselves but very little about men. What does this desolate heath know or care about men, and how can these wild paths know where people want to go? They run on, now to the right, and now to the left, like a forsaken child or a wandering dog; often, too, only until they get tired, and then they stop suddenly before a sand-hill or a snow-pond, and that is the end of it!"

"What a place! And to be exiled to such a world forever!" said Ferdinand to himself, half-aloud.

The forester drew his cloak closer around him, then began a quick motion with his feet in the stirrups, and then drew out a short pipe, with a wooden bowl, which he filled and lighted, the quiet pace of his horse allowing him to use his hands freely.

"If one's feet did not get so cold in the stirrups, we could get along very well," he said. "A short, quick trot would be too hazardous; Heaven only knows into what hole under the snow the nags might step, and if we should have an accident I shouldn't like to meet that postmaster again; he is as obstinate and hard-bitted as if he had trotted before his mail-wagon himself for the last dozen years; it's a great wonder that you prevailed on him to lend us these two old nags."

"That was, indeed, a good-natured thing for him to do. He would certainly not have lent us the horses if it had not been for giving you an opportunity to carry your good news to the forester at Vellinghaus. Does he know him, this Herr Drausfeld?"

"I do not know; he may know him, and he may not. He will trouble himself very little as to whether the forester, Drausfeld, receives the news to-day or a year from now; he did it entirely from love of your bright thalers, you may be sure!"

"But you know him, Herr Drausfeld?"

"I know him, and so I know what it means to him—such a paper as I have in my pocket for him. Fifty thalers increase of salary—that is all the world to people in such circumstances. For the husband and wife and the bevy of children, who have heretofore had to live on four hundred and fifty thalers, together with their rent, the use of a garden and meadow, and six cords of fire-wood—it is all the world."

"Four hundred and fifty thalers in this horrible, desolate wilderness?"

"Do you think it so very little?" said the forester, smiling. "Well, the science that one of us has to bring to such work, and the amount to be done, are very well paid for with four hundred and fifty thalers. But I can tell you, sir, the management and skill necessary to keep house with such a sum and not run behind—four hundred and fifty thalers will not pay for that! But what would you have? Dransfeld was thankful enough to get the place. He had not many claims on a position, and, poor as this was, there were applications from others as well qualified as Dransfeld. In any other place he could hardly have succeeded. If his forest had not been so far out of the world, he could hardly have kept away the wood thieves; and where there are poachers, a flute blower, piping half the night to the moon, would hardly be the right kind of an officer. But I will say nothing against him, although he is no more fit for a forester than a sheep is for a snipe-catcher, and the Lord only knows by what cousinly influence he obtained the place; but he is a kind-hearted and courteous man, who wishes well to every one. Beside, the poor fellow cannot hold out much longer; whether it is from blowing the flute too much, or what, his lungs are affected, and when he begins coughing, it is enough to scare one away. Well, you must know him well, or you would not have been so determined to go to him, and have persisted, in spite of this wretched weather, until our postmaster brought out his old nags."

"Which I should not have succeeded in," said Ferdinand, evasively, "if you had not happened to come along with an errand to the forester at Vellinghaus. The close-fisted fellow," he added, laughing, "has in you a security that I will not run away with this jewel of his stables."

The forester made no reply. He may have thought his companion a little too reticent and mysterious about the reasons that led him on such a day through this snowy wilderness to the forester of Vellinghaus. He, therefore, kept silence. Why should he allow himself to be drawn out about his flute-playing colleague by a man perhaps related to him? It was well known that Dransfeld was from a good and once wealthy family, and if nothing had even been said of it, it would have been evident from his fine and gentle manner, notwithstanding his negligent appearance, and the unbrushed clothes that hung around his emaciated form.

The forester had smoked out his pipe; he put it away, and began again to work his feet in the stirrups, saying:—

"How thick the fog is growing! It is well I saw the tower of Ehleru, and the corner of the forest to which we must ride; as the air is now, we might easily lose our way."

"Like the man, or woman, rather," said Ferdinand, looking down beside him at the snow, "who left these tracks. They run along in a wild and uncertain way across our path."

"That is true," answered the forester, checking his horse, and observing, closely, the deep tracks in the snow. "Some woman must have lost her way, for these tracks were evidently made by a woman's shoe, a fine shoe, too; notice the narrow sole and the small, high heel. Our peasant women do not wear such."

"Singular," said Ferdinand. "How can a lady have been lost here? It is incredible!"

"It must have been yesterday," continued the forester. "There is a little water in all the tracks." He raised himself in the stirrups in order to see the direction of the steps as far as possible.

"They come from the left," he said; "from the direction of the Vellinghaus forest. Here, not far from where we are, she must have lost the direction, perhaps, to Stavorn, the station from which we came. From here she kept more to the right. God grant she got to Ehleru; otherwise it may have gone hard with her."

Ferdinand, who had rode a little distance in the direction of the steps and observed them carefully, said:—

"It is, indeed, not only the foot, but the gait of a lady; of one, at least, whose walk has been trained. How regularly the toes are turned outward! But here and there the tracks are noticeably wider, the foot has been planted uncertainly and raised again; the wanderer must have been very weary."

"It is very strange," said the forester; "if I had not seen it with my own eyes, I could not have believed it. In this wilderness !"

"In truth," said Ferdinand, thoughtfully, "it is very strange, and there is something very uncanny about the footsteps here in this desert of fog and snow. I should not be surprised if we should presently meet a pair of bewitched little boots, condemned for their past sins to wander forever on this desolate heath !"

"Then they would have each other for company," answered the forester, smiling; "but the person that left these tracks was entirely alone, without a companion, guide, or protector."

They rode on, and as from time to time the footsteps again became visible in wide curves, the forester said at last:—

"I see they come from the forester's lodge at Vellinghaus, and it could have been no one else than the forester's wife wandering here on the heath—Frau Drausfeld. She is the only person for leagues around here who could wear such shoes. Yes, yes, it must have been she. God help us ! The poor woman must be crazy to run about so in the snow !"

Ferdinand shook his head. "Crazy ? One might well be after being exiled here for years. And what if her husband had treated her badly, which even the best-natured one might come to in such circumstances——"

"He ? Oh, no; he could not treat any one badly; and, as far as I know, he has

never had any trouble with his wife, though they are badly enough suited to each other. When he had been forester here for a year, he must have found that without a wife, and all alone with his flute-playing, it was absolutely unendurable, and then, they say, he advertised in the newspaper for a wife, and so he happened to get a former lady's-maid in a noble family; people thought she would have a hard time of it in the quiet lodge, and would have to play the termagant, if only for diversion. But no; the little woman has held herself bravely, and has brought up their large family well and in the fear of God—all except the oldest boy, who is a good-for-nothing, and is said to have run away from his parents two or three times already."

Ferdinand had listened in silence, and the conversation was now dropped. The horses ploded along through the wet snow, till at length they came to a broad, straight forest road, through a melancholy, unmoving fir wood, which seemed to stretch out endlessly before them. The foot-tracks appeared again beside it; after a while they were doubled, one row coming into the road from under the fir trees, and leading toward the forester's lodge.

"She got back to the house safely," said the forester, "here, straight through the forest. The tracks run here to the house. We shall soon reach it."

They reached it in about ten minutes. It lay to the right from the road; a little garden enclosed by a paling lay in front of it; some pines stretched their heavy branches over the roof; they had caught and held the snow on their broader needles better than had the firs in the wood. In front of the little windows on the gable-side of the house stood a pair of leafless linden trees, their branches twined together above as a protection against the summer-sun. Behind the house, and at the side of the little stable, lay quite a large garden, and on the other side an orchard, with crooked, moss-covered fruit trees. No living creature was visible.

When the riders had dismounted and tied their horses to the garden paling, the upper part of a door in the centre of the house was opened, and a boy looked out. His long, blonde hair hung over his projecting forehead in tangled locks, and his eyes surveyed the strangers with a sullen and hostile expression.

"Good day, my boy," cried the forester, stamping with his benumbed feet on the ground; "how goes it? Is your father at home?"

The boy did not answer. His looks grew more hostile, but he opened the lower part of the door, and the men stepped in. They entered a clean and bright-looking kitchen, where a turf fire was burning on the hearth; a number of children were sitting around on low straw chairs and stools. They were remarkably quiet, and a half-grown girl, with a baby on her lap, showed by her reddened eyes that their strange quiet had some tragic cause.

"Where is your father?" asked the forester again of the boy.

The boy remained silent. The girl answered for him.

"Father," she said, and fell into such a violent fit of sobbing that the words she added could scarcely be understood, but they sounded like "Father is dead."

The boy stood and stared at the strangers as if to observe the effect of the words, and ready to fall into a passion if it should not be what he expected.

"What? Dead?" exclaimed the forester.

"Dead?" repeated Ferdinand, whose color changed visibly.

"There is mother," said the child.

A door was opened at the right—a glass door, with a curtain on the other side—and situated at the head of six steps; it was evidently the entrance to an upper room.

A thin little woman, in disorderly attire, came out and descended the stairs. Her features, which must have been originally pretty, were disfigured by the unmistakable impress of bitter sorrow, though her eyes were dry and firm as she looked at the strangers.

"What do I hear, Frau Drausfeld?" said the forester, with emotion, stepping toward her. "Your husband is dead?"

"He died yesterday—last night; between eleven and twelve. You are the first man I have seen since. He is dead, dead!"

She staggered and fell into the straw chair near her, as if crushed by the terrible fact.

"But, Heavens! how did that happen so suddenly, so unexpectedly?"

"Unexpectedly? I knew very well that it would soon be over with him. I thought in the spring, when the trees leave out and the young grass springs up, then it must end! But I did not think it would end so soon. Yesterday, at noon, he had a dreadful hemorrhage, and there was no one—no one to help him. I ran out, leaving the children with him, out toward Stavorn for help; for a physician. I ran a long way through the snow. But the fog was so thick on the heath I lost my way; I did not know where I was. I would gladly have lain down in the snow and died there!"

She said no more, but sat with her hands pressed convulsively together, and stared with her tearless eyes at the floor.

"Then they were really your footsteps that we saw," observed the forester, after a pause, during which Ferdinand had been looking at the poor woman, and trying to imagine the despair of that lonely wandering through the fog and snow; it was heart-rending.

"And how did you get home again?" asked the forester.

"God knows," she answered, in a lifeless voice; "at the last I thought only of getting home before nightfall; and just at dark I got home. It was like a dream!"

"And so you did not have the slightest assistance, and he died in the night?"

"He died," she answered, with a deep sigh. "He lies up there, in the alcove off the upper room. If you would like to see him, you can go up there."

The forester threw a glance at the door, a glance as of doubt and reluctance. Then he said:

"And no one knows that you are here in this deserted place, cut off from all the world, alone with your dead?"

"No one on earth. What is to be done, I do not know."

The forester shook his head. He seemed

to have need of time to comprehend such a situation and make it clear to himself.

"Take courage, Frau Dransfeld," he said, slowly and half-aloud, as if still deep in thought; "I will ride at once to Ehlern and arrange for everything needful. The neighboring foresters shall be notified, and everything shall be done for you that it is possible to do.

"If I had only been sent here a few days sooner—but it always takes such a fearful long time for the gentlemen to get all the writing done. See, there, what I came to bring your husband—an increase in his salary of fifty thalers a year!"

She took the official letter which he drew out and handed to her, and dropped it apathetically into her lap.

Her son was standing by her, leaning with his shoulder on the back of her chair. He took up the letter, opened it, and read it through slowly, without saying a word. Then he laid it as quietly in her lap again.

"It comes too late, too late!" she said, with an expression of complete despair.

Complete, utter despair was the expression of her entire appearance. She showed no violent grief; she did not weep or sob; as she sat there with her look of fixed and stony grief, it was evident that there would be no outbreak of stormy despair; she was completely broken, perhaps even dulled in every feeling, broken in every power, by the cares and sorrows of past days, months, and years.

"It is too late!" she repeated, lifelessly. And then, after a pause, she said, "Will you go up, Herr Gellhorn? He lies there so still, and peaceful, and beautiful! His face looks as if something great and holy had come to him—something great and holy!"

At these words of the mother, Ferdinand was struck with the appearance of the boy at her side. While his face had previously worn an expression of wrathful defiance, he seemed to be strangely and completely overcome by what his mother said of something great and holy that had left its imprint on the still features of his dead father; he broke out in a terrible fit of sobbing, and threw himself on the stairs that led to the

upper room, pressing his forehead upon one of the higher steps, and giving himself up to a passion of sorrow.

Ferdinand looked at him with deep emotion. The forester, Gellhorn, might have thought, in his powerlessness to be of any assistance, that it would perhaps comfort the wife a little if he should do as she asked and go to the upper room; he might, too, have thought it a kind of duty toward his departed colleague to look for the last time upon his rigid features. So he went lightly up the steps, past the boy, and disappeared behind the glass door.

Ferdinand shrank from following him. Why should he expose himself to the shock of seeing again, under such circumstances, the man he had known, young, fresh, hopeful, in that other, happier life so long ago?

Frau Dransfeld looked into his face with a questioning glance.

"Your look," he said, "asks who I am and why I have come. My name is Ferdinand von Schott, and I was a friend of your husband's youth. Has he never mentioned my name to you?"

"I think he has," she answered; "I think so, for the name sounds familiar."

"Well," he continued, "I came to see him again and talk with him of old times. But not for that alone. In those times he was the confidant of two people, whom a strange fate threw together and then tore apart again; they were thrown so far from each other that the only connecting link between them was your husband. These persons were a lady of the highest rank, and a man who went to seek his fortune across the ocean. Both wrote letters to him, to Emil Dransfeld; he communicated with both, telling as much as it was necessary for each to know of the other, or as much as each desired the other to know. I have come to obtain these letters from your husband. I have a right to see them, to receive them. For, to tell you plainly, my whole future depends on the contents of those letters. My fortune depends on it, and through that my whole future life. The oral explanations I hoped to receive from your husband are now no longer possible. But perhaps I can obtain the letters. You must know where your husband kept his correspondence. Will you be kind enough to show me his letters?"

The woman had raised her eyes to him and listened with a kind of absent attention. She seemed to try to collect her thoughts before she answered; then she passed her hand across her forehead, and said:

"I know very little of what you are speaking of. Letters? Yes, he received some letters, but not many of them, and it was years ago. Sometimes he did not receive one for years. Sometimes they came from America—from an old friend, he said. But the last one came, perhaps four or five years ago. I do not know whether he kept them. They may be in his writing-desk."

"And if they are, will you give them to me?" asked Ferdinand, eagerly. "I am not a rich man, but you may be sure that I will not forget you, if you give me those letters."

"As you have come after them at this season and in such weather," said the woman, thoughtfully, "they must be of great value to you. But that is no reason that I should refuse you. No one will suffer injustice or sorrow by my giving them to you, sir?"

"No injustice will be done to any one; that I can swear to you!"

"Then," she answered, "you can look for them yourself, sir; there is my husband's room; I will take you into it."

"Let me, mother, I will do it," said the oldest boy, who was still lying on the steps, but who seemed to have gradually forgotten his grief while Ferdinand was speaking, and at the last had kept his dark and still tearful eyes fixed upon the stranger's face. He now sprang up and led the way across the kitchen to a door on the other side, which he opened for Ferdinand.

The room into which it led was not large, but was comparatively pleasant, being lighted by windows on two sides. At the right was a deal writing-desk, painted brown, and provided with compartments and drawers; it was covered with a confused mass of official and other papers. Some hunting implements were hanging on the wall at the farther side, and the round table in the centre was covered with books and sheets of music. The flute was leaning in one corner of the window.

"Had the unfortunate man been allowed to adopt the life to which his talents and his tastes impelled him," thought Ferdinand, as he looked around, "what a comfortable and even happy existence he might have secured by his talents! But no; those who attempted to provide for his future, compelled him to adopt a 'solid' calling, only to fail more miserably than he could possibly have done in the practice of his art. And how miserably!"

He sat down at the writing-desk, and began to search it. The drawers were all unlocked; and, in truth, they contained very little that would have been worth looking up.

There were old letters there, but not the ones that Ferdinand was seeking; and scattered through the drawers were articles hardly worth keeping, old pocket-books, knives with broken blades, broken pipes, single dominos, and a pair of old miniatures of Emil's parents, in frames whose gilding had long been worn down to the copper; locks of hair carefully rolled in paper, dried flowers, bronze medals won by God knows what forgotten relatives in what forgotten campaigns—the drawers were filled with this little *bric-à-brac*, which it is so foolish to keep, unless one has, like Emil Drausfeld, a sensitive heart to connect with them remembrances inseperable from the outward tokens.

In the middle of the writing-desk was a small door which was locked. Ferdinand looked around for his guide to ask him for the key. But the boy was gone, and Ferdinand stepped back into the kitchen to ask Frau Dransfeld for it. She was still standing by the hearth, talking with the forester Gellhorn, who had returned to the kitchen. When Ferdinand asked for the key, the boy was just coming down the stairs from the upper room, and he answered for his mother:

"Here are the keys!"

"You have them, Carl?" asked his mother, as if surprised.

"I brought them from my father's

pocket," answered Carl; "for I thought the gentleman would want them."

It was an attention that Ferdinand would not have expected from the boy, after what he had seen of him. The boy handed to his mother a ring, with three keys on it. She gave them to Ferdinand, but went with him into the room, to assist in the rest of the search. Carl, in the meantime, had disappeared, having passed up a steep, narrow staircase at the side of the fireplace, leading probably to the attic.

Ferdinand opened the little door in the writing-desk with one of the keys. It was filled with papers: Emil's appointment, orders from his superiors, a few letters from his relatives, his wife's certificate of baptism and recommendations from employers, and an open, lidless box, containing a small sum of money—the entire amount of property left by Emil Dransfeld.

"There is nothing here," said Ferdinand, breathing heavily and greatly excited; "no trace of what I came for."

"Then I cannot help you," answered the woman, apathetically. She was standing by him, but her thoughts seemed to be far away from what he was doing.

"But the letters must be in existence," exclaimed Ferdinand, in feverish excitement; "they must be; your husband has certainly not destroyed them. Perhaps there is some other place where he may have concealed them—some closet, or bureau, or trunk?"

"There is a closet up there in the alcove," she said, "at the foot of the bed. He kept there the books he used to read himself to sleep with evenings. Whether he put the letters you are looking for in there, too, I do not know. We can go and see."

She went in advance, and Ferdinand, his spirits a little revived by this renewed hope, followed her across the kitchen, up the steps, to the upper room, which served as the family sitting-room—a room whose scanty and cheap furniture was even now in miserable disorder—and into the alcove, the double glass door of which stood wide open.

Ferdinand threw a glance of awe at the bed, on which lay the corpse of the friend of his youth, who had come so near to him in a great crisis and misfortune of his life; he was thankful that the face was covered, that he was spared the pain of looking into the rigid features of that friend whose days had ended so sadly in this poverty-struck dwelling, in the midst of this forlorn and deserted waste.

Emil's widow, who had taken the keys, opened the closet which was made in the wall of the alcove at the foot of the bed. Ferdinand busied himself with the contents, consisting of books, memoranda, fragments of an herbarium, old almanacs, a pair of old silver candlesticks, the relics of better days, and a beautiful cut-glass drinking-cup, with a broken standard; the contents of the closet were very much like those of the writing-desk, and, unfortunately, it was quite as empty of what Ferdinand sought.

"You do not find what you are looking for?" asked Frau Drausfeld, as Ferdinand turned away, with a deep sigh.

"No," he said, in a tone of such complete discouragement and despair, that the woman, notwithstanding her apathy, looked at him with a puzzled air, and said:

"And these letters are of such extraordinary value for you?"

"Of the very greatest, as I told you. Everything depends on them for me—everything on my finding them!"

She shook her head.

"I pity you from the bottom of my heart. But I cannot help you any more. If the letters are not in the writing-desk and not in the closet, then my husband must have destroyed them."

"That must be the case, and it is very unfortunate for me that it is so. But, if you should find the letters, some of which are from America, and are signed Philip Bonsart, and others from places in Germany, and probably have no signature, but are in a lady's handwriting—if you should find them, send them to me at once; I will give you what you ask for them; I will do anything I can for you, if you will get me those letters; they would perhaps enable me to give a more fortunate turn to your fate, and that of your children——"

"My God!" interrupted the widow, "if

those letters are of such extreme importance to you, it is truly a misfortune that they are lost. He certainly could not have dreamed of such a thing, and must have burned them; for otherwise they would be here or in his writing-desk. I have not the slightest hope of finding them——"

"But if you should find them, here, take my address; send the letters to this address, without delay!"

Frau Drausfeld took, with a nod, the card Ferdinand handed her, after he had added a few words with a pencil.

They then returned to the kitchen. The forester was anxious to go home at once: it was time, for they must ride by way of Ehleru, from whence he was to send the necessary assistance. Frau Dransfeld insisted on placing on the table such refreshments as she could offer—bread, butter, and cheese. Ferdinand would not allow her to trouble herself to prepare anything more; he contented himself with the old rye-brandy which she brought, though it was with reluctance that he took the unaccustomed drink which the forester urged upon him.

During this time Carl had returned to the kitchen. He stood leaning against the fireplace, looking sullenly at the strangers. Ferdinand, whose thoughts were entirely occupied with the fruitlessness of his journey, let his eyes pass absently over the boy's features, at first; then fixed them on him intently and thoughtfully, as a vision of his old friend's face rose before him and looked sadly and reproachfully at him from the features of this boy; and, innocent as he was of the fate of his friend, it came upon him with a certain burden of responsibility, as a load upon his conscience, as human misery will reproach us; we cannot alter fate, and yet how much we might change, were we only more helpful, more warm and active in our sympathy! With this feeling, with the thought of what might become of this boy, whose character seemed in such urgent need of discipline, Ferdinand was impelled to offer his assistance.

"It would be easier for you, Frau Drausfeld," he said, "if you were relieved of the care of at least one of your children, would it not?"

Frau Drausfeld looked inquiringly at him.

"It would be hard for me," she said, "to part with one of them; but whether hard or easy, one is seldom asked in this life," she added, with a sigh. She had seated herself again and was looking apathetically at the floor.

"I should like to do something for your husband's children," answered Ferdinand. "Would it suit you, if I should take your oldest boy home with me, and prepare him for some occupation for which he has the taste and ability? I would provide for him until he should be able to take care of himself. I am not rich enough to open to him any very brilliant career. But I would see that he has good instruction and a respectable position in life."

"Your offer is exceedingly kind, Herr von Schott, and I thank you for it," answered the widow, without, however, expressing the slightest gratitude by the tone in which she spoke. "It depends on Carl himself," she added, "whether he will go with you. The boy has a will of his own."

"Then we will ask him," said Ferdinand. "How is it, Carl, will you go with me, so that I may send you to a good school, and afterward put you into some business where you will soon be able to take care of yourself and do something for your mother and your brothers and sisters?"

The young fellow looked with a shy and undecided glance from his mother to Ferdinand, and back again to his mother. It seemed as if the prospect opened before him was not what he would have taken from his own free choice, as if it presented not the slightest resemblance to his dreams and fancies of the future. As he had wandered among the pines and firs around his home, he must have drawn quite different pictures of what awaited him in the great world, and the wind piping through the trees, his only comrade, must have sung more romantic songs of fortune and glory than any he found in this tame promise of school and business.

He looked at his mother, whose eyes

rested upon him without expressing any expectation, any anxiety in regard to his answer; they expressed nothing but dull, utter despondency. But in that very expression there seemed to be an eloquence that melted everything hard and defiant in the boy; there was a quiver in his face, as from the violent suppression of rising tears. He stepped up to his mother, laid his hand upon her shoulder, looked long and searchingly into Ferdinand's face, and said:

"I will come to you, if my mother thinks best, hereafter; to-day and to-morrow I will stay with my mother."

"Very well, that is right," said Ferdinand, affected by the boy's manner. "You ought to stay with your mother now; and then she can send you to me. Give me your hand upon it."

Carl took the offered hand without much warmth. Ferdinand gave the mother directions about sending him, and then the two men took leave, and mounted their horses to ride back through the woods and over the snowy moor. The fog had rolled up into thick, heavy, dark gray clouds which covered the plain as they emerged from the forest. The forester took the direction of the church-tower of Ehleru, now distinctly visible. Ferdinand was obliged to take the circuitous route with him; he could not think of attempting to return alone by the direct route to the mail and railroad station from which they had come, as night would overtake him on his way.

— So he rode silently along beside the forester, who was also thoughtful and self-absorbed under the impression of what he had just witnessed. Ferdinand's thoughts were busy with the days when both he and Emil Dransfeld had dreamed so little of the turn their lives were to take; when Emil had lived for the present, so careless and unconcerned for the future, as if borne upon the waves of the music within him, an *anima candida!* And how had he been punished for his want of energy and the indolence that seemed inseperable from his talent and his disposition?' It was, indeed, a hard fate. To be sure, he had brought it upon himself. The duties the world imposed upon him and which were repellant to his nature, he had performed badly; he had not strength to master his inclinations, to cast behind him his love of art for the sake of bread, to contend in the struggle for existence with those that were stronger than he. These were crimes that could not weigh very heavy in the balance of the infinite Judge; they were not necessarily connected with an evil heart; it is possible to be such a criminal and yet have a heart full of love and a helpful hand for all with whom one is thrown into contact—to be a faithful friend and a self-denying husband and father, to be what Emil Drausfeld had been through life.

But it was Emil's misfortune that these are the very crimes most cruelly punished in life—the very crimes that the avenging hand of circumstance never spares, which it pursues with relentless rage to the very last, and for which it inflicts more stripes than for the most heartless and soulless villany !

CHAPTER VIII.

IRENE.

Ferdinand von Schott had returned from his winter excursion, and was once more within the four walls of his home, four strong, massive, firm walls they were. This house was perhaps sixty miles west from the barren waste where Emil Drausfeld's life had closed, not far from the Rhine, and in a region somewhat renowned for its scenery. It was a broad valley, inhabited by an active, industrial people; a rapid river, which had been made navigable at great expense, flowed through it; it was enclosed on both sides by hills, not very high, but thickly wooded; still it was far from being a secluded vale; on the contrary, the ruling powers of the time had taken possession of it; whatever idyllic charm it might have had, was destroyed by the railroads and factories, and the bran-new villas that stretched along both sides of the river. In looking over the valley from one of the heights, the attention would have been drawn especially to three points. On the right bank of the river was a little town, with a great, many-towered cathedral, seeming disproportion-ately large for the size of the city. Enclosed by a wide circle of gardens with pavilions and little villas, or larger country-houses, it had long burst through the enclosure of its ancient fortifications, of which only a tower here and there still remained; the finest and largest projected into the water of the river, that washed around its base. The second point was a castle with a wing on either side, whose long rows of shining windows looked down from a slight elevation, the spur of a higher one beyond; a double line of lindens extended from the height to the gardens of the city, like a broad band by which it might hold fast the busy, restless little town. To-day, perhaps, the citizens would have little cause to think of anything emblematic in this green band, but there had been times when the relation between the castle and the city would have been aptly symbolized by it.

Opposite the castle, but below on the other side of the westward flowing river, was a large, new villa, rising above high terraces on the gently sloping side of a mountain, and appearing to be surrounded by extensive grounds laid out for a park.

This villa was the residence of a celebrated manufacturer whose immense factories lay farther up the river. The castle was inhabited by a prince formerly sovereign, and now mediatized—that is, it was his residence when, as now, he was in the place, and not in Nice, or at his villa on Lake Como, or at the capital, where he spent a large part of his time.

The house to which Ferdinand von Schott had returned, was at the upper end of the city; it was a long, old, unpretending building; the office of the royal landrath occupied the lower story; the upper was used by him as a dwelling; it made up in the size of the rooms and passages for what it lacked in light and cheerfulness, in modern conveniences and comforts.

In one of these rooms, the windows of which were darkened by the dark-gray rook-haunted walls of the cathedral which rose dismally near to them, and looked out at the right upon a dry grass-plat, two ladies were seated. The older one, who might have been somewhat over thirty, was seated on the sofa and engaged in some feminine occupation; the younger was leaning back in a low rocking chair opposite. The beautiful and serious face of the elder, whose somewhat too colorless features bore some resemblance in form and expression to those of Ferdinand von Schott, were bent over the material on which she was engaged. The other was a girl of not more than seventeen or eighteen, with a round, rosy face, full of life and grace, and blonde curls: as she rocked gently back and forth in her bright blue dress, she looked like a blue flower swaying in the wind.

But her face was far from wearing the careless expression of a flower, for the tears stood in her eyes, and her brows were drawn together and her lips quivering with sorrow.

"And I have told you everything, Aunt Adele, everything, that I have not told to any one else in the world—not even to my mother or my Aunt Elsie, and now you have no help and no counsel for me!"

"Is confidence always enough to bring help, you foolish child? It would, indeed, be very pleasant, if, by our confidence, we could always give others the power to help us!"

"Oh, but you certainly could help us if you only would. For there must be some way to help us. It is all so strange, so unnatural and mysterious, that it only needs a real sensible person to come and set everything right with a few kind and sensible words. Herr Kronhorst threatens to send William abroad for three years if he has the least reason to believe that William has any more thought of me. And now, just tell me why is it? why should William be forbidden to think of me? And my mother, instead of standing by us, hates Herr Kronhorst; she hates to have me mention his name, and takes care to avoid every place where she might meet him. And Aunt Elsie, since she noticed how it was with us—with William and me—has not invited

Herr Kronhorst to the castle a single time when we were there, although you know yourself, Aunt Adele, how the prince likes him, and likes to talk with him better than with any one else. Now, is not all that mysterious? What have they all against it? Are not William and I suited to each other, and does he not love me, and am I not always good to him? And I am rich, as you said yourself, Aunt Adele, and why is Herr Kronhorst so opposed to it? And why does my mother hate William's father, and why is Aunt Elsie so opposed to it? Tell me, Aunt Adele, tell me; I am no longer a child. Explain all this to me."

"I cannot explain it to you Irene, believe me," answered Adele, looking up and letting her work fall in her lap, as she rested her elbow on the arm of the sofa, and supporting her chin in her hand, looked up at the old cathedral wall. "These people of whom you complain are not all as open and confiding toward me as you are. Not one of them has entrusted his secrets to me; and as to the grounds for their actions, I have not the slightest suspicion."

Irene looked doubtingly at her, and interrupted her with—

"But, Aunt Adele, you are so shrewd; if you only would——"

"If I would what, my child?"

"If you would ask them—if you would speak for us. Oh, it must be they would see how foolish they are, that William and I love each other too dearly to be separated; that it is unchristian, abominable, tyrannical, to try to separate us, and that they will never, never accomplish it; that we will die sooner than give each other up!"

Adele's eyes turned from the dusky old wall, and rested on the excited face of the girl with an expression of lively sympathy; the passionate words were followed by a violent fit of sobbing.

Adele laid her hand on Irene's arm, and said, softly:—

"Is it, then, so serious, so tragically serious, Irene?"

"Do you not believe it? Must I throw myself into the pond there under the old poplars to make you believe it?"

"Why, child, how passionate you are!"

exclaimed Adele, startled at Irene's violence. "Control yourself; I did not think you were taking the matter so much to heart; a seventeen-year-old heart forgets so easily. What is more natural than that I should think the little pearls in your eyelashes were only the drops of dew on a rose leaf, which the wind brushes away in an hour? Heavens! do these children know what deep, ineradicable love is? But, Irene, do not look so angry and excited because I am a little incredulous. It is not for your advantage, my poor child, to convince me that the matter is so extremely serious."

"Advantage? What do I care for advantage or disadvantage?" answered Irene, half angrily, half sadly, as she dried her eyes with her handkerchief. "I only want to show you how unhappy I am. I only want you to know all, all; to see how I suffer——"

"But," interrupted Adele, "that is the very thing. If I can believe that it is only one of the ordinary fancies of a young girl, who, when she meets with obstacles, sheds a few tears over the hard-heartedness of parents and the terrible cruelty of the world, and then forgets her sorrow over the question whether she shall wear a rose-pink or a sea-green dress at the next ball, then I could be your friend, and do my best to help you by my advice to be reasonable, and to forget and overcome the unhappiness connected with this little episode in your life. But, if you convince me that you are so serious and desperate in the matter, so that I am obliged to conclude that all my advice is entirely useless, and that opposition will only make matters worse, then nothing is left for me but to forbid you to talk to me about it. What else can I do? I cannot help you to resist the will of your mother, or encourage William to act in opposition to his father's express command. I should be abusing most shamefully the confidence placed in me by your mother and your aunt, in allowing you to brighten so many of my lonely hours. Do you understand, little obstinacy?"

"Oh," answered Irene, poutingly; "I only understand that you are all against us. I only wish I understood why!"

Adele shrugged her shoulders.

"I am not against you, Irene, not at all. On the contrary, you both have my full sympathy. I have told you that I myself cannot understand the opposition of your mother and of Herr Kronhorst. So far as I can see, you are very well suited to each other. But as your parents have reasons for thinking otherwise, you owe it to them to believe that those reasons are so important and decisive that you ought to submit to them."

While Adele was speaking, Irene had given little attention to the sympathy expressed in Adele's whole look and manner; she had listened absently, half absorbed in her own thoughts. She had taken one corner of her handkerchief between her teeth and was pulling at it, her face still cloudy and sullen; suddenly she said, bitterly:—

"Do you, then, really believe, Aunt Adele, that my mother has 'important and decisive reasons,' as you call them, to be against William? Poor mother? I believe she would have nothing against it if she did not have to obey Aunt Elsie in this as in everything else. What Aunt Elsie wills is law to her; and why it is so is another riddle to me. My mother is so free, so independent! She might act her own pleasure, and do exactly what seems right in her own eyes. But she does nothing but what Aunt Elsie wishes. It seems as if she could not think without Aunt Elsie! What pleases Aunt Elsie has to please her."

"That is not so very strange, my dear child. Your mother has no other relatives, no one else in the world but your Aunt Elsie and you. Your father, my cousin Alexander, died so early; and we, my brother Ferdinand and I, are so distantly related. It is, therefore, natural that she should cling to the sister she loves——"

"Loves? Aunt Adele, do you believe that my mother loves Aunt Elsie so exceedingly well?"

"Why, of course! Do you not believe it? Why should she not?"

Irene shook her head, doubtingly.

"Well, now, what do you mean by that mysterious face, you foolish child?"

"Only," said Irene, lowering her voice, "that I believe my mother fears Aunt Elsie much more than she loves her!"

Adele shrugged her shoulders again and shook her head.

"She has not the slightest reason to fear her," she said, fixing her eyes, with an expression of wonder, on the girl's face. She may have been thinking how observing and sharp-sighted love had made this young girl, heretofore so careless, so unconcerned about anything beyond the passing hour.

"She cannot have the slightest reason," she continued. "Your mother is the older sister; she is rich and independent. Why should she fear your Aunt Elsie? But, think; your Aunt Elsie has become a princess; every one pays homage to her, admires her beauty and her talent, or flatters her because she is the ruling spirit in the prince's house. Hence it is natural that your mother, the widow of Major Schott, whose rank is low compared with that of your Aunt Elsie, and who, moreover, is naturally so gentle and yielding—what is more natural than that she should adopt the manner of others, and should show a deference to her sister which looks, to the eyes of children like you, as if she feared her."

Irene shook her head.

"Oh, no, no, Aunt Adele. I know she fears her," she answered, decidedly, and then was silent again. And Adele, who did not seem inclined to push the question farther, was also silent.

Presently they heard a carriage rattling over the pavement, and then suddenly audible only by the sound of wheels passing over turf or gravel. Irene rose and stepped to the window looking into the open space.

"There is the carriage to take my mother and me to the castle," she said. "I must go. It is too bad of you, Aunt Adele, to send me home without any better comfort."

"How can I give you any better comfort than I have, my child?" answered Adele, helping Irene on with a warm wrap that had been lying on the arm of the sofa. "Shall I see you soon again? To-morrow?"

"Yes, Aunt Adele, if I possibly can; at this time."

"I shall expect you. You know you always come into my dark rooms and my dark days like a sunbeam, though to-day the sunbeam shines through the rain. But the rain-clouds will soon pass off—we will hope so—if God will."

"Oh, but they will not pass off, not at all," answered Irene, with a tragic sigh; "on the contrary, they will keep growing thicker and blacker, and at last they will roll up into a terrible tempest, and scatter lightnings and thunderbolts."

"Oh, not so bad as that, I hope," answered Adele, smiling. "And now good-bye, my dear child."

She kissed her young friend; Irene embraced her cordially, and then went down to the door where a liveried footman helped her into an elegant carriage, drawn by two spirited black horses.

CHAPTER IX.

BROTHER AND SISTER.

When she was gone, Adele resumed her place by the window and took up her work again; but after a little she let it fall into her lap, and looked thoughtfully through the window at the dark old pillars of the cathedral and at the gray stone bishop standing opposite, on the column at the corner, his weather-beaten face staring sullenly into the damp winter air. Time had robbed him of his entire right arm and the hand that had held the shepherd's crook; to reach him at that height, the bold plunderer must have employed a crowd of street-boys to do his malicious bidding. But with his remaining hand the stone man clasped to his breast a ponderous volume, his only consolation—containing, it must be, promises and pledges enough of certain and terrible future retribution to be visited upon Time and his crowd of malicious gamins. Moreover, he was backed by the mighty church, with which he revengefully cast deep black shadows on everything around, and spread melancholy and gloom over the whole neighborhood. The heavy shadows reached far into the great room where Adele sat.

She was thinking of the question put to her by her young relative, who called her aunt, though the relationship was much more remote. It was, indeed, difficult ot understand why Herr Kronhorst, the great manufacturer, who controlled the industries of the place, should so determinedly oppose a marriage of his oldest son, William, to Irene—why the heir of the great villa we have mentioned as one of the chief ornaments of the valley, should not marry a girl with a property of perhaps a hundred thousand thalers. Herr Kronhorst was a man of genius, a great and strong character, who had risen from straitened circumstances to a position almost princely. He was the originator of the great iron industries of the region, their head and controlling spirit; and with this his ambition seemed to be fully satisfied; he had persistently refused offers of civil honors and promotion in rank, and had kept his plain burgher name. What, then, could he have against Irene, who was, indeed, the daughter of a major, but was also the niece of a princess? Perhaps he thought she had become spoiled by spending most of her time at the court of a petty prince. But he himself stood in the most friendly relations to that little court, and was a friend of the prince; and even if Irene had learned to live in a little too grand a style, if she had become accustomed to luxury, what was that to a man whose wealth was almost incalculable? And, then, why should Irene's mother, formerly Matilda von Melroth, and now the widow of Major Schott—why should she refuse to hear of such a thing? Why should her younger sister, Elsie von Melroth, now the reigning Princess of Lohburg-Achsenstein, who, as Irene herself had observed, influenced and controlled her yielding elder sister in everything? She could imagine no reason for it. There was, it is true, a mystery about the former life of the princess—a mystery that threw darker shadows on her brother Ferdinand's life than the old stone bishop could cast into the lonesome street, with the great minster behind him. But even all these dark and improbable suppositions, with which her brother was tormenting himself, and which were making him a gloomy, unhappy, embittered man—even if they were true, as Adele could not believe, even then she could find no explanation. There was nothing in any of them that could constitute a reason for Herr Kronhorst angrily forbidding his son to think of such a thing as a union with the innocent Irene Schott.

Adele sympathized most strongly with the girl. She knew how strong her feelings were, how deep and constant her nature was. Toward strangers Irene's manner was quiet, shy, and reserved—warm and open as she was at times to her friends. She was subject to peculiar changes of mood, much more than is ordinarily the case with girls of her years; she was, moreover, somewhat obstinate, capricious, self-dependent; this was, however, partly a result of her education, which, as Irene had often complained to her brother, had been as faulty as possible. Irene's mother had always striven to fulfil her duty to her daughter, conducting her education with conscientious regularity; but her sister Elsie had counteracted the influence of all that, by the irresponsible way in which she attracted Irene to herself, by indulging all her caprices, and giving way to all her obstinacy. Irene was much less under the care of her more sensible mother than under that of her indulgent aunt. It seemed as if Elsie, who had no children of her own, could not live in her great castle, with its spacious, lonesome rooms, without Irene. She spent most of her time at Achsenstein, shared her aunt's pursuits and went with her on her journeys, sang and read for her. When there was an unusual number of guests at the castle, Elsie allowed her niece to remain with her sister. People thought it cruel and selfish in the princess to take the child from her lonely mother, and weak in the mother to allow it.

Adele reflected on the effect this first great opposition to her wishes and inclinations that Irene had ever met with, must produce on a character like hers, whose natural tendency to obstinacy and determination had been so injudiciously fostered by Elsie's indulgence; possibly this very opposition might develop a strength of passion of which otherwise she would have been wholly incapable. Adele, the only one with whom Irene was perfectly frank, had a difficult task, to console and cheer, to advise self-denial and renunciation, and to preach reason, which is as hard for a young head as resignation for a young heart.

While Adele sat thinking, the shadows thrown into the room by the old church walls had grown deeper and deeper, and now a light rain began to draw gray lines down the dark surface of the wall, increasing the darkness and making deep twilight in every corner of the melancholy room. It seemed as if the stuccoed beams that supported the roof had settled down, making the low room still lower, and as if the dark, high wainscoting around the walls had grown browner and gloomier. Adele arose shivering. She stepped over to the fireplace to stir the glowing coals, when her maid came in to announce Frau Groebler, the wife of the police inspector. She was followed by an energetic step, and a lady came bustling into the room—the same who, in the old merry days in H., had recited her adjectives with such a peculiar pathetic emphasis—then Fräulein Theresa Holbrecht, now a wife and mother, the life-companion of Herr Groebler, who had been promoted for his services in behalf of the public safety. Herr Groebler had failed to capture that traitor years ago; he had been too late to lay his hand on the dangerous fugitive; but in countless other cases his services in behalf of the insulted public conscience and of moral principle had been signal, and so he had been promoted from police commissary to inspector, and removed to E.—for what reasons we shall see hereafter. Theresa Holbrecht had accompanied him as his wife; and she had come at this twilight hour, to inquire whether the Landrath von Schott had returned in safety from his winter excursion, and to express her anxiety about her husband, who had gone away several days before in this dreadful weather, without leaving any word as to where he was going, and had not yet returned, though the weather was so stormy and cold, and though Groebler ought .to think that he should spare himself and remember his wife and children, and ought to consider that the iron constitution on which he presumed might at last be broken, while he would still need it so long in his calling. While she was saying this, Frau Theresa loosened her water-proof and the strings of her bonnet, and took a seat before the fire on the chair which Adele had moved up for her. The features of her long face, which had grown sharper and thinner, shone in the blaze on the hearth at which she was warming her gloved hands.

"My brother," said Adele, in answer to her inquiries, taking a light cane chair beside the fire-place, "my brother returned two days ago. He had a very sad journey. He went to seek out an old acquaintance, and found him dead; he had died in poverty and in most miserable circumstances—the poor fellow, on a dismal heath——"

"Ah, do you not mean Emil Drausfeld?" cried Frau Theresa.

"That was his name. I never saw him, but from all my brother says of him, he must have been a noble, generous man; Ferdinand returned very much depressed."

"Emil Drausfeld dead!" said Frau Theresa, sadly. "The poor, poor fellow! How sorry I am!"

"Ferdinand," continued Adele, "found the family in such a destitute condition, that he offered to take the care of the oldest boy. The boy will be here in a few days."

"That is kind of your brother, very kind," answered Frau Theresa, softly, without turning her eyes away from the glowing coals into which she was looking, thoughtfully and absently. After a pause she said, "And had your brother heard how hard it was going with poor Emil, and did he go to see him once more before he died?"

"No, not that; he had no idea of his condition. He wanted to talk with him and get some explanations in regard to a matter that no one but Dransfeld could explain."

"Ah!" said Frau Theresa, turning quickly toward Adele, "and these explanations

concerned—do you know whom they concerned? Did your brother tell you?"

"I," answered Adele, evasively, "I did not ask, and if I have any conjectures, I——"

"I am much too discreet to tell them to the curious, you were going to say," interrupted Frau Theresa, with a rather disdainful smile. "You are right, you are right," she continued, moving her hand as if to ward off Adele's answer; "but I think we need not be more discreet toward each other than our masters and tyrants are between themselves—if you have no objections to my giving that name to your brother as well as to that sly husband of mine!"

"I have no objections," said Adele, looking at her intently, "so go on."

"We need not be more discreet toward each other than' they have been between themselves," repeated Frau Theresa, "and discreet they have not been, for I can guess at the connection between these two journeys. I can guess what sent them both out in this dreadful weather."

"What do you guess?" asked Adele, surprised, and observing anxiously the sharp profile of the face that Frau Theresa turned to the fire again.

"That I am partly to blame, for one thing. And I will give Groebler a good lecture when he comes back for not keeping to himself things that his poor, innocent wife confides in him in hours of weakness; because, instead of forgetting them, he makes a note of them and puts them to such a bad use!"

"And what can you have confided to him that has driven them both out in this weather? You confided to him that you knew Emil Drausfeld at the time you were so much at the house of the Melroths—my brother has told me about those times—you were a circle of merry young people—and then?"

"And then," said Frau Theresa, "I told him more about Emil Dransfeld; of his appointment to the Vellinghaus forest; and how, in the first few years, he had found it so hard to stay there, that from time to time he had asked leave of absence and had spent a few days at H. ; and how he had staid for hours talking to me, and had put it a little plainer, perhaps, than he needed to—the poor fellow! that he would be very happy if I would follow him into his Vellinghaus pine woods, while of course I couldn't think of such a thing as going there to shrivel up into a pine-cone; and how we had talked about the others, who, after Father Melroth was taken away, had been scattered like leaves in the wind; of your brother Ferdinand and of Elsie Melroth most, and how Emil Drausfeld had confessed to me that he sometimes had news from Elsie Melroth, short communications not really intended for him, but for an old friend of Elsie's who had gone across the ocean; and that this old friend of Elsie's, who was now entirely forgotten in H., wrote to him also from time to time, that he might send news of him to Elsie. All this I confided to that doubting Thomas, Groebler; for why should I not, after I had given him my promise, why should I not tell him all about my past life and the people I had known in my then short experience? But I could not tell him any more, for Emil had been strangely silent and reserved in regard to everything else about the matter. Probably he had pledged himself to keep it secret. When I asked him why those two people did not write directly to each other when they had communications to make, instead of employing a third person, he answered, 'There are circumstances in life, Fräulein Theresa, where it is preferable to do so; when people no longer like to speak directly to each other or look each other in the face, and yet there are circumstances which compel them from time to time to send word to each other; then it is easiest and most discreet for them to confide in some good-natured friend, and make a sort of speaking-trumpet of him.' That was all the explanation Emil would give me; and when I said the only such case I could imagine would be that of two married people who had separated, and yet might have to communicate with each other in reference to their property, he said I must not think of it, or talk any more about it; that he had already talked too much about the matter, which he had promised to keep secret. That is what I afterward told

my doubting Thomas, when I had become acquainted with him. Emil Drausfeld's visits had ceased then; he had found another girl, who was willing to go with him to the Vellinghaus forest, and the trips to H. were probably too expensive for the poor fellow. That is what I told Groebler, and now when he comes home, I will find out whether these two gentlemen have been trying to make capital out of that, and have been out to the pine woods of Vellinghaus to rake up old stories out of the snow that do not concern them, and which may in the end expose the princess most cruelly, and make her trouble with her husband, if he should hear of it. It would be abominable in them——"

"It would be abominable in us to suspect them of dishonorable designs," interrupted Adele, " and it would be very hasty in us to judge of the subject from what little we know. As you say yourself, it is only a guess of yours, that these two journeys have some connection with the information you gave your husband so long ago, and as we know nothing positive about it, let us leave it to them to carry out what they have kept to themselves as an official secret."

Frau Theresa nodded. "Oh, yes," she said, "that is your quiet, gentle disposition, Fräulein von Schott. But I am not so yielding. It vexes me to have my husband play the mysterious in an affair that he would never have known of but for me, and that he knows I have more interest in than almost any one else. And if I find out that they are intriguing against the princess, I will make his life such a burden to him, that all the stories they tell about Frau Xantippe will be thrown completely into the shade!"

"You have a good, warm heart for your old friends, Frau Groebler," said Adele.

"Not always, and not exactly for all of them," answered Frau Theresa. "But this proud and self-willed Elsie Melroth, who has climbed up to her princely station by her pride, I am sorry for poor Elsie. When I came here with my husband, I went to call upon her, with a presentiment of the kind of reception I should meet with, of the insulting condescension and coolness and half-cordiality with which such people hold out two fingers to their dear old friend, while they are inwardly execrating the stupid fate that has thrown her again in their way. And when I saw her, I couldn't help envying her for the wonderful beauty she had kept all these years. She had scarcely changed at all; she had the same forehead, with the rich dark hair waving over it, and the same bright, young eyes; she was the same 'Flame,' at which, as Emil Drausfeld once said, the moths used to burn their wings. She was only a little paler, a little more delicate and slender. She embraced me and greeted me without the least affectation or reserve; she was not as lively and brusque in conversation as she used to be; she was more quiet and serious and self-controlled; but there was nothing unnatural in her manner, not the slightest attempt to put on airs of superiority. That touched my heart, from the woman now so far above poor Theresa Groebler, and I talked cordially and openly with her about everything; and then, Fräulein Adele, I found that this great lady is not happy with all her splendor; and that something has happened to her that her pride cannot get over, and there is something broken that all her wealth and elegance cannot heal. That is what I found out, and since then I have been sorry for her; and woe to my Thomas if he is meddling with things that she would not for the world have a detective meddling with!"

Adele was silent at these words, which were spoken with a warmth that spoke well for Frau Theresa's heart. If she was in her brother's confidence, and if she knew that he and the "doubting Thomas," as Frau Theresa called him, were meddling with things that the princess must wish to leave dead and buried, then her brother must have imposed strict secrecy upon her; for she said nothing, but sat looking at the glowing coals on the hearth. Theresa, too, had become thoughtful, and looked in silence at the tips of her boots, which she had stretched toward the fire. At length Adele said:

"And when Emil Drausfeld told you about the letters he had received from Elsie Melroth, did he tell you nothing about the man that wrote to him from over the ocean—letters whose contents were intended for Elsie Melroth? Or did you know him yourself?"

"Philip Bonsart? Did I know him? No, I did not know him. I never saw him. But I had heard enough of him to know whom Emil meant when he began to tell me about those letters. Philip Bonsart: there was a time when they talked of nothing else in H. He was from the same place as Elsie Melroth, and they must have grown up together. Afterward, he was sent to school and to the university, and then, in the spring of 1849, I think it was, the disturbances broke out, and they told how the son of this steward—or perhaps he was already the proprietor—of Asthof was going about in the city, speaking to the working-people, and trying to organize them into a body, to unite with some from other parts of the country, and march to the capital, where they were going to found a republic and nobody knows what all! The men were all beside themselves, some in anxiety and distress, and many jubilant and enthusiastic, and, moreover, very drunk. This lasted a week or so, and they hung a great flag, black and red and gold, from the window of the council-house, though I never saw it, for my aunt, with whom I lived, kept the house closed all the time; she thought a wild mob might break in at any time and lay hands on her great silver teapot and her old damask cloak, with the sable trimming, her two greatest treasures. But, one evening, at twilight, a tall, weary-looking man, with a great staff and a shining knob on it, passed by our house; and this man saved my aunt's peace of mind and her teapot, and her cloak with the sable trimming; for more weary men came behind him, with hollow-sounding drums hanging against their knees, which were covered with white calfskin. And then came more weary and dusty and hungry-looking men, with bayonets on the guns they carried on their shoulders; and when they reached the market-place, and let their guns fall on the pavement, then the wild days were at an end, the flag disappeared from the council-house, and the anxiety from the hearts of the good burghers who had silver teapots to lose; nothing more was heard of the republic and the army of freedom, and Philip Bonsart had left for parts unknown. Some said he had gone with the boldest of the insurgents to the highlands, where they were still more wild and daring. That is all I know of him, and all that Emil Drausfeld professed to know. Afterward, as Herr Groebler told me, he returned to H, and to Asthof. Groebler got wind of it, and tried to arrest him; but Bonsart was too sly for my sharp husband. Perhaps he came to see Elsie Melroth again; I do not know as to that, and did not trouble my head about it. But I do know that, if there ever was anything between them, they were wise to separate, and go each his own way, with an ocean between them. What could they have in common, that proud, aristocratic woman, and that wild, crazy insurrectionist?"

"Certainly, Frau Groebler," said Adele; "and they must have seen that soon enough to refrain from taking upon themselves ties which would have made them unhappy for life."

"Ties? What ties are you thinking of?" asked Frau Theresa, looking up. As Adele did not answer immediately, she continued, as she drew her watch from her belt and held it to the firelight: "What do you mean? But it is six o'clock—nearly six— how the time passes when one is chatting so, and how my lambs will be crying for me, poor lambs! I must go back to them."

She rose hastily, put on her wraps, with Adele's help, and departed, probably to forget, among her children, all such dark subjects, which, as well as the course of the outside world, trouble a mother very little when she is among her "lambs."

When she was gone, Adele seated herself in her corner again, and rested her chin in her hand. There was very little in what Frau Groebler had said that was new to her; her brother had told her as much in hours of confidence, when he had given her a glimpse of his inmost heart. She was thinking only of what Frau Theresa had said of the impression the princess had made upon her. There was something broken that would not heal, as Frau Theresa had expressed it, and was not that the best word for what Adele herself had felt when she had talked with the princess, as she had done only a few times and at long intervals? There seemed to be something broken in her which could not be healed. There was a sore spot in her soul; there was something at which her heart bled, and over which she threw the veil of a lofty pride, but without being able to deceive an old acquaintance like Theresa Holbrecht, or a nature of such fine perceptions as Adele's. And around this wound in Elsie's heart, what he called her secret, her poor brother's thoughts were constantly revolving. He saw a crime lying deep below it all. Something not to be thought of! Something that Adele's pure and clear soul rejected as wholly impossible. And he was trying to get upon the track of this crime. He had bent to that end all the energy of his obstinate will, all the fire of his nature. What impelled him to it? What was the real motive that made him so restless, so eager in the pursuit? This was what Adele had brooded over for long, lonely hours in these dark winter days, here in the shadow of the old church-walls, where he had sent for her to come, to share his lonely and laborious life. Was it what he represented to her—what, perhaps, he made himself believe—the prospect of wealth that the discovery of a great deception would put into his hands? Adele believed she understood her brother's heart well enough to know that it was not that alone; yes, even that it was not that at all; that he was animated by a totally different impulse; that a fatality chained him to the steps of this woman, and that he could not rest, not live, without penetrating to the cause of her secret trouble, in which he certainly saw, whether he acknowledged it or not, the reason of her being so hard and cold and icy toward him, the cause of the deep gulf that yawned between them. That was it, Adele said to herself; he wanted to bring light into the gulf that separated them, as if the light would avail to fill the gulf!

She was about to ring for lights, when Ferdinand entered by a side-door, and, extending his hand to her, placed himself by the hearth with his back to the fire.

Adele arose and went to order lights; then, returning, she placed her hands upon his shoulder and said—

"How gloomy you look, Ferdinand; have you had vexatious work to-day?"

He put his arm gently around her, and, looking into her face, answered, somewhat absently, after a pause—

"Vexatious work? Really, I should have to think a while before I could tell you the subjects of the documents I had to look over to-day; and I think that is the most vexatious thing of all—to be obliged to worry over work that is so little adapted to our nature, is so little like that we would have chosen in accordance with our own tastes and tendencies, that we forget it as soon as we rise from the desk."

"Do you think that is the reason, my dear, discontented brother, that you forget it so soon?"

"What else?"

"Ah, you have other things in your mind, things that torment you, that draw all the sunshine out of your life, destroy all your pleasure, deaden all the ambition you need as a spur to interest and activity in your business—ugly, wicked, mad ideas, in whose power you lie captive like a poor, nerveless man, chained by sleep and lying helpless in the power of the vampire that is drinking his heart's blood!"

"Oh," answered Ferdinand, with a forced smile, "it is the way of women to exaggerate! I have been thrown by fate into this corner of the earth, where I have again come into contact with people in regard to whom it is my duty to ascertain facts on which your and my fortune depends—or your and my misfortune, I might better say!"

Adele was silent. She could have made many objections to Ferdinand's view of his "duty," to his idea of fortune and misfortune for them both, and of the facts on which they depended. But what would it avail to talk about it? She said nothing, but sighed deeply.

"How sadly you sigh, Adele," said her brother. "Really, the sunshine does not come to your face any oftener than to mine. And how could it, after all that has passed?"

"But it could, it could, Ferdinand, if you would think as I do. Think," and she laid her head upon her brother's shoulder while her eyes were turned thoughtfully to the slowly-burning coals, "think; with our fate it makes much less difference what it is than how we take it. Let us take ours on the best side. What if I were a poor girl, alone in the world, growing old, and sick perhaps, with no prospect of anything better, living in some garret and supporting myself by the labor of my weak hands—would it not be my ideal of happiness to have a brother, to be loved by him, to be relieved by him from every care, to be in a position where I have everything, and more than everything of what habit has made necessary, and where I am relieved of all anxiety for the future; and knowing, too, that I am not living in vain, that I have the opportunity of brightening life for my brother, of helping him, of giving him the care he needs—what an ideal of happiness such a life would seem to me! I often think of this, and when I have such a life before my imagination, I think to myself, you have all this and should you not be perfectly happy?"

Ferdinand looked down at her lovingly, and bending down kissed her forehead.

"How good you are! What a warm, noble heart you have!"

"Does it show a noble heart," she asked, smiling, "to count up one's treasures and rejoice in their possession? It shows nothing but reason; and you, too, ought to have this reason——"

"And do you think I haven't it? Do you think I do not appreciate the treasure I have in such a wise little sister?"

"Oh, the little sister is only a small part of the possessions that ought to make you happy. There are the friends you have made, your honorable position in the world, your office which——"

"Which," interrupted Ferdinand, smiling bitterly, "is so many hundred times better than, for example, that of a poor forester at Vellinghaus. In fact, the journey I have just made, the thought of the way poor Emil Drausfeld tried to go through life and ended by complete shipwreck—that alone would be enough to make me happy and convince me that I am one of fortune's favorites, if I had my sister's angelic disposition. Well, Adele, I will do better. I am not so bad as you think. I thank God every day that I have you. Does that content you? And now, tell me, has Irene been with you?"

Adele resumed her seat by the fire-place as she answered:

"The poor child has been here, in bitter distress over a scene William Kronhorst has had with his father, who forbade him most positively to think of marrying Irene. Irene was in despair. Their attachment, I am afraid, is much too strong for much to be effected by any such prohibition. I am afraid they are only adding fuel to the fire."

"Quite possible," said Ferdinand.

"And the more," continued Adele, "as Herr Kronhorst gives his son no satisfactory reason for his opposition, and William is not the one to submit to a merely arbitrary command."

"And Irene's mother is also opposed, I believe?" asked Ferdinand.

"Yes, and the princess, too," answered Adele. "Can you imagine the real reason why they have all, as it seems, conspired against the young people?"

"Perhaps," said Ferdinand, after a thoughtful pause, "Herr Kronhorst suspects the condition of affairs as I do; a man with his immense influence and resources has a thousand ways of getting on the track of such things, and does not want a daughter-in-law with a dowry that does not belong to her. And probably the two women are afraid to have the keen eyes of such a man turned on their affairs."

Adele shook her head doubtingly, but Ferdinand went on, more excitedly:

"Have we not been told that, before our arrival here, Herr Kronhorst was extremely attentive to Irene's mother, and was supposed to be her suitor? But the friendship was suddenly broken off. What had happened? Had Frau Schott told him things that had frightened him away? Or had he quietly made inquiries about her past life,

and been more successful than I have been? If he is now so decidedly opposed to his son's marrying Irene, without assigning any reasons, that will go to confirm such a conjecture, and it is also a confirmation of my suppositions."

"Of your suppositions!" said Adele, in a somewhat mocking tone, but with a sigh. "You certainly need all the confirmation you can get for them; they rest on such a weak foundation!"

"That they do not, my wise little sister. I think I have confoundedly strong evidence for them!"

"That Irene does not look as if she belonged to your family; that in her features you cannot trace the slightest resemblance to what you call the physiognomy of the 'clan'——"

"Yes, that is one evidence."

"And that the princess likes to have Irene with her; and that seems to me so natural."

"It is so natural, too, that the mother should so resignedly give up her child to the princess, leaving her entirely to her sister's influence, and waiving all her own rights!"

"That is not so bad as you imagine," said Adele, shaking her head. "And if Irene prefers to stay at Achsentein, what is more natural than for such a young girl to prefer the brilliant life of a prince's court to the lonely and monotonous life of her mother's house?"

Ferdinand took a cigar from a box on the mantle, and as he slowly prepared and lighted it at the lamp, he said:

"It is curious that in this affair we have exchanged *rôles*. Usually women can see through a thing much sooner than men; but here it is I who am most sharp-sighted, who put this and that little circumstance together, and draw my conclusions from them!"

Adele shrugged her shoulders.

"It may be," she said, sighing again. "But what good does it do us to discuss it again and again? The best way would be to put it all out of our heads—and hearts. But I cannot persuade you to do that!"

"No," answered Ferdinand, quietly, beginning to walk slowly up and down the room.

"Frau Groebler has been here," began Adelè, after a pause. "She was anxious about her husband's remaining so long away. But she left, fully decided to give him a most stinging lecture when he does come."

"I expect him back any moment," answered Ferdinand. "But what has the good fellow done to draw down his wife's indignation upon him?"

"Frau Theresa is sharp," answered Adele. "I had no sooner told her that you returned very much depressed at Emil Drausfeld's death, and that you had hoped to get information from him on a subject that interested you greatly, than she began to suspect what the explanations were that you went for."

"How is that possible?"

"How is it possible? You have just said yourself that women have keen eyes. She may have observed your former attachment to the princess, and have often asked herself about it, and now, when she sees you going through the storm to that desolate Vellinghaus forest for information of some kind, it was natural for her to think of that strange correspondence of which Emil Drausfeld had spoken only to her, and of which she had told her husband, your beloved Groebler. And the discovery that Groebler must have been indiscreet toward you, excited Frau Theresa so that she told me all she knew of the matter."

"Did you confirm her suspicion that I learned that from him?"

"I neither confirmed nor denied it. I let her tell me what she pleased, and kept as quiet as I could. And then—but some one is coming."

"Perhaps Groebler has come back," said Ferdinand, eagerly.

A servant came in and announced that the police inspector was in the landrath's office, and wished to speak with him.

Ferdinand went at once to his visitor.

CHAPTER X.

HERR GROEBLER'S REPORT.

When Ferdinand entered his office he found the police inspector standing at the lower end of the room with his back to the stove. Herr Groebler acknowledged his presence only with a slight bow. As Ferdinand went to turn up the lamp on his writing-desk, he said, in a voice of half-suppressed excitement:—

"At last, Herr Groebler, I thank God you are here to put an end to my suspense. I am grateful to you for coming at once. You must be just from the cars. Take a seat."

"You must thank my wife for my coming at once. I went home, and had just taken off my overcoat and begun to taste a cup of hot coffee, when I discovered that the army was fully equipped for war and on the move."

"That is to say——"

"That is to say that a campaign was designed. The *casus belli* was the betrayal of revelations of a secret character to a hostile power."

"Oh, I understand," said Ferdinand. "She is angry at you because——"

"Yes, she is angry, my good woman, and as a woman's anger is best conquered by flight, I hurried away here. What a quiet, happy asylum such a bachelor's room is!"

"And yet you have become so spoiled by your good wife's care, that you would not take very kindly to bachelorhood now! But, first, make yourself comfortable in this asylum, as you call it. Take the chair there," said Ferdinand, throwing himself into the arm-chair in front of his writing-desk.

"Let me stand here and warm my back," said Herr Groebler. "The world outside is cold, and it is well to have a reserve of something warm at one's back."

"That is true," said Ferdinand, "one does need something of that kind in this cold world; and in the struggle for existence a reserve force of heart. Is that what you mean, Herr Groebler?"

"About that," answered Herr Groebler, whose appearance and manner would lead one to expect philosophical observations. In the course of years he had grown much thinner and sallower; his black hair, that used to fall over his forehead in pleasant contrast with the tint of his complexion, had entirely disappeared in front, and grown gray at the back; and the small eyes had retreated far back in their sockets, as if they had missed the protection of the bushy locks above them. On the whole, Herr Groebler, with his weary eyes, which however, could, on occasion, send out swift, arrowy glances, with his bold, deep-cut features, and his yellow skin, which seemed to have been prepared for greater durability by the application of some powerful acid—on the whole, he looked like a man that would be a dangerous antagonist in the struggle with life, and that it would be well to think twice before engaging with him.

"But now to business," said Ferdinand, breathing deeply with excitement. "What news do you bring me, Herr Groebler?"

"Not much, but some. Nothing actual, but a prospect——"

"Not much, indeed! What is it?"

"I was at Asthof several days. As I had nothing else to do there, or, rather, nothing at all, I prepared a book of heraldry."

"A book of heraldry!" exclaimed Ferdinand, in surprise.

"Yes, indeed, for all Lower Saxony. What could have taken me to that stupid place in mid-winter except something of that kind? The clergyman, with whom I soon made friends, comprehended very readily that it was a great want, and that I should be performing a great and needful service by filling this yawning gap. He gladly placed at my disposal what he knew or could learn of the genealogy of the von Melroth family, to whom Asthof formerly belonged. There were old gravestones in the churchyard and on the walls, old writings in the sacristy, and a few books, not quite so old, containing the records of the christenings, marriages and burials of the parishioners. I searched them all through,

of course, for my work. There was no record of a marriage between a Fräulein Elsie von Melroth and a Herr Philip Bonsart."

"It had been removed; the passage was cut out, or the entire leaf torn away?" cried Ferdinand, hastily.

"Nothing of the kind," said Herr Groebler, quietly. "It was not there, and had never been there."

"Are you sure of that, Groebler?"

"Quite sure, Herr von Schott. I inquired whether there were any such books in the chapel at Asthof, containing records of such ceremonies that had taken place there. No; such ceremonies did not take place there. The manor-house belonged to the parish of Asthof, and the proprietors belonged, like all the other parishioners, to the village church. They could conduct private worship in the chapel, but nothing more. I asked whether marriage had not occasionally taken place there. No, not that the clergyman knew of, and not that the sacristan knew of, and he was an old man, old enough to be the father of the clergyman, who has been there but eight or nine years. I let the subject drop. When we were sitting over our wine in the evening, I talked to the reverend gentleman about the necessity of having the records kept by civil officers, as the old custom of having them placed in church-books by the clergymen was not adapted to modern times; the records of the most important events of life for the last twenty years were inaccurate and defective. It was natural that the clergyman should defend the old custom very warmly; I defended my assertion quite as warmly; he grew excited and I grew vehement. It was also natural that, in order to clinch my argument, I should at last refer to a case, which, however, was to be kept entirely secret—a case in his own parish; a case, too, not concerning poor farm-hands, whose marriage a clergyman might easily forget to record, if he happened to be very busy; but concerning a son of the last proprietor of Asthof and a daughter of the one just preceding, who were married there in the year 1852, as I had learned past all doubt in my genealogical researches, and of whose marriage, as I had found that morning, no record had been made in the books. The pastor laughed at my assertion, but his ambition was aroused, and in the following days he began investigations; as every one in the parish knew him too well to be reticent or suspicious, he could, of course, succeed much better than a stranger writing up a book of heraldry. And the result of his inquiries was that absolutely no one knew anything of such a marriage; that no one had heard of Philip Bonsart ever being married either in this country or in America, whither he had fled many years before; that not a syllable in regard to it had ever been uttered either by this clergyman's predecessor, or by the father or other relatives of Philip, who had remained at Asthof five or six years after the death of his father. They have since moved to a city in Pomerania.

"The pastor triumphed over me, and I had to leave him his triumph. I could not do otherwise than acknowledge myself beaten, at least as regarded the proofs of what I had asserted. So we began to talk of other things till I said, as if suddenly reminded of the circumstance again:—

" 'It strikes me that we could easily get light on the question we have been disputing by asking Philip Bonsart himself.'

" 'Philip Bonsart himself!' said the pastor, in astonishment.

" 'Why not? Will he make a secret of it? I do not see any objection, whatever. Did he have any reason at the time to keep his marriage secret?'

" 'You still persist in talking of this marriage.'

" 'I persist in it. But I mean that if he then had reasons for keeping it secret, they cannot surely have any force now, after all these years. Where is Philip Bonsart? Get his address for me, and I will write to him, in the hope that my letter may find him among the living.'

"The pastor shook his head. 'What an obstinate man you are,' he said. 'But——'

" 'That belongs to my trade,' I answered. 'To get the exact length of a certain term of years or a correct date, a genealogist must climb walls on which he spies some old inscriptions, descend into ancient tombs in which he may break his neck, clear musty parchment with acids which may make him blind, and submit to be turned out of doors by churlish householders, on whose windows he has discovered old escutcheons. In comparison with all this, what is the trouble of sending a letter to America?'

" 'A dangerous trade,' said the pastor, laughing. 'But, unfortunately, I know of no one here who could give you Philip Bonsart's address.'

" 'No one? Only think; there must be men in the place with whom he associated when he was a young man. Who were his intimate friends?'

"The pastor shook his head again.

" 'You know of no on?' I asked

" 'No. If he left acquaintances here, as I do not doubt he did, still I am convinced that no one has kept up communication with him, or did for any length of time after his disappearance. He was pursued by warrants as I have heard. It would not have been advisable for any one to send letters to his address. He himself would not have thought it prudent to give his address to any one who might have betrayed him by mere thoughtlessness, even.'

" 'On the other side of the ocean he was certainly safe.'

" 'Possibly. But here you will hardly be able to learn anything about him; you will have to go to his family in Pomerania, which, indeed,' he added, laughing, 'you are just the man to do, merely for the sake of confuting me.'

" 'Then I should first have to find out the name of the place in Pomerania where they live.'

" 'That,' said the pastor, 'will probably be easy. Your only landlady must know the name of the place.'

" 'My landlady?'

" 'Your landlady, old Frau Rose, was formerly house-maid at Asthof, and after she married the landlord of the Golden Duck, she always maintained—as it gives her great pleasure to say—the most friendly relations with the family of the proprietor, the Bonsarts. Her happiest recollections are of her friendship with these people, and she likes to talk of them. You can get her to talk without running any of the risks which, as you say, you are accustomed to encounter so boldly in the pursuit of your researches.'

"I took leave of the clergyman and went home to see what Frau Rose would have to say. It was not necessary to play the genealogist with the little old gray-headed landlady; a book of heraldry was beyond her comprehension, but it appeared perfectly natural to her that a sensible and experienced stranger of a thoughtful turn should listen with interest to everything she had to tell of the good old times when the Melroths and the Bonsarts lived at the manor-house of Asthof.

"After I had talked with Frau Rose for a while in the sitting-room of the inn, by way of awakening her garrulity, she took me into her private parlor and refreshed me with tea and little pan-cakes while she was quenching my thirst for knowledge with the history of that noble house. The details she gave were mainly of a human and personal interest, without any claim to historic importance. The pastor was right. She had been a housemaid of the Melroths; she had known Matilda and Elsie well. She told how much she had had to bear from little Elsie, who, as a child, had a peculiar talent for getting into all sorts of dangers, including that of being most mercilessly beaten by her playmate, Philip, the son of the steward, when she had teased and tyrannized over him till the wild boy was wrought into fury. From other dangers, Frau Rose said, she was often rescued by the wild boy himself, and they had been constant companions even after Herr von Melroth had quarrelled with his steward, Philip's father, and Philip was no longer allowed to visit at the manor-house. And then Philip was sent to school, and Elsie grew more quiet and reserved, and was at length sent to a boarding-school. Some years after Herr von Melroth left the estate which his steward had bought, and moved into the city.

"'And Philip and Elsie forgot their childish fancy for each other?' I asked.

"'No, indeed, sir; no, indeed,' said Frau Rose, significantly. 'No, sir, I do not think they forgot each other. They wrote letters which—why should I not tell you?—which passed through my hands; and the schools to which they were sent were in the same place. I don't believe they forgot each other there, either. And then, afterward, when Philip cut up such mad capers, and every one was talking about him and saying he had stirred up rebellion and what all, and that it would cost him his life if he were caught—even then I do not believe that Elsie forgot him; no, not even then!'

"'What! such a wild, crazy fellow?' said I, incredulously.

"Frau Rose shook her gray head mysteriously.

"'Yes, that he was,' she said, 'that he was; but after all, as I have always said, and will until my dying day, he was a boy with a good, true, brave heart. I was still housemaid at Asthof, for when the Bonsarts moved in they kept me in the service, for they knew me, and knew they could rely upon me; so they kept me in the house, and it was as pleasant for me as before, for they were good, well-meaning people, and not at all haughty, though they were the masters now; and as for what people said, that Herr Bonsart, the father, you know, had taken advantage of Herr von Melroth so dishonestly, until he had wronged him out of everything and could buy the estate—that I do not believe; people will talk, and they like to speak ill of their neighbors. And the Melroths—the Lord knows they never knew how to manage, and to squander their property was a lesson they had learned from their fathers and grandfathers. But what I was going to say—I was only a house-maid, and yet I know that if I had said, Herr Philip, I am in great distress, and I need some one to ride three miles for me this stormy night, and no one can go but you—I know that Herr Philip would have put on his hunting-boots and have gone for me. That was Herr Philip, sir; and now if you think he could have forgotten Elsie——'

"Frau Rose did not finish her sentence; she only indicated what she might have said by a funereal shake of the head and a very significant expression.

"Then I said, suddenly, in a very different tone, which astonished Frau Rose not a little: 'Perhaps I know more of Philip Bonsart's later life than you do, my good woman! I know about his flight as a rebel, of his return in the year 1852, and that he came home to be married to Elsie Melroth in the chapel at Asthof.'

"'Ah!' cried Frau Rose, her round, good-natured eyes starting out in astonishment; 'ah, you—you know that?'

"'I know it, Frau Rose.'

"'In Heaven's name, then, you know more of the matter than I do, though I could have told you the most of it. Then they were really married in the chapel? You have found that out? Really, I have never been sure about it; and, least of all, did I ever dream that a strange gentleman would come and tell me that. You know it?'

"'I know it,' I said, 'for I helped him over the ocean; I got a pass for him and his young wife, who, however, did not use it.'

"'No,' answered Frau Rose, in excitement, 'she did not use any pass. She did not cross the ocean with him, that I can assure you of. But she was here to be married to him, and she stayed here—here in my house, up stairs in the attic-room that looks out on the garden; I kept her there three nights. And Philip came and spent a great deal of time with her, and they made no secret of it to me, that they were to be married in the chapel late in the evening, when every one was asleep, and that it must be kept a perfect secret, not only because Elsie's father was not to know anything about it, but also because not a soul must know that Philip was here in the country. They made no secret of it to me, that is, Herr Philip did not, for I had taken care of his letters so long behind his father's back, and he knew me; and knew that he could rely upon Lisette Rose, and so he had brought Fräulein Elsie to me; he brought her from W. one evening in the twilight, in a one-horse carriage, and I took her up to the attic-chamber, as I told you, and waited on her as well as I could, and carried up everything to her that she could wish, I myself, all alone; for why? She was the child of my old master, and she had grown so handsome, so tall and handsome, I should hardly have known her, and though she was sparing of her words, and cold and short in what she said, I was sorry for her; for I saw very well, in spite of her pride and her cool manner, that her heart was not at ease about the matter, and more than once when I went up I saw that she had been weeping, and I knew how one must feel to go away from one's father against his will, and go over the sea into a strange world, and be married so quietly at night, as if it were something to be ashamed of, and to have no bridal day before all the people, and no wedding dress, no wreath, and no veil, but go at night into the church in a dark-blue travelling dress of alpaca, and a common hat, and then right away on the journey in a stage and all that—one of us can see how any one must feel, sir, and I, for my part, I would never have done it, never, even if Rose, my dear departed husband, had wanted me to; I should have said to him: No, Rose, I will do much for you, very much, but not this; no, not this; but Rose, he would not have asked it, for he was a good, kind-hearted man.'

"Frau Rose raised the corner of her handkerchief to her eyes, smoothed her hair back from her forehead, and, gazing at the flame of the lamp, fell into a revery.

"'But now tell me,' I asked, after a pause, 'why did not the young lady cross the ocean with him after they were married?'

"Frau Rose shrugged her shoulders.

"'If you were so intimate with him, did he not write to you himself, or let you know in some other way how the affair turned out?' she said, throwing a half-distrustful glance at me.

"'No,' I answered, 'I had prudently forbidden him to communicate any longer with me. I myself was not then in the best odor with the police, you must know, and letters to people once registered in the black book might in those days have been very easily read by eyes for which they were not intended.'

"'So, so,' nodded Frau Rose, knowingly.

'Oh, yes, that is easily understood. And so you do not know what happened afterward, and why she did not go with him?'

"'I know nothing of all that, Frau Rose. I never heard about it. When they were once married, I think she ought to have gone with him, don't you? For where the husband is——'

"'Once married?' said Frau Rose, thoughtfully. 'But were they? I never was sure about it.'

"'Do you doubt it?'

"'Certainly I doubt it. For, you see, this was the way of it; Philip told me everything, and I have often thought of it since, and think of it too often now to have forgotten it. This was the way of it: there was a young chaplain with our pastor then —afterward he was pastor himself—Herr Chaplain Heimdal, but he went away to the Catholic Church in Hamburg, and he died of cholera when it was there three years ago. And this young clergyman was a friend of Herr Philip; they used to hunt together, and Herr Philip had coaxed his father, who would not let any one hunt in the park at Asthof, to give the chaplain permission; and, beside that, they had been together a great deal, and were great friends; they had been at school together. And so it happened that the chaplain had promised to marry Elsie Melroth and Herr Philip secretly. It was to be in the chapel at Asthof, very late in the evening, when there was no one about. And then they had two witnesses, old Grundmeyer, who, even then, hardly had the use of his senses, and now has grown very childish, and Stephen Elms, Herr Bonsart's groom, a crafty fellow that Herr Philip was going to take away with him. He had gone to his father's to put his affairs in order and take leave of his friends and relatives. He was to come back the third evening, and then they were to be married, and leave here at daybreak.

"'I remember, as if it had happened to-day, how everything was arranged and prepared; and then one evening, it was about six o'clock; it was quite dark, for it was a gloomy, rainy day, and the wind blew fearfully around the house, and Rose, he had a sore throat then—he suffered so much with it, the poor fellow—Rose had gone to bed; and a gentleman came into the house, a young gentleman, just as if the storm had blown him in; he looked wet and dirty, and tired to death, as if he had come a long distance through the storm; and before I had scarcely caught a glimpse of him, he was beside me, as I was standing in the kitchen door with the lamp, and calling to the servant to shut the back door that goes into the garden, because the wind would blow out my lamp; and the gentleman said, panting, and in a half-whisper, "Madam," said he, "I have learned at the manor-house that Herr Philip Bonsart must be here in the Golden Duck; pray take me to him. I know that he is here, and he is my friend. I beg of you, take me to him at once." I looked at the man, and did not know what to do, for it was nothing to strangers, you know, that Herr Philip was in my house, and that he had come back and was here in the country, no one was to know that. So I looked at the young gentleman and thought—he looks honest, to be sure. And then he said again, so beseechingly, "I beg of you, take me to him. I am his friend, and have something of the greatest importance to say to him; something that he must know this very hour, and I have come out from H. for that alone, madam." So I made up my mind, and I took him up stairs and showed him the door; and he knocked, and then he disappeared, and I came back with my lamp, and heard and saw nothing more for perhaps an hour, and what passed between the three I do not know.'

"'Could you describe this young man to me, Frau Rose?' I asked.

"'Describe the young man?' she said, looking up, 'I think he must have been a handsome man when he was in dry clothes and had not just come for miles over a dirty turnpike in a storm. He was tall and slender, and I think blonde, with a light full beard; and I think he looked to me as if he must be a forester, or something like that, though I cannot say why I thought so——'"

"There is no doubt," here interrupted Ferdinand von Schott, "that it was the faithful Eckard, Emil Drausfeld, who came to warn them."

"From all that you have told me," answered Herr Groebler, with a resigned and melancholy smile, "I think it must have been the faithful Eckard, whom you had sent to warn them against a faithful officer striving to fulfil his official obligations, Herr von Schott!"

"Certainly; but now go on, Groebler," said Ferdinand, turning a face of suspense toward the faithful officer.

"Frau Rose," he answered, "soon finished her story. The gentleman remained at least an hour with Philip Bonsart and Elsie Melroth. Then Frau Rose heard them all three coming down the stairs. To light them out, she stepped with her lamp from the kitchen to the door. She saw Elsie going out into the night between the two young men, with slow and tottering steps. She looked after them and saw them stop outside, and Philip, talking excitedly to her, just as if he were trying angrily to remove some doubt or win some promise from her, or overcome some opposition. The stranger stood by without saying a word. And then they went on, on into the darkening night and the storm, until they became only three black shadows to Frau Rose, and at length disappeared in the shadows cast by the houses in the lonesome village street. After a full hour they returned, but not all. Only Fräulein Elsie von Melroth and the stranger. returned. Philip Bonsart had probably remained at his father's to make preparations for his journey; this was Frau Rose's first thought, though it seemed strange that he should not at least have accompanied his young wife back to the Golden Duck, but should have left that for a stranger to do. Elsie went to her room, and the stranger took lodging for the night. She did not see Fräulein Elsie again that evening, nor in the morning. At early dawn, the stranger came down and sent a servant for a carriage; then he took breakfast and called for his bill, and Fräulein Elsie and Rose got up to make it out, and the servant brought it in. The stranger paid it, and when the carriage came—Frau Rose had in the meantime made herself presentable in morning costume—then the stranger sent up for Fräulein Elsie's baggage, and

5

brought her down himself, and she was closely veiled, and bowed to Frau Rose and waved her hand in farewell, and then the young man helped her into the carriage and they drove away to W., where she had come from a short time before—not to Hamburg or Bremen with Philip Bonsart, as it had been designed.

"That," said Herr Groebler, in conclusion, "was Frau Rose's story, to which I succeeded in getting only a few unimportant additions. The driver said when he came back, that he had driven them to the stage in W., and that they had taken seats for H., where Elsie must have gone back to her father's as if she had just returned from the visit to her friend. Frau Rose had never seen anything more of Philip Bonsart; the groom, who was to have been a witness at the marriage, had been seen at Asthof the next day, after returning from his father's, and then he, too, had disappeared. He must have accompanied or followed Philip. On the second day after Elsie's departure, the chaplain appeared at the Golden Duck and took his early glass with some guests, and as he was going away he secretly handed Frau Rose a little article folded in a paper, and whispered—

"'It belongs to Fräulein von Melroth; she left it lying on the sofa. But send it to her so that it may not fall into the hands of some one else in the family and betray her. It must not come from here, from Asthof. Have it sent from W., by the stage; or give it to the messenger there—that will be best.' The young clergyman whispered these words to Frau Rose, and was about to go away; but she held him by the arm, thinking that she, who had waited on Elsie Melroth for days, had kept their secret for the two young people, and to whom Philip had told everything—that she deserved a little confidence from the chaplain, too, as to what had happened, why the young people had not gone away together after the chaplain had married them, and why the marriage had been hastened so. Whereupon the clergyman had answered only with exclamations of anger that Philip had been so thoughtless as to talk of a secret marriage, which must cost him, the chaplain, his position if it should become known; nothing had come of the intended marriage; Philip had been warned that police officers were on the way to Asthof—Frau Rose did not imagine," threw in Herr Groebler, "that I could testify to the truth of this part of her story—Philip had been obliged to take himself off at once, to go on board a ship, so as not to find his way beset by the police, even in Hamburg. With this, the chaplain had gone away in anger, and all that Frau Rose could learn afterward of that occurrence and of Philip Bonsart, was as good as nothing; little could be learned from the family at Asthof, for they did not like to speak of Philip—nothing but that he was in North America, that he had been in a good many kinds of business, seeming to be fickle and unsteady, but that he seemed to be getting along well; afterward the Bonsarts had left Asthof, the father having died about seven years ago."

"So these are your discoveries, Herr Groebler," said Ferdinand, in a tone expressive of anything but satisfaction with the results of Herr Groebler's journey.

"These are my discoveries," he answered. "Will you allow me, before we go any farther, to take one of these cigars, and have some sort of fluid brought, so that I may moisten my organs of speech, which have been somewhat severely taxed?"

"Oh, pardon me for not thinking of it," said Ferdinand. "My interest in your report was to blame for it."

He sprang up and pulled a bell.

"Will you have red or white?"

"If it is not all the same to you—if you have only one kind at hand, then it's all the same to me; I drink both. But if it is all the same to you, then it's not all the same to me; I prefer red. Red is the wine of temperate people."

Ferdinand smiled, and, by ordering the servant to bring some red wine, indicated that it was all the same to him.

Both were silent for a while, until Herr Groebler had emptied a glass of the wine, and then leaned back in his chair and sent up a few clouds of smoke from his cigar.

"Those are your discoveries," repeated Ferdinand, at length, "and if we sum them up we shall arrive at the result that we are no farther on than we were before. There is no record of the marriage, and there seems never to have been any. Frau Rose had it from Philip's own mouth that it was to take place, and that the preparations were all made. That, indeed, is a stronger evidence than I can give from what Emil Drausfeld told me. But Frau Rose was not a witness of the ceremony. Thus we have not a single witness. An old man was to have been one, and he is now childish; a groom, and he went over the ocean with Philip Bonsart, and probably has been entirely lost sight of. Moreover, it is a question whether this groom really did serve as a witness. He seems to have been absent at the time of the marriage, which was a day sooner than was first intended, and Emil Drausfeld seems to have taken his place."

"So it appears," said Herr Groebler.

"And Emil Drausfeld is dead."

"Ah! dead? The forester Drausfeld dead?"

"I returned yesterday from Vellinghaus forest."

"And you did not find him?"

"I found him—but dumb, silenced forever, and a broken-hearted widow, and crying children."

"That is bad, bad for our business."

"That it is, Herr Groebler."

"But the letters that were sent to Drausfeld; did the widow——"

"The widow could not give them to me, for they were not there."

"Pest!" ejaculated Herr Groebler, between his closed teeth; "then we are almost at the end of our string. I should think we were at the end. What do you think?"

Ferdinand took his glass, which was still full, held it against the light, and looked into it, as if he could read an answer to the question in the purple blood of the vine.

"And I must confess to you," continued Herr Groebler, after a pause, "that the affair seems doubtful now to me——"

"The affair? What affair?"

"The marriage."

"Ah! you doubt——"

"Yes. It is clear that the program of this secret marriage, which was first fixed for the next day, was disturbed. You sent Emil Dransfeld to warn them, and Philip Bonsart heeded the warning, and was up and away that night, which was very sensible of him, for on the next morning I had made arrangements to have all the roads leading from Asthof watched by some of my people. He went the evening before, whether as a married man or not, I do not know, but I think it doubtful."

"But did not Frau Rose tell you that they went away late in the evening, and stayed an hour or more, and did not the chaplain admit that they were with him? Why should they have gone to him if not to have the ceremony performed at once?"

Herr Groebler shook his head.

"Then would not the young lady have gone with her husband? Or, if she shrank from the fatigues and dangers of a sudden flight, or feared that she would be a hindrance to him, would she not have followed him soon after over the ocean?"

"I am convinced," answered Ferdinand, "that Philip Bonsart, who had come from America for this very purpose, had made that long journey, so dangerous to him, for no other reason, would not have gone away again after the preparations were all made, without having accomplished his purpose. He was a passionate, energetic, strong-willed fellow. He was not so timid as to be frightened by Emil Drausfeld's warning, so as to lose his head and rush away without knowing what he was about. He must have kept in mind the object of his coming, and have made it his first business to carry out what he had been so energetically striving for."

"But the lady," said Herr Groebler, after a pause; "the young lady! You do not take her into account. It sometimes happens that young ladies, too, have wills and energy of their own. I think that such an one might not have found this quiet 'aside' as much to her taste as the brilliant dramatic effect of a public wedding; and that she, if she must run, would—let him run! The chaplain, too, denied to Frau Rose that the marriage had taken place——"

"Not expressly, it seems. And if he did, what of that? He could not do other-

wise than deny it?" said Ferdinand, warmly. Herr Groebler knit his brows, and looked as sharp as if he were inwardly cutting the matter into infinitesimally small pieces. Then he took a long breath, drained his glass, and, putting his hand into his breast-pocket, said:

"Here you have all that I have brought back from the journey—two keepsakes, one of Frau Rose, the other of Fräulein von Melroth."

He handed Ferdinand a folded slip of paper and a very small parcel. The first was the address of Philip Bonsart's relatives, who lived in a small town in Pomerania. The parcel contained a small locket with some dark hair in it, apparently of very little value.

"The address," said Herr Groebler, "I obtained from Frau Rose. The locket is what the chaplain gave her as having been lost by Fräulein von Melroth. You will probably," he added, with a slight mocking smile that looked a little like a nervous quiver of distress, "you will probably receive the thanks of the princess if you restore it to her."

Ferdinand looked at it a moment in silence. "The landlady of the Golden Duck gave it to you?"

"She gave it to me when I told her that I could have it delivered to the princess, and would be very discreet about it."

"Then she knew the later life of Fräulein Elsie von Melroth?"

"She knew it; she had heard that Fräulein Elsie had bewitched a prince, and had been raised to a throne, but only as a rumor. She did not know the name of the prince."

"And now," began Herr Groebler again, after a pause, "you have a circumstantial account of my journey, and I suppose I may withdraw. My wife's wrath is probably over by this time, and I can betake myself to my domestic hearth, and await your farther pleasure."

He was about to rise, but Ferdinand, who had risen and began to walk up and down the room, pressed him down again into his chair and said:

"You must, of course, be tired, and in need of rest, and I will not keep you any longer, only for a few moments, just for a question or two. First, what would you do now, Herr Groebler?"

Herr Groebler took on the sharp expression again, and, raising his glass, looked at it as if trying to cut it in pieces. Then he said, thoughtfully—

"I would first put a question to myself, which must be a little difficult to attack. For men in general are not inclined to trouble themselves with such a question. It is a little distasteful, a little heretical. That is, in general. In our case it would not be so, but you would be no more than wise——"

"Well, out with this great question. What is it?"

"It is: Do I believe, or do I know? And I should act according to the answer I should be obliged to make. Exactly in accordance with it."

"That is to say?" asked Ferdinand, stopping before him.

"That is to say: in case you must give this answer—and I think it will be your answer, as it would be that of most men who are honest with themselves—in case you must say to yourself: I only believe, then let this matter drop; I have failed to find living evidence, and you have failed to find written evidence. Let it drop; and say to yourself that it is too difficult a task to find proofs for things we only believe—so hard for a human brain that many, originally sound, have been wrought to madness in the vain attempt!"

"And if I can give myself the answer: I know—what then?"

"If you can give that answer, then— why, then, go on with your search. I am at your command. If you want to send me to America, to get upon the track of this Philip Bonsart—as we have the address of his relatives, we may succeed in finding him and getting his secret from him—well, I have nothing to say against it. I will even go across the ocean, if that is your wish. I have long had a desire to get a sight of that wonderful world over there."

Ferdinand nodded.

"It would certainly be the best, the very best plan," he said. "But it would cost a great deal of money."

"It would cost money," said Herr Groebler.

"And I am not rich enough," said Ferdinand, with a sigh.

"Then," said Herr Groebler, "we must hope that your self-examination will lead you to the conclusion: I only believe, and to the determination to leave the matter with the Lord. Then we shall not have to fret because we are not rich enough to afford a little trip to America. So good evening, Herr von Schott."

Ferdinand offered his hand with the words, "How shall I thank you?" His visitor pressed it with unwonted cordiality, and left him alone.

Herr Groebler's advice was good. It certainly was. Ferdinand said so to himself more than once as he walked back and forth in the lonesome room. If he knew, if it were an incontrovertible fact to his deepest convictions, the proofs of which he was seeking, then he could go on searching and investigating with some prospect of success. For every event leaves traces behind it which may at last be discovered, which may at last be brought to light by a firm, persistent will.

But if he only believed, if he must admit to himself that he might be in error, that his entire chain of evidence might be but cobwebs of the brain, mere illusions of an imagination grown morbid by constant brooding over the same subject, the deceptions of little coincidences which he had caught up and interpreted too eagerly—then it were better to give up the investigation in which he had been so unsuccessful, in which everything seemed to conspire against him, in which a demoniac fatality seemed to have carried away, killed, annihilated everything that could have thrown light on the subject!

And so he took counsel of himself, seeking to weigh everything as coolly, as quietly, as impartially as possible. But the result of all his reflection was an aspect of the case of which Herr Groebler had not thought, something that could neither restrain him from farther search nor encourage him in it. He did not merely believe, and yet he did not venture to say he knew. He believed he knew. His conviction did not proceed from the facts he could cite; there was nothing incontrovertible in the evidence which he now summoned up anew; but there was something in his heart and in his soul that would not release him from those facts and evidences. It was this something in his heart, partly clear and definite, partly dark and strange to his own consciousness, that chained him irrevocably to the steps of this proud Elsie von Melroth, this Princess of Achsenstein, that lay upon him like a yoke he could not cast off, like a curse of destiny, and forced him to track her steps, from the moment when her path had first crossed his.

We will now turn back a little and relate the events in his life, now passing through his mind, in this solitary hour, when, in accordance with Grœbler's advice, he called himself to account and set them in order before him.

CHAPTER XI.

AN UNEXPECTED MEETING.

Without meeting any serious difficulties Ferdinand von Schott had carried out the plan of life he had cherished in his youth when we saw him preparing for the assessor's examination. After leaving H., and passing that examination, he had been stationed in several cities as *attaché*, as secretary, and as deputy of the ambassador, had gained the title of secretary of legation and was expecting soon to be appointed counsellor of the embassy, when a heavy stroke fell upon him, crushing his hopes and changing the whole course of his life. This was the sudden death of his cousin, Johann Heinrich Schott, the banker, whose nearest relative was Captain Alexander Schott, the only son of his dead brother. But the banker had never been very strongly attached to Alexander's father. Even as boys they had never got on well together. The young soldier and officer had been overbear-

ing toward the young clerk; and Johann Heinrich, whose quiet and reticent, but ambitious spirit by no means yielded to the arrogant claims of his spurred and epauletted brother, had never forgotten it. He had, therefore, clung the more closely to his more distant relatives. Colonel von Schott, who had been ennobled, had always treated the active and business-like young burgher with fatherly affection and care. After the death of Johann Heinrich's father, he had taken the boy and his mother into his own family. It was natural, therefore, that the banker should regard himself as a member of his uncle's family and should look upon the children, Ferdinand and Adele, almost as his own. Their mother had died young, and Johann Heinrich's mother had supplied her place to them; he himself, when he was a young man, had shared their plays; and afterward, when he had become independent, they had always clung to him as their nearest and best-loved relative. So it had seemed a matter of course when their father, the colonel, died without leaving them anything that Johann Heinrich, who had been remarkably successful in his business, should care for the two children and treat them as if he had tacitly adopted them. Adele lived with a relative of her mother, and the banker supplied her with all she needed for her personal expenses. Ferdinand finished his studies at his cousin's expense, and was then provided with the necessary funds for entering upon the career he had chosen. It was also understood, from repeated intimations of the banker, that Ferdinand and Adele would be his principal heirs.

This state of affairs was changed at a single stroke by a most unexpected event. Death surprised the banker before he had carried out his intention of making a will; and accordingly his property, valued at over one hundred thousand thalers, fell to the heir of his nephew Alexander, who had died, leaving a daughter, Irene. Ferdinand and Adele received nothing.

Ferdinand saw only too well that his career in his chosen profession was at an end. He had not advanced far enough to be independent of his cousin's help; his salary was too small to cover his expenses in the capitals to which he was assigned, where the cost of living was generally high. Moreover, he was now the only support of his sister. To get along by practicing niggardly economy, leaving Adele to provide for herself in some servile position—that might have been possible to some, but not to him. It was contrary to his education and his nature.

The disposition to spare and save, to hoard the pennies, and grow rich by economy, is not a tendency that shows itself spontaneously; it is an inheritance, formed and developed by the steady practice of preceding generations. In the Schott family no such practice had ever prevailed; no such hereditary talent had ever been developed. Ferdinand saw at once that the only thing for him to do was to leave Florence, where he then was, and seek some position in his own country, where he would be relieved from the expenses inseparable from his present position.

He had taken the initial steps toward a change, and had applied to the ambassador for temporary leave of absence, when, one day, as he entered the ambassador's rooms, he found two strangers, a gentleman and lady, the sight of whom called into requisition all the self-control his profession had taught him in order to conceal his embarrassment. The minister introduced the strangers as his highness, the Prince of Achsenstein, and her highness, the Princess.

The princess was Elsie von Melroth.

The Prince of Achsenstein was a man over sixty. His appearance was by no means prepossessing. He was scarcely of medium height and was thin and bony. His short neck carried a head in perfect harmony with his form; it looked as if a strong pressure had been applied to the top of the skull in childhood, which had extended the features permanently in breadth; the forehead was broad and low, the nose broad and short, the mouth broad and ugly, the chin broad and stumpy; the round and prominent gray eyes had been forced far apart by the pressure. This general tendency to divorce of the two sides of the head, was vainly resisted by the thin gray locks brushed together to a comb on the top of the head. But they did their best to add to the general oddity of the prince's appearance; and the effect was still farther heightened by the unpleasant hoarseness of his voice. He talked very much and very rapidly, passing frequently from one language to another, French, English, Italian, evidently imagining that he used them all with equal fluency and skill, and, in fact, speaking in all with the same dreadful accent and the same indifference to grammatical forms. The ugliness of his appearance, which bore the manifest stamp of vulgarity, was heightened in Ferdinand's eyes by the great number of ribands of various orders which he wore; a whole millinery shop must have been plundered to supply them.

A few minutes' observation was enough to show that Elsie, notwithstanding exalted rank and polyglot culture and honorary ribands, had sold herself!

And Elsie herself—she seemed to have grown taller and more beautiful, more dazzlingly beautiful; she seemed to him to be surrounded by a luminous splendor, but unapproachable, with the cold repose of a marble statue. She bowed her head but slightly as Ferdinand was presented; he would have known beforehand that she would meet him so—so stiff and cold, so armed against everything that might have betrayed her to speak a word of the past, or even express surprise by a look; he could have imagined this haughty air; he would have painted it just so, if he had thought beforehand that he should meet her suddenly—this noble Princess of Achsenstein. And yet it gave him a keen pang, a feeling of terrible humiliation, as an intentional affront, that she did not utter a single syllable in acknowledgment of their former acquaintance, and, without looking at him again, turned away and continued the conversation with the wife of the ambassador, which had been interrupted by his entrance.

He had seated himself, and took part in the conversation only when the ambassador appealed to him. He feared to betray the convulsive beating of his heart by the trembling of his voice.

The strangers remained for some time. When Prince Achsenstein had once begun to talk, the stream of his thoughts, which was ready to flow at any moment, in every direction, did not soon become exhausted. It was a real pleasure to him to turn the lantern of his intellect in any direction where a flood of light might be needed. It would have been fortunate for his hearers if he could have spoken stenographically; his desire for imparting information could have been sooner satisfied.

At length the princess rose. As Ferdinand looked at her now, he saw that he had perhaps done her injustice. Her face had more color than it had had before. He saw that she must have turned pale a little at his entrance. Turning to him now, she said, still coldly, but in a lower tone than she had used before:

"Herr von Schott, you must not be surprised if I make a little more of our remote relationship here in Florence than may perhaps be agreeable to you, and tax your friendship for the help one needs in an entirely strange city. Will you give us your cousinly attention and assistance? Herr von Schott," she continued, turning to her husband, "is a cousin of my brother-in-law."

"Ah," said the prince, shaking Ferdinand's hand, with apparent cordiality, "that is exceedingly fortunate, exceedingly; happy meeting; I am delighted, highly delighted, indeed!"

And then he turned again to the ambassador and finished his conversation, with the air of a man who has most nobly fulfilled a duty of politeness and need give no farther attention to the object of it, for which he no longer exists.

At last they went. An almost imperceptible nod was Elsie's parting salutation to Ferdinand. The ambassador and his wife accompanied their guests to the outside steps. Ferdinand took advantage of their absence to disappear and escape the questions he foresaw would be asked in regard to his relationship to the Princess of Achsenstein. He wanted to be alone, with the storm of thoughts and feelings he had to contend with.

In all these years the memory of Elsie had been alive in his heart. It had fastened itself there with a hundred tendrils. She had become the wife of Philip Bonsart, or had not; he had never had the heart to inquire. But she had not followed him to America. She had afterward become the wife of a prince, as rumor had long ago reported; perhaps Philip Bonsart was dead. At any rate, she had married a prince with whom she had become acquainted at a watering-place, where she had gone with her sister; the prince was an old man, who had persuaded her to join her youth and beauty to his decay, after he had buried two wives. Ferdinand had looked upon her love for her old playmate as an unalterable fact, which he tried to forget; her marriage with the prince seemed to him a hateful crime; he had hated her for it, and then had tried to forget this hatred.

And yet he had not forgotten her and had not hated her; he realized that he did not hate her by the angry resentment that now filled his heart; he realized it by the sudden storm that seemed to have stirred his soul to its very depths.

This storm was too great to allow him to be in very great haste to respond to her invitation, and call upon her. Not until the second day after did he feel that he was master enough of himself to meet her coolly and calmly—to meet her upon the only footing on which they could meet now, as perfect strangers, as if they had never seen each other before, but were drawn together by a kind of relationship; or perhaps as old acquaintances, who maintain friendly relations on account of common recollections, without taking any more interest in each other than either would take in a dozen other friends of youth.

Elsie might decide; it should be as she wished; he would accommodate himself to whatever tone she chose to take; he would show her that he made no claims, that nothing in the world could be more a matter of indifference to him than the degree of graciousness with which her Highness might choose to condescend to him.

And so he went, and ascended, with a gloomy face and firm, quick steps, and yet with a beating heart, the marble steps to the first story of a fine old palace, where the prince had taken apartments. He was received by a lackey in green livery, who requested him to wait and went to deliver his card; then a *valet*, in black, appeared and opened for him the door of a large parlor, partitioned with curtains. Ferdinand heard voices on the other side of the curtain, at the right, the voices of the prince and of Elsie.

"You understand that I can take no farther notice of this relation," said the prince, who had evidently received the card; "beside, as he is a Von Schott, it would be wanting in tact to remind him of his burgher relatives; and it is only through them that he is connected with you."

"What tender consideration!" said Elsie, in a sarcastic tone. "No one asks you to take any notice of a relationship that reminds you of sister-in-law with a burgher name—that is what makes you so exceedingly considerate! The best way for you to save your own feelings would be to carry out your plan of joining the noblemen's club into which you were to be admitted to-day."

"If you think so, I will do it," answered the prince, dryly.

"I foresee," said Elsie, "that you will spend the greater part of your time there; meanwhile, I desire to enjoy the art-treasures of Florence; I came for that, and I need a guide; I do not want to be left to go about alone while you are telling your hunting-stories in your club. Herr von Schott will do me that favor, and while I am talking with him and arranging the program, you would only disturb us!"

"So much the better," answered the prince, in a tone that indicated a slight shrug of the shoulders; "so much the better. Just as you think, child!"

The voices were silent. Ferdinand thought less about the somewhat humiliating *rôle* of an unpaid *cicerone*, which Elsie was imposing upon him—he was accustomed to that, the nobility seeming to regard the secretary of legation as appointed for that purpose—than about the remarkable way in which Elsie seemed to treat her husband.

It was evident that she ruled him, that he offered no resistance to her sway and was accustomed to obedience.

When the *valet* came back into the *salon*, he requested Ferdinand to follow him. In the next room, through which the servant conducted him, he saw the remains of a breakfast which the lackey was just carrying away. He found Elsie in a *boudoir* back of this room, reclining on a sofa, apparently absorbed in a journal. The prince had obeyed her and disappeared.

Although it was noon, Elsie was still in her morning toilet, in a morning dress of white cashmere with blue facings and a blue cord at the waist; she looked more charming in it than she had looked the day before in her elegant visiting costume. The years seemed to have taken nothing from her, but to have given her features more of soul and intellect.

"This Italian newspaper," she said, throwing the journal aside, and motioning Ferdinand to a seat without looking at him, "this Italian is so easy to understand, and the poets are so difficult for me! Why is that? Or isn't it so with you? You have been in Italy so long, that you must be able to use the language with perfect ease. But why do you not take a seat?"

"The poets," he answered, seating himself, a little puzzled at the extremely unconstrained manner in which she began the conversation, as if she had seen him but a few hours before, "the poets are hard to understand in any language. If the reason were not so obvious, because of the artistic form of their works—I should say it is because they are accustomed to write of such an incomprehensible thing—the human heart."

She nodded, and after a moment's pause, said, smiling:

"That is true. It is hard to understand poets' hearts—that is, for us prosaic people. Indeed, we often cannot understand ourselves. Is the incomprehensible in us—what we often regard as unreasonable because we cannot comprehend it—is it, after all, the best we have, the poetry in us?"

"There is objection to such an interpretation—at least, not for ladies, who are not expected to be self-critical. It would be harder for men to pass off their instincts and passions and the perverse things they do under the influence of them, for the poetry of their nature !"

She raised her eyes to his with a searching glance, and a slight flush overspread her face; she seemed to suspect a slight reproach in the words. In a tone in which there was something hard and condemnatory, she answered:

"Men should have no instincts and no passions. They should be clear-headed and self-conscious and able to control themselves. Self-control is the beginning of all wisdom. Do you not think so ? You are a diplomatist ; it must be familiar to you."

"Yes, I understand that; I understood it before I became a diplomatist, and I shall hold fast to the principle when I leave the profession, as I shall very soon."

"As you shall soon ? What do you mean by that ?"

"I shall enter some other profession."

"Indeed ! And why ?" asked Elsie, rising from her half-reclining position and looking at him in evident suspense. "Does not your position suit you ? Is it not as pleasant as you could wish ? Do you, here in Florence, regret our foggy atmosphere ? Or has your profession failed to meet your expectations, as you once described them to me ?"

It was the first time that Elsie had mentioned the past; it seemed as if she had been surprised into forgetting a determination never to allude to it.

"Not that I leave my position with the greatest regret, to go to handle dismal documents at home there in our foggy atmosphere, as you say. You can understand with what feelings one must tear himself away from Italy, never to see it again. But what can I do? I make no secret of my reasons; the death of my cousin, the banker, has destroyed my prospects. I have to provide for myself and my sister. To be a diplomatist, it is necessary to have a rich cousin, or to be his heir."

"Ah ! I did not know that—I did not know that !" said Elsie, drawing a long breath and sitting more erect, while a re-markable pallor overspread her face, making it of a marble whiteness. "I did not know that !" she repeated again, with white lips.

"Did not know what ? That my cousin is dead ?"

She did not answer. She looked at him with a peculiar fixed glance, and then dropped her eyes before his open gaze.

It was singular. She who had just said that self-control was the beginning of all wisdom, now betrayed unmistakably that there was something in Ferdinand's information that affected her deeply. What could it be ? Her sister's child was the banker's heiress. Why should that affect her so ? How could she help it if Ferdinand had lost what her niece had gained? There was nothing in that to shock her, nothing that could be humiliating or unpleasant to her. Could he believe that she had so much personal sympathy for him, that his misfortune could affect her so deeply ? It would be folly to think of such a thing. And yet what other explanation could there be for this strange emotion ?

She looked at her rosy finger-nails as if questioning the little white spots upon them what her reply should be; then she looked at the floor again, as if to reflect on their advice. At last she said, in a low voice, whose suppressed tremor did not escape Ferdinand's notice:

"If the property of your cousin, which has fallen to my sister, is so necessary to you in your present circumstances—as I did not dream, then——"

"Oh, I beg your highness," interrupted Ferdinand, "do not think that I came to entertain you with these matters. You asked me a question, and I gave you a straightforward answer, as I saw no reason for not doing. Now, if you please, we will let the matter drop. I beg of you not to allude to it again. Any farther discussion of it would be most painful to me."

She was silent and seemed again engaged with the spots on her finger-nails. At length she said:

"Why do you suddenly call me 'your highness?' you showed so much delicacy and tact in not doing so before. I beg of you, do not call me so, when we are alone."

Ferdinand bowed. "As you prefer," he said, surprised again. "You can understand that it comes a little hard to me," he added, and then colored at the words, which admitted of an offensive meaning, as well as of one quite the reverse.

Elsie did not show how she took it; neither did she return to what she was saying when Ferdinand interrupted her. Having entirely regained her self-control, she began to talk of her intention to make her stay in Florence as beneficial as possible in the way of self-culture, and to spend as much time as she could in studying the art-treasures of the beautiful city of the Arno. She counted upon Ferdinand's help; she could not rely upon her husband for any; thorough studies of things not merely to be talked of, but to be reflected upon and felt, were not in his line, as she said, with remarkable frankness. "The prince," she said, "has not been accustomed for years, perhaps never in his life, to withdrawing into himself, only to going out of himself, if the expression is admissible."

A wicked jest was at the end of Ferdinand's tongue.

"If your time is not too much occupied," she continued, "I would like to ask you to be my *cicerone*, when you are in a mood to do a favor to an old acquaintance. May I count upon your services?"

"I am at your command," answered Ferdinand. "Only I would like to make the condition that you will actually command me, that you will tell me definitely when and where I can be of service to you. I shall then be sure of not coming at times when you are occupied with quite different things from excursions to art-galleries."

"Indeed! you think my purpose is not very serious?"

"Oh, certainly; as serious as is usually the case with ladies in your position."

"'Ladies in my position,'"—that is to say, ladies accustomed to give way to every caprice, and troubling themselves only with the externals of a brilliant but really hollow life—who, at the best, are themselves deceived with the idea that they are interested in something higher, but usually only assume such an interest to deceive the world

or their admirers! You are mistaken in me, Herr von Schott!"

"As to that, I have not expressed any opinion, nor formed any in my own mind; therefore, I cannot be mistaken."

"Very well; it is wise to be slow in forming opinions. Then you will allow me to invite you to an excursion very soon?"

Ferdinand bowed silently, and soon after took his leave in a peculiar mood. He could not conceal from himself that, notwithstanding all the studied coldness with which they treated each other, as if they had met here for the first time in the world, yet the old sparring tone, the old intellectual combat, had been resumed—that he would suffer by it now as intensely as he had enjoyed in his happy and confident youth, and that the end of the play would be that he would be defeated as he had been defeated before. He felt that he was a fool to expose himself to her witcheries, to court his defeat again. He knew that it would be the greatest good-fortune for him, if, when he got to his rooms, he should find his leave of absence awaiting him, and should then pack his trunks and be off. But he did not find it. And if he had found it, he would not have gone. Why not? Did he himself understand why not? No, he only felt that he was chained; the why and the how must belong to the incomprehensible and unreasonable that Elsie had called the best in us and the poetry of life.

And then he thought of the strange emotion Elsie had shown at what he had told her of his circumstances—an emotion which the proud princess either had not tried or had been unable to conceal. How was it to be explained? Ferdinand stopped in perplexity as he thought of it on his way home. Had the haughty woman, after all, so much sympathy for him, that the turn in his destiny affected her so powerfully? Or did she feel humiliated at the thought that her sister had received what had been intended for him? It did not seem possible; and yet it must be one of the two.

If it were one of the two, then the extent of the emotion Ferdinand's information had produced was remarkable—the violence of the excitement whose expression he did not ee, but which the walls of the little room ooked upon after the door had closed be-ind him. She sprang up and walked ex-itedly up and down the room. At times he stopped, and, resting her hand upon the ack of a chair or the top of a table, looked xedly with her white face toward some ob-ect on which her eye happened to rest, vith half-open mouth, as if she were listen-ng in her distress for counsel from these lumb witnesses of her desperation.

"There is nothing, nothing at all to be done; he is defrauded of his rights and must remain so," she whispered, at length. "Oh, that this man must come in my path again to tell me that! This man, who has once before plunged me into a cruel strug-gle, whose influence first made me suspect that I was on a wrong path where I should never have allowed myself to be drawn, who even then began to gain the ascendancy over me, and who comes in my path again now, to compel me to confess to myself how despicable I have grown, how low I have fallen!

"And what can I do? Run away and escape him? I cannot do that; O, my God! I cannot do that, until I have succeeded in compensating him in some way for what he has lost, until I have found some way of atoning in part for my guilt, of keeping him in the profession he is about to re-nounce on account of his poverty!"

She dropped into her chair and sat watching, with half-closed eyes, the strip of blue sky visible from her window, over which fleecy clouds were floating lightly, as if their careless movement had some comfort in it, and were saying: "So men wander at the breath of fate, to reach at last the goal, unknown to them, and yet destined for them from eternity, and stead-fastly awaiting them in the far future."

CHAPTER XII.

FLORENTINE STUDIES.

Ferdinand was surprised the next day at receiving a note adorned with a crown and a monogram, in blue and gold, containing a brief invitation from Elsie to accompany her the next day on a visit to one of the galleries. He appeared punctually at the time appointed; she met him with a quiet, cool friendliness, growing more animated only in talking of the works of art they went to see. Ferdinand soon found reason to say to himself, with some surprise, that she really seemed quite in earnest in her plan of self-culture by the study of the works of art in the famous city. She not only desired to visit all the galleries and churches, but she studied into details, and busied herself with the lives of the greatest artists, with the history of the finest works of architecture, and of the city, and asked many more questions than Ferdinand could answer. She gave her opinions and criti-cisms with so much frankness and decision that it was natural for Ferdinand to feel, after a few days, as if they were on the old footing—not that of admiring homage and deference to be paid by the one and gra-ciously received by the other, as a footing of equality between friends who do not scruple to differ and carry on conversational warfare in support of their opinions. He often told her, in answer to her questions, that she knew much more of the subject than he, that she was fitted to adorn the chair of a professor of the fine arts; that without her he would have returned from the land of ideal art like a barbarian or an Englishman; that if she should delay her return till she had studied all Italy as thor-oughly, Germany would never have the good fortune of seeing again her most learned daughter.

"You say all those things so sarcastically," was Elsie's answer to one of these remarks, "that it is plain enough you think a femi-nine head cannot hold all these things, and would do better not to attempt it—to spare itself the fruitless task."

"Perhaps I might think so of a fem-inine head," answered Ferdinand. "But yours is not a feminine, it is a masculine head."

"Is that a compliment or a reproach?"

"A compliment, undoubtedly. A being with the head of a man and the heart of a woman, would certainly be a most perfect one."

"But only when the head and heart are in unison; if they are at variance, there may be no creature more unhappy."

"That is true. And they would very easily fall into discord, I am afraid. But what would you have? Perfection in this miserable world must be paid for with wretchedness and sorrow."

"And why must a masculine mind and a feminine heart easily fall into discord?" she asked.

"Because the two have different needs and different standards. But if they are developed to equal strength, then any conflict that may arise cannot be quieted, because each is too strong to yield."

Elsie nodded, without answering. After a pause, she said:

"It is true, the heart urges to action, and the mind criticises and vetoes. If the critic is as strong as the impulse to action, there must be a balance of forces, and nothing can be done. To escape from such a dilemma," she added, smiling, "one would have to alternate—giving the heart full sway for a time, and then for a time yielding wholly to the control of the intellect."

And you, princess, you live by that rule; for the present, you belong entirely to the intellect; when will it be the turn of the heart?"

"Ah," she said, smiling sadly, "the heart tries every day to enter into its right; but, as I have said, the mind criticises and vetoes."

"Then send him away—give him a furlough, and let him have a rest. I think he has been long enough in your service, and you ought to be willing to discharge him."

"How mockingly you say all that! Is, then, a man wholly incapable of ideality enough to believe that a woman can really be serious, about serious things?"

"Oh, certainly, when her age and circumstances leave her nothing else to busy herself with but serious things; then, certainly."

She shook her head.

"But not otherwise? Otherwise, a woman is only coquetting with intellectual interests? Well, I know that is the theory of men. And as they are all infallible, what can be said against it? It is stupid, to be sure, and absurd. But has it ever been an objection to a theory that it was stupid an absurd? But it will not help you any."

"How should it help me?"

"You only talk so to restrain my zeal for studying Florence in my own way, so that you may be released from your service a cicerone."

"If you were not the Princess Achsenstein, formerly Fräulein Elsie von Melroth I should answer you by declaring that this service affords me the greatest pleasure But as you——"

"But as I am Elsie von Melroth, you are too shrewd or too honest to say it, and thank you for it."

"Perhaps neither too shrewd nor too honest, but too proud."

She threw a quick glance at him, as of surprise—not at all unpleasant surprise, or as if she were hurt.

"Then I thank you still more," she said.

"Why?"

"Because I can build more on a man's pride than on his honesty."

"If you will build on me the basis of your confidence is a matter of indifference to me. I am content if I can show you that it is well-grounded."

She dropped the conversation and turned to other things. But that she did place confidence in him with less and less reserve, Ferdinand could not but see, although he sought to avoid betraying the emotion with which it filled him. She did not try to conceal the estrangement between herself and the prince, or, rather, she made no secret of the symptoms of that estrangement, which, indeed, were exhibited far less by her than by the prince. It was evident without very close observation or very great knowledge of men, that the prince had a somewhat coarse and extremely vain and violent nature, and when his vanity was wounded, might be very dangerous and take most unaccountable freaks. But it was also clear that nothing was farther from his intentions than to gain an ascendency for this coarser nature over Elsie's higher and finer one. In the beginning of their married life, he might, perhaps, as would have been no more than natural, have striven for such an ascendancy of his will and his ideas, and might, perhaps, have struggled for it. If this were the case, it was evident that he had been defeated in the struggle, that the result had not been such as to flatter his vanity. Hence, probably, his indifference toward her. At least he let her alone, and not that only, but he seemed to have a certain fear of her, to avoid her as a lively critic of his conduct, of his not always princely words, and acts, and tastes.

When two differing natures are brought together and held together by any kind of tie, it is seldom that the lower nature yields to the influence of the higher; the higher usually sinks toward the level of the lower. In the relations between Elsie and the prince this was reversed; the lower nature yielded to the force of the higher; but it showed, too, that it felt the force. He often alluded jestingly to "my little governess," "our most royal auditor-in-chief,' in a way that Ferdinand saw as mixed with some bitterness. Ferdinand often received the impression, too, that, in the marked, and often exaggerated courtesy shown him by the prince, there was a taint of bitterness; that he was gratifying a sort of revengeful spirit, by showing so openly and so often how well pleased he was that his wife had found a friend to relieve him of the duty of attendance. Elsie gave no indication that she noticed this; Ferdinand noticed it and felt a sort of indignation at it; he felt it as a sort of personal insult, though he could not, or would not tell himself exactly why.

And as Elsie did not try to throw any disguise over the nature of her relations to her husband, she talked with him on many subjects with the frankness of a sister to a brother. She seemed to take a peculiar satisfaction in humiliating her own pride by an apparent self-contempt—a kind of malicious pleasure, a certain triumph, in showing Ferdinand her worst side, as if it were a gratification to her to let him see what a complete fool he had been in ever feeling any attachment or reverence toward her. Ferdinand did not at all understand this conduct. It was a very strange kind of malice, if she thought to humiliate him by accusing herself; it indicated a wonderful self-conflict, almost morbidness. The explanation would have suggested itself that Elsie only found fault with herself in order to make Ferdinand contradict her and pay eloquent homage to her fine qualities. But that could not be the explanation; for he never contradicted her in the least; the whole tone of their conversation made anything like homage or gallantry inadmissible.

One day they had made an excursion to Fiesole. The princess was accompanied by a kind of court-lady, a quiet, unassuming creature, who never took part in the conversation without being directly spoken to. They mounted to the Church of Sant Allessandro and the Franciscan cloister on the site of the old Acropolis. From a broad arched window they looked down over the picturesque court of the convent upon Florence and the valley of the Arno. After a long pause, in which she had seemed absorbed in the contemplation of the wonderful scene, Elsie said:

"What a strange charm there is in this scene—it is almost fearful! I shall never forget it!"

"Nor I, princess," said Ferdinand, with evident emotion. "Though I have often been here before and looked down on this same scene, yet the impression it has made on me to-day will never fade from my memory!"

She threw at him a quick, sharp glance, that passed over his features like the convulsive flash of an expiring flame.

"In what," she said, "does this powerful charm lie? It cannot be in the mere natural beauty of the scene, for there are views of greater beauty. It must be the charm of association, the consecration of historical memories that rests upon the valley and

the city. Strange, that the past can move us so, has such a poetic power over us !"

"Do you call it strange ?"

"Is it not so ? What real interest has it for us ? What superiority has the past over the present ? One is old misery and the other is new misery. That is all the difference."

Ferdinand shook his head.

"What an 'idea!" he exclaimed. "Can you talk so, princess, you who are studying so zealously the art, the monuments of the past ? What are they but memorials of the intellectual development of men to freedom and beauty? what but footprints of the genius of humanity as it moves through the centuries, with ever firmer and more consciously sovereign tread? What draws you here, if not the perception of this? History is the picture of the conflicts and victories of ideas, the great epic of the human race, and should there be no poetry in that?"

She nodded and said, smilingly, "Well said. Go on and explain to me."

"Explain to you ! How ironically you say that ! Women, they say, always form their judgments from personal grounds. So look at it in a personal light. Imagine a man with a past full of ' old misery,' full of intellectual struggle and soul-conflict—in a word, a man with a history. Would he not have a greater attraction for you, a greater charm, than a man without a history ?"

"Certainly; you are right and I am ashamed of my stupid remark," she answered. "You see now how thoughtlessly and superficially a woman judges—how illogical she can be, and how limited, how hollow——"

"And," interrupted Ferdinand, "how mysterious, in being able to find enjoyment in such self-accusings."

"Oh, yes, that is stupid, too," she said, in a tone of contempt. "Give me your arm; we must see the Church of Sant Allessandro.".

As they drove back to the city she did not speak. Ferdinand's eyes rested thoughtfully on the valley, from which the hollow murmur of the great city began to reach

their ears, while a light fog rose from th Arno, and spreading a thin veil over th roofs and even the dome of the cathedrs and the tower of the *Palazzo del Signoria* on which the full glow of the sunset rested took on a rosy splendor in the sunlight, s that the mighty building was transfigurer with the crimson glory.

"See," he said, "even the life of to-day the 'new misery,' as you call it, is clothe with a rosy splendor. One has only to loo and have an eye to see it."

She looked full in the direction he indicated, but gazed with an absent air, as her thoughts were far away from the scene

A powerful sympathy began to mingle with Ferdinand's feeling toward her. He unsparing severity to herself was a riddl that constantly tormented him. With so earnest a character, this self-contempt mus proceed from deep internal discord, from a conviction of failure in life through its own fault, from complete disgust at itself; and moreover, it was evident that, in her zealou pursuit of mental culture, she was onl seeking distraction, and forgetfulness of he own thoughts. That Ferdinand's attach ment to her was only made more intense by his sympathy, was natural. The longing to bring help to her in her helplessness acted upon his love like wind upon flame. A man wants to support, to help, and guide where he loves, and where he can do this, he loves from it alone. So long as she was the proud, cold Elsie, sufficient to her-self and in need of no one, his feelings to-ward her had something angry and hostile in them. Since she suffered, and accused herself so bitterly, even in her pride, his deepest and strongest feelings mingled with and intensified his attachment.

CHAPTER XIII.

RIDDLES.

Although as day after day passed on in this way, Elsie seemed to have grown so accustomed to her guide as to regard him as an indispensable necessity; still Ferdinand could not but acknowledge to himself that what he had longed for, to find for himself a place in her heart and soul-life, was a hopeless desire. Though she often spoke of herself in a tone of the coldest mockery, if the conversation turned upon sentimental and enthusiastic friendships, upon heart-affairs and love.

"Believe me," she said once, "every love-affair is a struggle for the mastery; what men call love is only the caprice resulting from the most varied accidental motives, to gain complete sway over just this or that person and make him our slave. The first coquetries are the measures for finding out the strength of the enemy. Thereupon the weapons are crossed and the conflict begins; and it is conducted in the same way as the conflicts of parties and nations. The greatest anxiety of each side is to appear stronger than it is."

"Stronger?" said Ferdinand; "I think they are wonderfully willing to confess their weakness toward the other side."

"No, no; they represent themselves as stronger—that is, better, nobler, more amiable, more intellectual, more ideal than they are. While each is so intent on deceiving the other, neither is shrewd enough to say to himself that the other must be engaged in the same game. How stupid that is! And there they vie with each other in self-sacrifice, generosity and sensibility. At length, they get wearied out and conclude an armistice, and this time of suspension of hostilities is generally taken advantage of to have the marriage ceremony performed. Then the conflict begins afresh and continues until one party succeeds in vanquishing the other."

"What a prosaic, skeptical, heartless view that is!" exclaimed Ferdinand.

"Is it?" she asked. "It may be. But it is a woman's opinion, the conviction that comes to her from her own consciousness.

Men may have more heart, more sensibility in the matter, they may be less selfish and egotistic. These poor men—but listen, I will read something to you."

She went to a table in the corner of the room, where several books were lying, and took up a thin, elegantly bound volume. As she turned over the leaves, she said:

"These are the poems of Germany's greatest living poetess, B. Paoli. And now hear what this woman says:

'I saw them sport with slimy, noisome things,
Hissing and hateful, armed with poison-stings;
I saw them trust to woman's fickle mind,
Their honor, fortune, life itself, in blind
And mad devotion; saw them basely vie
In slavery to princes—till the lie
Was seen, the sting; the chain was felt too late,
And helpless now they struggled with their fate.
How strangely blind, perverse, infatuate!'"

"Better," said Ferdinand, smiling, "that they should be blind than wise enough to heed such a warning. What would become of the world if what you call a warfare and I the desire for peace, for the gratification of the soul's deepest longings, should vanish out of it? Rest cannot be found in the world, and hence the longing of every human soul for 'rest in the beloved.'"

"As if love gave rest! As if it were not the source of endless pain, anxiety and torture!"

"And yet the deep sea in which we sink all the pain, anxiety and torture of life."

"Our views are so different, so radically different," said Elsie, shrugging her shoulders, "that we cannot possibly find any way of reconciling them. Nothing remains but for us to tolerate each other's views and avoid all mention of them. Are you tolerant and wise enough for that? Are you sure enough of yourself to engage never to make any attempt to convert me?"

As she asked the question, she looked into his eyes with such a sharp, significant, flashing and almost angry glance, that he gazed at her in perplexity and let a minute pass before he answered:

"I can be sure that I shall always conform to your wishes and that my desire to please you will always be stronger than my solicitude about your errors and prejudices."

"That sounds almost like a compliment, and on that account is hardly satisfactory. But let it pass. We will drop the subject now and forever. Come, our carriage is waiting to take us to San Miniato. You need not give yourself the slightest trouble to please me. But to help me, instruct me, and show me that I have a friend in this strange land, who, while our paths run side by side for a few weeks, will help me to pass the time pleasantly and with profit—that is the task that you cannot escape now."

She spoke coldly and haughtily, and Ferdinand, deeply wounded, answered in an unmistakably sarcastic tone:

"Your highness has, of course, only to command!"

She took no notice of the sarcasm, but let him conduct her down the steps to the waiting carriage.

Ferdinand was, in truth, deeply hurt by her manner toward him, and this more and more the deeper he became involved in the struggle that always comes when a man thinks he has a claim to a place in a woman's heart, and sees that claim continually unrecognized and despised by her. The worst of it was that he could not express his feelings, could not confess what was in his heart. The whole tone of their intercourse, the footing on which they had placed themselves, excluded all sentimentality. He could not complain when, as so often happened, she wounded him most sorely by talking as if she regarded his interests and hers, his likings and opinions and hers, his whole life and hers, as wholly foreign, radically and forever unlike and apart from each other.

He suffered inexpressibly from it. Once in a while he took a little satisfaction by accusing her of terrible pride. She answered once:

"That is true. I am proud, proud to excess. It is my most prominent failing, but I cannot help it. That fault may be the destruction of me, but there is nothing to be done. I can confess it to you, for you know that it is not a ridiculous weakness that has come over me since I have been called 'your highness,' but that it is a natural trait of my character that showed itself eve when I was a young girl. It must make m offensive and unendurable to other people.

What could be done in the face of suc frankness? Should he betake himself t the ordinary weapon of lovers, to sulkin when she had wounded him too deeply, ar enraged him by her cold way of ignoring h feelings, and passing on to the order of tl day? He would not do that, he would hi self be too proud—and yet he fell more an more into the habit of it.

He suffered terribly in this state of thing it was so utterly hopeless. And why was hopeless? Because this Elsie, beautiful an intellectually charming as she was, utter: ignored all feeling, all the heart-life th makes a woman truly a woman. There w: something abnormal and perverse about he something under which she herself suffere She seemed to be at war with herself, an to be conscious of inward desolation. Wh did she not flee from it into the warm regio of heart-life? What kept her back? H sense of duty to her husband? But Ferd nand had not the slightest idea of interfe ing with her feelings toward her husban Moreover, she despised him too thoroughl to admit, in her pride, that he had any righ to control her intellectual and emotiona life. It must be that very pride that mad her so cold and abrupt. And he felt a ma longing to break her pride and conquer he perversity—to compel her to acknowledg the claims of the heart that must be there.

That must be? He did not suspect hov bold the assumption was. As if every wc man must have a womanly heart! Hov many men who know very well that ther are men without a single manly quality suffer shipwreck because it never occurs t them that there may likewise be women with out a single womanly quality!

It did not occur to Ferdinand, and a every day he became more deeply involve in this unhappy complication of feeling, h was more urgently impelled to set right th perversity in Elsie, to tear her away fror the icy solitude of her own heart, to compe her to open her soul to a life of the emc tions, in which he saw the only hope for he and for himself. He lost no opportunity t tell her what he thought of the destiny of women, of their vocation to live for the affections, of their only way to happiness. She did not protest against such talk as something they had agreed not to discuss; but she listened with a condescending smile, and, at times, indeed, with an absent expression, as if she were not hearing.

The leave of absence he had asked had long since arrived; he no longer thought of using it.

But he had seen in the German papers that the office of landrath for the district in which the Castle of Achsenstein was situated was vacant. As the place suited him, and as it would keep him near Elsie, he applied for it. Being one day alone with the prince he told him that he had done so. The prince, who had the chief voice in regard to filling the position, promised at once to use his influence in procuring it for Ferdinand.

So the Rubicon was passed, the first step from his present position in life to a totally different one was taken. Ferdinand thought little about it; everything not immediately connected with Elsie had come to be of subordinate interest to him; he had but the one thought, that his new position would take him to her present home.

And yet this step brought on the crisis of his relations to her.

Several days had passed, when, one day, as he entered to walk with her to the Gardens of Boboli, she received him with the words:

"What do I hear, Herr von Schott—you have asked the prince to take steps for securing to you the position of landrath in our district? The prince told me so to-day; I have heard nothing of it before. Why were you silent about it?"

"Because you have given me no right to trouble you with my personal and business concerns."

"Oh, what an abominable answer! A sulky, simple revenge you are trying to take! How can I help troubling myself about your personal affairs? Heavens, how petty, how childish such a man is! But, I tell you, nothing will come of it. It is my

6

decided request that you withdraw your application."

"Ah!" exclaimed Ferdinand, growing a little paler, and recoiling as if from a sudden thrust. "Why, if I may ask? Do you object to my being in your neighborhood? Can you not tolerate me there?"

"That has nothing to do with it—nothing whatever."

"And what is the reason, then, if not that?"

"The reason is, that I do not want to see you in such a place."

"And this will of your highness is to be enough for me?"

"The highness has nothing to do with it. It is the will of a woman who has shown you—openly and unreservedly, I think—that she is your friend, your friend in the most prosaic and sober sense of the word, if you will, but truly and genuinely, a friend to whom it never occurs, even in a dream, to give you a rose, or a ribbon, or any such tender *souvenir*"—she uttered the words with unspeakable contempt—"but who would be ready, if it were necessary, to knit you a pair of warm socks, or run about the woods for hours to find an herb to make tea for you, if you were sick and needed it. You told me yourself that it made you very unhappy to be obliged to leave your profession—that only necessity drove you to it. But necessity shall not drive you to it. You shall not leave it for the want of a little miserable money. I have money in abundance. I spend it lavishly. I throw it away for trifles, for the mere gratification of whims—and not even that always. My spending money has often nothing to do with gratifying a whim or a wish. I have so few wishes, that I should thank God if I had more, so that I might strive to gratify them and have something to do. No, I often spend money as a mere matter of habit, of tradition. A princess is expected to buy every useless thing she is asked to; to give her help to every foolishness that any society may invent to force themselves upon public notice; to allow herself to be duped by every attempted imposition upon her purse; and I am too indolent to disappoint such expectations. And with all this, how can I endure that, for want of this money, which people get away from me for such useless purposes, you should be lost in an occupation repellant to you, and unsuited to your nature and your tastes—which must make you doubly unhappy after you have for years occupied one much pleasanter and more brilliant, and have looked forward to such a different future? No. It shall not be. You will receive an annual income from me. You must. Do not refuse. You have only to say whether you consent to have me send it to you at certain times, and that it may pass through the hands of my sister Matilda. That would be most agreeable to me, and you can have no objection to her knowing it."

Ferdinand shook his head, smiling. But she anticipated his answer, and exclaimed, with passionate warmth, "Do not say anything against it; you hear me—I insist upon it; it is settled; and now go at once to the prince and explain to him that you have no more thought of taking the position he is trying to get for you."

"Most gracious and august lady," said Ferdinand, when, at length, he found an opportunity to speak, "you forget that the days when a poor subject was obliged to submit to such arbitrary interference in his affairs are over. Our relations are quite different: I am a nobleman, and you a high-born lady, and I will take no money from you. You say that you often spend your money on account of traditional usage, of custom. For the same reason, you must submit for once to see your money refused."

"Ah, then, you will not; really will not?"

"No."

"What foolish obstinacy! It is perfectly childish. No, it is more than that. It is reckless, it is rude of you to repulse me so!"

"Rude! The expression is a little strong."

"But it is the right one. You see how much in earnest I am, how I have the matter at heart; so much, that your refusal is a wicked insult to me. Is it any satisfaction to you to know that, from henceforth, I must say to myself, 'You have this wretched money, and cannot put it to any use that

will make it of value; you are powerless with it; you cannot even help your nearest friend with it?' What can you enjoy in this humiliation for me? What miserable pride! You will rock yourself in the consciousness of having withstood my will; isn't it that? For the sake of this miserable pride, you will plunge recklessly into your misfortune. Heavens! how childish, how stupid, how silly! Do you require me to humble myself so far as to beseech you, to fall on my knees to you?"

She said all this with flashing eyes and with a strange emphasis, that made Ferdinand look at her in surprise and perplexity.

"You do me cruel injustice, princess," he answered. "I see that you have an extremely poor and thoroughly false opinion of me. I certainly cannot take money from you without feeling humiliated. But, still, I would be ready to make the sacrifice for you, and if my acceptance could make you happy, as it seems, I would even be willing to deny my pride, and do as you desire. But, fortunately, I do not need to make the sacrifice, because the assumption on which you base it is a mistake; for, to speak frankly, I shall give up my position here with pleasure; the prospect of spending my life near your Castle Achsenstein is infinitely more alluring to me than all the attractions of Florence and all that I could hope for in my present profession in the future; and I will not give up the prospect."

Elsie rose at these words; she threw up her head; her form seemed to have grown taller as she looked down at him from her half-closed eyes, with a gaze of anger and contempt. Half-audibly, she whispered:

"You are as despicable as other men!"

Ferdinand quivered at the look and the words, as at the sting of a serpent.

"That is a strange answer to a frank and very natural avowal," he said, in an almost defiant tone. "You know very well, Elsie, that I loved you devotedly when we were both young, and you know equally well that, for natures like mine, such things happen once for all. Since that time you have been to me the ideal of womanliness—the only one for me. It is an ideal that no man can break away from; and so I have remained fettered to you, and will follow you as long as I can!"

She rose and. stamped lightly upon the carpet, saying, as if to herself, in a tone of angry despair:

"All, all in vain!"

Then she turned her back to him and went to the window.

"What is in vain?" he asked.

She did not answer. She stood gazing into the street, with frowning brows.

"Tell me, princess, what is in vain?" he repeated, after a pause.

She suddenly turned her head.

"Are you there yet?"

He arose slowly. The flame in her manner had brought the old fire in him to a blaze. He felt that what he had said ought not o have offended her. She must know him well enough to know that he was not making any declaration of love unworthy of her, that he did not forget what separated them. Should he defend himself, should he attempt any explanation? No. He took his hat and gloves, and withdrew, silently, with a slight bow.

He went with a heart full of excitement and anger. What right had she to treat him so? What right to treat his manfully controlled affection for her with such contemptuous *hauteur*? What was there offensive or humiliating to her in simple faithfulness? Had she not herself done enough to call out his frank declaration? Had she not openly shown him the coldness between herself and the prince? Had she not shown him the desolation of her heart with a frankness that was almost a challenge, and so awakened in him an irresistible longing to fill the void in her heart, to restore harmony to her soul, and give her at least somewhat of that happiness, the want of which she evidently felt so deeply? What had she meant in her daily conversations with him by those self-accusations, by those expressions of bitter self-contempt, which were an indication of perfect confidence? Was she so ignorant of the logic of the heart that she could deceive herself as to how he would take them? And if all this had not been, if his declaration had come to her as a complete surprise, as something

incredible and unexpected, what gave her a right to treat him with such insulting, aggravating haughtiness, as if the deepest and most sacred feelings of his soul were only fit to be trampled upon by her princely feet?

They had been right in naming him Fire; he was Fire—a fire that Elsie's treatment could not extinguish. He did not think of giving up, vanquished, of quietly withdrawing, as if hopelessly defeated; that would have been contrary to his nature; he would have been driven to despair if any unconquerable necessity had forced him to withdraw then. It was only the beginning of a campaign; he had lost the first battle; it was bitter, but nothing had been lost with it but a strong position, and this must first be regained.

He let a few days pass before he went back. To avoid a *tête-a-tête* the first time, which would have been somewhat painful, he went at an hour when he would be sure to find the prince at home. He realized that, hard as it would be, he must court the favor of the prince a little, in order to retain his gracious good-will. It would have been a disastrous blow to him if Elsie had instigated the prince to defeat his election to the place he had applied for, and on which now all his hopes depended. He must anticipate anything of that kind by showing the prince how important the matter was to him. The thought that she might already have been working against him almost filled him with despair; he well knew how she controlled the prince.

When he arrived, he found them at breakfast, and in a lively debate. The prince, without allowing himself to be disturbed, reached a hand over his arm, while Elsie's eyes rested coldly upon him, merely as if she took his appearance as a matter of course, and was no more surprised at it than she would have been at the entrance of the waiter.

"Have a seat with us," said the prince; "and, Hermann, a glass; let Hermann give you whatever breakfast wine you prefer; I drink Marsala, though I like good Burgundy much better; but what can you do? We are the slaves of ideas: we are in Italy, and think we must drink their bad wines—a mere notion; so, take a glass; and now let me tell you that I have a bone to pick with you."

"A bone to pick with me, your highness?"

"Yes, with you," answered the wordy man, who considered himself a slave to ideas. "You have been playing the *cavalier servant* to my wife, and have entertained her so badly that she has suddenly found Florence to be tedious, absurd, and intolerable. Well, I have nothing to say against that. That, too, is an idea; it is her idea; and because man, as I said, is the slave of ideas, it is necessary to accommodate one's self to the fact, and I must give up to this idea of hers. So we will go. But you should not have allowed her to get such an idea into her head; it is your fault, Herr von Schott! I am afraid you have played the German professor too much, have talked too much about the Renaissance, and art, and the Medici, and Bramante, and Dante—by the way, when I see that Dante, in his great hood and his long frock, I always think his name would be better without the D; well, Dante or Auntie, you must have lectured her so much about them that she is tired of it. Have you ever admired one of her toilets? Have you? Say, Elsie, has he?"

"Oh, you are absurd!" said Elsie, contemptuously, without looking up.

"Well," continued the prince, unruffled by her manner, "my wife is bored here, and we shall travel. To speak candidly, I have nothing against it. But the idea of travelling is like a carriage, to which our wishes are harnessed, like horses, in front and behind; the princess is in front, pulling southward, and I am behind, pulling northward. What is to be done?"

"The carriage will have to remain stationary where it is—here in Florence."

"Oh, pshaw! Not at all. Now see how little you know about women. When a woman is harnessed before an idea, she is always stronger than any man; believe me, there is nothing more terrible than a woman harnessed to an idea; resistance is of no avail; no animal can compare with them!"

"You are getting lost among dangerous metaphors, dear Gottlieb," interrupted Elsie. "The fact of the matter is, Herr von Schott, that we are to pass the latter part of autumn in Sorrento. The prince expressed a wish to be at home at the beginning of the hunting season; but he has had the kindness to agree to a compromise, so that we travel southward now, and go home in time for the great hunts later in the season."

Ferdinand looked at her with an expression of surprise. She avoided meeting his eyes.

"That is very unfortunate for me," he said.

"You see," said the prince, "that is your punishment. Why did you let her take the idea into her head that Sorrento would be more amusing than Florence?"

"I do not think people travel through Italy to be amused," said Elsie, half aloud.

"Well, well, I beg pardon for the expression, child; I did not intend to offend your seriousness of soul and your intellectual dignity," said the prince, and Ferdinand detected in the words something like angry vexation—the result, perhaps, of former discussions of the kind; "not at all! But do not take it ill of me that I place some value on my amusement. And that we shall have, late in the autumn and in winter. I should be very happy, Herr von Schott, to see you at our hunting-parties; our arrangements will please you; I have an excellent head-forester, an incomparable fellow, and a very fair supply of game in my grounds; red deer, unfortunately, are rather scarce; well, you shall see, and, I promise you, you shall be amused. When we come back, I hope to find you installed as our worshipful magistrate; I received news, day before yesterday, that there would be no difficulty about your election."

"I thank your highness most heartily for your kindness in the matter, and this favorable news puts me under the greatest obligations to you."

"Not in the least, Herr von Schott; the princess and I wish nothing more than to see you settled near us. After our intercourse here, which I am sorry to have broken off by our departure, you may be assured that we shall be very happy to find you at our home."

While the prince was speaking, Ferdinand looked fixedly at Elsie. This time she did not make the slightest attempt to evade his searching glance. She regarded him with such a look of repose, such an equable, self-assured glance, that Ferdinand was at a loss how to interpret it. It was certain, at least, that she had not made the slightest attempt to influence the prince against his appointment. Was that her pride? And was her pride, too, the key to her present manner? Did she want to show him that, looking down from her icy height, she saw nothing more of what was passing in his heart? Was that to be his punishment? But that was not possible. How would that harmonize with her departure, whose suddenness was tantamount to a confession that he was the cause?

Ferdinand could not understand it. She was a true sphinx, this woman, with the half-closed eyes, betraying so much inner fire, and yet looking out on the world so coldly and wearily. There was no opportunity for him to speak with her alone. The prince said he intended to make some farewell calls with his wife directly after breakfast.

"And to-morrow," added Elsie, rising from the table, "we must have our packing done. If you should come, you would find it uncomfortable here in the confusion. So we will take leave of you now. Good-bye, Herr von Schott; I thank you for all the trouble you have taken for me. The prince will call on you to take leave; we shall drive by the embassy."

She made a slight, formal bow, and withdrew to her little *salon*, where she rang for her maid to bring her hat and wrap. Ferdinand thought he saw in the prince's face a little surprise at this cool leave-taking of the man who had been obliged to be at her service so long as *cicerone*. It might have occurred to him that this conduct of his august wife was a little too openly in the style of "The Moor has done his duty; the Moor can go." But Prince Gottlieb of Achsenstein had long since given up criticising his wife's actions. He pressed Ferdinand's hand the more warmly as he took his leave.

Ferdinand went, quite bewildered at the enigma of Elsie's movements. Her journey was manifestly something like a flight from him. And yet, again, she allowed him to come into her neighborhood, granted him a place near her home, where she could not avoid frequent meetings with him; for the prince would certainly have yielded to her influence if she had decidedly opposed Ferdinand's appointment. Did she want to intimate to him that she despised what he had said too thoroughly, that she looked upon it as too foolish and senseless, to be moved by it to interfere in arrangements already made? But why, then, should she leave it to be so naturally inferred that she was now leaving Florence on his account?

And, then, how to reconcile the angry and contemptuous manner of her present treatment with the strange sympathy she had shown before, the concern about his lot that had driven her to betray such deep emotion? What was it that gave such a sudden stroke to her proud nature when he first told her that his poverty was throwing him out of his chosen profession? And now, again, why her stormy violence when he had so firmly refused her offer of money to enable him to remain? Was it only a mortification to her pride, which could not endure the thought that her princely privilege to set all obstacles aside, to make all crooked places straight, by money, was not recognized and yielded to? Or did it all express a deep heart sympathy, as had her previous frankness, and was her anger at his avowal only an instinctive development of her woman's pride?

Ferdinand spent the following days absorbed in these questions, and naturally more and more inclined to be convinced that the answers most agreeable to him were the true ones. Prince Achsenstein, with his wife and his suite, had disappeared from the city of the Arno; and Ferdinand started soon after, going first to the capital of his state, and then to visit his sister.

Ferdinand had found no difficulty in carrying out his design of leaving his diplomatic position. His withdrawal was regretted and his application granted with the best wishes from the foreign office. He had already been notified by the department of the interior, that the assembly of the district of E. had recommended him to his Majesty as a candidate for the vacant office of Landrath. The king's confirmation of the appointment reached him in the little town where he was visiting his sister Adele, and he hastened to enter upon the duties of his position. His sister followed him in a few days to take charge of the melancholy old dwelling that was to receive him, and which soon assumed a brighter and more cheerful appearance under her active and skilful hands. This was the more fortunate, as it was now late in the autumn, and Ferdinand felt deeply the change from the sunny and beautiful city of the south to his own duller skies at this dreary season. The old cathedral, with the complaining rooks hovering around it, looked into his windows with such an unspeakably gloomy and dismal expression; on the open space in front of his dwelling, covered with a scanty growth of grass, cold winds swept the damp, yellow leaves together, then threw them eddying far upward, and at length, as if weary of the foolish sport, gathered them into a thick cloud and threw them into the muddy water of the pond. On the edge of this pond stood weary ducks, their heads under their wings and one foot hidden in their feathers, almost motionless, except when, in sudden desperation at the unendurable monotony of their existence, they plunged into the muddy water, and then uttered their long-drawn lamentations with peculiar energy, as if complaining that a duck when tired of life could not even have the poor consolation of drowning itself. How November-like it all was, and how drearily soon it grew dark in the great rooms with their low ceilings and deep windows! And to add to the dismal effect the old cathedral produced with the shadows of its black pillars and walls, a half-crazy organist spent hours in tormenting the organ into most dreadful chorals. Adele's sitting-room had the most direct benefit of this musical treat. When Ferdinand sat there beside the fireplace in his

leisure hours, his sister sitting quiet at her work, these surroundings filled him with unspeakable sadness. He seemed to himself like a condemned soul suddenly plunged from an existence full of sunshine and love into this dark, cold prison-house under a dull, northern sun. But these moods did not last long. His nature was too strong and elastic to give way to them for any length of time. The mere fact that this turn in his fortune was a benefit to Adéle, that she was evidently happy in once more having a home and a definite purpose to live for in the caring of her brother and being near him, helped Ferdinand to overcome his own despondency. And then, too, so soon as the burden of the day was over, there was the thought of Elsie to help him forget where he was and what kind of a world surrounded him.

He had time to become quite well acquainted with this world before Elsie returned from Italy. When the prince was not at Achsenstein, the central point of the social world there was the house of the Privy Councillor Kronhorst, a widower with several children, who lived in a large and luxuriously furnished villa, and around whom, as around a sun, all the men, the industries, and the interests of the region seemed to turn. As a matter of course, the landrath of the district was frequently thrown into contact with him; and Ferdinand was not a little impressed by the energy and genius of the man, who was, nevertheless, so mild in his judgments and so far removed from everything like boastfulness. He had also found here his cousin's widow, Matilda von Melroth, with her daughter Irene, the fortunate heiress of the banker, Johann Heinrich Schott. She lived in an elegant house in the city, in order to be near her sister, her only other near relative. When Ferdinand and his sister made their first call, he found nothing in her manner to remind him of the simple and frank manner of his old acquaintance Matilda. She seemed strangely ill at ease and constrained; in her expressions of friendship and her protestations of joy at seeing her relatives settled so near her, there was an unmistakable uneasiness, an expression of anxiety and pain. The greetings of the daughter to her hitherto un-known relatives were perfectly cordial and unconstrained.

"What a strange woman," said Adele, as they were going home; "it seemed as if in her solitude she had become so unused to society, that our call threw her into the greatest embarrassment."

"It was probably the thought of the in-heritance which was intended for us but had fallen to her, that made her so con-strained and embarrassed," answered Ferdi-nand.

"It is possible," said Adele. "But we will soon show her how far we are from taking it ill of her, who cannot help it, or from envying her. Her daughter is a charming girl. I am sure I shall learn to love her very much, and I hope I shall see her often."

"She is indeed very pretty and agree-able. What joy my poor cousin Alexander would have had in such a lovely daughter!"

In the farther intercourse between the two families, Matilda's constraint gradually wore off, though, as Adele felt very keenly, it did not entirely disappear. Matilda related to Ferdinand the story of her life since they had lost sight of each other; and how Elsie, who lived with her after the death of their father, had made the acquaintance of the Prince of Achsenstein at a watering-place; how the prince had become a passionate ad-mirer of Elsie, had shown her great atten-tion, and soon offered her his hand; how she had at first treated him with cold *hau-teur*, but had afterward "listened to the voice of reason," as her sister expressed it—Frau Matilda seemed to have contributed not a little to give the voice of reason a pow-erful resonance; how Elsie's principal ob-jection, that she was too proud to be re-garded and treated by the relatives of the prince as an interloper—to see constantly by their manner that they considered it a wholly undeserved honor that she should have the privilege of throwing a princely mantle over her simple escutcheon—that this objection of Elsie's was removed by an elder sister of the prince, a lady of strong character, who had told her how gratifying it would be to the whole family if Prince

Gottlieb, on whom, as head of the princely house, the welfare of the whole depended, should again come under the influence of a wise and strong-willed wife, and not fall into eccentricities by living longer that kind of bachelor life. The sons of the prince, two well-trained young men, now in the mil-itary service, had also taken means to let El-sie know how well satisfied they were with their father's choice; and so she had at length consented to wear the princely dia-dem, and had now been married five years. She was thirty when she was married, but the years did not count with Elsie; she was as beautiful now as when she was twenty-five.

"Years of conflict count up twice as fast, those of inner peace with only half the swiftness," said Adele.

Matilda made no reply to this remark, but as she talked more of Elsie, it was evident how her sister and everything relating to her filled up her life and busied her thoughts, and formed her supreme interest.

It surprised Adele that in her present loneliness from the absence of her sister, Matilda did not mingle in the society whose centre was the house of the Councillor Kronhorst. She never spoke his name, and never joined in a conversation relating to him; she also kept Irene away from that so-ciety; it was so surprising that Adele men-tioned it to her brother. He knew from Herr Kronhorst's own expressions how very friendly were his relations to Elsie and to the whole court at Achsenstein. Ferdinand did not think the matter important enough to trouble his head about. But Adele soon afterward found a solution of the enigma. The little society of ladies had benevolently given Adele the benefit of the current gos-sip of the place for some years past; and, among other things, they had told her that some time ago, when Frau Schott had first moved there, Herr Kronhorst had been ex-tremely attentive to her, and it was sup-posed that they were to be married, when, suddenly, the strong friendship between them had turned into marked estrangement, from some unknown cause.

Frau Matilda Schott did not now come out of her retirement on account of her newly-come relatives; but she seemed to be very glad to have her daughter Irene in Adele's society. Irene had formed a great attachment to Adele, which soon grew so warm and confidential, that Adele could not but think the girl would not be so devoted and so frank toward her, unless she missed a true motherly feeling in Matilda. And yet that would have been exceedingly strange and quite inexplicable, since Matilda was so isolated from the world; how was it possible that she should not find her all in her only child? And yet Adele became more and more strongly impressed with the idea that Matilda did not regard her child with real motherly warmth of affection, and that Irene felt it, so that there was no true confidence between them. She told Ferdinand of this impression, and said she thought this cousin Matilda must have a strange, unloving nature; but Ferdinand assured her she was mistaken and told her how amiable, frank, gentle, and yielding Matilda had been when a young girl, how she had allowed Elsie to control her, and how modestly she had always kept herself in the background, and allowed her more brilliant sister to throw her into the shade.

So some weeks passed, when, one day, there was commotion at the former summer-castle of the princely abbesses of E., which had now fallen with all the domain belonging to the Prince of Achsenstein; the shutters were thrown back, the long rows of windows were opened to the air, and everything was activity. The gardeners raked the autumn leaves from the paths in the park, the grooms brought the horses back to the stables, the high chimneys sent up clouds of smoke, and the beautiful road that joined the castle to the city was lively with servants, carriers, wagons and carts.

To the busy city the news that the prince would soon return for his great hunting-parties, was not very exciting news; but it was for Ferdinand. It came to him with such a shock that at the first he was enraged at himself, at this demoniac power of which he felt himself to be the victim, which he had allowed this princess to gain over him, this Elsie whom he had better never had seen. So at least he told himself in this

moment of awakened pride; but a moment more and he was thinking of nothing but how their first meeting would be; what would be her manner toward him and his toward her; as if it could be anything different from what might be predicted beforehand of their characters; for no quality is more simple and definite, and more easy to reckon upon, than pride, and it was the most prominent quality in both.

Their pride helped them both over the first meeting and those that immediately followed. Ferdinand had little opportunity to see Elsie alone. The prince invited him to the hunting parties, ending with luxurious dinners, at which the ladies were not visible. They, Elsie, her companion whom Ferdinand had met in Florence, and Irene, who was at the castle nearly every day, occasionally appeared as spectators of the chase. When Ferdinand came to the castle for a call, or on business with the prince, he nearly always found Irene with Elsie, and Elsie often withdrew and left him alone with Irene. She frequently commissioned him to take the young girl to her mother's in the city; if Irene did not happen to be there, Elsie would talk about her. It seemed, at length, as if she and Ferdinand had no interest in common except that in Irene. She avoided all allusion to the past, to the days they had spent in Florence; they appeared to lie for her beyond a great gulf, of which she would not think, now that it lay behind her. She was very friendly toward his sister; she seemed to be strongly attracted toward her; yet it was contrary to her character to show a sudden and strong warmth of friendship to any one; and Ferdinand had to content himself with the measure of good feeling she manifested for Adele. In the first days of their acquaintance, Adele said of Elsie that there was something sphinx-like about her, that she was hiding either a great passion or a great secret, or both, and that her attachment to Irene was singular; that she loved her niece with a warmth remarkable in one of her character; that there was something gentle and tender in her way of speaking of Irene that seemed to be foreign to her nature.

"It seems," said Adele, "as if she were

sensible of the dry and hard in her nature, and sought in the fresh, childish heart-life of the girl an element whose want she feels in herself; perhaps, too, she likes to escape from the shadows of her own inner life into the sunny world of youth."

It was evident, at least, that Elsie could not be contented without having Irene with her several hours each day. Matilda seemed to give her up without opposition and usually remained at home; she showed her usual resignation to her sister's will, too, in allowing Irene to spend many hours with Adele. Elsie had often said she was glad the young girl had become so attached to Adele, whose influence she thought would be most beneficial to her; and so, as it was Elsie's wish, the mother seemed to claim no right to object.

Days passed on, and it was almost Christmas, when, one day, Ferdinand received an official notice that very pleasantly surprised him. As his district was filled with a large industrial population, in which the number of crimes of a bold and outbreaking character was constantly increasing, he had petitioned the authorities to appoint some particularly capable and experienced police-officer; in answer to this, he was notified that the urgency of his requirement was recognized and steps would be taken to fulfil it. On this day he received notice that the Police Inspector, Thomas Groebler, of H., was appointed to the same position in his district. Herr Groebler appeared a few days afterward, to announce his arrival and readiness for duty. Ferdinand expressed to him his satisfaction in being supported by so energetic a man, and one, moreover, from his own former home. Herr Groebler was very much rejoiced, too, and they began a very lively conversation about people and affairs in H., whence Groebler had just come, and about the work to be done first in Groebler's department, until he asked the question:

"I would like to ask a little advice of you, Herr von Schott. I shall have to call upon the prince, as a matter of propriety?"

"Certainly. You are not officially under obligation to do so, since, as you know, the prince has resigned his official rights in these matters; but it is still an obligation of country——"

"So I think. But would you advise me to take my wife with me and——"

"Your wife!" exclaimed Ferdinand, in surprise. "You have a wife, Groebler? A wife! Really, I should never have thought of such a thing as your having a wife. You always gave me the impression of being the very type of a bachelor—the bachelor in the superlative degree!"

"Why? Why shouldn't I have a wife? Police officers are always married. You will always find that poets and police officers are married."

Ferdinand laughed. "Poets and police officers! Do you mean to say that they of all people have the greatest need of love?"

"About that, yes. For, you see, they are both isolated in the world. The poet has no actual tie connecting him with the people around him, and the detective is separated from them by his calling, which makes them shy of him. They are both, therefore, thrown back to their own hearths for sympathy, and must have a peaceful domestic atmosphere in which to cool their brains after the heat of the day's work and care."

"There may be some truth in that," said Ferdinand. "At any rate, it is a strong point in favor of the police that you ascribe to them such a need of love. And you would like to know whether you ought to present your wife to the prince?"

"Not that; but whether it would be in good taste, and would be well received, up there on the hill, if she were to call upon the princess? Her highness, you know, is said not to be very condescending. My wife, at least, says that when she was a young girl she gave promise of developing a peculiar talent for trampling other children of men in the dust."

"Ah! does your wife, then, know the princess?"

"Yes. My wife was formerly very intimate with the Melroths; her name was Theresa Holbrecht; you will remember her; you knew her, too?"

"Ah, most certainly I remember Fräulein Theresa; we once spent so many hours together at Herr Melroth's house. I shall rejoice to see her again, and I think the princess would have a right to be angry if she should not go to greet an old friend. So Fräulein Theresa is your wife; who would have thought it? Fräulein Theresa Holbrecht!"

"Who would have thought it? That is what my wife often says when she thinks of her old friend, Elsie von Melroth, becoming a princess; and, after all, that is more curious than that Theresa Holbrecht should become Frau Groebler."

"Certainly, certainly," said Ferdinand; "do not think that I intended to hurt you because I thought it curious."

"I did not think of taking it so, Herr von Schott," replied Groebler. "I only called this princely marriage curious, because my wife has told me all sorts of strange things about the former relation of the present princess to a rabid demagogue, whom I was once on the point of catching: it was in the Manteuffle times, you know; at the time when your cousin's bank was broken into—I learned in connection with that; but you must remember yourself; you were present when——"

"I know, I know," interrupted Ferdinand, turning a little pale at the recollection of those days, so painful to him, "and what did your wife know of it? Was she Fräulein Elsie von Melroth's confidant in that affair, of which no one else, so far as I know, was informed?"

"But you seem to have known of it, Herr von Schott."

"I—well, I was initiated only by accident."

"I can, then, speak openly to you about the matter, since you know of it?"

"I wish you would, Groebler. It may be regarded as an official secret between us. Then your wife——"

Herr Groebler nodded. "Let us, then, regard it as an official secret," he said. "My wife was not the confidant of Elsie von Melroth, but of a gentleman whom you knew very well at the time, and whom you used to meet at the house of the Melroth's—of the forester, Emil Dransfeld."

"Emil Dransfeld—certainly, certainly I knew him; and he was then more trusted by Fräulein Elsie, our princess, than any of us others. How is he getting along, the good fellow?"

"How he is getting along God only knows; probably very badly; he has a wretched place in a desolate region; such a starvation post, you know, as invariably makes a man fall into the chemical process in which he is eaten up by a morbid development of all kinds of acids."

"Poor fellow! He was the confidant of the princess, I know; and of Fräulein Theresa, of your wife, also?"

"Yes. They were distantly related. Their fathers were cousins, or something like that; and although they had not been very warm friends, yet afterward, when Dransfeld was forester at Vellinghaus, he showed quite a strong attachment to my wife. The loneliness there was almost unendurable, and drove him back, from time to time, to his native place; but after the Melroths had gone, he had no intimate friends there; so then he looked up his cousin, and used to spend long evenings there, complaining of his misery and talking of the better days in the past. They naturally talked a good deal of Fräulein Elsie, and Herr Drausfeld confided to my wife that Elsie—she was then living with her sister, to whom she had gone after her father's death—that Elsie corresponded with Philip Bonsart, but not directly, strangely enough, not directly, but by way of Vellinghaus. They both wrote, from time to time, to Emil Drausfeld, who then forwarded them the letters—or not the letters themselves, but an account of their contents, for the two stood on a war-footing with each other, and there were only some special reasons, some special common interests, that held them together."

"That sounds strange," said Ferdinand. "They kept up communication and yet were on a war-footing?"

Groebler nodded. "That often happens that such a pair of hostile parties still cannot quite get free from each other and are compelled to keep up some communication——"

"And what did Dransfeld say of the

special reasons, the common interests that held them together?"

Groebler shrugged his shoulders.

"That I never understood, nor my wife either. Dransfeld would not explain it."

"Would it make it clearer to you," said Ferdinand, "if I should add to it the facts I learned? At the time when you found that Philip Bonsart was in the place and tried to arrest him—at that time he had returned to Europe to be secretly married at Asthof to Fräulein Elsie von Melroth, and to take her with him to his new home across the ocean——"

"Indeed! For that?" interrupted Groebler, without, however, manifesting any great astonishment.

"Yes, for that; and if nothing came of it it was your fault, Groebler; or, if you will, it was mine."

"Yours, Herr von Schott?" asked Herr Groebler, now evidently more surprised.

"Mine. I was overcome by sympathy for Fräulein Elsie. When we were at the bank I saw how completely the harpy spirit of the detective had taken possession of you; the fate of the poor girl if her lover should be seized and lost to her forever touched me; so I went to Dransfeld, who was already her confidant, and was initiated into all their secrets and plans, and told him what a dark cloud was hanging over them, so that he might warn Philip; Elsie had already gone to Asthof. Dransfeld at once started off in the storm, the kind-hearted fellow, and got there soon enough, I suppose, to warn Philip that he must be up and away at once if he wanted to save himself. That was the way of it, Herr Groebler, and the reason you lost your prize. But what came of the intended marriage I do not know."

"Well, well," said Herr Groebler, slowly: "that you had a hand in the game is quite new to me, Herr von Schott. I thank you sincerely for it."

"You thank me in earnest?"

"Yes, in earnest. For, you see, in the heat of the combat, a man will strike his adversary dead; but the rigid face haunts him afterward. Though I am not exactly of a sentimental turn, which would spoil me for my occupation, still one cannot help having some sympathy for poor devils one has placed for years behind locks and bolts, although if they were free they would not disturb the peace, or set houses on fire, or make the highways unsafe—people like this Philip Bonsart, who is said to be really a good and noble fellow. So you, you gave him double freedom, then? you rescued him from the chains of the police and of matrimony? For nothing came of the marriage?"

"Of the marriage? Hardly! Fräulein Elsie von Melroth could not have been Princess of Achsenstein if anything had come of it."

Herr Groebler thoughtfully stroked his dark hair, now mingled with gray, behind his ear.

"The matter is doubtful," he said.

"Doubtful? Then Philip must be dead."

"That he is not. From all I have heard, he is perfectly well."

"Indeed! And you believe——"

"I believe that the matter is questionable. For, you see, when I arrived at Asthof, with some people to assist me, I found that the bird had flown. I could not reach him, for the world was not so well arranged as now, and there were no telegraph wires at Asthof or at H. But I learned that he had been at Asthof for several days, and that a young lady had been at the inn two or three days, and he had visited her often. Now, it seems to me, that if this was Elsie von Melroth, and they were to be secretly married, there was time enough for it in those two or three days. That is my opinion, and my wife hasn't much to say against it; on the contrary, she is tempted to believe it from what Dransfeld said, who betrayed enough to show that there was some tie between them, though he would not tell frankly what it was."

Ferdinand looked at Herr Groebler with wide-open eyes.

"Ah!" he exclaimed, "those are wild suggestions, Herr Groebler. The lady we are speaking of cannot have married Philip Bonsart, for he, as you say, is still living, and she is the wife of the Prince of Achsenstein——"

"The conclusion is logical," said the other, "very logical."

"And yet it does not satisfy you?"

"I think it may satisfy us both, as we have no farther interest in the subject. We both have sympathy for our fellow-creatures, Herr von Schott, especially when they are beautiful women of high rank, of whom, after all, we can prove absolutely nothing. If we were to search farther into the matter, we should only make trouble for the poor forester of Vellinghaus, the only one, perhaps, who knows all about the affair."

"If they had been married," said Ferdinand, half aloud, after a pause, and as if it went against him to utter the words, "she would surely have followed him."

"Probably. Though it is possible that she remained behind so as not to impede his flight, and was to follow afterward; and that when he was gone, and she had time and opportunity to reflect, she recoiled at the thought of going alone to share his adventurous life beyond the sea. I can very well imagine that to be the case with such a young girl; cannot you, Herr von Schott?"

Ferdinand looked thoughtful, and made no answer at first. Then he shook his head.

"It is nonsense. Let us drop the subject, Herr Groebler. My sister will be delighted to have you bring your wife to us, and I shall be very glad to meet my old friend again. Please remember me to her, and come to see us very soon."

Herr Groebler understood that Ferdinand wanted to be alone, and withdrew. It was well that he did, for Ferdinand could not have concealed any longer the excitement the discussion raised in him. The moisture already stood upon his forehead. It was extremely hard for him to give his voice the tone of cool indifference in which he had to talk with Groebler on the subject. It was too horrible and monstrous, the thought that this policeman, with his diabolical suspicion, had put into his mind; it had gone to his heart like a dagger. When Groebler was gone, Ferdinand breathed heavily as if to come to himself again. He hastily paced the length of the room, then turned and crossed it a few times, saying to himself:—

"No, no, no! that is too mad, too insane, too absurd. It is infamous to think of such a thing!"

At length he stopped in the centre of the room, clasped his arms with his hands, and, looking at the floor, said, quietly:—

"But it is thought—and said! What this Groebler has only intimated to me, he must have long ago talked over freely with his wife. And he had a definite ground for suspicion which cannot be reasoned away; this strange correspondence through Emil Drausfeld, which would not have been kept up unless there had been something to bind them to each other—something that retained its power through all circumstances and changes. Did she have to help him? No; for they say he has always been successful over there. It cannot be that. What is it, then?"

He was too much affected by the affair to be able to control himself enough to talk of it even with his sister. To avoid confessing to himself that he had not the requisite composure to talk of it coolly and rationally with her, he told himself that he must regard it as an official secret between himself and Groebler, and treat it as such.

The next day he was obliged to go to Achsenstein; he had to see the prince's revenue-collector, and make some arrangements relating to a recent survey for determining the boundaries between the prince's woodlands and those of the crown. After he had been there some time, and was coming to a satisfactory arrangement with the officer, the prince himself appeared, in order, as he said, to assist the gentlemen, and help the matter along. After spending half an hour interfering with what was already satisfactorily arranged and settled, and throwing everything into confusion, he took his departure, saying to Ferdinand that the princess had commissioned him to "require" his services for her entertainment at tea, as he jestingly expressed it. Ferdinand had not received so direct an invitation from Elsie before since they were in Florence. He accepted, but looked forward with anxiety to meeting her while his seething, rankling suspicion was in his heart.

When he went up, he found her sitting by the window in the parlor, with an illustrated journal in her hand. The prince was sitting opposite, exercising his ingenuity on a sort of puzzle, and Elsie's maid-of-honor was helping him with suggestions. The puzzle was a little arrangement consisting of a couple of wires, on which a number of connected rings had to be arranged in order. It required some ingenuity and skill. Now the prince, and now the young lady would feel sure of having discovered the trick, but would directly see that the triumph was premature, and that the wicked rings had fallen again into their old confusion. Elsie beckoned Ferdinand to her side, and gave him a seat next to her. She asked after his sister with apparently very sincere interest. He answered her questions, and, while his eyes rested upon her face with a shy and unsteady glance, he told her that a lady had just come to E. from their old home—their old acquaintance, Theresa Holbrecht, now Frau Groebler.

Elsie expressed pleasure at the news. She would be heartily glad to see her again, provided she should not come with too many claims on her intimate friendship, and too many expectations of social intercourse, which their unequal positions in life would make impossible. Ferdinand assured her that Herr Groebler's modesty would already have repressed any too ambitious expectations his wife might have formed. Herr Groebler had asked him whether he thought it would be proper for his wife to call on the score of their old acquaintance, and he, Ferdinand, had told him he thought she should by all means do so; whereupon Elsie assured him that she should receive Frau Theresa with a great deal of pleasure.

The servant interrupted them by bringing the tea which the young lady had just made and poured out at the other side of the room, while the prince was rattling and clattering the bewitched rings at the other window.

"You will be glad, too," continued Ferdinand, "to hear through Frau Groebler of another old acquaintance of ours, whose kindness of heart won the sympathy of all of us. You know whom I mean?"

"You mean Emil Drausfeld?" said Elsie, raising her eyes and casting a full glance at him; whether her color grew a little paler at the name, Ferdinand was not so sure as that there was something like a question in her look.

"Frau Theresa cannot give you any very good news of the poor fellow," he said. "He was sent to a very inferior position in a wild and desolate region. You know his relatives compelled him to be a forester, quite in opposition to his tastes, which inclined him to music."

"I know; he could not pass the examination, and so was forced to take a situation under miserable conditions."

"And that," said Ferdinand, "made him very unhappy, at least at the first. Sometimes his loneliness grew unendurable, and then he went to visit his old acquaintance, Fräulein Holbrecht, the only one remaining of his old circle of friends in H., to tell her how miserable he was. They became very confidential friends."

Here Elsie raised her eyes to his again with the same questioning expression. He noticed that the hand that held her cup trembled slightly, so that the spoon rattled; as if to conceal it, she handed the cup to him quickly, and as he rose to set it away, she said, with a certain hard irony of tone:

"And this forlornness of Emil Drausfield affects you so deeply, Herr von Schott?"

"Yes, naturally; but from what do you draw your conclusion?"

"From the tone in which you speak of it. Your voice sounds as if you were completely broken down over it! Well, I am sorry, too, for the kind-hearted fellow, although I have heard that he is married, which may make his life there more endurable. And if, as you say, such a confidential friendship has sprung up between him and Frau Theresa, that would be the best channel for sending him some help, in case he should be willing to receive it. I will talk with her about it; have her come to see me soon. But, Gottlieb, I beg of you," she said, in an irritated voice, turning to the prince, "are you not done with those rings? The clatter and rattle, and your wonderful patience in such an utterly useless task, make me nervous; it is unendurable!"

"Well, well, my most illustrious wife," answered the prince, in manifest embarrassment at the violence of the attack, "you know that when I have once undertaken a thing, I carry it through, useless or not. But if I disturb you in your conversation with Herr von Schott, I will gladly take my rings and leave the field to you. Come, Fräulein Eugénie," he continued, rising, "bring my tea into the cabinet; we can go on with our work there. I must finish it, if it takes till dark!"

He passed into the cabinet with emphatic steps, and Eugénie followed him, carrying his tea. Elsie motioned to Ferdinand, who had risen, to be seated again, and said to him:

"I want to talk with you, Herr von Schott. I want your advice in a matter that lies near my heart. It refers to Irene."

Ferdinand was too much occupied with the observation he thought he had just made—the impression his mention of Emil and Frau Theresa's confidential friendship with him had made upon Elsie, and her annoyance at which had been visited upon the unfortunate prince, to allow him to listen very attentively to what she said. But she probably did not expect an answer.

"Irene," she continued, "has become wonderfully intimate at your house; when she comes here and I inquire where she has been, the answer is always, 'With Adele Schott.' She must enjoy herself very much there, and I am delighted that she does. What do you think of her; how does she please you?"

"Fräulein Irene? We, my sister and I, are delighted with her frankness and sweetness, and her fresh, clear, natural manner, which is so superior to that of most young girls. There is not a drop of poor blood in her; her nature is as pure as gold."

"That is enthusiastic praise," answered Elsie, "but I believe she deserves it. And the fact that you are so pleased with her is another proof of the old saying, that such feelings are always mutual. She is enthusiastic in her praise of you, Herr von Schott——"

"Of me! Indeed, I do not know how I have deserved that."

"And yet that is the case. But you have not told me how her appearance pleases you."

"Her appearance! I should think there would be no need of saying. Fräulein Irene is such a beautiful girl!"

"Very well; if you think so, I will go on —as an old friend, Herr von Schott, who, at the same time, must speak for her sister, for she cannot speak the first word on such a subject as freely as I can. To come to the matter directly, you can understand how my sister is distressed at the thought that a large property, which you had every reason to expect, should have fallen to her, or rather to Irene."

"Let us not allude to that again, Princess," interrupted Ferdinand, in a somewhat hard voice; "whatever vain hopes I may have had should not disturb your sister's assurance of her own clear and perfect right."

"And yet that is the case, and I think it very natural. But there is a second thought that is also very natural—a thought that my sister has cherished from the beginning, and of which I cannot but approve; and because I approve of it, and think it very desirable that it be carried out, I will speak freely of it to you. It is the question of making up to you the loss you suffered by the unhappy accident that your cousin was called so suddenly from the world without leaving a will. This could be easily done by an alliance which could bring nothing but happiness to all parties."

Ferdinand looked at her with wide-open eyes while she spoke these words with a peculiarly hasty, anxious, and eager manner.

"Ah!" he said, in a tone of extreme astonishment, "you do not mean——"

"My meaning cannot escape you. I have told you what a favorable impression you have made upon Irene, and you may leave it to me to intensify it."

"No, no, no; that cannot be your serious desire, Princess!" he exclaimed, springing up.

"Not my serious desire? And why should it not be? It is my most sacred desite, and my most ardent wish. I assure you, I have weighed it long and carefully. And why should I not express it? I might, indeed, have gone to work more diplomatically, I might have gone to your sister; but I have always found that frankness is the best policy. You do not seem to recover from your astonishment. Why not? The only objection you can make is that you are considerably older than Irene, but what of that? Irene, as you can see for yourself, has a very earnest character, and will not expect you to roll the hoop or play blindman's bluff with her. Her mind is well developed enough to make her happy with a man forty years old."

\ Ferdinand had risen and had been looking for his hat. He stood silent now, his eyes wandering restlessly around the room. He felt almost as if he had received a deadly insult, and yet powerless to express his sense of the insult; he would have liked to break out in unbounded anger, but his deeply-wounded pride closed his mouth and kept him dumb.

"Well?" asked Elsie, almost angrily. "You answer such an overture, which shows you my complete friendship for you, by running away?"

"I believe, in truth, Princess," he answered, with white lips, "that it would be best for me to go away silently. If I should tell you openly how your words have hurt me, I could not help giving my words as much emphasis as you have given to the affront; and then—well, then the end would be that you would call me a stupid, brainless man, who gets angry when he is offered the best prospects for making his fortune."

"Well," said Elsie, coloring deeply, "I am, indeed, almost tempted to call you so."

"Oh, yes," said Ferdinand, hardly able to control himself, "women are incomparable, admirable, when they stand smiling and radiant with all an angel's consciousness of virtue, and look down serenely on us poor fools, after they have treated us with the most utter heartlessness, and driven us to desperation!"

"Herr von Schott!" exclaimed Elsie, trembling with anger, "control yourself, control yourself, or——"

She turned abruptly, and without finishing her sentence, began to walk up and down the room.

"I said it would be best for me to go," said Ferdinand, suppressing his voice; "you kept me and made me speak."

"Stay, I desire you to stay," answered Elsie, forcing herself to composure, and seeming to have gained her wonted self-control. "Let me speak with you as your true friend. What you say of my having put a grievous affront upon you, that is in reality nonsense, and your anger at it is forced, in part, at least——"

"Forced!" exclaimed Ferdinand, in angry astonishment, and quivering as at the fang of a serpent.

"Yes. I have shown you plainly that I have entirely forgotten certain things you were bold enough to say to me in Florence, as they deserved to be forgotten. Now you conceive that you must confirm those declarations by your anger, and show me the sincerity of your feelings as you expressed them then; and so you affect· to be indignant because I take the liberty not to show the slightest respect for them. In part, indeed, you may be sincere in your anger, because it may wound your vanity to see that your declarations have made so little impression upon me."

Ferdinand stood benumbed. To see his wrath at the insult offered him, the deep wound in his heart, treated as something forced, was too much; it was one of those feminine tricks that a man has to be accustomed to not to be beside himself at them.

"But, I beg of you," continued Elsie, "let us leave all that folly and nonsense behind us. We are mature and reasonable people; let us talk together as such. Think as badly of me as you will; think that it is only my love of power which is determined to carry out a plan once formed; add to this that sympathy and anxiety for Irene impel me to it; the girl is spoiled here at Achsenstein, where she is indulged and accustomed to ways of living to which she is not born; my sister and I must think of her future, and you—now, really, it is not possible that, with the hand of such an amiable, rich, and beautiful girl, you will refuse a happiness that——"

"Say nothing farther, Princess," said Ferdinand, in a most determined tone, but with a voice whose tremor betrayed how hard it was for him to control himself. "Say nothing farther. It is useless. May I go?"

Elsie looked at him. Her brows were knit; her face, which had been deeply colored, had grown pale. There was an expression of pain and desperate struggle with herself in her features. She was silent for a few moments. Then she said, turning suddenly away:

"Well, go, then; go, in Heaven's name, and may you never have cause to repent your folly!"

He did not answer, but bowed proudly, and went.

He little dreamed with what strangely altered features Elsie looked after him; how all anger had vanished from them; what a deep, proud seriousness, as of great, ideal satisfaction, a comforting and inspiring thought, came into those features as a slight color returned to them. And how she whispered words that accorded poorly with the satisfied and somewhat triumphant expression of her face; for they were unsatisfied, despairing, complaining of fate.

"All in vain!" she whispered. "All! Even though I do what is hardest, most cruel for myself; though I bind my own heart with iron chains, and drag my own deepest feelings to the sacrifice; though I do more than human nature can endure—it is of no use!—I cannot free myself of this burden, this inner degradation! How grandly and nobly he thrust away the temptation! And yet, if I had had lightnings to send, I would have struck him down for very wrath and desperation at myself!"

CHAPTER XV.

A SUSPICION.

Ferdinand went out into the darkening evening, without thinking of returning to his home. Trying to control the storm within him, he wandered up one of the poplar-lined roads running along the river through the valley, into the night and the darkness, in the face of the cold, sharp, evening wind. Whatever idea Elsie might have of his feeling for her, it was a passionate love, and he had never realized it more or more painfully than now. The insult she had offered him by taking a step which said so openly, so cold-bloodedly, that she had nothing but contemptuous incredulity for all he had told her of his exclusive regard for her—he believed that he should never get over that insult. He had not asked for a return of his love; no, not with a syllable. She was the wife of another man; he had never forgotten it. He had not rebelled, not persecuted her, not once complained when she had treated him so coldly, when she had so suddenly left Florence, only on account of his declaration.

But for her to tell him: "I do not believe your professions; it is all a lie, a trick"— that was too much, she had no right to do that. To say to him, "I believe, in spite of all the beautiful sentiments you say you cherish for me, that you will quietly accept from my hand a beautiful girl when she has a beautiful fortune"—that was an insult unendurable to Ferdinand's deep, passionate, honor-loving nature. It seemed incomprehensible to him. It threw him out of all his ordinary tracks of thought. He might struggle for composure as he would, he could not succeed, even in gaining enough to deceive his sister when he returned home after some hours of walking.

She noticed that something extraordinary had affected him, and at length she questioned him about it.

"You have been up at Achsenstein; what has happened to make you look so pale and gloomy? You have been looking into the fire a quarter of an hour without saying a word to me. Has Princess Elsie turned into a Princess Ilse and put you under a

wicked enchantment? Or did Prince Gottlieb pour out his wit and eloquence on you
so lavishly as to take all the life out of you?
Tell me, Ferdinand. I want to know what
the matter is; why you have come home in
such a gloomy mood while I was anticipat-
ing so much pleasure in telling you about
Frau Groebler's visit and all she told me
about H. She told me all about how splendid you were in those days, how you were
the manager of all kinds of amusements,
.and, moreover, the *primo amoroso*, and
how you made the storm and sunshine in
the Melroth house, and how—well, how
clearly you betrayed to all the world, by
your eternal strife and dispute with Fräulein Elsie, that you were hopelessly in love
with her. Frau Theresa Groebler—and, by
the way, she might speak a little lower and
laugh aloud not quite so often; she cannot
possibly be happy, the happy do not advertise their happiness quite so publicly—Frau
Groebler saw Irene here about half an hour.
She says Irene does not look as if she belonged either to us Schotts or to the Melroths; she is very pretty, but not nearly so
pretty as Elsie was then; but not so haughty
either, and very lovely. She was delighted with Irene and praised her excessively. Irene was very much pleased with
her, too, and invited her to visit her mother very soon, and tell her more of the life
in H., about which Matilda and Elsie are
very reticent. Irene was especially delighted with some dreadful stories of a dark
old haunted hall in Herr Melroth's house,
of which Frau Theresa told us. You never
said anything to me about that, Ferdinand.
But to return to our subject: you are excited; something has happened to you, and
you must tell me what the matter is, Ferdinand."

While Adele had been talking on with
apparent carelessness, and as if to divert
her brother's attention, she had kept her
anxious eyes on his face.

"I have vexatious official business to
think of, Adele," answered Ferdinand,
pushing back the coals on the hearth with
his foot; "matters that cannot be of interest
to you."

"Official business! Well, if it is nothing

more than that, I will not trouble myself
about it. But it is wonderful how you have
suddenly set your whole heart on this official business!"

There was something in Adele's tone that
made him look up at her with a sharp
glance. She was busily counting stitches
in her knitting, and had her face bent
over it.

"Heart? Have we men, then, any
hearts?" he exclaimed, with unspeakable
bitterness.

"Has any one accused you of having
none? And that makes you so bitter?
But as a diplomatist you ought to know
that that only means: 'Show me more, give
me more of your heart!' But who could
have said that to you here? Certainly not
your old 'Flame!' I would wager that
that proud lady has at some time loved and
suffered; and it enraged her so that fate did
not make an honored exception of her, but
gave her suffering with love, like all other
mortals, that since then she has revenged
herself on love by the most extreme contempt, regarding it as her special and personal enemy; and that she would have no
objections if, for a change, some man
would make a little romantic episode in her
monotonous days by shooting himself
through the heart for desperate love of her.
But I hardly think any one can ever succeed
in reviving what seems never to have been
actively alive, her heart!"

"How sharply you women criticise each
other!" said Ferdinand.

"One judges best of his equals. If you
men would regard women as beings like
yourselves, as just human, not half children
and half angels, you could judge of them
better. If you want to understand a woman, translate her, as you would a foreign
novel, into your own language, give her
your own every-day dress. Imagine how
she would impress you if she were a man.
And then you can judge of her. Among a
hundred, ninety-nine would no longer
please you."

"I will do so, my wise little sister, if I
should ever be placed in a position where I
should need to form a careful and thorough
judgment of a woman."

A pause followed. Ferdinand sat silently looking into the fire. Adele's eyes passed anxiously over his features from time to time. Her keen observation had long since detected a revival of his old feeling toward Elsie. She knew that he had been to Achsenstein. His excitement, which was passing into a dumb self-absorption, told her but too plainly that something of great importance to him had happened. But she saw, too, that she could not draw it from him by seemingly unsuspecting chat. He did not allude to Elsie, and this was one of the principal symptoms that disturbed Adele.

"Your newspapers are here," she said, after a pause; "do you not want to read them? Read a little to me, will you not?"

"I am so tired, Adele!"

"Then let us talk. That will divert you best. Can you tell me how old Irene is now? Frau Groebler asked me, and I had to confess to her that I had no means of telling. Cousin Alexander did not honor me with a notice of his daughter's birth. But I was only one of the small-fry then."

"He did not write to you of Irene's birth?" asked Ferdinand, looking up. "That is strange, for he sent me no word either, though he was particular about such forms. And, afterward, when he wrote to me, he never mentioned his daughter."

"Indeed! that looks as if he meant to disown her. Perhaps he was disappointed in not having a son."

"It is really strange," resumed Ferdinand, after a pause. "Alexander was an affectionate man, and must have thought a great deal of his child. That he should never mention her is very singular. And Frau Theresa thought she did not resemble us Schotts in the least."

"She is right about that. It did not occur to me before, but now that my attention is called to it——"

Ferdinand sprang up, suddenly. He took a few steps through the room, and then stood suddenly still, staring down at the carpet.

"What is the matter, Ferdinand?"

Adele might have repeated her question many times without receiving any answer.

For the sudden thought that had gone like lightning through his brain and made everything clear. He would have been ashamed of it, as a fiendish suspicion, if he had put it into words and uttered it. But the thought clung to him, and made a deeper and deeper impression. Irene—so his suspicion said—was not the child of his cousin Alexander and Matilda. Elsie had married Philip Bonsart at the time she left her father's house with that intention, and this girl was their child. Then Elsie, for some unknown reason, had separated from Philip Bonsart forever, and her sister had adopted the child of this secret marriage, which the world must not suspect. And after this, his cousin, Johann Heinrich, had died, and as he left no will, contrary to the general expectation that he would make Ferdinand his principal heir, Irene, who had not the slightest claim, had, to the surprise of the sisters, become the heiress of the estate that would have gone to Ferdinand and Adele without any will, since Alexander, the only nearer relative, was dead. These were the combinations that shot seething hot through Ferdinand's brain, and drove the perspiration to his forehead; he could not shake them off, because they threw light upon everything, made everything most wretchedly clear and plain.

Groebler, indeed, had hinted the suspicion that Elsie and Philip were really married at Asthof. Who could know, then, whether Philip had really crossed the ocean, or had remained and kept himself hidden, until they had quarrelled, or something had happened to make them separate forever? And what was there to prevent them from breaking in secret the tie they had secretly assumed, and to exchange vows to regard it as though it never had been? If Matilda would allow herself to be so influenced by Elsie—and why not, since she had always yielded to her control?—if she would allow herself to be so influenced as to pass off Elsie's child as her own, then there was nothing to prevent Elsie to live on after that episode in her life without placing herself before the world in so doubtful and humiliating a light, and stake her wonderful beauty to draw from the lottery of life a more brilliant prize than a life with Philip Bonsart across the wide ocean would have been.

And she had drawn this great prize, so much more brilliant than she could have hoped. She had drawn and appropriated it—she, the wife of another! But why need she trouble herself about that? The ceremony was secret, and she was probably sure of Philip Bonsart, and whatever else there might be to give evidence against her, who could know what means she had taken to make it harmless, even if anything of the kind really existed to be feared?

And everything harmonized with this supposition. It explained Matilda's coldness toward Irene. It explained Elsie's tenderness for the girl, scarcely allowing her to pass a day without her. It explained Matilda's constrained manner toward him and his sister. But it also explained the most unaccountable of all—Elsie's manner and conduct toward him.

How fearfully her pride must have suffered when that most unexpected event, the death of the banker, suddenly gave Irene an inheritance that did not belong to her. Elsie and Matilda could not now confess that Irene had no claim to it, that she was not the daughter of the man for whose daughter she had passed. They could not confess it, for Elsie was probably already the Princess of Achsenstein. They could do nothing but silently allow matters to take their course, and take the property, which now gave their actions the character of a common swindle, which forced them to receive a large sum of money that belonged to others who must suffer greatly by the robbery. How dreadfully heavy must that have lain on Elsie's soul! With what a suffocating weight. And hence her pallor, her emotion, when he told her that time in Florence, that poverty compelled him to leave his profession. Hence her passionate desire that he should receive money from her. Hence to-day her astonishing proposal, so wanting, under the circumstances, in the tact so natural to her. It was a plan to put him in possession of Johann Heinrich's property. He was to receive it from Irene's hand. They wanted to roll the guilt from

their conscience by marrying him to a girl young enough to be his daughter.

And how the supposition threw sudden light, too, on the fact that Groebler had told him that communication had been kept up between Philip Bonsart and Elsie, not direct and immediate, but through Emil Drausfeld, the confidant of both. They had not personal interest in each other after their separation, but Philip wanted news from his child, he clung to her; and that was the reason they had written to Emil.

It was a fearful moment to Ferdinand when this explanation came suddenly into his mind. It took away his breath; he could not stay with Adele and control himself as he must in her presence; he went back to his office, to give himself up to the thoughts that tormented him till he lost all sense of what was passing around him. He did not see, therefore, that the door of the room opened and Adele stood on the threshold, observing him for a while; then she stepped in, turned up the light on the writing-desk, and, stepping up to him, laid both hands upon his shoulders, and said, firmly and earnestly:

"Ferdinand, something has affected you very deeply. I want to know what it is. I must know, you must not evade me any longer. Tell me."

He looked at her with a wild, unsteady glance, then passed his hand over his face and said:

"Well, then, if you must know what has happened to affect me, it is a thought, nothing but a thought; but a thought that nearly drives me wild!"

"A mere thought that drives you wild. In God's name, what terrible thought can have such power over a strong, rational man?"

"I will tell you. I believe that Elsie von Melroth was secretly married to Philip Bonsart; I believe that Irene is their child; I believe that she separated from him, and then dared, in her pride, to tread under foot the laws of God and man, and take a prince for her husband, as if her hand were free and her will independent—so soon as a prince came and offered himself. But this Bonsart is still living and Elsie is a Catholic; she could not be divorced from him, and, therefore, she has committed a fearful crime——"

Adele looked at him with a frightened stare.

"Do you believe that?"

"I believe it."

"And Irene is their daughter?"

"Irene is their daughter. But this witness of a marriage that her proud will chose to regard as annulled, and that the world must not know of, could not—this poor girl must be taken by Matilda under her wing, adopted by her."

"That would have been dreadful. And if it were so, if Irene were not the daughter of your cousin Alexander, then we should be the heirs of the property that——."

"We should be," interrupted Ferdinand, in a lifeless voice.

Adele dropped into Ferdinand's office-chair as if pressed down by the weight of this sudden revelation.

He took a few turns up and down the room. She followed him anxiously with her eyes.

"Well, tell me more," she exclaimed, at length. "Tell me your reasons; tell me everything!"

Ferdinand did not answer for a while. Then he began and told her, in broken sentences, everything in relation to the affair; what had aroused his suspicions, what circumstances and facts he had put together to arrive at the conviction so painful to him.

Adele sat silent for a long time. "I do not know whether you are right," she said, at length. "I cannot judge about circumstances and people of whom I know so little. But you must admit that what you assert is improbable—improbable in the highest degree—and that your attachment to Elsie has brought you into—do not be offended at the expression—into a morbid condition, and all your combinations, all these dark suspicions, may be only an unhealthy result of that. Until I have other and more convincing evidence than you have given, I shall not believe your assertion. I shall not contradict it; it is possible that you have discovered the truth; but I do not believe it."

"We will not dispute about it," said Ferdinand, stopping and looking down at her; "but you shall have the more convincing evidence. Do you think that I myself can be contented with the combinations of my 'morbid condition,' as you call it? Oh, no; I, too, want more convincing evidence, and you can be assured that I shall not rest till I have obtained it. I shall have no other thought from this time on but to obtain it!"

With this decision Ferdinand left his sister late in the evening; and early on the following day he sent for Herr Groebler.

Herr Groebler appeared. He always appeared, when his duty called him, with wonderful promptness. As it was a cold, blustering day, and he had come through the snow-drifts the night had been heaping up, he gladly accepted Ferdinand's invitation to take a cup of hot coffee with him and smoke a cigar by the warm fire. This was well calculated to give the conversation a private and confidential character. Notwithstanding the surprise that Ferdinand's statements must have caused Herr Groebler, he did not lose the expression of a man who finds himself in a very agreeable situation and is determined not to be disturbed by anything the outside world may find it good to do, until duty requires him to begin "official operations." He drank his coffee, listened to Ferdinand, and looked, with half-closed lids, into the blue clouds in front of him. Now and then he looked up at Ferdinand with the expression of an unmoving bird of prey that sees a dove flying past, and—lets it fly. At times he shook his head slightly, and at length he said:

"It is, indeed, possible, Herr von Schott. It is possible that everything is as you suspect. It is also possible that the personal interest you have in the matter may have led you into error. There is nothing that so confuses our clearness of insight in any matter as a personal interest. But as you evidently desire it, I will set aside this consideration, and suppose that you are right. Very well, then; we have first a case of bigamy—for I think this Philip Bonsart is still alive; he was, at least, when Fräulein von Melroth was married to the prince. We should, therefore, have a case of bigamy; that would be one side of the case. And then we have the fraud in regard to the child, that would be the other side. That would be material for a criminal process that would make a pretty good noise; don't you think so? I think it would make a frightful noise, and a much greater scandal than I should care to be mixed up in! How do you feel in regard to that, Herr von Schott? But, indeed, the case is different with you. For you, there is the third side, that of your private rights. You want the property you have been defrauded of."

Ferdinand stared at Herr Groebler with a peculiar expression. Herr Groebler did not understand the meaning of that strange, bewildered look. He could not know that the idea of a criminal process hanging over Elsie, which he had stated so directly and undisguisedly, of a publicity ruinous to her, had something in it ruinous to Ferdinand also—that the thought of interfering so fiendishly in her life, blighting and destroying it, brought horror and agony into his soul. Herr Groebler could not know this, and Ferdinand was far from wishing him to suspect it. And there was no need of it. It was easy enough to find a pretext by which to explain his burning desire to get light on all these things, to explain it to Groebler's complete satisfaction.

"You greatly misunderstand me, my dear Groebler," he said, "if you think my zeal goes so far that I would plunge with the delight of a novice into an investigation whose result would be a horrible criminal suit against a lady who is to be pitied, who has been led into error by feelings and motives that we cannot know. If what I have told you is true, then, believe me, the Princess of Achsenstein is already punished enough. For when she induced her sister to adopt Irene as her own child, she could not foresee, or even dream, that my cousin's property would ever fall to her. In this consequence of her act lies her punishment: the necessity of suffering this result to follow is, for so proud a nature, "the curse of the evil deed;" it is the tragedy of the story, the expiation of her guilt. And you must, therefore, understand the design of the steps I am about to take. I wish nothing whatever like a process against the princess;

I desire only to collect proofs; and, armed with these, I will go to the princess and Irene, when Irene is of age and can control her property without the interference of a guardian, and will say to them : Live in peace, but give me what belongs to me, me and my sister, whose rights I have to protect."

"There is nothing to be said against that, Herr von Schott," answered Groebler, "and if that is the case, we can pass on to the chief question—what is to be done to collect such proofs?"

"That, of course, is the question now. And in this I count upon your help. Two steps are to be taken at once. Search must be made in Asthof in reference to the clandestine marriage. And also in—what is the name of the place where Emil Drausfeld lives?"

"Vellinghaus."

"In Vellinghaus, then; he must be hunted up and made to speak; if possible, to give up the letters that are in his hands. This latter task I will take upon myself. Emil will see that I have a right to a clear understanding of the matter, and a right to take measures for getting what belongs to me."

"He will see that. His silence would make him an accomplice in defrauding you of your cousin's property."

"Therefore," continued Ferdinand, "I will start for Vellinghaus to-day. And you, Groebler, I beg of you to take on yourself the search at Asthof. You will be more skilful and successful than a novice like me, in work like that, requiring experience and professional knowledge. Will you do so much for me? The weather is not inviting for a journey, and so much farther east as Asthof and Vellinghaus lie, it must be still more wintry, but——".

"But," interrupted Groebler, "for the police there is no such thing as weather, as there is no day or night for them. I will go to-morrow, or, if it must be, will join you to-day in your journey, eastward. Please get me leave of absence for six or eight days."

"I knew I could count upon you, Groebler," answered Ferdinand, extending his hand gratefully. "Let us go together, then, this afternoon. By that time I shall have arranged affairs so that my secretary can take my place for a few days."

Herr Groebler withdrew to make preparations for his journey, and at dark they were both in the train, bound eastward.

We have seen what the result of Ferdinand's journey was; how he arrived at the end of a tedious journey only to find that he had come too late. We have also heard Herr Groebler's report, which threw very little light on the matter and did not advance it a single step. We have also heard Herr Groebler's advice to Ferdinand, to ask himself whether he were really convinced of Elsie's guilt, and ready to drop farther investigation than to pursue a shadow.

Induced by this advice from his helpful and zealous friend, Ferdinand had now passed all these circumstances in review. In the morning, when Herr Groebler reappeared, Ferdinand was ready to say to him: "I do not, indeed, know that it is the truth, but I believe it so firmly that I cannot give up seeking for the proofs of its truth. The nearest way lies open before us. We must find out where Philip Bonsart is. This man will not refuse to tell me the truth if I make it clear to him that I am entirely free from hostile feeling toward the princess, but only desire to recover what I have been defrauded of—when I tell him that by denying or keeping silence he will be a party to the fraud."

"Would not this man," answered Groebler, thoughtfully, "would he not know, assuming that Fräulein Irene is his daughter, would he not be likely to know that she has become the heiress to a property to which she has no right? And, by keeping silence so long, has he not given reason to fear that he will be silent in the future?"

"I do not think," said Ferdinand, "that he knows it. I do not think the princess would communicate to him a fact so humiliating to her; for that would give him an opportunity to answer or have Emil Drausfeld answer. These are the consequences of the audacity with which you tore apart the tie that bound us; this humiliation, this degrad-ing thought, that you must be a criminal

against your own will, is the punishment of your faithlessness to me. Believe me, Groebler, the princess would not have given Philip Bonsart such a triumph, would not have exposed herself to such an answer."

"That seems reasonable," answered Herr Groebler. "And so our business is narrowed down to a hunt after Herr Philip Bonsart?"

"You took the introductory step when in Asthof; it now remains for you to take the farther steps, my dear Groebler."

Groebler nodded. He was perfectly ready. His advice to Ferdinand to drop the matter had been given yesterday in the fatigue from the journey, in the discouragement consequent upon the fruitlessness of his search. To-day the detective instinct was awake again; he would have had no objections to being sent through the cold and storms, away to Pomerania.

But there was no need of that. The business could be transacted by letter. Philip Bonsart had nothing more to fear. There was no reason why his relatives should conceal his present place of residence. Herr Groebler, therefore, went home to write a letter to those relatives. Until the answer came, Ferdinand could do nothing but seek to divert his thoughts by his business, and escape the sad brooding over all these things that brought such strife into his heart. The ultimate purpose of this chase after the traces of a crime supposed to have been committed by Elsie von Melroth—did he know what it was, had he expressed it clearly and definitely to himself? Did he only desire to know nothing farther than to be clearly convinced? Did he want to recover what was his right, and help his sister to hers? Or did he want to know whether Elsie had offered him help that time in Florence from sympathy, from the pressure of affection, or only from the pressure of conscience? Whether she had offered him Irene's hand in cool calculation, or whether she had done it against the voice of her heart, under the sting of her conscience again? Did he want to be sure of that, or only to gain a powerful weapon to humble her pride, to gain the ascendency over her, to prepare a triumph for his own pride? He would certainly have found it hard to answer all these questions to himself. One thing only he knew, and that was that he could not find rest, or escape his constant torture, until he had discovered the truth.

CHAPTER X

ELSIE.

And what of Elsie all this time? The gloomy winter days had been passing over her unsuspecting head with leaden wings, while Ferdinand and his zealous assistant had been restlessly diving into the obscurity of her past. The prince devoted himself to the pleasures of the chase for which he had turned his back on sunny Sorrento; he lived for nothing else. He had invited a motly throng of gentlemen from the city and the neighborhood, with very little regard to their culture or their conversational talent, if they only knew how to shoot and to listen to him. Elsie kept her own apartments, entirely absorbed, as the prince said, in recollections of her Italian travels, in journals and photographs she had brought home. He seemed to intimate that he thought she contemplated writing a learned book about her travels. It is certain that if she had cherished any such design, she would have been very little disturbed by Prince Gottlieb Anton. He seemed to indulge her desire for solitude very willingly; the shadowy presence of her attendant could not disturb her greatly; Irene only came every day and read to her; her sister Matilda came much less frequently, and often let several days pass without appearing at Achsenstein. She had been greatly rejoiced to meet her old acquaintance, Frau Groebler, once more, and they kept up a quite lively intercourse.

One evening at twilight, Elsie had found her sister at her rooms when she returned from a walk in the park.

"I thought to find Irene here," said Ma-

tilda. "She intended to call on Adele on the way, and she must have stayed there."

"Then send the carriage down to bring her. You came in our carriage?"

"Shall we not leave her down there," said Matilda, "if she takes so much pleasure in passing her time in that dark old house? I think nothing could suit us both better."

Elsie shook her head.

"It cannot do us the slightest good, dear Matilda," she answered; "not the slightest, to leave her there."

"Ah! Then you gave up the plan that we discussed so thoroughly?"

"No; so far from giving it up, I talked openly about it with Ferdinand von Schott."

"You did? And——"

"I did—and was refused!" answered Elsie, going to one of the darkening windows and looking out.

"Indeed! Is it possible? Why, pray? Ferdinand would be a fool if——"

"A fool? yes, he is one. He took my proposal as a deadly insult."

"As an insult? That you offered him Irene's hand? That is still stranger. What is the reason?"

"You know that long ago, when we lived in H., he paid some attentions to me."

"Yes, indeed; they were marked enough."

"That was long, long ago, and many things have happened since which might have made him forget it. But when I met him again so unexpectedly in Florence, the thought of it troubled me somewhat. He was still unmarried, and he has an obstinate, tenacious nature. Hence I did all I could, when I thought I saw a spark of the old fire glimmering under the ashes, I did all I could to put it out. I regulated my whole conduct for that; I told him that love was nothing but a mutual deception, a sham display of good and noble qualities and charming sentiments, an assumption of a beautiful ideal character, and then I did just the opposite; I frankly showed him self-contempt and hard-heartedness, and the utter deadness of all feeling in me. I gave myself all the qualities that make a woman repulsive in a man's eyes. Oh, an idiot would have known that I did not want his love, that every word I spoke meant that and nothing else. And yet—yet——"

"Did you see him often there?"

"Yes, I had to; in order to make it impossible for him to return to his old feeling, I had to do everything I could to draw him into a confidential and unreserved friendship. I had to place myself on a footing with him where I could in some way restore what we have robbed him of."

"What you have robbed him of, not I!" said Matilda, half aloud, with a sigh.

"Both of us, for you are in possession of the plunder, and hence it must lie equally heavy on both our consciences. But, if you please, I only—what is the difference? Well, then, what I robbed him of: it was my one thought, day and night, to make him my friend, my brother, in a sense, so that I might restore what belonged to him."

"And you failed, as you told me. His pride rebelled against taking a gift."

"His pride rebelled because, in his masculine vanity, he imagined that my whole manner was only a coquettish trick to challenge him to re-animate the dead heart, and heal the wounded soul with his love. That must be what he imagined. Oh, men are so silly, so incredibly blind where their vanity is concerned! Well, he refused my offered gift, and honored me with a declaration! It was enough to drive one to desperation. I repulsed him in a way that ought to have cured him. I left the place, and when I found him here on my return, I avoided him. I did everything to show him, in the most humiliating way, what a fool he had been. In the mean time, I had settled it with you that nothing was to be done but to take the one course remaining to us—to give him Irene's property with her hand. Irene's friendship for him and his sister seemed to make it easy; but when I attacked him on the subject, he grew excessively angry."

"He loves you yet?"

Elsie shrugged her shoulders, contemptuously.

"He loves me yet? Yes, if you call that love. From the circumstance that I quietly allowed his appointment here, though I could easily have defeated it through Gott-

lieb, his vanity seems to have drawn some hope, and so he felt humiliated when I quietly offered him a wife. He believed his declaration had made an impression on my heart, and this proof that I did not think it worth the trouble of remembering made him angry. He thinks it due to his honor to show me, by acting as passionate and desperate as possible, how deep and ardent his feelings were and are yet; I am to be completely crushed by the consciousness of my utter heartlessness and frivolity in doubting the sincerity of such holy feelings. If you call such trickery, such vanity and egotism, that seeks to conquer because it cannot bear the humiliation of a defeat—if you call that love, then he does love me yet!"

Matilda was silent a while. She had listened with surprise to her sister's violent words, and was probably trying to make clear to herself the real ground of Elsie's excitement.

"However you may analyze and revile it in your bitter and unsparing way, Elsie, that does not alter the fact," she answered, at length. "I prefer to call it by the name it takes for itself; it is, at all events, the shortest. So, then, he loves you, and our plan to arrange matters so that we could consider ourselves half-way honest again has failed. If this could have been foreseen, it would have been better for you to defeat Ferdinand's appointment through the prince."

"It was not foreseen. I could not foresee that he would be such an idiot."

Matilda shook her head. "We will not dispute about it. Other men have been in love with you without your getting so fearfully angry with them for it. You usually take it with cool indifference. You are as beautiful as ever, Elsie, and your very indifference and contempt has the effect of a challenge. And 'true love never dies!'"

"Love!" said Elsie, with contempt. "When I have once made it clear to him what I think of this love, and how thoroughly I see through it, then he must see that Irene——"

"And you have not yet given up that hope? Do not think that he will acknowlodge his folly by taking Irene from your hands. No, not such a man as he! And then, too, I must confess to you that I fear we should meet with opposition from Irene if we should try to carry out the plan."

"From Irene? How is that?"

"You certainly know about William Kronhorst?"

"But I thought you had long ago explained to Irene——"

"Explained! What good does that do with such thoughtless young creatures?"

"You believe they are keeping up that nonsense?"

"I fear they are. Observe for yourself when the Kronhorsts are here, or when you meet them anywhere else."

"I will," said Elsie. "That must, by all means, be stopped."

"Yes," answered Matilda, with a sigh, "by all means! Kronhorst will never consent to a marriage between them."

"And Irene," said Elsie, "shall not be made unhappy by really losing her heart to the young man. If your suspicion is confirmed, something must be done at once. We could send Irene away——"

"Where?"

"We might send her for a year to a boarding-school—as far away as possible; to Belgium perhaps; to one of those convents of the Sisters of the Sacred Heart. I should like it if you would, in the meantime, make inquiries about them."

Matilda promised to do so, and soon withdrew, leaving Elsie to her thoughts, which to-day seemed to give her no rest. For when she had gone to her bed-chamber she sat a long time before the dying fire, that had thrown its red light so merrily over the great canopy of the bed when she entered, and was now gradually sinking into ashes, while the castle-clock announced one quarter after another to the dumb night without and the dumb sleepers within the silent building, dying away in a long, melancholy murmer, as if complaining that the simplest truths, truths simple and irrefutable as those it was proclaiming, find ever the fewest hearers.

Elsie probably did not think long of what Matilda had said of Irene. She believed very little in juvenile love; she thought its enthusiasm nothing more than the love of pleasure, the thirst of vanity gratified by a "conquest." It seemed to her that no one could love fully whose illusions had not already begun to fade, who sees that the happiness he dreamed of in youth is a chimera, that the world he meant to make tributary to himself is engulfing him. Then, first, she thought, could the affections spring up and come to their full strength; then first the inextinguishable fire be kindled that deserved the name of love.

Then she thought of Ferdinand and his anger at the step she had taken with reference to him. She felt impelled to take an entirely different view of it from that she had expressed to her sister; and she thought over the evidences that lay in his anger. He had, at least, not deceived her; coldly and contemptuously as she had treated his attachment, cuttingly as she had talked to her sister about it, she confessed to herself now that there was something genuine and true in it, and, at the same time, something strong and powerful in its manly self-control that challenged her respect. And thinking of it, she fell into the old torturing train of thought over the whole course of her life, as it had led her, in devious paths, to this to-day, as lonely and sad and desolate as yesterday had been and as to-morrow would be. She thought what a different turn her life would have taken if she had met Ferdinand soon enough to give him her first affection. She painted to herself the kind of life she might have led with him; and as she quieted the thirst for happiness natural to every human heart and remaining even to the end, with these pictures of a life at Ferdinand's side, her idea of his character took on a brighter and nobler coloring.

At length she rose, shook back her hair, as if to shake off all such thoughts and send them far away, and went to push aside the curtain from her window and look out into the clear light of the rising moon. A softened expression came into her eyes as she slowly raised them and looked at the white clouds passing across the sky. The shade of sadness on her face deepened, till at length her eyes grew moist and tears hung on their long dark lashes.

A few detached sentences that fell from her lips betrayed what was passing in her mind.

"If my mother had only lived!" she whispered. "She would have guarded me from Philip; she certainly would. A mother would have watched me. Then I should now have been Ferdinand's wife. I think I should. Perhaps I should be happy —oh! how many times happier than now, at all events; than now, when I have not even the poor consolation of complaining. For at every complaint I must tell myself, with bitter contempt, 'You have gained a far higher place in life than you are worthy of. All that you could make of yourself you have made, and it is far more than you deserve.' And this man loves me! How blindly we can stare at the ruins of our lives without seeing the meaning that stands out so clearly written upon them!"

CHAPTER XVII.

THE YOUNG PEOPLE.

While Ferdinand was waiting for the answer to Groebler's letters, a remarkable looking figure was one evening ushered into the room where he sat reading to Adele from the daily paper. It was a boy of fourteen or fifteen, in whom Ferdinand, after a little, recognized his *protegé*, Carl. His sturdy form was half hidden behind the great hunting-pouch of worn sealskin that hung at his side. He wore a gray-green hunting-jacket, probably made by some country tailor from an old garment of his father's, with more reference to freedom of movement than elegance of style. With his hair hanging in dark, stringing locks around his expressive head, Carl looked at his patron so boldly from his dark, flashing eyes that Adele was a little frightened about this addition to the household. But after a little the bold and apparently deep and strong character of the boy began to attract her. The pouch, with some things his mother had given him to bring, was laid aside, and his hunger appeased with tea and all kinds of eatables; after this he thawed a little and answered Ferdinand's questions about his mother and the younger children. He had a letter from his mother to Ferdinand, which he now drew out of the hunting-pouch, and which Ferdinand eagerly tore open. But he found in it only the certificate of Carl's baptism and a few anxious words from Frau Drausfeld, in which she commended the boy to his kindness and begged some indulgence for him if he should be at first a little stubborn and untractable; he had never been under the control of a strong and firm will, and so had always been like a young savage; but he was wise and thoughtful enough to bend if he were met by force that could master him —his good father had not been able to do so. The letter showed more culture than Ferdinand would have expected from Frau Drausfeld; but it made him a little anxious about the success of the work of education he had taken upon himself in the warmth of his sympathy for the destitute family. "I have not found," wrote Frau Dransfeld, in a postscript, "any more letters among the papers left by my husband."

While Ferdinand was busy with the letter, Adele had begun to ask Carl about those he had left; he told her that his father's colleagues from the lodges near had all come to the funeral, and even the head forester himself; and that this gentleman had assured his mother that he would arrange it so that she could remain a whole year longer ·in the forest lodge at Vellinghaus, and should receive a pension; and then she could go to Ehlern, where the younger children could go to school, and his mother could earn a great deal by working; for there was great need in the village of a skilful woman who could not only sew but cut out clothes. This, indeed, was not all stated at once by the shy boy, but was drawn out piecemeal by Adele's questions.

"And what shall we do first, Carl?" said Ferdinand. "You will have to attend school a few years until you are prepared to go into some business, either to be a forester like your father, or a soldier, or clerk, or machinist, or miner, or an overseer in a factory perhaps, if you are good and industrious. There will be time enough to decide about that. It is now too late in the year for you to go to school; we must wait till Easter, when the new classes begin; and in the meantime I will give you something to do in my office to keep you busy."

"What shall I have to do there?" asked Carl, in a low voice.

"Write."

"Only write? And then shall I have to go to school?"

"A few years you must. But that is the fate of every one—to be a prisoner in school for a few years. You must forget the forest and its freedom. The sooner you make up your mind to it, the sooner will you be independent and be able to help your mother. If you are very diligent and faithful, in ten years I can make a bailiff of you, and then you will be respected and envied by many."

Adele saw a peculiar quiver pass over Carl's face; she thought, too, that she saw tears on his lashes. She did not believe they were tears of joy at the prospect of some time being a bailiff, and so she laid her hand kindly on his arm and said:

"I see that all this does not please you, Carl. So tell us freely what you really would like."

"I would rather not go to school; I want to go to sea and to strange lands to hunt wild beasts. I have read in books how they do it. And when I had a lot of them together, lions, tigers, and hippopotamuses, then I would bring them to Hamburg, where you can sell them for a great deal of money—for zoölogical gardens—sometimes they get many thousand thalers for them."

Adele smiled and Ferdinand said:

"Provided, my boy, that you had the money for such costly expeditions to distant countries, which unfortunately none of us have. But I am glad to see that your desire to go so far away and battle with the monsters of the wilderness is not a mere romantic notion, but is connected with a business enterprise. That speaks for your ability to understand the spirit of the time, and adapt yourself wisely to the circumstances around you. There I must yield you the palm. At your age I was not thoughtful enough to give such a practical turn to the flights of my imagination. We shall see if you will still be inclined to this rather unusual occupation when you are grown up. In the meantime you must admit that you have first very much to learn; first, you must learn foreign languages, so that you can make yourself understood in those countries; then, geography and natural history, and many other things. And so, after all, we shall have to begin first at the real school. What do you think?"

Carl looked at him with flashing eyes. There was evidently something in the ironical, jesting tone, that irritated him. Then he turned his face to Adele, and, raising his eyes with a full and trustful look, he said, after a pause:

"Do you think so, too?"

"Certainly. It is just as my brother has told you, Carl. That you must see yourself."

He nodded. "Then I will go to school," he said. "And if I must write till then, I will write for you."

"For me? Very well, you shall. Only I must tell you that the most I ever have to be copied is a pretty verse that I have read, or a good recipe for cooking; for these you shall be my secretary. But as it will take very little of your time, I may ask you to help my brother in your leisure hours with his writing, may I not?"

Carl nodded and continued to look at Adele, just as if he were trying to make out how she managed to make people do as she wanted them to, till she took him to the little room assigned to him, where his weary limbs were soon quiet in sleep.

When Adele returned to her brother they talked a long time about the peculiar manners of the boy, in whom a childishness behind his years seemed strangely mingled with premature calculation and cunning, and of the task of giving the right development to this wild plant, a task which Adele saw would fall mainly upon her. With the burden that lay upon Ferdinand's heart and kept his thoughts so intensely busy, he would certainly have been but an indifferent tutor.

In the afternoon of the following day Adele was expecting a visit from Irene. She sat at the window in the shadow of the old minster listening, half-against her will, half attracted by the wonderful strains of the crazy organist who was once more giving expression to his strange fantasies. But Irene did not come; and Adele was left to enjoy her solitary and melancholy art-entertainment, and to listen to the strange voice with which the old decaying pile confided its reflections on the things of this lower world to the wind that drove through its arches and over its roofs and then piped out in scornful impertinence what the old church had been murmuring in the tone of a penitential psalm. It was like the storm of time, rushing forward and brushing aside, in wild contempt, what the voice of old civilizations is whispering from the dead centuries.

Irene had not come, but she was not far away. She, too, was listening to the sounds rolling through the old building and dying away in its arches; or, rather, she might have heard them, if her attention had not been claimed by quite a different voice, which, although just now not much more cheerful than the dismal notes of the organ, was more grateful to her ears than any other voice in the world; it was that of William Kronhorst.

In one of the angles of the minster an arched door opened into a passage leading to the former burying-place of the sisters of the convent. It was a picturesque bit of mediæval architecture, its arched roof resting on double columns and decorated with quaint devices. At the farther end a door led into a narrow street, so that the passage was used by many of the congregation as they came from the cathedral services; but at this hour the church was deserted and the quiet place seemed made for the secret tryst that Irene and William Kronhorst must have appointed here—Irene certainly not without misgiving and secret anxiety; but she could not possibly help it, she must

speak to William, and this must was so imperative, so dreadful!

So they were sitting under one of the open arches on the plinth projecting from the wall above which the columns rose; an old elder tree behind them threw its superfluous shadow here into this realm of shade. William's arm rested on the simple gray wrap that covered Irene's shoulders, while she held in her trembling hands a paper that both were reading with anxious faces, or Irene read, and William followed the words with his eyes as she spoke them half-aloud.

"Now, my dear child," she read, "I have given you some idea of the life I have led, and which has made me what I am to-day—a man that has come out of the battle with many scars and from toil with hardened hands, but who feels that he can no longer work for the mere sake of work, or go into the conflict for the conflict's sake. A nature like mine can endure to live for a long time without happiness in the present, and in hope of the future as confident as it is indefinite and obscure. But at last an hour comes when such a nature sees that the current of its life, instead of growing broader and more powerful, is narrowing and drying up and threatening to lose itself in the sand. This is the hour when it cries out with Faust, 'Cursed be hope, cursed be faith, and cursed above all be patience!' But these are not words to write to a young girl. You will understand me better if I tell you, in plain words, that in my solitude I long for a life of the affections such as happier men have, who look at the faces of wife and children beside their own hearth-fires; and after contenting myself for years with thoughts of you, I must at last give words to my thoughts. Tell me, then, how you live, how you feel toward those who have the care of you, how much happiness you receive from your surroundings; tell me all this, and tell me, above all, whether it would break your heart if a man having a sacred claim upon you, more sacred than any other, should assert his claim and ask from you the love and confidence of a daughter. The decisive question is whether it would make you forever unhappy to leave your present life, or whether the thought that you would be bringing unbounded happiness to a solitary man could make up to you for your loss. If you cannot leave your present life, then I must try to gain strength to forget my rights and suppress my desire as a selfish one, and wait till we are thrown together in some other way—a hope I cannot abandon. I might say a great deal about how dear you will be to me, but I will leave that now. I have put my question plainly and simply and I will add nothing to bribe you or make your decision anything but entirely free. A heart as young as yours is easily awakened to enthusiasm, and my words might lead you to extravagant ideas of the life that awaits you with me, if I should try to describe it; and if then you should find it simpler and less satisfactory than you had imagined, I should be very unhappy. But I hope it is unnecessary for me to use much eloquence to influence your decision; your heart must determine, and I trust it will speak loudly for me, now that I have told you how near we are to each other, and what natural claims we have upon each other. Answer as soon as possible. I need not remind you of the promise you gave me in your last letter to be silent about our correspondence. My address is the same as before:—P. B., Newcastle-on-Tyne. To be left till called for."

It was a strange letter from which the two young people had just read this extract, and if Irene had promised silence in her answer to a former one from the same source, she can hardly be blamed for confiding in William in her deep emotion at this sudden shadow that had fallen on her young life.

"I cannot tell you, William, what distress the affair plunges me into," she said, looking up and meeting the eyes that looked down upon her full of dumb perplexity.

"You do not need to tell me, for I can understand perfectly," answered William. "Poor little Irene! It is strange, terribly strange. I cannot understand how the man that writes these strange letters can have the heart to torment you with them: it is cruel and inexcusable to give you so much sorrow."

Irene sighed and shook her head.

"Probably he cannot help it," she said. "He has no one whom he could send to me as a friend. You see how sadly alone he is. Oh, I have so much sympathy for him. He could not write to you; he knows nothing of you. So he had to write directly to me; for, you see, William, he certainly has claims upon me; that seems clear."

William nodded. "It seems clear to me, too; undeniable claims; we can guess what they are. It will not help us to refuse to understand that."

He said no more, and Irene was also silent. She laid her head upon his shoulder; he drew his arm closer around her, and they sat there silent, looking into the darkness that descended like a great curtain, growing ever heavier and heavier.

"You love me, William, don't you?" said Irene at last, raising her head. "You only, no one else. If they did, why have they left me so long in ignorance about such dreadful things? Why is there not one to whom I could go and ask, and learn the whole truth? Do you think my mother or my Aunt Elsie would tell to me the truth?"

"You have given your word to say nothing to them. And the fact that they have not told you that there was something dark and mysterious about your origin, you cannot regard that as coming from a want of affection. But I think it heartless and selfish of this strange man to write such letters to you; it is abominable to shock and distress you so!"

"It does not shock me so much as you fear, William. I do not think so much of this man, who seems to have some claims upon me, as I think of you. You have better claims on me, William, have you not? I think I belong first to you; say so, William; to you first, to others afterward. Will you say it?"

"I will," answered William, touching his lips to her forehead; "I have the first claim to you, for you are my life and my soul; and no one shall interfere with this claim, whoever it may be—even if it were all the fathers and all the mothers in the world. My father is good and kind, Irene, and I love him more than I can tell. But I cannot let him interfere with my right to you."

She raised her face, and, clasping his head in her hands, drew his lips down to hers.

"Now, tell me, William," she said, after a long pause, "what shall I do? I will do as you say."

William considered a while.

"It is possible," he said, at length, "it is possible that all there is in these letters is only a cunning plot, a strategem, to deceive you and perhaps cheat you out of your property, or for some other dark and wicked purpose. It is possible. But the tone of the letters, their whole tenor, make that improbable; and we both have the impression that it is the voice of true and honest feeling."

Irene nodded.

"I have," she said.

"You have and I have, too. Therefore, if I were in your place, I would answer that you will not refuse to write the information required when the matter is made clearer to you. Only half the truth has been told you and you require the whole. I would ask permission, too, to talk with others about it. With Adele von Schott, for instance. Even now you ought to talk with her, to whom you can confide everything. It would certainly be well for you to have the advice of such a friend about your answer now."

"It would be well," answered Irene; "but I dare not now. But go on, William; tell me how you would advise me to write my answer."

"As I said, you must demand unreserved explanations."

"And then, if he gives them?"

"Then we must consider farther. We must see whether they are such as to cause a complete change in your position and destiny. If they should be, then, I think, we need not despair. For, see, if you were suddenly placed in an entirely different position, with another name, in an entirely new world——"

"It would be dreadful, horrible!" exclaimed Irene, as if suddenly overcome by the thought, covering her face with both hands.

"It might be terrible to your feelings a the very first," said William; "but you real world, the world of your heart, woulc remain the same. Nothing can change ou love. And then, think, then my fathei would certainly look at you with quite different eyes, and it would, it must, produce a change in his will, in his firm determination to separate us!"

"Do you believe that?"

"I hope so confidently."

Irene was silent. But William's words must have been a great consolation to her. She raised her head, dried her tears, sprang down from her seat, and with the words:

"I must go back; it is high time for me to hurry home," she pressed her lips lightly to his cheek and hurried away through the dark passage till her form was lost in the shadows.

CHAPTER XVIII.

HERR KRONHORST'S PARTY.

A few days after this, a large party given by Herr Kronhorst assembled at his villa the first society of the city and the surrounding country. Elsie had wished to excuse herself, but the prince had expressed a strong desire to have her go, giving as a reason that her absence would be taken as a slight by Herr Kronhorst and his guests. Elsie yielded, and in her court-toilet, which had for a long time been laid aside, took the carriage for the villa, accompanied by the prince and her attendant. From the avenue leading from the castle to the city, they could see the brilliantly-lighted villa on the opposite bank of the river. The light from the windows shone far out into the night, and the broad terraces between the dwelling and the bank of the river were furnished with torches which made the grounds as light as day, and were reflected in shimmering rays from the dark stream below. After a drive of about twenty minutes, the carriage reached the gate; a telegraph signaled the arrival to the host, giving him time to take his place at the head of the broad steps of the villa to receive the prince and princess. Drawn up on the left and right, in military form, was a company in bright uniforms, the fire department of the Kronhorst factories.

After the first salutations, Herr Kronhorst gave the princess his arm and led her into the hall and up the broad marble stairs which led upward through what seemed a forest of exotic plants; the prince followed with the maid-of-honor, into the apartments decorated with all the splendor that modern art in the service of wealth could furnish. There was a time when not only the palaces of royalty but the dwellings of the richer citizens were adorned with similar products of art; when nearly every private dwelling was filled with the antique furniture, embroidered tapestries, carved mouldings and sculptures, now so eagerly sought for by antiquaries. But the storms of the sixteenth and seventeenth centuries impoverished our people, and gave to the dwellings of fifty and a hundred years ago an appearance of extreme plainness and bareness. The present has changed all that with almost magic rapidity; the time of the Renaissance has returned in the arts as in intellectual life, and will not the products of this second Renaissance be prized by future antiquaries as indicating a much finer artistic sense and much more highly developed technical skill? With all the honor due to great names, still it must be admitted that such luxury as surround Herr Kronhorst's guests in his parlors and dining-hall far surpassed the work of the old goldsmiths of Florence, the glass-blowers of Venice, or the potters, colorists, and enamellers of Pesaro and Faenza. The splendor of these hundreds of beautiful things, these marble statues under the shade of tropical leaves, the silver table-service, the carpets and the silken hangings, was so far beyond the means of the modest income of an ordinary princely house, that it could not inspire Gottlieb Anton with envy; it lay far beyond the bounds of envy, and, on the other hand, far below the summit to which an aristocrat of the highest rank is raised by his serene princely consciousness. The prince envied Herr Kronhorst one thing only—his stables and horses. The prince had a special passion for fine horses, and to be outdone in this aristocratic specialty by the plebeian manufacturer, was a little hard for him. When Herr Kronhorst had conducted his most honored guests to the seats reserved for them at the upper end of the large drawing-room, where they were soon surrounded by a kind of small court, the prince began to ask after his old acquaintances, the fine animals in the councillor's stables, and to display his hippologic wisdom. Elsie, in the meantime, was answering somewhat laconically the compliments of the noblemen and officers around her, while her eyes wandered as if seeking some one among the many-colored groups that filled the room. She looked wonderfully beautiful and brilliant. A shade of sadness rested on her slightly-flushed features which remained throughout the excitements of the evening, an evidence of the strength of her nature to resist all exterior excitements and influences.

Ferdinand, who was observing her from a distance, was reminded of the expression that had so affected him years before, on the day of her sister Matilda's betrothal. It seemed that all the intervening years had failed to take anything from her beauty, but had rather given to it a noble seriousness and dignity. And with the tortures of remorse, the thought came into his mind that he was following this beautiful woman with a base suspicion, tracing her past like a restless bloodhound—that past that must have been so full of sorrow and conflict to her—ensnaring her with disgraceful detective strategy. The thought filled him with self-contempt; at this moment he would have fled from himself into another world, if only he had known of any other where he could have been sure of escape. Most gladly would he have gone to her and told her frankly of everything, and said: "Give me at least a knowledge of your secret as a right of friendship. Give it to me to guard carefully from all other eyes."

But would the proud woman take his offered hand and give, him the answer he craved? No, she would flash into fury; she would have but the one desire, to annihilate him and make herself forever secure from what he knew.

Meantime the dancing-music had begun, and Herr Kronhorst invited Elsie to open the ball with him. The prince followed with a noble lady of the neighborhood, whose husband led out Adele von Schott, and the endless line of the Polish closed up in parti-colored procession, to break up again after a long series of serpentine windings and leave the polished floor to the privileged younger people. Herr Kronhorst had found his way to the side of the chair Adele had taken to watch the dance; he had often shown an interest in Ferdinand's pretty sister. A peculiarly pleasant and attractive smile rested on his clear-cut features, which also bore the impress of great firmness and strength of will. She spoke of the beauty of the rooms, and he answered in a voice betraying some emotion, that he had originally had no taste for anything of the kind, and had been, he feared, a very rough, unpolished machinist, till his wife, who had now been dead several years, had given a more ideal turn to his tastes; and now these things had become in some degree a necessity to him—the more as he now connected the love of artistic beauty with the memory of his wife. Some inventions he had made after long-continued efforts, and through years of loss and anxiety and disappointment, the price of a toilsome life, had given him the means for gratifying those tastes in such abundance, that he regarded it as a duty to use his means for promoting art and science and every noble effort requiring money for the accomplishment of its ends. "If," said he, "you had by long effort, or only by accident, invented or discovered something that might be a benefit to thousands, a means of alleviating pain, or saving labor, or advancing science, you would certainly think it base and contemptible to lock up your treasure and allow it to benefit no one but yourself. I consider the rich man quite as contemptible who locks up his treasure in his safe instead of using it to promote noble efforts and so advancing the

interest of all as well as being helpful to individuals."

"I agree with you so perfectly," said Adele, "that I would not even say, it is nobly thought, but only it is justly thought."

"But," replied Herr Kronhorst, "one sooner becomes a martyr to this habit of thinking justly, as you call it, then you would believe. One soon becomes surrounded with such a multitude of things, that they are a burden; he can no longer keep up acquaintance with them all; they grow to be perfectly strange and the pleasure of possession one has with less is gone. The idea of property has only a certain amount of elasticity; it has limits beyond which the human mind is incapable of stretching it. It is a cloth according to which one can cut his coat when it is too short, but when it is too long, he cannot possibly get it all in, 'My property'—do you think I feel any pride and satisfaction in being the owner of all that men regard as my undisputed possession? Of these large sums of money that remain to me as profit after the accounts for the year are balanced? Not in the least; I look upon those sums only as a minister of finance at the figures of his budget; it never occurs to him to regard the money they represent as his own. I feel like a manager at the head of some great establishment, whose profits belong to the commonwealth of mankind, the ultimate proprietor of all."

"What you say leads me to think of something I have not hitherto thought much about—of 'property,' the subject our socialists are troubling themselves so much about. It seems your wealth has led you to the same conclusions others have arrived at through their poverty."

"It is possible," answered Herr Kronhorst, smiling. "The first result of this feeling is a very natural wish. If I cannot directly enjoy all that comes to me because we chance to live in a time one of whose first needs is for just the things my factories produce, and the millions of the State treasury have a peculiar tendency to throw themselves away on me for much coarser and clumsier metal; if I cannot myself eijoy this superfluous wealth, and often feel like a martyr to all the obligations it brings upon me, then I can but long to enjoy it indirectly, by making it benefit some other one whose happiness would be mine."

"But that again is bad," answered Adele, after a pause; "for one whose happiness could be found in all this wealth and splendor would certainly not be one who could make you happy. Neither could you easily find one who would be willing to accept such an office from you."

"An office?"

"Yes, it would be that; the office of your deputy in enjoyment, to taste for you the pleasures to which you are no longer sensitive."

"For which I am too *blasé*, is what you would say, Fräulein. That is too bad of you. I should not have taken you to be like all other women, who, when we open our hearts to them in confidence, begin at once to abuse us."

"Have you often had that experience?"

"How one has to be on his guard with you," answered the gentleman, smiling. "But I admit that your answer is a deserved punishment for my assertion. You are right; I have very seldom opened my heart in confidence to any one, and less frequently or never been repaid with abuse. I will, therefore, retract and apologize, at the same time acknowledging that I should have no objection to being abused by you a little more."

"Then you must first confide something more to me."

"What shall I confide to you?"

Adele looked frankly at him, and in the feeling of confidence the man inspired, she said:—

"I have an almost motherly tenderness for my young cousin Irene. I alone know that she suffers, and how she suffers. Can your confidence lead you so far as to tell me why she does not please you?"

Adele colored. She had spoken on the impulse of the moment; she felt directly how indiscreet the question was.

"Does not please me?" he answered, quickly. "Oh, do not think that. I think Fräulein Irene much more attractive than

all these light-footed and charming girls around us, far prettier and more attractive. But as you ask my confidence, and as I wish nothing more than to show you confidence, I will willingly tell you that there is a reason in Irene's circumstances that makes it impossible, forever impossible, for me to consent to a marriage between her and my son. Unfortunately, I cannot tell you more, or, at most, only this, that an inquiry into those circumstances, the reason for my determination, would be entirely fruitless. There are some things in life that we can confide to no one, because they are not our secrets. Give me your hand upon it that you will not be led by your sympathy for Irene to search into the facts I have hinted at, will you?"

Adele silently took the offered hand.

"I will give you the promise," she said, then, "if you will promise me to forgive and forget the interference I was led into by my love for poor Irene."

"That I certainly shall not do, Fräulein von Schott; your confidence has given me too much pleasure for that. But I have forgotten to see whether our prince has found a partner for his game of whist. Excuse me, please."

Herr Kronhorst went away to his duty as host, and Adele looked for her brother, to whom she would have liked to report the conversation. But Ferdinand was just then engaged, and Adele was soon joined by William Kronhorst, who took advantage of the moment the dance ended to slip into the chair at her side and enter into a conversation, whose ultimate object, as Adele could easily guess, was Irene. And, in truth, he soon turned the conversation upon her. Adele talked freely to him of her feelings toward the girl; the young man's frank face, with its dark eyes and heavy dark-brown hair curling around it, inspired her with sympathy; he assured her that Irene was enthusiastically fond of her, and had often told him she trusted no one on earth more completely.

"No one? Do you believe that?" asked Adele, smiling slily.

"Why should I not?" he answered, coloring deeply. "I have heard from her all

8

she has confided to you, and I know I can talk openly with you, since you have been so kind to her. I am anxious to know what you think of the letters."

"Of the letters? What letters?"

"Why, the two letters she has received from England."

"Letters? From England? That Irene has received?"

"Why, has she not talked with you about them?"

"She has not said a word to me."

"Oh, then I have been too hasty. Then excuse me from saying anything more about them; it is not my secret, but Irene's. I thought she had already told you. She has received two letters from some one she does not know, that is all," and, ashamed of his indiscretion, he looked away embarrassed.

"Perhaps she will tell you yet," he added. "If my father would only speak," he continued; "if he only would speak! But he will not."

"Oh, do not blame your father," said Adele; "a man like him will neither speak nor be silent without the most important reasons, reasons that demand our respect."

"He has reasons," said William, "and I can think what they are. He was once very attentive to Frau Schott, Irene's mother. She must have told him some facts that induced him to break off his friendship with her, and to refuse me so cruelly when I spoke to him of Irene. She told you of that?"

"Yes; and I have done what I could to comfort her and convince her that we must be resigned to what is unavoidable and unalterable."

"Unalterable?" said William, with a gloomy smile. "That would be too hard. I can assure you," he added, with a determined look "that neither Irene nor I look upon it in that way."

Adele was about to answer when they were interrupted by some gentlemen who came up to speak to her, and William withdrew.

Ferdinand, in the meantime, had exchanged greetings with his acquaintances and the few ladies with whom politeness required him to pass a few words. At length,

as he turned away from the last one, he saw Elsie near him, walking slowly through the room, accompanied by an old gentleman, profusely decorated.

"I assure your highness," said the old gentleman, "to make room for his villa, Kronhorst, like a Vandal, tore down an exceedingly picturesque ruin of an old castle that stood here on the bank and commanded the river. When I was a boy it had some very well preserved towers with roofs; I have often climbed up into them. It was the family-seat of an old family whose last representative lost his life in the Thirty Years' War; he did not fall in battle, but was murdered. He was stabbed by the hand of a woman. It is a very strange, tragic story. And now, is it not dreadful to destroy such a beautiful relic of feudal Christian architecture, to make way for a Baal's temple of sinful modern luxury?"

"Do you think, then, my dear count," answered the princess, "that life in those old castles and in the times when women had to defend themselves with knives, was any less sinful?"

"No," answered the count. "But the sins of that time were grander, wilder, more poetic. Let us take as an example the story I have just mentioned, the murder of the last of the House of Tratzberg. He was at a great banquet given by the officers of an imperial regiment, the night before they were to leave the city where they had been in winter quarters. He was stabbed there by a passionate girl, who could not be resigned to his leaving her. Then she drowned herself in the waters of some neighboring river or pond."

"Ah, and that story is true!" exclaimed Elsie, and in her astonishment she turned to Ferdinand, saying, "I beg of you, Herr von Schott, hear what Count Langendorf has told me."

Ferdinand had turned slightly pale as he heard himself called so suddenly and unexpectedly by the princess. He stepped up, and Count Langendorf repeated the story of the death of the last of the Tratzbergs. "There is no doubt that the story is true," he said, in conclusion. "It is mentioned in several old local histories, and I heard it from my grandfather when I was a child. The arms of the Tratzbergs appear very often on our ancestral roll."

"And what do you say to that?" said Elsie, turning again to Ferdinand; "isn't it very strange that we should come upon this dark and horrible deed again here?"

At this moment Count Langendorf was drawn away by a lady who begged him to give her his arm for a promenade through the rooms. Elsie also made a movement to go, and, by a slight motion of the head, gave Ferdinand to understand that she wanted him to accompany her. In the next room she sat down on a sofa standing somewhat apart beside a pyramid of exotic flowers, then said, smiling:—

"You would not honor me with a word the whole evening, Herr von Schott. Now the death of the last Tratzberg has drawn us together by force, and I think all resentment should be silenced at a grave, should it not? So take a seat here, and let us gossip a little."

"Gossip, princess? At a grave?"

"Oh, that wretched man, who, after all, only received what he deserved, cannot expect to keep us under restraint, although it is remarkable that we should have come upon his track here again, as if he were pursuing us."

"More correctly, as if we were pursuing him. I hope there is nothing prophetic for us in his story. Perhaps our guardian angels send us this old tradition of his death as a warning."

"As a warning against every passion, it is possible. We are both hot-headed, Herr von Schott, therefore take care; it would be bad for us both if you should enrage me so by acting unreasonably, as, for instance, you did recently, that I should first murder you, and then throw myself into the river."

She spoke in a jesting tone, but with a slight tremor in her voice.

"You are right, princess," answered Ferdinand, "it would be bad for us both; the more as we could so easily get on so peaceably together. Therefore, let us try this latter plan."

"Try? I think it would become two reasonable old people like us better to say, let us resolve it. A trial presupposes the possibility of failure. And I do not think we need to fear that. Neither of us, I think, could be reproached as lacking in strength of will or self-control."

"That may be. But it is a sad fact that we have only one-half ourselves in our own power. Would you like to have me give you my theory of it as well as I can? A man is like a planet that has two distinct motions; the one turns him around himself with all the force of his egotism; the other sends him in a course he does not himself understand, around some other object. But, after all, this does not express what I want to say. He is rather like a being half plant and half human, like Daphne, when, with her feet in the earth, she stretched her arms toward Heaven and prayed to Zeus. Man is half a plant, half a free, conscious being. This free, conscious being is controlled by his reason and his resolution. But the plant must be allowed to grow in its own way. Whatever it may grow into he has no power over it, no knowledge of it. He must be resigned to suffer this dark, mysterious growth, this plant-life, or unconscious part of his existence. He has as little power over it as has the beetle in the heart of a rose-bud over the development of the rose. When this part gains the ascendency —as sometimes happens—over the other part, the part controlled by reason, men call it passion; they have written many wise, beautiful, and moral things about the demon that carries them away at such times, from the earliest antiquity down to to-day. But, with all this, they have come no nearer to discovering the real nature of the demon or finding means to break his power."

"Oh, you make me dizzy with your confused talk: you seem to have grown so yourself, perhaps from watching these endless circles of the dance. Why do you distress me with your absurd theory? Do you think I should be afraid of your demon?"

"No, I do not think you are afraid of it, princess; but I am."

"Perhaps, then, it will help to quiet your apprehensions to see how calmly I look upon this mystical and, to me, not at all dangerous being."

"Perhaps. But can you always do that? Will you always be able to look coolly on this demon in the soul of a man, filling it with a morbid restlessness, compelling it to be forever buried with you, to trace every step of your life in the past—a demon that is an actual demon, a monomania, if you will, an insanity——"

The princess raised her eyes slowly and looked him full in the face.

"You are right in saying that it would be a monomania, an insanity—and who could be entirely composed in the presence of a lunatic? No; in that case I am afraid I should be seized with terror and should run away and leave the lunatic to himself and his lunacy."

"You would not rather try to cure him?"

"How could I do that?"

"Easily, I think—by confidence; by drawing him away from his researches into your past and his thoughts about your future, as you could do by really making the friend of him that he would like to be. To have common intellectual interests, as we had in Florence, no friend can be permanently satisfied with that; only common interests of the affections can bind men into real and permanent friendship, and such a community of interest is not conceivable without confidence regarding the past and the future."

It was a sharp, flashing glance that she sent into his face while he was speaking. Then she lowered her eyes and said:

"I am afraid I was not born to 'minister to a mind diseased.' I should certainly not fail in good-will and zeal and honest sympathy. But after having once made the trial —God knows how sincerely—to heal the sick, I lack the courage and perseverance to begin again, seeing what an utter failure my first attempt has been. You cannot certainly ask that. To struggle with a demon! Great God, how can a woman do that? To have a community of heart-interests with a lunatic! What an idea! No, no, Herr von Schott, nothing remains for me but to take to flight, and wait till reason returns of itself to the afflicted, and shows him what a fool he has been to waste his time searching into a woman's past, when there are so many things incomparably more worthy of a man's attention!"

She rose and withdrew. Ferdinand looked after her terrified. How angrily her voice had trembled at the last words! And so he had gained nothing he had hoped to gain; he had but deepened the gulf between them. His hope of gaining her confidence so that she would frankly tell him of her life was at last entirely destroyed. And her anger—was there not something in the coolness with which she had listened to him, something that told him he was really a fool and a lunatic with all his infamous suspicions? Would he not do well to hold to his own theory of the double nature of man, one-half being under the control of reason, the other governed by passion, and often the slave of demoniac fantasies, fixed notions from which it cannot free itself, and in which there is nothing real but the unspeakable wretchedness they bring? As Ferdinand said this to himself he was seized with despondency; he would have liked to escape, not alone from this suspicion against Elsie, but from himself, to flee afar off into the wide world, into nothingness. He felt that he was fast being driven to desperation; and how was it all to end? Was he at last to arrive at the truth, at certainty in his investigations? The very thought of those investigations filled him with disgust!

And yet the very next moment took him back to them. A gentleman stepped up to him and took the seat the princess had just left; as he looked up he met the sharp eyes of Groebler. It went to his heart like a dagger. Groebler seemed now like an accomplice in guilt, like an incarnate reproach, like a reflection of his conscience. Was it not shameful that, spurred on by his demon, he had gone so far as to let such a man into the secret, to use him as a bloodhound upon the track of the woman he loved? Poor Groebler had very little suspicion of any such thought. He began, cheerfully:

"Now, see how much a man may have to thank his dear wife for. Because my wife is from a good family, and has had a friendly reception from you and Fräulein von Schott, and the privilege of calling on the princess, a poor police-inspector gets an invitation to a party like this. You can imagine how I am flattered by it. To be a guest in these rooms! It is like a dream, a lovely dream! Do you know what I would like?"

"Well, what would you like, Groebler?"

"You will laugh at me. I would like it if I could place all these people, these finely dressed, brilliant, noble people with all the claims on our unbounded reverence expressed by their diamonds, their silken robes, their stars and uniforms—I would like, by some diabolical sorcery, to place them in the various cells and dungeon holes which I have hitherto provided with inmates by my official efforts. And, on the other hand, I would like to bring all those poor devils from their cells and place them in these brilliant parlors and at those tables in the dining-rooms, and keep them here till morning; then I would have the rascals back behind their bars and these honest people in their warm, comfortable beds."

"What a wonderful policeman's imagination you have, Herr Groebler! What satisfaction could you take in that?"

"What satisfaction? Why, you see, one can't help having some heart, and when I have nothing better to think of, my mind turns to my foster-children, who owe to me their reception into a moral, domestic circle. To be sure, they are in reality the foster-children of the state; but I cannot get rid of the feeling after I have secured their adoption, that they are my *protegés* or wards. Now I think my foster-children would be very much amused here. Do you not think so, Herr von Schott?"

"Undoubtedly. It would be excellent amusement for them."

"Yes, and it would have such a good influence on them to let them see how pleasant life is for honest people—people that have never come under the ban of the law —what a reward 'unbankrupt morality' has even on earth."

"But for that purpose you would not need to shut us all up in your cells for the night, your landrath most disrespectfully included."

"True, I should not need to. But who can resist his own demoniac impulses?

They are stronger than we. That is another fancy of mine. I was standing up there near a large group of gentlemen. Scarcely a word was spoken that did not make me think, 'How healthy a short sojourn in a cell would be for you!' You may call it pure insanity, but I could not help thinking it. Two of them were talking about eating, and one of them said he could not eat oysters without chablis. 'To the penitentiary with you,' thought I. The other couldn't endure lobster-salad without sliced tomatoes, 'To the cell for a night or two,' I thought. Do you see that stout party there, with a blue wart on his cheek? He said his interest in Perlhuhn & Co. brings him in thirteen hundred thalers every month. Every month! 'Into the cell,' I thought; 'to the cell with you!' And these women with the fabulous chignons, that grew on other people's heads, and with these puffed-out air-bags behind; don't you think a little solitude in a dark hole would be good for them?"

Ferdinand smiled.

"You express, a little roughly and harshly for such a company as this, a thought something like Göethe's in the lines, 'Who never ate his bread with tears.' It is, then, from pure philanthropy that you want to put all these people where they can see the serious side of life. But how do you know how many of these noble, finely-dressed, haughty people have already learned to know the 'heavenly powers?' In such society, at a party like this, every one is masquerading."

"All but us two," said Herr Groebler, nodding; "us and Herr Kronhorst; I was looking at him when he was talking with your sister, observing him closely, and he looked so frank and so sincerely benevolent, it did me good to see him. And as for you, Herr von Schott, you look so fearfully dismal—if it is not disrespectful to say it—that no one would say you were masquerading in a festal face. Perhaps I can cheer you up a little. I have news for you."

"Ah! from Pomerania?"

"From Pomerania. The people there answered my questions very willingly. Philip Bonsart is not now in America; he has been in England for some time, at New-castle-upon-Tyne, where he has an agency for a firm in New York. His address is Dean street, Queen's Place, No. 13. He is still unmarried, they write me."

Ferdinand looked at him almost in amazement. It seemed to him as if something entirely strange to him had been spoken of, something he had been entirely unprepared for. Then he dropped his eyes to the floor, as if to collect himself and reflect upon his answer. At length he said, slowly and absently, "In England; that would be much nearer than we thought. Very well, Groebler; let me reflect what is best to be done now; we will speak of it again—see what a commotion there is there in the other parlor—we will speak of it again; 'Dean street, Queen's Place, No. 13,' you said?"

"That is the exact address," answered Groebler, looking at the movement in the next room to which Ferdinand's attention had been attracted. The various groups there were crowding together.

To explain this movement, we must go back to Prince Gottlieb Anton. He had been at a whist-table in the room back of the dancing-hall, and at the last had been playing with Count Langendorf and two other gentlemen. After the last rubber was played, he rose.

"I am afraid," said he, wiping his forehead, "that I have taken too much of that excellent punch, à la Romaine. I feel very warm and distressed for breath. Let us go into the open air for a little while, count."

"We can get it," answered Count Langendorf, "by stepping into the conservatory. The air is purer, and it is very quiet; the music can scarcely be heard there. Herr Kronhorst has it arranged beautifully; there are some lovely places for a tête-à-tête in among the leaves."

He stepped forward to the high glass door, one side of which stood open, and led into the large conservatory, dimly lighted by lamps above; there was no one in it, and it seemed like a quiet world by itself, a tropical palm-land apart from the noise and excitement of the festival.

The prince followed and the count passed on, talking, to the end of the conservatory, where there was a light table, holding a smoking-set and surrounded with Japanese chairs, low stools, and rockers.

The gentlemen seated themselves and each lighted a *cigarette*. Count Langendorf talked on, while the prince, contrary to his custom, was silent. At length, throwing away his *cigarette* and wiping his forehead again, he said:

."Don't you feel a draught here? The door there cannot be closed."

He pointed to a glass door that led from the conservatory to the great balcony in front of it. At the same time he rose and, approaching the door, said:

"I was right; it is ajar. One of the guests must have gone out before us to get a breath of fresh air. Let us follow and take a turn or two on the balcony; it will do me good. Come."

They stepped out upon the broad balcony, with its parti-colored floor, which was flooded with the light from the windows and the lamps at the door. The prince went straight across it toward the outer balustrade.

"The air blows over cursed sharp from the river, your highness," said Count Langendorf; "you are so heated, are you not afraid of getting a rheumatism, or something worse?"

"On the contrary, it does me good; I feel better."

"But we are thinly dressed, and I can't say that this cold night air is agreeable to me. I will go, your highness; and if you will remain, I will send a servant with an overcoat. Allow me to do that."

"Very well; do so, my dear count."

Count Langendorf fled from a possible cold back into the conservatory, while the prince, who must still have been feeling uncomfortable, and whose steps were somewhat uncertain, as if from dizziness, walked on; having come to the balustrade he walked along beside it. Looking over he could see a dark balcony directly below the one where he stood; this lower one reached nearly to the bank of the river, whose steel-blue water shimmered through the night, receiving only the light that fell upon it from the villa; on the other side, the slender stems of the willows could be seen lightly rocking in the night wind.

When Prince Gottlieb reached the end of the balustrade, he stood at a rounded projection of the balcony, to the left of which a flight of steps led down to the lower balcony. Here he thought he heard a low conversation just under where he stood; supporting himself on the balustrade and looking over the edge, he saw two persons standing at the foot of these stairs, or, rather, one, the form of a young man, was standing, the other, a woman wrapped in a mantle or shawl, was sitting on the lowest step. They could not have heard the prince, for they were absorbed in their conversation, and the prince's step, usually firm and heavy, was now weary and lingering; they continued speaking in an animated and excited manner. Prince Gottlieb bent down over the balustrade as if he recognized the voices, and wanted to hear what they were saying.

Whether he succeeded, and what he heard affected him so seriously, or whether it was a mere accident that the illness he had felt before, and the consequences of the change of temperature to which he had exposed himself now made themselves felt; at all events, when Count Langendorf returned after a while in his overcoat, and accompanied by a servant carrying one for the prince, he at first saw nothing of him; after looking around here and there, his eye happened to fall on the inner curve of the projection, and, to his terror, he saw the prince lying upon the floor. He sprang to him and tried to raise him and to get some explanation of what had happened; but the prince made not the slightest sound; he seemed to be paralyzed in every limb and entirely unconscious. They succeeded, however, in raising him, and the servant knelt and supported him while Count Langendorf hurried back into the rooms, and, meeting Herr Kronhorst, whispered to him what had happened, and then looked among the guests for a physician. He soon found one and took him to the balcony where the prince still lay unconscious and in death-like rigidity in the arms of the servant, who was now assisted by Herr Kronhorst. The four

men carried him back to the conservatory and laid him down on a sofa. The physician took off his cravat, and after feeling his pulse for a long time, said:—

"A fainting-fit, only a fainting-fit I hope. Tell the princess. Nothing can be done at present. It will be best to take him home, and there, perhaps, bleed him. The first thing to be done is to order his carriage; he can be carried from here out over the balcony, so that the company need know nothing of it, and the party need not be disturbed."

"It is most sadly disturbed for me, at least," said Herr Kronhorst. "If this were a mere fainting-fit, he would already have recovered. It is a stroke of apoplexy, doctor."

The doctor shrugged his shoulders and bent down quickly to place his ear to the patient's mouth. The prince had turned his eyes, which had before been fixed, and moved his lips as if to speak; but he could make no intelligible sound. Kronhorst hastened to tell the princess what had happened and order the carriage, as well as to send servants to the balcony in front of the conservatory to carry the prince to his carriage. He was as quiet as possible, but the attention of the company was attracted when he gave his arm to the princess, whose features plainly indicated strong emotion, led her into the conservatory, and closed the door behind them. This had caused the assembling of the excited groups mentioned. In a short time Herr Kronhorst returned and relieved the general suspense by announcing that the prince had fallen in a fainting-fit, which would probably be attended by no serious consequences, and that he had just been driven back to Achsenstein with his wife and the physician, who had insisted on accompanying them as a matter of precaution.

This satisfied the company. The players returned to their games, the young people to the dance, and the others to conversation, which was turned into a general exhaustive discussion of all kinds of fainting-fits and like attacks; but the dreadful word apoplexy was carefully avoided as if by a general tacit understanding, as if no one would be thought so wanting in tact as to utter the word in such a glad and brilliant assembly.

CHAPTER XIX.

STROKE UPON STROKE.

And yet no one who thought for a moment of the stout form of the prince, of his short neck, and his face flushed with luxurious living, could doubt that he would be liable to a stroke of apoplexy; and it was already perfectly clear to the physician as he sat beside the prince in the carriage and supported his paralyzed limbs, that such a stroke had actually fallen upon him, and that it was one of most alarming severity.

And, in truth, the prince rallied very slowly after arriving at Achsenstein, where everything possible was done for him. One side of his body was paralyzed. His tongue stammered, and the functions of the brain were so disturbed that, in trying to call for what he wanted, he made the strangest mistakes. Elsie did not leave him; she was the only one that could guess what he meant, when, with painful stammerings and impatient gestures, he called for things he could not possibly mean, asking for a horse or money when he wanted his handkerchief or his lemonade glass. It was a dreadfully exhausting task, the care of him, and Elsie slept scarcely two hours a night. And yet she kept her place firmly; nothing seemed too great for her persevering devotion, and no injunction of the physician to spare herself more, no offer of Matilda or Irene to relieve her for a night, could induce her to leave the post to which her sense of duty assigned her.

Only at times she stepped with a deep sigh to the window, and, clasping her hands convulsively, looked out in tears at the wintry valley below, at the bare trees, and the smoky and sooty city, with its roofs and gables and chimneys, and its dusky minster, no longer softened by the green veil of summer foliage. Perhaps, too, her eyes may have sought the cathedral, and rested upon the long building near it, the house of the man who might have been her friend and some comfort to her now, if he had only understood her, if he only would have understood her. Perhaps she thought angrily and bitterly, and yet with the longing of a woman who feels, in spite of all that surrounds her and all offers of help, that she is alone, forsaken; and, in spite of all the assurances of the physician, threatened by a dark experience, perhaps she thought longingly of this firm, ready, and inflexible man, now when she felt the need of a firm nature on which to rely; and then again angrily that in his mad passion he had made himself more an enemy than a friend and helper; because, notwithstanding the calm reason she had tried to make him listen to, notwithstanding the kindness and sympathy she had shown for his misfortune, and the effort she had made to secure his future happiness, was now threatening to pry into her past life, with a selfish desire to humiliate her, and gain an ascendency over her; and to this Princess Elsie was the last to yield.

For his words had indicated nothing else than this. She could not see that they were prompted by quite other feelings than a selfish desire for triumph; she could not understand the meaning that trembled through them—that he acknowedged himself vanquished, and was begging only for peace, if only she would show him with one word of confidence that she understood him. But she had not understood; she had turned away in anger, and was suffering from the unspeakable bitterness with which her interpretation of his words had filled her.

As the prince recovered, regaining the control of his limbs on one side, and being able to sit up and even to walk across the room when supported by a strong arm, it was surprising how little gratitude he seemed to feel for Elsie's faithful care. His eyes often rested upon her with an unmistakable expression of resentment; when she spoke to him, he would often stare at her and then turn away without trying to answer, as if he saw a perfect stranger before him, and could not understand what right she had to address him. This continued several days, until one day when Irene was admitted to the room; formerly her presence had always been agreeable to him; he liked to talk and jest with her, and had never been sparing of his words when he thought her in need of information on any subject whatever; and he had often made her presents. He had never seemed to like the society of Irene's mother; his princely sensibilities were probably pained by such a reminder of the plebeian connections of his wife. But now he stared at Irene with a peculiarly hostile expression. He would not answer when she spoke to him, but followed all her movements with the same angry glance. She soon withdrew, and the prince said to Elsie, in a surly tone:

"You are very careless in regard to that child. Guard her better!"

"Guard her?" cried Elsie, in surprise. "From what? From whom?"

"From childish love affairs, secret meetings, and—but what does it matter to me? It is your business."

"Oh, I beg of you, go on, Gottlieb; what were you going to say?" said Elsie, anxiously.

The prince, who had spoken the words "your business" with a peculiar sharp emphasis, shook his head and laid it back on his chair, frowning and closing his eyes.

Elsie looked at him in anxiety. She had no key to his words. She could not know that a moment before the stroke he had been leaning from the balcony and listening to part of a conversation by two voices familiar to him, a conversation which no one could suspect of any connection, even the most remote, with what had happened to him there. The only explanation Elsie could think of was that Irene had had a secret interview with William Kronhorst, and that the prince had found it out by some strange chance; and she resolved to have Matilda send Irene at once to some convent school beyond the border.

In carrying out this plan, she met with as little opposition from Irene herself as she had from Matilda when it was first proposed. Having spoken again with Matilda and received her permission to talk with Irene, Elsie sent for the girl and explained to her that it seemed necessary, in order to complete her education, to take her away from her somewhat planless and irregular life in E. and at Achsenstein, and send her to the Convent of the Sisters of the Sacred Heart at B., in Belgium, that they might fill the gaps in her knowledge of necessary subjects.

Although Irene could not have been prepared for this disclosure, she took it with the greatest calmness. Elsie's representations of the advantages of the school, which was composed wholly of boarding pupils from the higher classes of society, seemed entirely unnecessary to reconcile her to the step which was to separate her for a whole year from her mother and the princess. This served greatly to quiet their apprehensions about the strength of Irene's attachment to William; it could not possibly be very strong when she consented so willingly to be sent away for such a length of time.

When the matter was arranged, and the day for Irene's departure fixed, (her mother was to accompany her,) Elsie hoped the prince would explain the reasons for the warning he had given her.

"You warned me in regard to Irene," she said to him, "and her mother has, therefore, concluded to send her to a convent in B. She will start day after to-morrow."

The prince looked at her with the stare now become habitual to him, without answering.

"May she come to-morrow and bid you good-bye?"

"I hope you will spare me that!" he answered, frowning.

"As you please. I thought you would desire it, as you liked Irene. It seems from what you said to me a short time ago about childish love affairs and secret meetings, that you must have found out something of which I do not know, and that must have entirely destroyed your affection and favor toward Irene. Will you not tell me," she added, as he did not answer, "what you have learned about Irene?"

He measured her with the hard, hostile stare, now almost his only look for her. At length he said, in a sarcastic tone, and with a malicious quiver about his lips:—

"No, my gracious lady, I will not tell you. It is best for me, a sick, broken-down man, to say nothing about it; and it certainly is best for you. So do not disturb me with your questions. And as for Irene, I hope never to see her again."

He closed his eyes and rested his head on the back of the chair, bringing into full relief his face, now uglier than ever, with its pale, sunken features.

Elsie looked down at him, pale and anxious. Every word had gone to her heart like a dagger. What did he mean? Could some fiendish accident have let him into secrets she would rather have had discovered by any one else in the world? She was filled with anguish at the thought that it might be so, that it must be so; for otherwise his words would have had no meaning whatever.

And what to do? To leave him so, with only half an understanding of the matter, which was all he could have gained? Or to disturb and torment him now in his illness with a full confession, with explanations of matters he would not comprehend—was it not wholly out of the question? No, she could not do it; she had not the courage. She went to the window and stood there in her helplessness, looking down upon the dark city; she laid her hot forehead against the cold glass, and sought with her eyes the roof under which lived the man who might have helped her if he had only been willing to be her friend; who might have spoken for her to throw light upon the prince's tormenting thoughts, and set right his distorted ideas. But he would not give her what she wanted, friendship, or help, or support; nothing but his stupid, idiotic passion, which filled her with anger, because it was only a selfish desire to humiliate and triumph over her. To be triumphed over by this man who was prying into her past life for that purpose, as he had insolently told her—the thought filled her eyes with angry tears as she looked from the night within to the darkening night without.

With a blind, vain desire for revenge she threw upon Ferdinand the blame of the prince's mental suffering, as if he alone were responsible for the suffering he might have healed.

It was the day before the one on which Irene was to start with her mother. She had made her preparations with a sort of defiant composure which apparently covered a peculiar excitement, while she did not betray the slightest objection to being sent so far away. But when she came to take leave of Adele, she burst into tears as she threw her arms around her most trusted friend. Adele drew her down upon the sofa, and said:

"What shall I do in my gloomy old house with my gloomy-faced brother, when I cannot now and then have a glimpse of your rosy face, Irene? You do not know how painful the parting is to me."

"Oh, I know, I know!" exclaimed Irene, clinging to her. "More painful than it is for my mother, who will now be all alone, or for my Aunt Elsie, who can send me away so easily that it nearly breaks my heart!" and she began to sob violently.

"You must not blame them, Irene, or think there is any want of love in it. They are making a sacrifice for what their reason tells them is right, and why should they let you see how hard it is for them, and so make it a great deal harder for you to go?"

Irene pouted sulkily.

"A sacrifice—their reason!" she said. "What they want is to separate me from William. And you call that reason, Adele? I tell you it is unreason. For whatever they may do, William and I will not be separated!"

"Why, Irene, you frighten me by your violence; and it is the best proof that it is time, if not to put an ocean, at least, a good stretch of railroad between you, and see whether you will not think differently when you return after a year; that is such a long time at your age."

"If I return I shall think just as I do to-day, dear Adele; you may be assured of that. If I return——"

"'If'—what is the meaning of that emphatic if?"

Irene threw back her head haughtily.

"Say, my wrathful little girl, what do you mean by that?"

"Nothing," answered Irene, avoiding Adele's eyes; "only that since they send me away so cheerfully, I should not wonder if they should never want me back."

"Oh, you are beside yourself, Irene. You are getting very unjust——"

"I am not unjust, dear Adele, believe me; if I could only tell you all you would say yourself that—that—I am very unfortunate!"

At these words she began to sob violently, and could not control herself. Adele put her arm around her and tried to comfort her.

"And what is it that you cannot tell me, my dear child?" she said, at last, as Irene began to grow more quiet.

"O much, very much; if I were not strictly forbidden to tell it to any one on earth; and so I must bear it alone, all alone!"

"All alone? And must not William know either?"

Irene looked slyly at the floor. "Nor he either," she said, with a sigh.

"Are you telling me the whole truth, now, Irene?" Adele asked. "William Kronhorst spoke to me of some mysterious letters that you had received——"

"He spoke to you of them?"

"He spoke of them; but you must not blame him. He supposed you had already taken me into your confidence."

"Heavens! he could not have thought so; he knew how strictly I was forbidden to tell, and I told him only a little of what was in the letters, only as much as I had to, so that he might be prepared, if, some fine day—but I cannot say any more, I really cannot."

"And you shall not," interrupted Adele. "I will not let you tell me any more. It would be dishonorable in me to urge you to tell me what you think it your duty to be silent about."

Irene embraced her friend, and, laying her forehead on Adele's shoulder, sobbed again. After a little, she sprang up, embraced Adele again in an excited way, kiss-ed her cheeks and her hands, and hurried away.

When Adele told her brother of Irene's visit and her excited manner, Ferdinand was greatly surprised.

"You see," he said, "that I am not chasing a phantom of my own brain. What do those letters mean? From whom do they come? Is it not reasonable to suppose that they come from some one who has claims upon Irene, and who is perhaps now preparing to assert his claim? And why are they sending Irene away? What is that for? To keep her in safety from this man?"

Adele shook her head.

"Why are they sending her away? That, it seems to me, is plain enough. To separate her from William Kronhorst."

"And why are they so anxious to separate her from William Kronhorst? Why is William's father, as you told me yourself after your conversation with him, why is he so firmly determined to oppose their marriage?"

"That I do not know," answered Adele. "And," she added, with a sigh and a sorrowful glance at Ferdinand's face, "it is not our business to search into it and brood over it."

Ferdinand was silent. But, deeply affected by Adele's information, and plunged into the depths of passionate torment by this new confirmation of his suspicion, he said to himself, at length, in desperation:

"But I must clear up this mystery; I must have light upon it, and peace!"

Peace, as if he could have secured it so!

He resolved to go to England himself. He would himself hunt up Philip Bonsart; he would talk with him and compel him to speak. He went zealously to work to prepare for his journey. But two weeks passed before he could get his business so arranged as to ask for leave of absence; it was several days more before he received it, so that some three weeks had elapsed since Irene's departure, and her mother had been at home again for some time, before he was ready to start. No one but Groebler knew the real object of his journey.

CHAPTER XX.

THE TELEGRAM.

The princess had heard of Ferdinand's journey, but there had been nothing to cause her to attach any special significance to it. Some days after his departure, she was walking alone in the afternoon through the park that surrounded the castle. The castle was on a spur about half-way up a mountain; the park rose behind it, and lost itself above in the wood that covered the summit of the height. Elsie walked with a leisurely but elastic step through the broad, well-kept gravel walks, which sloped upward, now gradually, and now with a steep ascent. The day was mild; the soft air seemed a prophecy of the coming spring. The willows already began to show their fragrant catkins, and the hazel-bushes their red buds, the first harbingers of advancing vegetation. Elsie, indeed, took little notice of them. The serious expression which had long since become habitual to her face had to-day passed into one of deep sadness. The evening previous the prince had had something like another stroke; he had been taken with dizziness, and had fallen unconscious from his seat to the floor, before any one could reach him. Not until morning had he recovered enough to speak coherently. Elsie had insisted on watching with him through the night. In the morning she had a talk with the physician, who had admitted that there was great danger to be feared from a repetition of these attacks. At this moment a notary was with the prince, who had called for one to make some alterations in his will, as he intimated.

Alterations in his will! It was a threatening word to Elsie. After the strangely cold and almost hostile manner he had recently assumed toward her, Elsie could not but fear that this boded little good to her. A bitter, scornful smile curved her lips as she thought that he would perhaps strike her out of his will entirely, that she would some time be a poor widow, burdened with a high-sounding title, with the curse of ludicrousness attaching to a high, pretentious position connected with extreme poverty.

It was true that, before her marriage, she had received assurances which were brilliant enough; when they had urged her to accept the prince's offer, they had explained the whole matter at length, and had dwelt with emphasis on its advantages; but was it really unalterable? If the prince would, could he not set the whole arrangement aside and take back what had been promised to her, leaving her only a small annual allowance, or even nothing at all, or make her dependent upon the bounty of her step-son, who would inherit his father's princely title and dignity? She did not doubt that the prince could do so if he would; she did not doubt that an able lawyer could arrange it all as he might desire—women have such wonderful ideas of the elasticity of the law and of written contracts! Occupied with this idea, she told herself bitterly that the reward of what she had done would be nothing but poverty and desertion; she said it with a sort of scornful triumph over herself, as if she had deserved exactly that, as if it were the most righteous punishment that could have been visited on an unworthy woman; as if it were the just vengeance of Heaven.

And she would do nothing to avert it; she would not waste a word on the affair; she would talk with no one about it. Indeed, she had no one with whom she could talk, no friend in the world, and she thought again, with anger and resentment, of the one whom, she believed, could have helped her. But now she would rather be destroyed than turn to any one for help; she would be destroyed; it would be a punishment to him; he should reproach himself that it had been through his fault, through the folly and obstinacy that had separated them.

And yet this anger and resentment were but the foam thrown up by quite other feelings—a feeling of utter helplessness, that seemed to banish her thoughts to him and keep them there. Since the day he had so angrily refused Irene's hand, she had in her inmost soul felt confidence in him; she had begun to understand something of the depth of his nature; and if he had met her in her present mood, exhausted by the sleepless night and tormented by the thought of her future, she might have had no words for him but a wild cry for help.

She had gone some distance upward, and had come to where the park passed into the fir-wood that covered the upper part of the mountain, where the gravel walks of the park ran into narrow paths, leading among the high firs, when she came suddenly, at a turn in the path, upon a boy, lying a little way aside from the path, upon the mossy ground under a tall pine tree, and busily engaged with something upon the ground. Elsie approached him; the boy looked up into her face in surprise. Whether struck with astonishment at the beauty of this unexpected face, or embarrassed at being caught in an unlawful occupation, the boy was evidently disconcerted; he opened his mouth, as if to speak, but could not bring out a word. Elsie, too, looked fixedly and silently at him; the dark head and the flashing eyes had a peculiar attraction for her; there seemed to be something familiar, something she had already known well somewhere, in this face, which gradually took on an expression of bold defiance. At length she said:

"What are you doing here, my boy?"

"I am catching squirrels," he answered, and raised a wire trap to show her; he had fastened it to a stake which he had driven into the ground, and placed it just over the root of a pine tree, so that an animal running from the root up the tree would be caught in it.

"And do you dare do that—set traps for these poor little creatures in a stranger's park?".

"Certainly," answered the boy. "Squirrels are a nuisance; they eat the young buds from the trees. It is allowed to catch them anywhere."

"Is it? And are there squirrels here now? I thought they stayed in their nests during the winter."

The boy shook his head.

"They ought to stay in their nests. But, you see, squirrels are the most careless of all animals. They lay up a store of winter food in autumn, but never enough; so that by February it is all eaten up, and then they have to leave their nests, and run about in the pine woods to pick up pine-cones and get the seeds."

"You are a great naturalist!" said Elsie, smiling.

"Oh, I know all about the forest and the creatures that live in it. I catch one or more squirrels every day. I have five of them now at home, alive."

"Poor unfortunates! You ought to give them their freedom."

The boy looked at her, smiled, and shook his head.

"I shall sell them," he said. "Will you buy one? I gave one to Fräulein Adele, and was going to give her another, but she didn't want any more. It is very pretty—so large! Will you buy it?"

"No, my boy. But who is Fräulein Adele? Fräulein von Schott?"

"Yes, the landrath's sister, Fräulein von Schott."

"Ah! and you know her?"

The boy nodded.

"And what is your name? You have not been brought up in this part of the country —you speak another dialect; more as at my home," she added, to herself.

"I do not belong here. I came from a long way off. I had to travel a whole day to get here, first on foot and then on the railroad. I was never on the railroad before. How it rattles and flies along! Have you ever been on the railroad? Oh, of course. How pretty you are! Prettier than Fräulein Adele. But she is pretty, too. Do you know her? She has been on the railroad often. And the landrath, he goes often, too. He went away just a few days ago; he hasn't come back yet, and he will not be here for several days. So much the better; I can stay here in the woods and catch squirrels; he would not let me; he makes me write in his office. It's so hard and so stupid to be tormented with that. And it's most all good for nothing—what I write. I write it wrong, and then the secretary throws it in the waste-basket. So what's the use of my being plagued with it?"

While the boy had been talkin Elsie had been looking intently into his face, which had grown more animated. Evidently he was so impressed by her beauty and the encouragement she gave him to talk freely, that he had lost the sullen and defiant manner he usually showed to strangers.

"You were going to tell me who you are and where you came from," she interrupted.

"Didn't I tell you? I came from Vellinghaus, and my name is Carl Dransfeld. My father was the forester in Vellinghaus forest, and as he died, and my mother couldn't take care of us all, Herr von Schott had me come here and is going to take care of me. Fräulein Adele takes care of me, too; she is very, very good, Fräulein Adele. Do you know her?"

"Then you are a son of Emil Drausfeld," said Elsie, surprised, and looking in his features for a resemblance to his father, of whom she had been vaguely reminded on first looking at the boy, without being able to define the recollection. "My poor boy!" she continued. "How noble it was in the landrath to relieve your mother of the care of you!"

Carl looked up at her with something of his usual defiant expression. He seemed not entirely to agree with the praise of the landrath, who kept him a prisoner at the writing-desk. He shook his head and answered:

"Oh, he knows what he is about! He did not come only for friendship to my father, as my mother imagines—that time when he came riding through the forest in the fog and snow, and my father had just died——"

"And why should he not? Your father was a good, brave man—you must always honor his memory—and he certainly was deserving that an old friend should make a journey even through snow and fog to see him once more——"

"Then did you know my father?" interrupted Carl.

"Yes, I knew him well, and used to see him often, though it was many, many years ago."

"Well, then I will tell you why Herr von Schott came that day when the weather was so bad and so cold, and we were all so sad. Shall I tell you? I have told no one else.

But, because you knew my father, and because I would like some advice—will you give me some advice?"

During the conversation Carl had seated himself on the root of the tree to which his squirrel trap was fastened. He looked up with a peculiarly wary and searching glance at Elsie, who was standing with one foot on the root and her hands resting on the handle of her parasol, looking down at him with an expression of intense interest in all his talk.

"Give you advice? Certainly, with pleasure; and I would gladly give you something more than that, something for your mother and your brothers and sisters. But tell me first what you were going to say."

"Will you never, never tell the landrath, truly? Will you promise me that?"

"I will promise it."

"Then make a cross on my hand," he said, extending his palm.

Elsie made the symbol, which she remembered had been considered in her childish plays as setting the seal of sacred obligation to a promise.

"Then I will tell you why the landrath came away out there to our house. He came for some letters. He stormily demanded some letters from my mother."

"Letters? What letters?"

"Letters my father had received from America, and others that he said were written in a lady's hand."

"Ah!" cried Elsie, in terror, "and the letters were there, and he received them?"

"They were there, but he did not receive them. My mother was going to give them to him, right away, for nothing. She did not know where they were, but she told him he might look in my father's room, in the writing-desk, and see whether he could find them. Wasn't that foolish to give them up so? When he was so anxious and excited about them, and had taken such a long journey through the snow to get them, how much they must have been worth to him! Must they not be very, very valuable? And wasn't it foolish in my mother to give them up so, for nothing?"

"Go on, go on," said Elsie, in suspense. "Then he did not find them?"

"No. I could not talk with my mother

about it, she was too sorrowful; it was all the same to her, now my father was dead. So I took the letters and kept them. While Herr von Schott was searching in my father's room, I ran into the alcove; they were there. I knew my father kept some letters locked up in the closet near his bed. I hurried and took the key from his pocket and got the letters, and carried them up stairs and hid them in my straw bed under my pillow. Then I took the keys to Herr von Schott, and thought, now you may look!"

Elsie took a long breath. .

"And where are they, where are those letters?" she cried, in desperation at the thought that Emil Dransfeld had not at once burned her letters to him, as she had so expressly begged him to do, but had saved them—she had believed so firmly in this man's loyalty, and he, too, had deceived her !

"Where are they?" answered Carl. "They are safe. I have them. I kept them from everybody and brought them with me here. I thought I would tell Herr von Schott that I had them, and then I could find out what they were worth to him, and what he would pay us, pay my mother for them—my mother is so poor—oughtn't he to pay for them—wasn't that right—we are so poor?"

"And then? Go on!" said Elsie, eagerly.

"And then, when I was here, I did not know how to begin. I wanted to speak to Fräulein Adele, but she would have told her brother right off, and instead of giving me money for the letters, he would have taken them away from me; perhaps he would have punished me for taking them and keeping them hidden so long from him. Don't you think he might be very angry if he should hear of it now? I am afraid so; I am afraid of him. And so I don't know what to do. Give me your advice, will you?"

"Certainly I will, Carl. You must not give him the letters; no, never, for Heaven's sake ! They are letters that were not written for him, but to your dead father, to him alone. It was wrong in your father not to burn them. But it would be worse, very

much worse, in you to sell them, and so betray their contents for money, to the very last people who ought to know them. Do you understand?"

Carl took his eyes from her face and fastened them upon the ground.

"But," he said, half aloud, "no one would give me money for old letters unless he had some interest in knowing what was in them."

"Money !" exclaimed Elsie. "You are detestable ! Would you be dishonorable for money ? How can such a child be so greedy for money ?"

"You can do nothing without money, buy nothing, go nowhere you would like to."

"And where would you like to go if you had money ?"

"I would like to go to the sea-shore and go on a ship."

"Ah ! you would ?"

Carl was silent for a while, keeping his eyes on her face with a dissatisfied look.

"Yes," he said, "I would like it. But I would give most of the money to my mother; she has so little; and it makes her so unhappy; she has so little for my brothers and sisters; often they have no shoes to put on to go to church on Sundays," and the boy broke into a sudden fit of weeping.

Elsie laid her hand on his shoulder.

"You are a good boy, Carl; I see that you are. I know you will be honest. You will bring me the letters and I will burn them. You will bring them to me, not for money, for that would be a contemptible trade—as you must see yourself—unworthy of you and of me. But I will reward you for acting honorably. I will give you something—a nice watch, and then we will both have a treaty together. Run home now and bring me the letters at once; come with them to the castle down there. Come right in; I will tell the porter to watch for you and bring you at once to me. And then we will sit down together, and you shall write a few lines to your mother and tell her that you have found a friend of your father's, who has given you a present for her; and I will put one hundred thalers in the letter and we will send it to your mother. Would you like that?"

Carl raised his tearful eyes with an indescribable look of gratitude.

"Will you really do that? One hundred thalers? Heavens, how good you are! Will you do it? I will bring you the letters—right away! I will bring them to the castle!"

He had already sprung up and was about to hurry away. Then, half turning back, he asked her:

"Are you the princess? I believe you are the princess. And you will give me a watch?"

"I am the princess. Now hurry. *Auf Wiedersehen!*"

He sprang away, down the mountain, taking a straight course through the trees and thickets, without troubling himself about the park-paths. In a few moments he had disappeared.

Elsie stood and looked after him. But her thoughts did not follow him; they were fixed on the crushing fact, that her secret was suspected, unravelled, discovered, that Ferdinand had discovered it, that he was not contented with knowing it, but was seeking for proofs of it, proofs to destroy her. To destroy her! That, indeed, he would be obliged to do if he were to regain his rights—his sacred, unquestionable rights, which she had most wickedly and recklessly invaded, against which she had committed a crime that cried to Heaven for vengeance! Why should he not destroy her? Who in the world could expect him to spare her? What was it to him if she were destroyed?

And yet, it seemed to her as if she had suddenly trodden upon a serpent. As if a horrible treason were hissing in her face. Yes, it was horrible! He had talked to her of his love! And all the time he was searching behind her back for means to destroy her. He had assumed the *rôle* of a passionate lover while he had really been playing the part of a spy. For his rights! For the sake of his inheritance! He had lied and played the hypocrite to ensnare her, to draw a confession from her! And all this to get his money—his wretched,

miserable, devilish money! Or was he not lying when he professed to love her? Had he been moved by that only in searching after her secret, in hunting the proofs, the means to her destruction? Had it driven him to adopt blindly any measures, even the most ignoble, to gain power over her?

Elsie's head swam, and her heart was filled with wild tumult. She was too excited to reflect as to who or what could have betrayed her secret to him—how he could have come upon the track of the letters she had written years ago to Emil Dransfeld. She did not ask herself that. She thought only of the terrible revelation of what she called Ferdinand's treachery and unfathomable business, and to which she felt herself to be a sacrifice. And that just at this time when her feelings had begun to change, when her thoughts had turned to him so constantly as the one able to help her. She thought of nothing else, and felt only the raging anger and contempt which tossed in her heart like foaming waves, over a horrible sense of utter helplessness.

Her steps tottered and trembled as she descended the mountain and approached the castle. She was incapable of considering calmly what was to be done against such an enemy; she could only say, "Oh, he has the right. And I am justly served. Why should not a deceiver be deceived? Why not pretend love to outwit, ensnare, and destroy her? Why am I too good to be treated so? What does a woman that has thrown herself away deserve but to be punished and destroyed?"

And yet it seemed to her that the heavens must grow dark and day turn to night at the revelation that he, even he, could play such a part!

So she at last arrived home. It was already deep twilight in the castle. They told her the lawyer was still with the prince. The maid-of-honor came and expressed her anxiety that this long interview might seriously excite and injure the prince. She did not listen. She left it to the young lady to go herself and look after him. Then she sent a servant to the city after her sister. She wanted to see her that evening.

Then the porter, with whom she had

spoken as she returned, came in, bringing Carl. The boy laid his cap on the carpet near the door, and drew a little packet of yellow letters from the breast pocket of his jacket.

"There are the letters;" he said.

She untied the cord that held them together and took them to the fireplace. By the light of the glowing coals she looked them over. There were not many of them, perhaps eight or ten, not more than a dozen at the most. They were short, too, most of them covering only the first page of the sheet. After looking them through she laid them upon the coals; they blazed up and filled the room with light. Carl looked wonderingly around at the splendidly furnished apartment, which the sudden blaze revealed to him; but it did not last long; the flames died away and the room was again in twilight. The princess turned and asked him:

"Did you read the letters?"

"I looked into them sometimes. The letters in the lady's hand told about a child, what it was doing, where it was, what it had learned, that it had been sick of scarlet fever, and such things; and that did not interest me. The other told about all sorts of things in America that I didn't understand, and so I didn't read much in those either."

"So much the better. And what you did read you may as well forget; it is not worth the trouble of remembering, and it is all about things of no consequence, Carl."

Thereupon she rang for a light; when it was brought she had it placed upon the writing-table and seated Carl there to write his letter. It was some time before he finished. First he had to breathe on his benumbed hands to warm them; then admire the costly and elegant writing materials; and after he had successfully finished the "Dear Mother," he could bring nothing out of the excitement and confusion of his thoughts that would make a good beginning. At length Elsie, who had been walking up and down, stepped to him and dictated the letter. She had him close with the words: "When you answer,

9

say nothing of this matter; the lady does not wish anything said about it."

The letter was finished at last. Elsie opened a drawer of her writing-desk and took out a bank-note, which she folded into the letter. She placed five seals on the envelope, and asked Carl for his mother's exact address. While she was writing it the floor seemed to burn under Carl's feet. He seized the letter as soon as she had finished to rush with it to the post-office.

"Wait, wait, my boy. You must have money for the postage, and do not forget to take a receipt."

"Oh, I know, I know; I often carry Herr von Schott's letters to the post-office." He had already reached the door with his letter.

"But you are running away and forgetting your watch!"

"Oh, the watch!" said Carl, hesitating; "yes, the watch!"

"Which you had forgotten in your haste to give your mother pleasure. That is a sign that you have a good heart. You shall have one so much the nicer. My servant shall go with you and buy one for you down in the city."

She rang and sent for the *valet;* when he appeared, she commissioned him to go to the city with the boy and buy him a good silver watch which he was to select for himself. Then she gave Carl her hand and said:

"Now you may go, and whenever you need advice again come to me, will you?"

Carl nodded and was about to go, when, as if something had suddenly occurred to him, he turned back again, and with a face blazing red, stammered, in confusion, "I thank you, too!" Then, his face beaming with satisfaction that he had remembered this duty of courtesy in time and had successfully discharged it, he went away in high spirits, rushing on down the steps ahead of the servant.

Elsie turned back to the fireplace, and gazed at the coals where the ashes of the burned papers still lay. Her excitement was over; in its place had come a defiant but still resignation to fate; he had the right, she told herself again, "Let him claim his right. What does it matter about me? What can come to me that I have not deserved? Have I a right to reproach him with lying and deception? I of all the world?"

She sank into a long reverie. It was strange that she could not keep this last thought, so simple and clear, in mind, could not resign herself to this logic. With any one else she could, but not with him. That he could have deceived her so and tried to entrap her by professing affection, there was something in it that overcame her, that extinguished all the light of life and joy of existence left to her.

And if it had not been so, if it had not so terribly crushed all her life and courage, as if the world had never before seen such an example of deception, then perhaps she would have given more attention to the thought that lay heavy upon her mind and yet which she had not the courage or the energy to look steadily in the face—the thought that the end of it all would be that she would be compelled to seek peace with Ferdinand, to tell him everything frankly, and then say:

"Now, do as you will; trample me under foot, if you will!"

Suddenly steps were heard outside in the hall, the door was suddenly thrown open and Matilda rushed in, evidently in the greatest excitement.

"What has happened, what is the matter, Matilda?" said Elsie, stepping up to her.

"There, read," said Matilda, out of breath. "Heavens, how I ran up the long avenue; I am suffocating!"

"She sank, panting, into a chair near the fireplace, while Elsie stepped quickly to the light with the paper. It was a telegram, and ran:

"*Mrs. Major Schott, E.:*

Your daughter, Irene, disappeared from the convent this morning. She seems to have been abducted by a strange man, of middle age, who was observed here yesterday. Will give particulars in a letter.

(*Signed*)   THE PRINCIPAL."

"What do you say to that?" cried Matilda, as Elsie dropped the paper from her trembling hands.

"It is dreadful, dreadful!" she exclaimed, her eyes resting wide and fixed upon her sister and her chest heaving.

"Abducted! She was abducted! And by whom? William Kronhorst is here; I saw him pass to-day. It cannot be he. 'A man of middle age,' the despatch says."

"No, it is not he," whispered Elsie, in a scarcely audible voice, "it is another man, and I know, I know who it is!"

"You know?"

"I know. It is Ferdinand von Schott."

"What! Ferdinand von Schott, cousin Ferdinand? In Heaven's name, Elsie, I beg of you, for what——"

"Do you not see, can you not see through it?"

"You think because he has gone away without letting any one know where, or for what——"

"No, no; but because he, he alone would be capable of the deed, he alone would have an interest in causing her disappearance, in putting her out of the world, in murdering——"

"Oh, my God, Elsie, you are raving!"

And, indeed, she was rushing up and down the great room like a lunatic.

"He knows, he has found out everything. He has known a long, long time, that Irene is not your daughter, that we have cheated him out of his inheritance, and he has done everything to find proofs of it. He did not succeed; the proofs he sought are lying there in the ashes. Now he has taken the last, extreme measure; he has carried Irene off; he has murdered her, or sent her over the ocean——"

"My God, what do I hear?" stammered Matilda, clasping her hands. "For Heaven's sake, tell me how you learned all this!"

Elsie told in hasty, broken sentences of her meeting with Carl, the boy's explanation of the object of Ferdinand's visit to Vellinghaus, but in the midst of it she stopped, clasped her hands, and cried despairingly:

"Oh! my God! my God! he will kill her! that horrible man will kill her!"

She hurried to the bell and pulled it violently. When the servant came in she ordered him to have her carriage brought around; then, in uncontrollable excitement, expressing itself in detached and wild exclamations, she walked rapidly back and forth through the room. Her sister seemed completely subdued by her stormy manner, so that she no longer expressed any idea of her own, but listened only to Elsie and echoed her thoughts; she was entirely carried away with the current of Elsie's passionate conclusions; she had no longer any doubt that it was a proved and settled thing —Ferdinand von Schott had carried off and murdered Irene!

"But where will you go, what will you do?" asked Matilda, when the servant came in to announce that the carriage was ready, and to ask whether he should call the maid-of-honor.

"Bring me my hat and cloak yourself— or a shawl—and do not disturb the young lady," answered Elsie, and when he was gone she turned to Matilda.

"Do you think I will take it all quietly and leave Irene to her fate? Do you think I will not try to save her from his hands, or at least to punish him for his crime—to send a spy after him, as he himself has played the spy on me?"

"You will start off at once and follow him?"

"I? No! Suppose I should, what power could I have? I will send some one after him that will have some authority. Come!"

Elsie threw on the wrap the servant brought, and Matilda rose, drawing up her cloak, which had slipped from her shoulders.

"Follow us," said Elsie to the servant, and as she stepped into the carriage, she ordered the coachman to drive to Police-Inspector Groebler's.

As the carriage rolled down the long avenue, both were silent. Matilda's cooler reflection, however, suggested the thought that, in consequence probably of her long attendance on the prince, Elsie had fallen into an excitable state of mind, and hence these horrible thoughts of crime and murder, which were too wild to stand the test of sober reflection.

CHAPTER XXI.

AT HERR GROEBLER'S.

In a few moments the carriage stopped at an old house in a narrow street not far from the cathedral, where Herr Grobler had found shelter for himself, his wife, and two or three children of tender age, the "lambs" before alluded to.

"You had better go in with me," said Elsie to her sister; "or, no; the coachman can take you home after I get out; I would rather see the man alone; you can drive home and send the carriage back."

Matilda made no objection, and Elsie alighted, sent her servant forward, and then ascended the steps to the rooms of the police inspector, while the carriage drove on.

The appearance of the princess at Herr Groebler's modest dwelling caused some excitement. Frau Theresa anxiously withdrew with her lambs to the innermost apartment, their toilets not being in court order. The servant-girl had to take the hall-lamp, with an apology, to light Elsie into Herr Groebler's office, and then vanish in haste to find some better light.

In the meantime Elsie looked around the dimly-lighted apartment. It was a neat, pleasantly furnished little room, evidently arranged by some one with a taste for flowers, pictures, and other pleasant little ornaments. The occupant, too, seemed to have taken care that there should be nothing more to remind one of his business than was absolutely unavoidable. His papers were stowed away in two cases with green curtains, and on the writing-desk lay only some open letters and official documents.

Herr Groebler, who came in buttoning the coat for which he had just exchanged his dressing-gown, seemed to be in some haste, and did not conceal the excited curiosity this unexpected visit caused him. He had too much tact to ask the princess to be seated, but waited until she should do him the honor. She seated herself on the haircloth sofa, and, throwing back her veil, began:

"Let us be seated, Herr Groebler; I want to talk with you. I come to you with confidence, although I have seen you but little. But for years I have heard you spoken of as a man upon whom reliance can be placed. And I come to place confidence in you as a friend."

If Herr Groebler could have been guilty of the juvenile weakness of blushing, his cheeks would probably have taken on a deeper tinge. It was so humiliating that the woman against whom he had twice in his life played the part of a spy should now come to confide in him as a friend!

He bowed and seated himself in silence opposite to her, at his writing-desk.

"I know that I can rely upon you," she continued; "that your sense of duty and honor will lead you to do your best, even though your services may be required in opposition to your personal sympathies, against people near to you, and whom you have heretofore valued and honored——"

Herr Groebler's eyes, which were fixed sharply on her features, expanded a little.

"Ah! against people near to me? What does your highness mean?"

Elsie did not answer, because the servant-girl just then stepped in with a large lamp, which she placed on the table near the sofa. When she had gone, Elsie handed the telegram to Groebler.

"Read that!" she said.

He read it and looked up in surprise.

"That is strange and, for you, dreadful news!"

There was a peculiar emphasis in the words "for you," and a peculiar sharpness in the glance he fixed upon her dark eyes.

She did not seem to notice it, but went on hastily: "How dreadful, you shall hear. Irene was not carried off by some man that loves her and wanted to marry her; it was by a 'man of middle age,' the despatch says; and this man wants to make way with Irene, to put her out of his own way, out of the world—God knows what! And this man is your colleague, your chief, your landrath——"

"Ah! Herr von Schott?" cried Groebler, entirely losing his official composure and jumping up.

"Herr von Schott!" repeated Elsie, firmly. "You will soon be convinced that this is the case. You know, do you not, that he was destined to be the heir of the banker Schott, in H. ?"

Herr Groebler nodded.

"Well, he was not. When the banker died, there was no will. The property went to Irene, as the daughter of his nearest relative, of Major Schott. Ferdinand von Schott and his sister received nothing. Now Ferdinand suspects that Irene is not the major's daughter, is, therefore, not the lawful heir, and hence the property rightfully belongs to him. He has spared no pains in the attempt to find proofs of it; but he has failed to find them. And since he has not succeeded in putting her out of his way by this means, he has resorted to others —he has followed her and carried her away?"

Elsie spoke in a tone of passionate certainty—with the emotion of a strong soul that has discovered a baseness past all forgiveness in one nearer to it than other men, one who has not only committed the baseness, but in doing it has robbed that soul of its last faith in the world and in humanity. And by speaking in this tone of certainty she entirely misled Herr Groebler; while she was speaking he yielded fully to the impression that it was all as she said, that his chief and friend was in reality the death-deserving criminal that Elsie saw in him. It was true—who knew better than he, Groebler?—that Ferdinand did really see in Irene a false heiress, who had wronged him out of what should have been his; it was true that he had been absent several days; it was true that the despatch said "a middle-aged man." To him, indeed, Ferdinand had professed quite a different object in taking the journey; but might he not have deceived him? Or, if not, might he not have taken a new resolve, have changed his plans while on the way? Was it not possible that, having seen Philip Bonsart and talked with him without gaining anything, he had now resorted, in desperation, to the most extreme measures?

Herr Groebler passed his hand over his forehead and looked at the floor in silence.

"And now," continued Elsie, as he did not answer, "now I come to you. I am but a weak woman and cannot go to contend with this man. I cannot pursue him to prevent a crime, and I have no one to send. You are the only one that can save Irene. If you will go, I will furnish all the money you need; I will pay you liberally if you get there soon enough to save her. Have no scruples about anything if they will stand in the way of this purpose. I am afraid of nothing. I will not shun anything to accomplish it. Even if the whole affair were to come before the courts, I would not shrink from the publicity; I would go forward as a witness.

"That, your highness," answered Groebler, lifting his eyes to her face, and speaking slowly and emphatically, "that you could not do!"

"Could not? Why not?" asked Elsie, defiantly. "How do you know what I could do, what I would do, to what I would subject myself, to put an end to a cruel, unendurable situation? But that is not the question now. I have told you that Irene has been carried away, that you are the only one I can send to save her and bring her back, and every minute is precious. Will you do as your position binds you to do, and go at once?—will you? Otherwise, I must myself see what I can do—I must go myself. And if I must, I will go to-night!"

"Compose yourself, your highness," answered Groebler, softly and thoughtfully, as if weighing his words. "It is not exactly my duty to go beyond our own boundaries on such an errand without first receiving instructions from the authorities. But an order can be obtained by telegraph, and I will consider it. Still, in order that no precious time may be lost while I am considering, I will go at once and send an agent this evening, one that will be the best we could possibly find for this business, and one whose zeal will far surpass mine. Will that satisfy you?"

"Who is this zealous officer?"

"You know," answered Groebler, smiling, "that the police owe their most brilliant successes to people whose relation to us is not known, and who, from that very fact, are able to accomplish more."

"A secret agent, then?"

"We will call him so.".

"Very well, then. You are, of course, sure of his discretion, in case discretion can avail to keep the whole matter private?"

"Perfectly sure."

"Then do not delay to talk with him," said Elsie, rising. "And when shall I know whether you yourself are going? You can send word to my sister, who lives so much nearer to you, and I shall hear at once through her. I should naturally distrust you. Herr von Schott is your principal, or, at least—I do not know whether he is officially your chief—your colleague. On that account you would feel like shielding him. But with men of your calling——"

"The bloodhound instinct tramples on all considerations of friendship and fraternity, is what you were going to say," interrupted Groebler, with a somewhat bitter smile.

"Not exactly that; I was going to say that, with men of your calling, the sense of legal right must be developed to such keenness and strength that such considerations cannot pervert it, and that your professional honor consists in the fact that you cannot be moved by entreaties or bribes. Hence I trust you. Will you help me?"

"I will do what I can, your highness; I give you my word upon it."

"Do you need anything to show that you are authorized?"

"I think not. But leave the telegram in my hands."

"As you think best. And my sister will give you any farther authority that you may need."

Groebler bowed, and Elsie drew down her veil again and turned to go. He gave her his arm and conducted her through the now brilliantly-lighted hall, where her servant was waiting, and down the stairs to the carriage, which had returned from her sister's, and now carried her swiftly out of sight.

Groebler returned to his room, and stood with his arms folded across his chest, and his small, twinkling eyes fixed upon the place where Elsie had been sitting. He had need of time to come to himself again, after this storm of feminine passion which had swept over him and carried him away into wild imaginations of horrible crime—imaginations in which Elsie's excited mind had revelled, as if she could thereby revenge herself for the wound given her by Carl's revelations, imaginations which Groebler must very soon reduce to plain common sense.

But only after long and cool deliberation —after mature reflection on the matter still so dark and mysterious, "She confided in me, that proud woman," he said to himself, "but what did she confide to me? the crime of which she believed Ferdinand von Schott capable. She confided her belief in that to me. But nothing more, not a word of all those mysteries. Did she intimate, by a single word, whether this Fräulein Irene is her sister's child or hers? Whether Ferdinand von Schott is right or not? No; but, Groebler, you did not ask her. Perhaps she was ready to tell the whole truth; she was excited enough to tell the whole, to conceal nothing. But you did not inquire. To be sure, it is nothing to you; you had no reason to trouble yourself about it, no right to catechise her. She came to make an accusation, and you had only to do with what facts she presented. You are not an inquisitor and she not a defendant. But yet, it was a little stupid of you, it certainly was. You might have asked why she should be so beside herself, as the matter primarily concerned Frau Matilda Schott; and why the mother did not herself come. You might have asked that outright, instead of putting in that sly innuendo which she did not understand."

After Groebler had ended this monologue he remained standing for some time motionless. Then he exclaimed: "I'll be hanged if I can see into it. But this much is certain: to regain an inheritance out of which he had been swindled, Ferdinand von Schott would never commit a crime. He is not the man for that; he is the last man to commit such a crime. But there is something more about it than he shows to me. He is absorbed, and swallowed up—he is completely lost in this matter as a reasonable man never would be. But what is not possible with us poor human devils, for every one of us has a demon in him. Perhaps he has

gone to say to this poor Fräulein Irene: you are not Frau Schott's daughter. You have been used to get wrongful possession of an estate. And the poor child has consented, in her desperation, to leave these people that have so shamefully used her existence for their own profit, and to disappear forever for them. After all, that is the most probable supposition."

Herr Groebler sighed. Then he took down his cloak that hung behind the door, wrapped himself slowly and carefully in it, took up the telegram, which he put into his pocket, and left the house.

He passed through the brilliantly lighted streets of the city, till he emerged from the narrow, irregular streets of the old part into a fine broad avenue with new buildings, and stopped before a house at the first corner.

It was a large, fine building; the entrance and the windows of the first story were brilliantly lighted; it was the club-house of the city, and at this hour most of the gentlemen of the better class of society were assembled there. Herr Groebler had had the honor to be elected by a considerable majority of white balls to the fortunate circle that were here repaid every evening for the burdens of the day with Moselle wine, cigars, and lively conversation with congenial friends. Herr Groebler ascended the stairs, hung his cloak among innumerable others in the ante-room, and passed into the hall, which was filled with tobacco-smoke.

Herr Groebler passed around the room, shaking hands and exchanging a few words with friends here and there, then glided unnoticed into a smaller room in the rear, where were several tables covered with a formidable array of newspapers. A young man was sitting on a stool in one corner, smoking a cigar. The inevitable glass stood before him, and he seemed to be absorbed in the daily paper he held in his hand.

In a moment Herr Groebler was seated beside him.

"Ah!" exclaimed the young man, looking up, "you come up, Herr Groebler, as if you were just going to lay your policeman's hand upon me."

"Perhaps I shall, Herr Kronhorst."

"Really? Well, now, who is safe from

you?" answered William Kronhorst. "What crime have I committed? My conscience doesn't accuse me of any, unless you call it one to read this paper, which is, to be sure, filled with stupid stuff that it ought to be a crime to read."

"You have committed no crime, Herr Kronhorst, and if I should lay hands on you, it would only be with the intention of getting valuable help from you in my difficult calling."

"Ah! that means that I am to give some information. Not about any of our people at the factory? Has anything happened there?"

"It is not information, but actual assistance that I want of you. I want to make you my secret agent and initiate you at once, this very night."

"How kind!" said William, laughing. "A secret agent of the police! Really, that is something they never sang in my lullaby!"

"Do you remember so distinctly?" asked Groebler, drily.

"Would you like to have me think it over? It wouldn't be of much use, for, granting that I should have to admit that it is possible, it would still be impossible for me actually to enter upon the honorable career you propose."

"We should not be hasty, my dear Herr Kronhorst," answered Groebler; "it is possible that before you think you may be fairly launched into the career, and may trouble yourself as little about whether it is honorable, as about what lullaby may have been sung over your cradle."

"You are getting mysterious, Herr Groebler. Come, out with it; what is it?"

"First I must beg pardon for prying into your secrets——"

"My secrets? I have none."

"That is true; at least, no very great ones, unless the feelings of a young man's heart, of which almost all of us have quite a lively idea from our own experience, may be regarded as a great secret."

"Ah, what do you mean?" cried William, in surprise.

"That I am aware of your preference for a certain young lady."

"You, Herr Groebler?"

"Do not be disturbed; there is no objection on the part of the police to that preference, and, if I were to express my private opinion, I should say it does you honor. Neither need it disturb you that I know of it. My wife, who is a friend of Frau Matilda Schott, has told me something of it—quite as a private, unprofessional matter. That is all, and we are not communicative. But to come to the matter in hand—you know where Fräulein Irene is?"

William looked at him with wide-open eyes, and did not answer.

"You know," proceeded Herr Groebler, calmly, "she is in B., or, rather, she was——"

"Was?" interrupted William.

"So I said. For at this present time, she is no longer there, unfortunately. Her mother has received a telegram to that effect. If you wish to see it, here it is."

He drew the paper from his pocket and placed it on the table in front of William, who devoured it with his eyes, while his hand trembled and his face grew pale. Springing up, he ejaculated:

"Oh, my God! That is dreadful; he has carried her off!"

"He? Who?" said Herr Groebler, quickly.

William turned his white, distressed face to the detective, without answering.

"Say, who? Who has carried her off?"

"Why, the man—the man mentioned here in the despatch," whispered William, turning from Groebler and sinking into his seat as if crushed.

"My dear Herr Kronhorst," said Groebler, after a pause, "you cannot escape me so. Your 'he' was some definite individual, some individual known to you, and in your mind at the time; and I must know who this 'he' of your thoughts is. You need conceal nothing from me, nothing at all. The princess has taken me into her confidence, and given me all the explanations necessary to enable me to act in the matter. Moreover, I know about all of the past history of the princess—not all, but the most of it. You will, therefore, commit no indiscretion by talking with me about persons who may, perhaps, have been connected with the princess in times past, or about matters you think it necessary to conceal from the rest of the world——"

"How should I know anything about such matters?" asked William, avoiding Groebler's eyes.

"I should think through Fräulein Irene, whom you love, and who loves you in return."

William did not answer at once; then he said, hesitatingly:

"And the princess has talked with you about the matter—has taken you into her confidence, not Irene's mother, Frau Schott?"

"No, not she; perhaps," he added, in a slightly ironical tone, "the princess may be thought to have more practical talent for business transactions; perhaps that was why she came. Perhaps, too——"

"What were you going to say?"

"Perhaps," whispered Groebler, in answer, "perhaps the princess stands in closer relation to the girl than we think."

"Ah!" exclaimed William, in astonishment, "do you know that?"

"I know nothing, nothing at all; all I want is to hear from you who this 'he' is. When you have told me that, we will talk farther of the matter—not before."

"Well, then," said William, forced to an answer, "this 'he' is one Herr Philip Bonsart, and is Irene's father."

"Ah!" cried Herr Groebler, half aloud, his eyes flashing at the declaration, and a start betraying his surprise at this definite assertion. "Really, then—you know that?"

"Yes. You must know that Irene has received several letters lately, signed at first, P. B., and afterward with the full name, Philip Bonsart. They came from England. The first was short, and said that a person nearly related to Irene had some information to give her, and would give it if Irene would answer the lines and promise to show them to none of her family. Irene answered, and gave the required promise."

"Which did not hinder her from showing the letters to you?"

"Yes, she showed them to me. I was not included among her family, and she was helpless without my advice in such a remarkable affair."

"Of course. And the letters that followed contained—what?"

"Herr Philip Bonsart, the writer, filled the next letter with a short sketch of his life—the life of a man who had made his own way in the world, and in doing so had passed through many hard struggles, and now, when the struggles were over, when he was enabled to enjoy the fruits of his efforts, had a new sorrow to contend with—the painful sense of being entirely alone in the world. He was originally from the neighborhood of H., was a son of a former proprietor of Asthof, had been a student, and in the year 1848 was among the——"

"Democrats, compromised himself in the Baden revolution, and then, when the reaction came, had to flee to America from the warrants that were out for his arrest——"

"Indeed, do you know all that, Herr Groebler?" cried William, in surprise.

"Certainly I know it," said Herr Groebler, smiling and nodding, "I had it from both official and private sources—very special sources—so let us come to the point, and dispense with Herr Philip Bonsart's biography."

"Very well, then; the following letters, which Irene awaited in suspense, as the warmth of feeling displayed in the others had filled her with lively sympathy for the man, told her that his longing to see her was so great that he had determined to make the attempt to get her back—for she, Irene, was his daughter!"

William had whispered the last word with still greater caution than the others, and he looked at Groebler as he said it to observe the impression the revelation made upon him. But Groebler's features did not show the least surprise. He only nodded with the same smile as before, and said:

"His daughter. Then so much is established. And what else? What more did this lonely, melancholy man write?"

"She had no right to the name of Schott. She was nothing at all to the people for whose child she passed. She was his daughter, and, therefore, he had a sacred claim upon her, and could establish his claim in open court, for he had never given up his right. But he would not claim her against her will; and as for carrying the case into court, he was prevented from doing that by circumstances of a peculiar character. He could not compromise the princess; he had to consider her, and he would injure her irremediably if he were to appear against her to assert his right to his child. Hence, he knew of no other way than to make a direct appeal to his child. Irene was to answer as to whether she would grant him an interview, so that they might see each other, and he could then explain many things that could not be written. He would leave it entirely to her whether she would go with him or not; she should be perfectly free to decide according to her own feelings and judgment; only he must have an opportunity to speak, undisturbed, with her, and explain everything."

"The poor child!" said Herr Groebler. "How cruel to tell her all that, and require such a decision from the child!"

"In truth," continued William, eagerly, "the later letters shocked and terrified Irene exceedingly. She was almost beside herself, and did not know what to do. She received the last one the evening my father gave his last party. Frau Schott and Irene were not at the party—they do not visit at our house. But Irene was so agitated by the letter, and so much in need of some one to confide in, and receive advice from, that she wrapped up in her veil and cloak and came to our house. I received a note by a servant, asking me to come to the lower balcony. I slipped out unnoticed, and found Irene waiting for me, in great excitement. We went to the farther end of the balcony, and Irene told me, with sobs, all that was in the letter. I could not read it for the darkness. You can imagine how perplexed we were; we thought it over and over; my advice was that Irene should first require further explanations and proofs of the remarkable assertions of the man, which she had already asked in her former letter; and that, until they were given, she should carefully avoid a meeting with him, because it was possible that it might be some one trying to deceive and defraud her. Irene promised to follow my advice, though I saw that the writer of the letter was making more and more of an impression on her feelings, that

she had a great deal of sympathy for him, and that her heart pleaded for him. I succeeded in quieting her excitement, and she was quite like herself again when I took her home.

"When I came back again, quite confused and anxious about this strange affair, which might have so much influence on my destiny through my relation to Irene, I found the company in great excitement over the sudden illness of the prince. I was dreadfully frightened when I heard that they had found him lying on the balcony in the projection at the corner; for Irene and I had stood just under that projection when she told me about the letter. I had heard steps above us, but had not thought much about them, because I thought I heard them pass away again. You can imagine how shocked I was, and how anxiously I have wondered whether the prince could have overheard us, whether it was possible that any part of our conversation which may have reached his ears could have had any connection with his stroke——"

Herr Groebler shrugged his shoulders.

"It is not impossible, to be sure," he said; "it is not impossible that a conversation like yours with Irene may have thrown a sudden light for him upon his wife's past history—a very peculiar light. But it seems to me that the man's nature is not sentimental enough to be crushed by any such revelation, which, too, could only have come to him in a very confused form. We may, therefore, set aside the subject of his attack, and trouble ourselves no farther about it. Let us confine ourselves to the facts; to the fact that it must have been Philip Bonsart who carried off the young girl he calls his daughter, and, therefore, that there is no need of either you or me starting out to-night to pursue him. That was what the princess desired me to do, and what I was going to propose to you, because I thought you would be the best and most active agent in the business of finding Fräulein Irene Schott, and protecting her or saving her from a crime. But since we know who the abductor is, we need not fear that any harm will happen to her, and may go to rest for the night in peace."

William Kronhorst did not look as if he expected much peaceful rest that night. He made no answer, but clasped his hands together, looked at the floor, and seemed more and more absorbed in thought.

"Well," said Groebler, at length, "what are you thinking of?"

"I am not thinking much," said William, starting up. "But I feel that I can no longer bear the dreadful suspense I have been kept in ever since Irene made those disclosures to me. When she went away, she promised me sacredly that she would not keep me in this painful suspense a moment longer than was necessary; she would give me an immediate and minute account of everything that should happen, and would not decide on any step without my advice. But she has not written a line——"

"Indeed! Perhaps the little nuns at B. have taken care that the young ladies shall not keep up correspondence with young gentlemen in painful suspense——"

"I have borne it till now," continued William, "but I can bear it no longer. I must and will know what has happened, where Irene has gone, what fate awaits her with this Philip Bonsart, and what my own fate is to be. You will not need to make me an agent; I will go as my own agent—this very night!"

Herr Groebler nodded. "It would be hard to keep you back, and I have no interest in keeping you. So go; take the telegram with you; it will serve as a credential with the nuns, to show that you are sent by the mother, by Frau Schott. You will have to make inquiries first of them."

William, who had risen, took the paper and put it into his pocket.

"You must be prepared," added Groebler, "to find this Philip Bonsart a hard customer, if you should meet him. And—do not hurry so, do not run away without finding out where the man you are going to seek keeps himself, where he lives."

"Why, do you know that? You know that, too?"

"Open your memorandum-book and write: Newcastle-upon-Tyne, Dean street, Queen's Place, No. 13."

William stared at him in astonishment.

"Ah," he said, "then you know all; you already knew this Philip Bonsart, you knew his relation to the princess, to Irene—for Heaven's sake, why do you not speak and tell me everything, as I have told you—all these things that are such a riddle to me—the real connection——"

"Why not?" interrupted Groebler; "simply because I only say what I know, and keep my conjectures, and suppositions, and combinations to myself. I pursue my calling a little as an art, my dear Herr Kronhorst, and an artist, you know, does not show his first attempts, his sketches and vague fantasies; he waits until he has fairly laid hold of his idea, and brought it out upon canvas. So, if you are determined to carry out your plan, go, and may God help you. I have nothing more to tell you that would help you in your work; if I had, I would not keep it from you; but what else I may know or think—that is a professional secret."

Herr Groebler offered his hand; William hastily laid his own in it, looking at the other with an uncertain glance. Then the detective passed out, wrapped himself again in his cloak, and went home to Frau Theresa's waiting evening meal.

CHAPTER XXII.

CONFESSION.

Herr Groebler rose the next morning in a very uneasy state of mind. Cool and undisturbed as he usually was, and accustomed to the shifting chances of human destiny, still he was strongly affected by what he had heard the evening before from the princess and from William Kronhorst. His thoughts had been so occupied with it that he had gone to sleep very late; then he was tormented by confused dreams—dreams that he could not distinctly remember, but which, judging from the impression they left on his spirits, must have been of a most disquieting nature; perhaps that all his wards and foster-children had escaped from their cells and were making his district so unsafe that he had to run himself nearly to death in pursuit of them; or that his salary was reduced by just the amount he had promised Frau Theresa for her summer wardrobe. He was standing now in front of the stove in the room where he had received the princess, warming his back and blowing smoke-clouds from his long pipe, while he thought over all he had heard the day before, and which, much as he had thought it over and weighed its probabilities before, had yet come to him as strange and almost impossible.

So Ferdinand von Schott had been right. It was all as he had suspected, divined, believed—all; Philip had been married to Elsie von Melroth that time at Asthof, and Irene was their child. They were Catholics and could not be divorced, and so Elsie von Melroth had taken the law into her own hands and divorced herself—boldly and presumptuously, as if the princely mantle would hide any sin! Or was still another explanation possible? God only knew!

And now, what would come of the matter? Could it be hushed up, even now? Perhaps. This Herr Bonsart had acted discreetly, and seemed to be a man who would not proceed without consideration; and if William Kronhorst were allowed to marry Irene, he would be quiet, too. But would his father consent, and would Philip Bonsart be willing to give away his daughter, just as he had gained her? As regarded Herr von Schott, he, too, would be silent if the property of his cousin were delivered up to him. "Nothing would remain," said Herr Groebler to himself, "but to explain the affair to Irene's guardian and to the Probate Court; that would be a difficult matter. Perhaps the prince will be generous and make up Herr von Schott's loss to him up to the time when Irene is of age and can give up the property independently, without appealing to her guardian and the Court. The prince! The poor devil! If the affair should come to his ears, he would strangle his proud wife! He is the very man for it!

"And then, at last," he continued, after a pause, "there would be no one left but Herr Groebler to be induced to hold his peace. Well. Herr Groebler is good-hearted. He would do a great deal at a friendly request. It's a pity that he is no better casuist. For, the devil take me, if I know whether I can help to hush up the affair. After all, the police is not an order of father confessors. People cannot confide their sins to their *subsigillo confessionis*, and so place a padlock on their lips. And they have their official honor, and their oath of office; they have their conscience and their ambition. And if, after all, the whole performance should come to light and it should be said: Groebler knew of it; they slipped a pretty piece of money into his hand to keep him quiet—then Groebler would be the victim of his good heart and would be ruined in expiation of the crime of making such a mistake as for a royal police-inspector and member of the fourth class of the order of the Red Eagle to obey the voice of feeling in preference to that of duty."

Herr Groebler passed his palm several times over the part of his head where the organ of secretiveness is thought to lie, as if involuntarily attempting to appease it by flattering caresses for his disregard of its monitions; then he began to send out still greater clouds of tobacco-smoke.

"Now, then," he began again, after some time, "we shall have to wait upon the princess, to report to her what Herr William Kronhorst has confided to us, and what this same Kronhorst, junior, has decided to do. It will quiet her completely as far as regards the horrible robber-story she has been spinning about the landrath; but, on the other hand, it may not be so pleasant for her to hear that this Herr Philip has so unexpectedly turned up again. I am afraid the name of Philip Bonsart will startle her a little. With his claims upon the young girl, whom she surely will not easily give up, unless she is compelled to—well, we shall hear what she says to it."

At this moment Herr Groebler's reflections were suddenly interrupted. There was a quick knock at the door and who should follow it but the very man Herr

Groebler had just been thinking of—Herr von Schott.

"Here I am," said he, extending his hand, "worn-out with the long journey, and as wise as I was before."

"You!" exclaimed the police-inspector, "You here! So much the better! When did you come?"

"Late last evening," answered Ferdinand, throwing himself into the sofa-corner the princess had taken the day before, "direct from Ostend."

"Then we should have the best proof of an *alibi* for you."

"An *alibi?* What does that mean? What is the need of an *alibi?* Am I accused of committing a murder or any other horror here?"

"Not here, but in B——."

"I? In B——? What has happened there?"

"Fräulein Irene has been carried off by a middle-aged man, supposed to be you."

"Carried off? Irene? And I——"

"You are said to be the rascal."

"Groebler—I beg of you—and who says so?"

"Go to her Highness the Princess of Achsenstein, and I have no doubt she will tell you so to your face."

"Now, by Heaven," cried Ferdinand, springing up, "I will; I would like to hear that from the princess herself! She—she accuses me of carrying off Irene?"

"She does. She accuses you of having been long prying into her affairs to destroy her, and now of having abducted the child. But, as I have said, you can prove an *alibi*. Yesterday you were on the railroad from Ostend here. And day before yesterday in England—were you? In Newcastle-upon-Tyne? What is going on there? What is this wonderful fellow, Bonsart, doing?"

"First tell me all about this abduction. What has happened to Irene?"

Herr Groebler told the whole story. While he was speaking Ferdinand seated himself again to listen. When it came to Philip Bonsart's letters to Irene, leaving no more doubt who the abductor of the girl was, Ferdinand interrupted him, exclaiming:

"Ah! Everything is clear now. It was

for that Philip Bonsart had left his home. I found his rooms in Newcastle empty. He had gone away to Belgium and France, they told me, for three, four, five weeks, they did not know how long. I was in a state of desperation, but what could I do? I had to decide to come home again, after staying there several days in doubt. And now we see why he was not in Newcastle!"

Herr Groebler nodded. "Of course," he said, "and everything agrees remarkably. It is a good thing I was not foolish enough to start off myself, at the beck of the princess."

"And young Kronhorst went, instead of you?"

"He would not be kept back, although I did not see that he could accomplish much. But who knows; perhaps he will succeed in overtaking them and coming to an understanding with Herr Philip. As the girl loves him, it is not improbable. You can console yourself now for having learned nothing at Newcastle-upon-Tyne. All you wanted to know is now open and clear, and for fear I may forget it, I will bow in humble admiration of your sagacity. You were right in everything. What your intuition saw and penetrated, is all proved true. The letters of Bonsart to the girl are evidence enough."

Ferdinand did not answer. Sunken in his sofa-corner, he seemed busy with his own thought.

"And I think," continued Groebler, after a pause, "we shall have a tangled story out of the affair. Herr Philip wants his daughter; Herr von Schott wants his property. 'My ducats and my daughter,' cries Shylock in the play; and what will the prince cry, as the third in the list for tormentors of the princess? I am afraid he will very soon call for something she will find it hard to give—explanation!"

"The unfortunate woman!" exclaimed Ferdinand, starting up. "The unfortunate woman! What can be done to help her? Poor woman!"

"Do you say that now, just as you hear that all your suspicions were well-founded? How to help her! I should think that would be your last thought, after you have been robbed by her and then deemed capable of murder!"

"And yet she must be now far more unhappy than I am, and—give me my hat, Groebler——"

"Where are you going?"

"Where should I go but to her? I will tell her what has happened, who it is that has carried off her daughter, and will see how I can help her."

"You will do that? Well, I have no objection, and you will save me the trouble—and a little embarrassment I should have felt at meeting her—for, to tell the truth, I never had less desire to make the most of a discovery, than with the one I should have had to report to her to-day."

"You shall be relieved of all that," answered Ferdinand. "Leave everything to me, everything." He hastily extended his hand to Groebler and hurried down the steps and out of the house. The sharp wind that blew through the lindens along the avenue to Achsenstein, cooled his heated face and enabled him to breathe more freely. The wild chaos of his thoughts and emotions seemed to subside under the frosty current of air. He had the feeling of being justified from the sin against Elsie in prying into her past life; not justified by the fact he had just learned from Groebler that he was right in every one of his suspicions; no, not by that; but justified because he believed he understood the secret of her life clearly because of this very prying, and it was fortunate for Elsie that he did see it clearly. He could now go to her and say: It will no longer avail you anything to conceal the facts from me; I know everything, and you must now take me as your only friend, the only one who can interpose for you and help you.

He was absorbed by the one feeling of unbounded satisfaction as at a great conquest, in the belief that he could reassure and protect her, that she would be obliged to accept his help, that he could convince her of all that he could be to her.

There was, perhaps, some selfishness in this feeling. There was, perhaps, mixed with it, a considerable proportion of pride in being able now to heap coals of fire upon her head; perhaps, too, a considerable proportion of the love of power that makes a man desire to conquer where he loves. But Ferdinand did not examine his motives; he only stormed onward; and if he had tried to put into words the real object of his present visit to Achsenstein, he could have answered only: "To reassure and comfort and help her in her suffering!"

At his arrival he was told that she had not been seen the whole morning, and he would hardly be received. But he insisted on having his urgent wish to see her announced to her by her maid. The servant returned and beckoned to Ferdinand to follow him up to the princess' parlor. Ferdinand awaited her there with a beating heart. He stood at the window from which Elsie had so often looked down in sadness on the city roofs and the minster. The whole view seemed to Ferdinand to-day like a picture in a dream, as something uncertain and dissolving that he saw and did not see, that his eyes refused to receive the impression of as something real and defined. Elsie came at last. She was still in her morning dress; her hair was loosely tucked under a cap; she had not even taken the time to tie the strings; they were fluttering over her shoulders as she stepped in hastily.

"What is it you wish, what have you come for?" she asked, in a voice trembling with anger, as the door closed behind the maid, and she stood opposite Ferdinand in the middle of the room.

"To tell you first, princess, that I did not carry off Irene; and then to tell you who did."

"Ah! and who was it?"

"Philip Bonsart."

Elsie grew deadly white. With a trembling hand she reached for the back of the nearest chair.

"Ah!" she said, controlling herself with surprising power, while her breast heaved and her eyes flashed upon Ferdinand, "he—and you know it; it was probably you who informed him, who induced him to come; you incited him to act, you were his assistant, his accomplice. It was for that you were prying around at Vellinghaus—to accomplish, at length, this grand deed—to destroy me through Philip Bonsart, and then get possession of your money, your miserable money——"

"No," answered Ferdinand, whom her violent words had helped in regaining his own self-control; "but I am not offended at you words. On the contrary, they are agreeable to me. The worse you think of me, the more cruelly you treat me, the lighter grows the weight of my shameful offence toward you—the offence of searching in Vellinghaus for the knowledge of your past. Not for my money, not to gain possession of my miserable money, as you think—no, most certainly not—but in obedience to the demon within me, that has given me no rest since I saw you again, but has tormented me, day and night—that has made my life one continual torture! In a word, that which I have done, and which you are so angrily reproaching me with, I did it because I could not help it; because I could not live without trying to get a clear understanding of these things. I wanted to know whether the generosity that led you to urge upon me first money, and then Irene's hand—whether all that sympathy came only from a consciousness of guilt, from a conscience trying to relieve itself of a part of its burden. That is what I wanted to know, and, truly, nothing farther. And, in order that you may see that the money has nothing to do with it, I tell you now: I know everything; I can destroy you at any moment, princess, by coming forward and demanding that 'miserable money.' But with this power over you, I have only come here to compel you to hear my solemn declaration that I would rather cut off my hand than raise it against you; and that I will do my utmost to strike down any other hand that may be raised against you."

Princess Elsie sank into the chair beside which she had been standing. She looked at him with glance whose calmness indicated a peculiarly sudden disarming; the clear, open eyes resting full upon her face, and the earnest, decided, manly tone of the words, seemed to work upon her with peculiar force. They seemed to subjugate her, to break her pride. There must have been a force in the words that made her feel

that she had found her master—a feeling Elsie von Melroth had never before experienced; she silently bowed her head, resting her forehead on the high arm of the easy-chair, and began to weep bitterly.

Ferdinand was silent for a long time. At length he said:

"Control yourself, princess. "We have to talk, to consider. First, I ask you to give me your hand as a friend whom you trust. Do you trust me, princess?"

She extended her hand, and, without looking at him, or lifting her forehead, she said:

"Yes, I trust you. Go on."

"Well, I will tell you what has happened. I wanted to ascertain your relation to Philip Bonsart. For that purpose I hunted up Emil Drausfeld, because I knew that you and Philip had exchanged letters with him. I found Emil Drausfeld no longer among the living. I, therefore, hunted up Philip Bonsart himself. I went to England where he now lives; but I did not find him; he had gone away for some time. Last evening I returned. And here I learned, through the man whom you took into your confidence, that Irène had been abducted, and that it could only have been done by Philip Bonsart, who had been writing letters to her which she had kept secret, and in which he had claimed the rights of a father. She had shown these letters to only one person, and that one was William Kronhorst, whom she loves. Groebler looked him up yesterday after his conversation with you, and learned all this from him. William, however, has gone to B. to learn what he can about Irene's fate, though it seems to me that there is no need for any great uneasiness in regard to it. You see that for the present you have no occasion for anxiety. Your secret is safe with me, with Groebler and William Kronhorst; it remains only to keep Philip Bonsart away and silent, and not to irritate him by useless resistance to the right he claims. It becomes necessary, therefore, —it may be extremely hard for you, but it is absolutely necessary—that for the present you should submit to the loss of Irene. There is good reason to hope that she will be William Kronhorst's wife, and then you will have your daughter here again."

"My daughter!" exclaimed Elsie, starting up. "My daughter? Why do you say 'Your daughter?'"

"Why—your daughter—Irene!" answered Ferdinand.

"You think Irene is my daughter?"

"Why, certainly; how else could it be? What other explanation can there be?"

"So you believed that? That is what you were trying to prove—and you, you believed it! Well, how could you help it? The suggestion was so natural—there was no other explanation!"

She covered her face with her hands, and the tears trickled through her fingers.

"And is she not—is Irene not your daughter?" asked Ferdinand. "But, heavens! Do I not know that you were secretly married to Philip Bonsart at Asthof—does he not call Irene his child—and did you not yourself confess that my cousin's property rightfully belonged to me, as it would not if Irene were your sister's daughter?"

With a deep sigh Elsie uncovered her face, and, turning to him, said, calmly:

"Yes, yes, you could not do otherwise than think so. I am not angry about it, my friend. And it is perhaps a just punishment for me that you think so. I have long had an impulse to give you my full confidence. Why did I not do so? But why were you not there at the times when I longed to talk openly with you and to find in you the heart of a friend?

"Why, when you were there, did you excite my anger by professions of love? Otherwise I should have confessed everything to you long, long ago, and should have asked you for help—you, against whom I have sinned the most. But could I ask you for help when you were talking to me of love? And the consequence is that you have formed—God only knows what unworthy conceptions of my past life!"

She stopped, clasping her hands and dropping them wearily in her lap, and looked in silence at the floor.

Ferdinand looked at her with a peculiar expression of pain and suspense, not venturing to answer a syllable. There was something crushing in this discovery that he had been so completely deceived and had so sinned against her in his thoughts.

"Do you wish me," she continued after a pause, "to tell you the whole story, all that has made me so unhappy? If you do, listen, and I will tell you:

"When I was a young girl at Asthof, a wild girl, without a mother's care, Philip Bonsart was my constant playmate. We ran about the yard and the gardens, played all sorts of wild tricks, and were constant allies in teasing and tormenting the harmless people in the world around us. This bound us together, though we were, in reality, very different in our natures, and were constantly at strife. But at that age, who inquires whether a companion is really congenial, when he needs him every day for the fun and pleasure that is everything at that age? I, at least, did not; and when Philip was at length sent to school, I gave him my word that I would be his wife when he should have finished at school, and have become a man in business and dignity. As it occurred to him to ask this promise before he went, I should have been obliged to give it, for if I had not, he would probably have given me a beating. But I was a little affected by the parting—too much affected to refuse it. He wrote letters to me, now and then, some of which I answered and some left unanswered; when there was any fun to report, I wrote; when the days passed along quietly and monotonously, I did not, for there was nothing to write; nothing came from my heart that I was impelled to write to him. Gradually he began to feel this. As he grew older, he complained of my hardness and coldness toward him. Even when he was at home during vacations, I had to hear these complaints, and the answer I gave was generally worse treatment than before, until it came to passionate scenes which ended in our making peace—I had to make peace to put an end to his passion, which bored me. He tormented me, too, with petty jealousies, and in return I reproached him with his wild life at the university, of which all kinds of stories were told, and then we sulked—or I treated him as badly as I could, till at length we were reconciled, only to begin again shortly, with the same performance. Whether he loved me, I do not know. I do not think he knew himself; it was, perhaps, only a demoniac desire to gain the ascendency over me, to conquer me, and so to revenge himself for all the pain I had given his heart, or, perhaps, his wounded vanity. This state of affairs continued till the year forty-nine, till the part Philip played in the events of the spring and in the summer months, on the Rhine—the name he made for himself as the people's hero, suddenly gave me a wholly different feeling toward him. I began to respect him, as I had never done before, to admire him; I fell into a state of fanciful fanaticism, I could have borne everything with him, could have struggled and fallen for the great cause of the fatherland, for German unity and freedom. I was often almost on the point of running away secretly to follow him into the conflict for our ideals. Who can tell what would have happened if his *rôle* had not so soon come to an end at H., the city so near us, and to which my father afterward moved? He fled from H., and we exchanged the most high-flown letters, which passed through the hands of one of his friends in Switzerland, until Philip, having escaped from the wreck of the revolution, arrived in Switzerland himself, and at length concluded to turn his back forever to Germany, which he did not now dare to enter, and to try his fortune in America. My enthusiastic admiration for him continued; it was heightened by sympathy for his misfortunes; and so our relation remained the same, and I continued to regard myself as his future wife, and was ready to follow him when he should come to claim my hand. This lasted a year or two. The letters he wrote me were full of hope and courage; I enjoyed them, and waited patiently and contentedly; and yet I was terribly shocked when I, one day, received a letter saying that he was about to sail shortly to take me back with him. It suddenly seemed to me to be a dreadful criminal venture—to go in secret, a fugitive, into a new world, against my father's will, and forever separated from those I loved. That new world seemed to me suddenly so dangerous, so uncertain, so

changeful, the whole future so threatening, and Philip's character so wanting in everything that would secure happiness to us both. And yet, could I now say no—now, when he had been counting upon me for years, when all his efforts to build up his fortune in his new home were animated by the thought of me? I could not, I had not the courage; but I told him, and remained firm in the resolution, that I would go only as his wife. This made it much more difficult for him, when at length he came; it kept him much longer here where his safety was constantly threatened; he had to engage a priest and some witnesses, and to make some preparations that kept him at Asthof several days. He came to H., and I saw him again; he tried to quiet my anxiety, and I promised everything, agreed to everything; under the influence of his imperious personality, I ventured no opposition. On the day appointed, I went to Asthof, under pretence of visiting a friend not far from there; he had provided for my entertainment in an inn, kept by an old servant of his family. But my heart bled when I left my home; I was more dead than alive; and a single warning cry, a dissuading word, would have kept me under my father's roof. But the warning was not spoken. My sister and my father were perfectly willing I should make the visit to my friend; my father helped pack my trunk, and my sister accompanied me to the stage; and I went alone, out into my uncertain future."

"And do you think," said Ferdinand, half aloud, as Elsie paused, "do you think I suffered less during those hours than you did? I was in despair, that day, for I knew everything. I had learned everything through your confidant, Émil Drausfeld."

"Ah! You knew everything, you!" cried Elsie, in extreme surprise.

"Yes, I knew everything—except that a word of dissuasion, a warning, could have held you back; if I had known that, the one to warn you would not have been wanting; he would even have thrown himself under the wheels of your carriage to keep you back. I know, too, what happened afterward. Philip Bonsart's return was discovered by the police; again, I was the only one that knew it; if I had obeyed the impulse of my jealous passion, I should have quietly left him to his fate; but I thought his misfortune would strike you, too; that his lot would thenceforth be yours; and so I went to Emil Dransfeld and sent him to you and Philip with the warning news."

"And do you know that that news, that warning, saved me?" cried Elsie, eagerly. "I may call it saved, for it is clear to me now that Philip Bonsart and I were not suited to each other, that we should have made each other very unhappy. Two characters in which pride so predominates should not be joined together; for neither can yield enough to make the other happy. Yes, that warning saved me. It opened my eyes to the dangers of what I was about to do. I saw the danger of being with him, pursued by the police, treated as a criminal and put into prison, or being obliged to read my name with his in the warrants which would be sent after us; of dishonoring my father's name, and destroying my sister's happiness —her husband could no longer hold his position as an officer—no, all that was beyond my strength, the strength of my pride, perhaps, but it was beyond it. I urged Philip to fly at once to the nearest port, not to make his flight more difficult by taking me, to leave me. At this, he flew into a violent passion, and from distress at this passion, at the sorrow he showed, I consented to go with him to the clergyman who was to marry us, and Emil Drausfield went with us. But this clergyman, who had made the promise to Philip very reluctantly, came to my relief most unexpectedly. He could not perform the ceremony at such short notice, because the chapel was not ready, because one witness was lacking, and there was no other at hand, as he declared, of whose secrecy he could feel assured—in short, he was as anxious to be released from his promise as I from mine; and at last, Philip, in great wrath, declared to me that he would release me from all my promises to follow him afterward, that he would give me back my word, that I should be free forever—only that he should require in return another, and sacred promise; and this promise was, that I should take his

10

child and give it a mother's care. His child! It was a little girl, two and a half years old, that was living in the cabin of a field-watch at Asthof, with the parents of her mother, who had died soon after her birth; the child was sickly, poorly cared for, and miserably neglected. This child, of whose existence I had never known before, lay on his heart; I was obliged to give him the promise he required—my God, what would I not have promised at that moment—I promised everything and swore it, and then he rushed off to his father's, took a horse from the stables, and fled through the darkness and the fog.

"The next day, I returned to my father's, quite broken in spirit by the exciting scenes I had passed through, and yet saved, by the revelation I had received of Philip's character, from regretting that I had at last faithlessly broken my word to him. I tried to care for the child as well as I could; to take it into our house was, of course, impossible; I had to find a family in the city who would take it and be quiet about it; when this was done, I told all to Matilda, and she helped me in the care of the poor child, until she married your cousin and went east with him. After that, my father died. And then I learned that my care of the child, notwithstanding all the precautions I had taken to keep it secret, had been discovered and rumored about, and the worst construction placed upon it. It was not enough that I was left alone, unprotected, and orphaned, and doubly helpless through my poverty, for our affairs were thrown into confusion at my father's death, and I was a beggar—that was not enough, but the world must add to it this horrible wrong. Nothing remained for me but to go to my sister's. Matilda and your cousin received me kindly, and, as they had no children, they were glad to receive Irene also. In the little half-Polish place to which your cousin was transferred immediately after, people troubled themselves very little about the child's origin. It passed for the daughter of your cousin and Matilda; that was natural, and it was quite as natural that neither Matilda, nor your cousin, nor I should see any occasion for explaining to them the real state of the case. Matilda and your cousin soon became so accustomed to the *rôle* of Irene's parents, that they hardly realized it was a *rôle*. I heard from Philip Bonsart, from time to time, through our confidant, Emil Drausfield. He wanted information about his daughter, to whom he seemed very much attached, and I gave it by writing to Emil, who then sent word to him. A direct correspondence would have been so painful to us, that we had decided on this way for Philip to hear from his child.

"And then came the time when Matilda was left alone, when your cousin Alexander died. We then left that place and settled in a little watering-place, K., in Thuringia. We were in very straitened circumstances, for we had to live on the interest of the settlement your cousin, the banker, had given Matilda's husband at his marriage, and a very small pension Matilda received. To this was added a small amount, a few thalers a month, for their daughter Irene."

"Ah, she should not have accepted that!" exclaimed Ferdinand.

"No, she should not ; but what could she do? She did not ask for it; a friend and comrade of her husband had attended to her business affairs after his death, and had made all the statements and allegations necessary; her pension and this money for Irene were paid to her without anything farther; and as she had to provide for me as well as for Irene, and pay for her education, we did not discuss the propriety of taking the money very closely."

"You acted like women, who are deficient in the sense of right men have in such matters, and believe that law can always be twisted to fit circumstances," interrupted Ferdinand.

"The next year," continued Elsie, "I became acquainted with the prince at K., and was weak enough toward myself and toward others who beset me to accept the hand he offered me; I was so poor, so forsaken; I did it, God knows, with the noblest intentions. I believed I could exert the influence on him which I had been assured I could. In my vanity, I believed that from such a lofty height I could shed a

benign influence over a wide and grateful circle, like a guardian spirit. I saw a wholly ideal life before me. What would not a girl believe when a princely crown was offered her? What, until she finds that she has sold herself to the coarse nature of a man that mocks at her ideal dreams, that, notwithstanding all the self-denial he requires of a wife, will not make the slightest sacrifice himself, and must always be what he was and is, leaving nothing for her but self-contempt for so idiotically throwing herself away! But something still more dismaying than this discovery was yet to come. Your cousin, the banker, died, without leaving any will. Matilda had not had the slightest doubt that everything would be left to you; her husband had often assured her that it would be so, when suddenly the entire property fell to her as the mother of Irene, the nearest relative! The court at H. appointed a guardian without delay; the guardian accepted the care of such a property with pleasure, and manifested great zeal in it. No affirmations or proofs were required of Matilda; the matter was regarded as unquestionable, and all Matilda has had to do is to sign certain papers and receive the money sent her by Irene's guardian.

"Matilda had moved here; it was natural that, being so lonely, she should desire to be near me, and I wanted to attend to Irene, as I had promised Philip Bonsart. You can imagine how we two women were frightened, and how helpless, how at sea we felt, when this dreadful inheritance came. What could we do, what, in Heaven's name? The property did not belong to Irene; it belonged to you ; you alone. There was no will, but there was no need of one; since my brother-in-law had died childless, you and your sister were the nearest relatives. But could we now come out and say: Irene is the daughter of a poor servant girl at Asthof; I had put myself under obligation to take the care of her, and then my sister adopted her as her child? It was impossible; wholly impossible. My sister would have exposed herself to criminal prosecution for claiming and receiving the money for the child's education. I should have been completely ruined; for how would the prince have borne it if I had told him the truth; if he had known me to have been engaged for years to a republican and demagogue, who had fled to America, if he had known how near I had been to becoming his wife, that I had stolen away from my father's house for that purpose, how would he have received that? And that was not all; what I feared more than his anger, was his distrust—the incredulity with which he would meet my statements in regard to Irene. He thinks so badly of women! I thought shudderingly of what I had experienced in H., of the calumny I had drawn upon myself by my care of Irene. The end would surely have been that the prince would have rejected and ruined me. That would have been the end of the long struggle between my pride and his coarseness, for that is what our married life has really been—the end would have been irremediable humiliation for me and I should have died in the disgrace.

"And so, so, then, we were too weak to come to a decision, and we let the days pass and became criminals—were silent and took the inheritance that belonged to you. At first we were oppressed and could hardly breathe under the burden, but gradually we grew accustomed to it, and quieted our consciences with the thought that, in the first place, you and Adele, so far as we knew, were not in want; that you had a good position, and that in four or five years Irene would be twenty-one; then she would come into full possession of the property, and then we could disclose everything to her, and quietly put you in possession of what belonged to you.

"So matters stood when I met you in Florence and heard from your own lips how I had sinned against you—that just the loss of that inheritance had entirely ruined your prospects. Not until then did I comprehend the crime I had committed in its whole extent.

> "'Where does the real wrong begin?
> Where man has harmed his fellow-man.'

"That is the principle by which a woman always judges of right; a wrong that harms no one seems very trifling to her, while she feels keenly one that injures or makes any one unhappy, or ruins his prospects, as did mine toward you. What could I do? I tried to gain your friendship, in order to have the right, as a friend, to restore at least a part of what you had been defrauded of. But you did not understand me; you spoiled my plan by your foolish refusal; and afterward you spoiled the second plan I formed to make good your loss to you. Since then I have lived in wretchedness and self-contempt, every morning dreading the new day, and every evening seeking self-forgetfulness in rest the night would not bring—until yesterday, when an insane sense of desperate satisfaction took possession of me, as I found myself on the verge of a catastrophe that must put an end to the unendurable state of affairs. You had discovered our crime, you had taken steps to obtain proofs which would expose me, you had been trying to get possession of my letters to Emil Drausfeld; I had deserved it all, but it excited me inexpressibly; there was so much artifice and hypocrisy in it; it gave me the right to despise you and the whole world as I despised myself; and with this angry contempt was mingled a feeling of satisfied revenge toward myself, as I cried out, in my senseless excitement, 'It is he who has been trying to get the girl into his power, and your deception has driven him to it; and the end will be the ruin of us all.' I was on the verge of madness yesterday. Oh! I suffered unspeakably!"

"Poor woman!" said Ferdinand, softly, and in a tone of heartfelt sympathy.

"Is that all you have to say after you have learned how you have been defrauded and how unjustly I accused you yesterday?"

"That is all; for, truly, you were all the time more unhappy than I; and that not through your own fault, but through a fatality, through the combination of circumstance with the peculiarities of your character; and is not our character, too, a fatality? The character has often an original, unavoidable tendency; if we would only recognize this truth, how much more peaceably we should often get along with others.

We two have sinned against each other—you against me, and I against you, by a hateful, unworthy suspicion. In this we are quits. Let us now throw all that behind us and help each other to meet the future. There is no ground for despair at the prospect. You have no enemy here, no one who would lift a hand against you. Irene, indeed, has been carried away by her father; but need the world, our world here, know anything of that? Groebler will be as silent as the grave. William Kronhorst has no interest in acting against you; on the contrary, he, as well as Philip Bonsart, owes you gratitude for what you have done for Irene. What would her life have been without you?"

"And you—you yourself?"

"I," said Ferdinand, with a bitter smile, "I am mean enough to use the advantage I have over you. I require you to throw all the care and responsibility upon my shoulders. I will talk with Groebler, and then with Philip Bonsart. He will not want to give up his daughter. But as for injuring you in any way, surely——"

"Can you, then, find him so easily?"

"Yes, I know where to find him. He lives in England. I have just returned from an unsuccessful journey to see him."

"Ah!—you hunted him up?"

"I did not find him. I wanted an explanation from him."

Elsie looked at him with large eyes, but said nothing.

"And will you now allow me," he continued, "to go to him, and prevent him from doing anything that may embarrass you?"

She rose and gave him her hand.

"Do I need to tell you that I will? Have I not given you the right to act for me by giving you my unreserved confidence? Do now as you think best. Arrange the matter of the property as you will; I shall be satisfied; provided only that this burden is taken from me, that I know you have received what belongs to you. When that is done, I shall thank you from my inmost heart; and, till then, I will await what the future may bring, with confidence."

Ferdinand held her hand in his while she was speaking, and tried to meet her eyes. But she did not raise them from the floor. He stood a while, unable, in his emotion, to say more. He felt that it would be best to go in silence.

He left the castle, and passed down the long avenue to the city, his eyes fixed upon the grass and the dry leaves at his feet. He felt as if the burden Elsie had spoken of was now rolled upon him.

How could it be otherwise? It was too overwhelming, what he had heard—this look into Elsie's open heart, the thought of what she had passed through, what she had suffered, and then of what he had done against her, in his blind, mad passion. Every wretched, distrustful thought he had cherished against her gnawed at his heart like a poisoned tooth; every word he had spoken against her in his insane suspicion came back to his memory like the stroke of a dagger.

And what was to come of it all? What was to come of him and his feelings toward her, that the last hour had made a thousand-fold more intense? Could she ever forgive him the suspicion he had cherished against her, and the steps he had taken as an unfriendly inquisitor? No, a proud and haughty heart like hers would never forgive it. What would it help him to show generosity in reference to the property she had defrauded him of, to make a parade of unselfishness? She would regard this generosity and unselfishness as the price he felt under obligation to pay to free himself from the shame he must feel for his treatment of her.

But whatever price he paid, he could not clear himself in her eyes. It was impossible. Though the circumstances had compelled her to accept his services and give him her hand as a friend, still she must always, in her heart, hold him in contempt for talking to her of his love while he was secretly plotting against her.

And he could not explain to her what had driven him to this secret action; he could not expect her to believe it, even if he could speak of it; but he had lost the right to speak to her from his heart.

He could not complain of this; he had

deserved it, fully deserved it. If he should search his inmost consciousness for the ultimate motive of his action, he could find no other answer than that he had been prying into the secrets of her life in vexation at her coldness, because he was hurt and angry, and wanted to revenge himself by humiliating her; and so he had nourished the meanest suspicion, had been absorbed in it for months, and had made himself contemptible; and now she was so nobly justified!

When he reached his home he told his sister the whole story. She was startled at the depth of his feelings; he was usually so reticent, she had not dreamed of what was passing in his mind. But now his reticence was broken; he felt that he could not live without confiding in the one he felt sure would understand him. She heard him in silence. She felt that she could say nothing that would be in harmony with the mood his words betrayed. Passion was a province she did not understand, and which she shrank from looking upon. But he did not want an answer; he was not talking to receive consolation or excite contradiction. He talked only as the wounded deer moans.

At length, when he had finished, and sat broodingly looking at the fire, she said:

"Ferdinand, are you going to do nothing now?"

"Do? what shall I do?"

"Do what there is most urgent need of doing; and that, I think, is, to help this poor woman, instead of sitting there in despair and brooding over the matter; to put an end to this hateful story of our lost property in such a way as to take that, at least, from her conscience."

"And how shall I do that?" he asked, eagerly.

"Wisest of brothers! Do you ask advice of me, an unpractical woman? You must know best. Or ask Groebler. That matter must be settled, for that is the very thing that presses most heavily upon the princess; it could not be otherwise. If I knew you would receive advice from me in a business matter, I would make a proposition."

"What is it, Adele? Tell me, I beg of you."

"Let Frau Matilda Schott write to the Probate Court at H. that you are her nearest relative, and as you now live in the same place with her, and as she has confidence in you, and would like your assistance in the care of Irene, she begs the court to appoint you as Irene's guardian and give you the care of her property. I do not think the court would make any objection. The present guardian will then have to give everything into your hands, and then the princess and Matilda Schott can breathe freely; the matter will be off their consciences. When Irene is of age, she can renounce her right. Everything will then be arranged, and no one else need be the wiser for it."

Ferdinand looked at her in surprise.

"In truth," he said, "that is a thought so simply practical that I admire you for it, Adele. That makes everything smooth and easy——"

"I am glad you think so. You do not believe the court will make any difficulty about it?"

"No. The nearest relative has a right to a voice in the guardianship; and if Matilda expresses a wish to have the change made, the court must grant it."

"Then make arrangements at once to have it done. Talk it over with Matilda."

"I will, I will," said Ferdinand, springing up. "I will go and make it clear to her that the affair can be best arranged in that way. Let me embrace you, sister, for your good advice."

He kissed her forehead and went away. Adele watched him as he went, rejoiced that she had succeeded in arousing him from his despairing reflections and sending him off with such an elastic step in a practical errand.

CHAPTER XXIII.

WILLIAM KRONHORST'S JOURNEY.

It was not the most pleasant time of the year to take a pleasure trip, but William Kronhorst had run the risk of his father's surprise at such an idea, and left home the evening before, telling his father in a note that he was going to visit a friend on the Rhine. At noon the next day he reached the convent in Belgium to which Irene had gone. He sent his name to the superior as a messenger in behalf of the friends of the young lady, and as he had the telegram to show in proof of it, he was at once received. When the superior found the messenger to be a handsome young man, and one whose name indicated no relationship between him and the young lady, she possibly felt a little distrust; but she gave him, without hesitation, all the information she could; she had already sent it in a letter to the mother. A man probably from forty to forty-five years old, somewhat above the medium stature and strongly built, with an open face, tanned by wind and weather, and a full dark-blonde beard, had come a few days before on the day of the week appointed for the pupils to receive visits, and had asked to see Irene. He spoke German, but not very fluently, a little in the singing tone peculiar to Americans, and called himself Asthof. When Irene was informed, she was manifestly very much startled, and said, excitedly, that he was a near relative, and she would see him. She had a long conversation with him in the parlor; the next visiting-day he came again. As he was a man of mature years and prepossessing appearance, there had seemed to be no reason for denying him another interview. This, too, had lasted some length of time. The only noticeable thing about it was that Irene had been very quiet and apparently depressed that evening; she had eaten nothing at supper, and had not slept at night, but tossed restlessly about, as her neighbor in the dormitory reported. The next morning the young ladies, of whom there was a large number in the convent, had spent an hour in the garden after the first lesson-hour, and when

they returned to the school-rooms, Irene was missing. They inquired and searched for her, but in vain; she must have gone into the shrubbery of the large garden—William could look from the windows over this garden which formed a moderate sized park—and must then have stolen through the gardener's house, which was the only place of exit, the entire garden being surrounded by high walls. The gardener and his assistants had been out at their work, and could not have seen her. Closer inquiry had brought out the fact that at the same hour a close carriage had stopped on a turnpike, about ten minutes' walk from the convent. There was, therefore, no longer anything mysterious about the matter, except Irene's motive to an action, so incomprehensible and unjustifiable, raising such a commotion in the institution, and so injurious to its reputation.

"And what direction did the carriage then take? Was that noticed?" asked William.

"Yes," answered the sister; "not toward the German border, but westward, into Belgium."

That was all the good sister could tell him; she was anxious to know what should be done with Irene's effects which she had left behind. William assured her that Irene would most probably write to her to apologize for the step she had taken; it could be explained by a strange and unusual complication of circumstances. Until that time he advised her to take no farther steps in the matter. He then took his leave, in order to continue his journey westward without loss of time. As the fugitives had little reason to fear pursuit and hasten their journey, he hoped to overtake them, at least by the time they reached the boat that should carry them to England.

And, in fact, when he arrived at Ostend late in the evening, having taken the shortest route, and went on the steamer which lay in the harbor all ready to cross the channel, he saw a man standing near the prow and quietly smoking a cigar, looking toward the light-houses that rose against the dark back-ground of the evening sky, and observing the dazzling play of the lights from the great reflectors. According to the description given by the sister superior at B., this could be no other than the man with whom Irene had gone. William approached him with a beating heart.

"Herr Asthof?" said he.

The man turned; as far as could be seen from the light of the lantern by which a sailor not far off was packing up trunks and boxes, his face did not indicate very pleased surprise. After a pause he answered, somewhat sharply:

"What do you want of 'Herr Asthof?'"

"First, that he will not be offended at my addressing him, even if I should call him by his right name, Herr Bonsart."

"Ah—you know me, then, well?" said he. "What is it you wish?"

"To introduce myself to you. My name is William Kronhorst."

Philip Bonsart, who did not seem the least inclined to deny his identity, bit his lips and looked at the young man with an expression rather hostile than encouraging.

"William Kronhorst!" he said, mockingly. "The dead, they say, ride fast, but lovers, I see, are not easily outdone. Will you have the kindness to tell me why you have thought it necessary to rush after me like a whirlwind?"

"I may assume that Fräulein Irene has mentioned my name to you, and also, I hope, that you will be kind enough to pardon me for following you in my anxiety about her, even at the risk of your displeasure, which would be exceedingly painful to me."

"Would it, indee Well, then, you can very soon put an end to it by turning around and going the other way, when I tell you that my daughter is well taken care of, that she is safe on board the steamer to return with me to England. I think that ought to quiet your anxiety."

William had grown a little pale at the man's words and his hostile tone. But he answered with so much the more determination:

"If she is under your protection, I need have no farther anxiety about her certainly. There remains only Irene's anxiety about me, and on that account I beg of you to let me speak with her."

Philip Bonsart looked steadily at him with contracted brows.

"Why?" said he. "Don't you think it would be better for you to turn back and leave between you henceforth this channel we are going to cross, my daughter and I?"

"I shall cross it, too; I shall accompany you on this steamer, and on your farther journey, until I have spoken with Irene."

"Plague!" said Bonsart, with a mocking smile; "you are a determined man; but if that is so, come."

He turned and led the way to the lower part of the boat, and showed William into the cabin, which was now empty, most of the passengers being in their state-rooms busy with their preparations for the night. Bonsart disappeared in one of these stateroom and returned immediately afterward with Irene, who uttered a low cry when she saw William; hurrying up to him, she threw her arms about his neck and exclaimed, amid a storm of sobs:

"You are not angry with me, William, tell me, are you? Oh, he will tell you all about it. I could not help it. When he tells you all, you will not be angry with me."

"Irene, how should I be angry with you? I was only anxious about you—my anxiety drove me in pursuit of you," whispered William.

During this little scene Bonsart folded his arms across his breast and looked down gloomily at the young people. It was probably a painful proof to him that he had only half won his daughter back, and must submit to it as unalterable; that his advice to William to leave the sea between them had so little prospect of being followed, and that he had come too late, if he had hoped to bind his daughter's life to his own.

He turned away with a sigh; then he beckoned to William, and seated himself on a *tabouret* near the table, under one of the lamps that hung from the ceiling; William sat down on the sofa at the other side of the table, and Irene beside her father. Taking his right hand and holding it fast in her lap, she whispered:

"Now tell him all, father; he must know all; tell him why I have come with you and belong to you alone," and she closed her eyes and laid her head upon his arm.

"I think it is, all things considered, best that I should tell you exactly how matters stand, Herr Kronhorst. Otherwise, I am afraid Irene would take it upon herself to explain, and I prefer to do it myself. She has told me that she showed you the letters I sent. They were, of course, not intended for you; but as the thing is done, we cannot help it now, and it will enable me to make my story shorter. You know, then, that Irene is my daughter——"

"I know that," interrupted William, drawing a long breath; "but who her mother is—the one to whom you referred only with dark hints in the letters——"

"I will tell you that, too. I shall be glad to talk of Irene's mother, for she deserved to be well spoken of—she deserves Irene's respect and love; she was, indeed, simple and unlearned, but she was a beautiful and affectionate creature. She was a fresh, sweet wild-flower, and if that dreadful, stupid political excitement had not come and carried me away in its current, and if the beautiful Elsie had not suddenly shown herself so sympathizing and enthusiastic toward the bold swimmer in the swift current of the time, and drawn him again to herself—just as the tin goose the children play with follows the magnet—then I should not have deserted that fresh wild-flower—reckless and wild that I was—for the splendid *centifolia;* and I should have been happier. But young men are stupid and seldom pass by an opportunity to ruin their future, when they are drawn on by vanity.

"Well, as I said, she was a simple peasant girl. All she knew of books was what she had learned in the village-school, and from the few volumes that had fallen into her hands and were used to pass away the hours on Sunday afternoons. She had learned refined manners at my father's house, where she was often employed as help, because my mother loved her and she was apt and intelligent and willing. And how beautiful she was! She had such an abundance of dark-brown hair, such a beautiful form, and clear gray-blue eyes, sometimes so roguish, sometimes serious; so shy and yet so trustful!

"It would have been better if I had never seen her, never noticed how beautiful she was—our wood-lark, as my mother often called her. But how could I help noticing it, wild and vain as I was, and with my vanity constantly wounded by Elsie's haughtiness? Elsie and I had grown up together at Asthof; we were accustomed to each other, we regarded ourselves as engaged; but enough of that. I will only say, this Elsie should not have treated me so. She should have made clear to herself what she really wanted; whether she could be my bride and belong to me for life or not; and then she should either have broken with me forever or have given me the regard and confidence due to her future husband. Instead of that, she held me fast by my ambitious passion, and yet never gave me a moment of the quiet happiness one feels in assured possession, in the consciousness that he can rely upon the heart he calls his own. She was always criticising and blaming me; when I looked for warmth and affection, she showed wit and coquetry, and the consciousness of superior rank; and especially the desire to rule; and we were eternally at war in our letters. I had always to be defending myself against her fault-finding; I was constantly bleeding from the wounds she gave my morbid vanity. And, at length, after a hundred secret outbreaks of anger and desperation, I gave up all hope of her; I renounced her and told myself that she was naturally unfit to be a warm-hearted wife to any man.

"And so it happened that I was the more attracted toward our wood-lark, Marianne, Irene's mother—attracted by the charm a vain young man finds in a woman's complete devotion. She was the exact opposite of Elsie; she trusted me and looked up to me; in her maidenly humility, she could not comprehend how a woman could be haughty toward the man she loved. I shall never forget Marianne; she was so much better to me than I deserved; I shall hold her memory in honor as long as I live; and some day, as soon as possible, I shall take

Irene to Asthof, and we, will seek out her grave together, and Irene shall kneel there and think of her as a mother most worthy the devotion of a child.

"Well, to make my story short, I had given up Elsie, and as good as forgotten her, though we still exchanged cool, objective letters, as old acquaintances; and so the time passed on—nearly two years. I was away from home most of the time, at the university, and busy with my preparations to enter on a political life; and then came the mad tumult of 1848. The storm naturally swept me on with it. Nature had given me hot blood, some gift at persuasion, and strong lungs; and that was all that was necessary at that time to make a man suddenly great. When I think of all the political nonsense I uttered and defended and grew angry over in my green youth—of all the excitement and dismay I and a crowd of other enthusiastic young fools brought into the venerable old swamp of that brave city H. ! I believe the Philistines we waked up there took me for a young Robespierre, only needing time for full development. Fortunately for them, I did not have time; for troops came very soon, and we were driven back and scattered. I went to Southern Germany, and played the same part there. When I think now of all the exertion and fatigue I went through, I console myself with thinking how much I learned from it and what a preparation it was for my experience in America.

"But there was one, at least, who looked upon the part I played with anything but disapproval: that was Elsie von Melroth. She, too, was full of patriotic enthusiasm. She was a fanatic in the cause of Germany's greatness and its resurrection as a mighty united empire; and she began to transfer a part of her enthusiasm to me, looking upon me as a warrior for those beautiful patriotic ideas, and very soon as a sufferer, a martyr. Her entire manner seemed changed; her old *hauteur* was gone; she was all fire and enthusiasm.

"At that time I was, in truth, something like a martyr. After a short time of glory, a short time of revelling in hopes of victory and ambitious delusions, I had become a poor fugitive, a poor homeless, wandering devil; I had to bear the heavy sorrow, too, of the loss of Marianne. She had died after Irene's birth, in the utmost need; while I, who should have cared for her, imagined it was more important for me to meddle with political affairs I did not understand than to do my duty at home. Of course my brain was too much excited then for my conscience to trouble me greatly. In the general crash and wreck of all things —for so I regarded the failure of the great plans we had made for the fatherland and the world—in this universal wreck it seemed to me to be but a kind of logical result that what I had personally held dearest should also be lost. It seemed to give me a final release from my country; in a word, it seemed to be only what must have come. I did what I could at that distance to provide for the child Marianne had left, and then I urged my father with redoubled persistence to send me the means for going to America.

"There," he continued, after a pause, "you have the explanation you desired. If you would like to know now why Irene was not brought up as a simple country girl after her mother's death, but as a sort of adopted child of Elsie von Melroth, I will tell you."

"Yes, I beg of you, tell me everything," said William. "You can imagine how anxious I am to hear."

"I have already explained it to Irene at length," answered Bonsart. "Yesterday and the day before I made it clear to her at B. how her fate came to take the turn it has. With you I can be more brief. It is enough to tell you—but do you know the princess, Elsie von Melroth?"

"Yes, I know her."

"She is still a beautiful woman?"

"Beautiful and charming—or, at least, she would be charming if her manner had something more cordial, and cheerful, and companionable. But that is lacking. Her serious manner and her reticence, which are naturally taken, in a person of her rank, as coming from pride and contempt for others, chill and repel, and so she gives only the impression of great and unapproachable beauty."

"The same as ever, then! Irene told me the same. Well, you can, then, imagine, how easy such a woman found it to bring back the man she had held for years in her chains—to excite his ardor anew. I had lost Marianne; I had lost my hopes and my prospects in life; I was banished from my fatherland; how could I help turning with all my heart to this beautiful Elsie, when she seemed suddenly animated with the most enthusiastic affection for me, when I waked up one morning and found myself her hero—I, who had had so long suffered under her contemptuous and haughty treatment! I was weak enough to forget it all, and devote myself to her with full confidence; and she knew how to reanimate my courage; my energy was reawakened; I began to hope for better fortune across the sea, and I felt strong to struggle with fate for her sake. We exchanged vows of faithfulness over and over again in our letters. So, at length, I went to America. To tell you all that happened to me there, would take days. It will be enough to say that, in that great republic, in its institutions and people and social conditions, I found a most discouraging contrast to the ideals of republicanism I had formed, and which I had saved from my political shipwreck. And was it not a bitter experience for me, who had made so many enthusiastic speeches about free government and republican blessedness—had studied, as I thought, so earnestly and profoundly into political matters, had gathered so many fine ideas in my head—I had to find that this real republic in the West could make no other use of my organizing capacities and my willingness for service than to give me the place of carrier of a red republican newspaper, without a single article in it that I, the carrier and errand-boy, could not have written better! But that was not my business; when the money I had taken with me was exhausted, I was thankful enough to get the place of errand-boy and printer's devil, as they call it. This, however, I kept only three weeks; then I obtained a place as a teacher farther in the interior, at a boys' institute, which, unfortunately, was broken up three months afterward. But one of the boys that had

been under my instruction recommended me to his father as book-keeper in a factory. This gave me a lucrative position, and as I emerged from the airy kingdom of my German ideals into the realm of practical things —to tell the truth, it was a kingdom redolent of soot and coal-gas—I advanced to still more lucrative positions. But I worked —worked like a horse—I had still one illusion left me, and that gave me no rest; the illusion that when I should have earned money enough and returned to Europe, I should find a true woman's heart to follow me and brighten all my future in that uncongenial world. An illusion, I say, for it was one. I made the journey to Europe two years after, only to return with a sense of bitterest disappointment and inexpressible anger—alone, as I had come. When I saw Elsie again, I found, to my dismay, that the meeting gave her very little of the happiness I felt; I found her faint-hearted and shy at the thought of a union with me, and of tearing herself away from her life here to go into a strange world."

"But that was only natural, father," said Irene, laying both her hands upon his arm and looking up pleadingly.

"It was natural, child," he answered. "You are right in that, and I no longer feel any resentment toward her. I have since learned to think differently from what I did then, and to understand how natural it was. At first I quieted her opposition by my passionate feelings, and the words they sent to my lips. Everything was prepared for our secret marriage. Elsie left her home under some pretext, and came to Asthof. Then, as ill-luck would have it, the police discovered my presence and began to search for me. There were some obstacles to an immediate marriage, and Elsie would not go until the ceremony had been performed. In the dispute about it I grew angry and gave Elsie back her promise, made her free forever, if she would swear to fulfil one condition——"

"To take care of Irene?" interrupted William Kronhorst.

"To take care of Irene," repeated Bonsart. "I had, of course, looked up the child when I came. I was dismayed to see how little the treatment she received, the whole surroundings in which I found the child, corresponded to the idea I had formed of them. And I felt so powerless to make it radically and permanently better; I had no one in the world to whom I could entrust her in perfect confidence. So, in the moment of our angry parting, I told Elsie all; I demanded that if she would not be my wife, she should at least be something like a stepmother to my child. I demanded it, without really thinking what a burden I was placing upon her. She vowed it—what would she not have vowed to put an end to the torture of that moment? I had not an instant to lose, and I left her and fled like a felon out into the darkness, with anger and despair in my heart. I reached the nearest seaport without being overtaken, and took refuge on an American vessel, where I was sure of protection as an American citizen.

"Now you know all," said Philip Bonsart, in conclusion, "all you can ask to know to clear up whatever mystery there has been about Irene's life."

"And," said William, eagerly, "I thank you most heartily for your unreserved confidence, Herr Bonsart."

"I wish," interrupted Bonsart, with a deprecatory movement of his hand, "I wish that, instead of thanks, you would do me a similar service, and solve the riddle that has been puzzling me since yesterday."

"Puzzling you? What riddle is that?"

"Tell me how it happens that Irene should be the heiress to a large property. How can she, my daughter and poor Marianne's, have inherited an estate? That is what I should like to know. How can she, without deception and rascality?"

"You would not think the Princess Achsenstein and Frau Schott capable of that," said William, emphatically.

Bonsart shook his head. "Not Elsie," he said; "no, not Elsie; she is too proud, much too proud to commit a felony."

"And Frau Schott?"

"I do not know her so well. But if you can answer for her, very well. Nothing remains but to suppose that matters were so arranged by Major Schott when Irene was very young that in case he should die be-

fore receiving some expected inheritance, it might not be lost; but there should be a child as heiress, and thus the property should not be lost to his widow."

William doubted that.

"It would be strange," he said, "for Major Schott to take upon his conscience an abominable deception which would be no benefit to him personally, but only to his widow after his death."

"Why not?" said Bonsart. "There are men who take pleasure in such intrigues, men to whom tricks and frauds give satisfaction for their own sake; or to look at the matter in a charitable light, perhaps the major, who had no children of his own, loved the one he had taken into his family and as good as adopted, the same as if it were his. Perhaps he grieved to think that a fine property would after his death be lost to Irene; and so she was falsely passed off as his daughter."

"That is possible," said William, doubtingly, while Irene said:

"I can never believe it; he was so good, so honest, so open-hearted, Major Schott; and I loved him so much when I was a little girl, and he used to play with me, and gave me dolls; and sometimes, even, he helped me to dress them."

"Perhaps, then," said Philip Bonsart, "it was his wife; she may have ruled him and have compelled him to make Irene heir to that estate by passing her off as his child, so the she herself might not lose it in case she should be a widow before it should come to the family."

"Frau Schott," said William, "is regarded as a good, quiet, and not very energetic woman, who allows herself to be entirely controlled by her sister, the princess."

"And the princess, again, I regard as a woman too proud and high-spirited to be capable of deception, or of consenting to it —notwithstanding all the experience I have had with her. And so the matter remains a mystery. I should not trouble myself much about it, but should be contented with simply regarding the connection between Irene and Frau Schott and her property as broken forever."

"But, father, you will certainly allow me

to write to Frau Schott, who was so long such a good and careful mother to me, and tell her how I shall always honor her and how I want to see her again?"

"Well, yes; that speaks well for your heart, child, and we can consider it and talk it over another time. For the present, I will only say that I was angry at myself yesterday, when I first heard of the matter from Irene. If I had dreamed that my child was being used as the instrument of some disgraceful deception, I should not have made so much ceremony with these women in my thoughts."

"But, father," exclaimed Irene, "how hard and hasty you are—how can you talk so and condemn them, when, as you yourself confess, it is all a mystery to you?"

"How I can condemn them? Why, I condemn myself for having been, even in my anger, such a soft-hearted, inconsiderate fool! So respectful of those women; so careful to spare them! You, Herr Kronhorst, will understand it. When I thought of Elsie and of Frau Schott, I thought of them as that good-hearted Emil Drausfeld represented them. You know—or do not know—that this good fellow was for years the only means of communication between me and Elsie and my child. After I had parted from Elsie, I felt too bitter toward her to write to her. She was still less inclined to a correspondence; she probably felt some regret for the whole affair, for her faithlessness, and I was a living humiliation, an eternal reproach to her, and so her pride could not consent to any communication with me by letter. But I had nothing in the world but my child, and I could not bear to hear nothing from her. So at length I wrote to Emil Dransfeld, with whom I was very little acquainted, but whom Elsie had taken into her confidence, and who had come, like a true warning Eckart, to tell me that I was discovered and persued by the police, that time when I was to be married to Elsie at Asthof. So I wrote to this Drausfeld from over the ocean, when I had become somewhat settled there, and begged him to get news of Irene from Elsie and then write to me everything in her letter that concerned the child; but he might

keep her letter and write to her that he should, so that she could write without constraint and not imagine that I wanted to hear from her, and was only making a pretext to renew our correspondence. I received the answer I desired from Emil Drausfeld; he told me what Elsie had written about Irene. In about half a year, perhaps, I wrote again, and so, to be brief, I kept myself informed in regard to Irene, and to Elsie also. I learned that Elsie—so at least she assured Dransfeld—was faithfully and conscientiously fulfiling the condition under which I had given her her freedom; that she had given the child to the care of a reliable family in H., where the Melroths lived; that she did not content herself with that, but very often went quietly in the evening to visit Irene herself. Then I heard that her care for the poor child had become known and had been maliciously interpreted. Well, that was no more than was to be expected in a gossipy little place like H., or, indeed, in any place where there are respectable people, the height of whose happiness is to torture and defame their dear fellow-men. Elsie lost her father shortly afterward, and went to live with her sister, who had moved with her husband to a forlorn little garrisoned city in Lusatia or Lithuania. I bought a map in Chicago to look out the place where my child was, and the little nest was marked in such fine print that I had trouble to find it; for Elsie had taken the child there with her, and the Schotts passed it off as theirs, which they had left behind under Elsie's care on account of the milder climate of their home in the west; that sounded plausible, and could not arouse suspicion in any malicious Wend or Lithuanian; and I had no objection to it; it seemed a very natural way of avoiding all difficulty. The years passed on; I learned that the captain had become a major, then that he was dead; I learned that the sisters lived together, and how Irene was growing up and developing; how she had grown to be a pretty and intelligent little lady, with a tendency to obstinacy and roguishness, how her musical performances left very much to be desired in the way of improvement, but that her talent for languages was more satisfactory; how she wrote a very neat, pretty hand, and could express herself on paper with ease, though her orthography was by no means faultless; I heard all that, beside a memorable, though unfortunate attempt to distinguish herself in some difficult cooking enterprise."

"Oh, father," said Irene, smiling, and giving him a slight tap on the arm, "how can you talk about all that now?"

"I like to talk about it, child; to think with what deep emotion I read all these little details, as Elsie condescended to send them to me, or, to be just, which she willingly gave in full, because her woman's tact told her what a father would like to hear about his child. But to go on with my story. I heard, too, the great news of Elsie's marriage; the poor girl who had once been so near giving her hand to a homeless man, a rabid democrat, had married a prince and put on a crown. Well, I could easily imagine how well a crown would become her proud head, and wished her all joy of her elevation, though I thought that real happiness could hardly be connected with the step that placed her on the throne of a petty, mediatized prince. To tell the truth, I felt a little humiliated; she could now have said to me, in triumph: 'You see how wisely I acted in being deaf to your entreaties, your reproaches, and your anger, that dark night, when you warned me of the consequences of my faithlessness, when'— but enough of that. Whatever might have been the feelings with which I heard of Elsie's brilliant marriage, I had long since accustomed myself to think calmly of her. I no longer condemned her. I had ceased to be an idealist, forming wholly false conceptions of women, and requiring impossible things of them. I had gradually been learning to know the world—the real, sober, practical, selfish world. America is a remarkably good school for such learning; and those American ladies, swaying idly in their rocking-chairs, had given me many a good and sensible idea about Elsie von Melroth that I never had had before. I told myself that it was, after all, better for both of us, that I could never have made her happy; we were both too hot-headed and

independent to get on well together, and America—at least that side of American life where I should be obliged to move—was not just the clear and peaceful lake for such a proud swan as Elsie to move upon."

Irene nodded wisely, and William remarked that one could often see a Providence in such turns of fate.

"If your very young experience has brought you to that conclusion," said Bonsart, good-humoredly, and smiling a little sarcastically, "we can regard it as settled. My altered opinion of Elsie's actions and character was not a little assisted, as I have told you, by what was written of her by Emil Drausfeld, who, of all men, said nothing but good, and, by the way, was, I think, a little in love with Elsie, or had been. But enough of that; I will make the story short; the satisfaction it gives me, after so many long, lonely years of isolation among strangers, to have an opportunity to talk freely, makes me talkative and prolix; but in a word: in the course of time I came to think of Elsie von Melroth with such a reconciled and grateful feeling, that I became a martyr to this feeling. The more I longed for the end of my isolation to come, for a heart that should be mine, the more I realized that I could never be happy in a marriage with any of the American ladies I knew, the more I longed for Irene, the more eager grew my desire to grasp the simplest and most natural means that presented itself to secure some domestic happiness, to give a purpose to my life, and not work on stupidly for the mere satisfaction of possessing a thousand or two dollars more at the end of the year than at the beginning. I wanted to reclaim my daughter, my property; Elsie should restore her to me; I would come back to the Old World to get her; this was in my thoughts for months—no, for years; and yet I did not venture to go about it vigorously and decidedly. I was so grateful to Elsie and her sister for all they had done for the child, for their years of trouble and care. The two childless women must have grown accustomed to Irene, must be devotedly attached to her. And, then, had not Irene, too, grown accustomed to them; was she not completely happy where she was—so near the princess, who must live in brilliant style? I imagined how it must be in a little court like that; how merry the life there might be, how many pleasures of all kinds, how many things to satisfy the little vanity of a woman, who would find it hard, after having been the centre of the homage and flatteries of an aristocratic circle, to be transferred to an entirely different world. So I felt that I would be doing a cruel and brutally selfish thing in taking the child from Elsie, and at the same time tearing Irene away from a happy and brilliant life. At last I came to a decision; I could apply first to Irene; I could learn what her real position was, and how she herself would look upon the prospect of a change. So I decided to write to her, at first only as an experiment, and in an indefinite way, that would betray nothing. Only when I had received answers that showed me I had formed very false conceptions of Irene's position—that her life was by no means that of a little princess, surrounded with attentions and revelling in pleasure—only then did I explain myself more clearly and go to work with decision to accomplish my purpose. Well, I need not tell you about the correspondence; you know already. Irene at length wrote to me that they had found it advisable to send her to B., to a large and celebrated school, kept by nuns. Of course, the first thing that suggested itself was that I go at once to see Irene and talk over matters freely with her, leaving it to her to decide then whether she would go with me or not. I accordingly went to B., and had no difficulty in obtaining an interview with my daughter. I need not describe my pleasure at seeing her—to you, of all men, Kronhorst—and my pleasure at the warm, hearty reception she gave me; to me, who must have looked a little strange and wild to her; her manner had nothing reticent or repellant about it; she told me openly and frankly what was in her heart. During our conversation, in the descriptions and accounts we gave each other of our past lives, and our discussions about what was now to be done, I learned a fact entirely new to me, one of which Emil Drausfeld had never

written a syllable—that Irene had inherited a large property from a banker, Schott, in H.—a man I remember, as I once transacted some business with him, never dreaming that his money would be the inheritance of my daughter; well, that Irene had received this property, and her supposed mother, Frau Schott, lived comfortably on the interest of it, and that Irene's expenses at B. were probably paid from the same source. I was inclined at first to believe that Irene was mistaken, that, with an ignorance pardonable in a young girl, she confused Frau Schott's possessions with her own. But I was most unpleasantly surprised when she assured me that she could not be mistaken; that the old banker had made no will, by which Frau Schott could have been the heiress, and that the major had made none, which was probable, as he died before the banker; but that she, Irene, received the inheritance because she was passed off as a Schott, a daughter of the major, as she herself supposed she was. This made it evident to me that Irene had been made the instrument of a fraud, that I had been a fool with my soft-hearted scruples about injuring Elsie and hurting her feelings, that I should have done better if I had interfered before and taken Irene away from a position where she was being made to play a dishonorable and villainous part. The explanation I gave Irene excited her and made her more inclined to conform to my wish that she should tear herself away from her present circumstances and those she had regarded as her family, and go with her poor, solitary father. So far, the affair would have been satisfactory, had not Irene given me some shy hints of another fact not altogether pleasant for me. In the picture she gave me of her life, a new and, to me, strange form began to appear on the canvas; it gradually advanced from the shadowy background where it had first come to view into a doubtful half-light; this made me a little suspicious; but at length a tremor in the voice and a peculiar embarrassment with which Irene pronounced the name, William Kronhorst, threw a blaze of light on the form of that fortunate youth.

" 'William Kronhorst!' I cried, startled

and vexed; and I am afraid my tone wounded my daughter's tender feelings a little——"

Here he was interrupted in his story by Irene, who exclaimed:

"Now, father, you are too bad, to talk so sarcastically of all that; you should not talk of it at all; if it must be told, I would much rather tell William myself.

Bonsart smiled good-humoredly.

"I was not speaking sarcastically, child," he answered; "not at all. If you think the impression made upon me by my discovery when we sat talking at the convent in B. put me into a joking mood, you are mistaken. Quite the contrary! The more you assured me that it was a very serious matter, and the more I became convinced that it was not a mere juvenile notion, the more dissatisfied and perplexed I grew about the whole affair. You cannot blame me for that, and if Herr Kronhorst blames me for confessing it so bluntly, I cannot help it; it is so, and I think it is very natural. I hoped to find my child whole and sound, and I find that a good share of her heart is lost for me; that I have come too late; that my fatherly care and satisfaction in finding a good husband for her will never be needed; that this gives me pain, no one can wonder or be offended at. But as I am not to talk about it, we will say no more on the subject. I will only add, to Herr William, that the end of it all was, I resolved to take Irene away from the convent at once. If they had recklessly passed Irene off for a Schott, to give her an inheritance to which she had not the slightest right, it was clear that I was under no obligation to stand on ceremony, or show them the consideration I should otherwise have had for the women who had taken care of Irene. I saw at once that it would be hard to come to an agreement with them; for, after what they had done, they would certainly make every exertion to continue the deception. If I had applied to them, they would have begun by removing Irene from the school, and have done all in their power to make it impossible for me to see her. I think that would have been the first result of a peaceable application to them. As you must agree to that, you will admit that the best and safest thing for me to do was to take Irene from the convent and bring her away with me. I succeeded in doing that without difficulty. Irene herself was so much excited about the *rôle* of heiress she had been made to play, that she was the more ready to come with me. Now, young man, you understand the whole affair; and when you hear the people at home talk it over and condemn my conduct, you can tell them how things stand and why I have acted as I have. However, if you want to spare the ladies, and that will be best, you may be silent about the matter. If you want to do still better for them, you may go to them, and say everything good in behalf of Philip Bonsart, and that, in case they do not provoke him by some unwise measure, they will be safe from all disturbance and all indiscretion on his part, and can be assured that he will think of them only with the most sincere gratitude for what they have made of this little blossom; and she herself will never forget——"

"Oh, no, surely not, never," interrupted Irene, eagerly. "I must believe my father when he says they have done a great wrong, but my heart remains the same for them, and I cannot endure the thought of being forever separated from them. I shall not be satisfied until my father has solemnly promised that I may write to them, and that when everything has been arranged by letter, I may visit them again—if they do not condemn poor Irene too severely because she could not do otherwise than follow her father, and are willing to see her again."

"Do not be anxious, Irene; it will all be settled satisfactorily," said William, taking her other hand. "There is nothing so very bad about it; and as regards the inheritance, we may assume, while we are waiting for farther explanations, that they can show palliating circumstances; perhaps they were forced to act as they did by circumstances that left them no alternative, and which we do not understand——"

"Oh, surely," said Irene; "it is surely so!"

"And now," continued William, "what I am most anxious about is, that Herr Philip

Bonsart should give me permission to talk about these altered circumstances with my father——"

"The great Iron Baron," interrupted Bonsart, "do you think he will be more inclined to grant your request when he learns that Irene is Philip Bonsart's daughter? That is a very bold presumption in you, young man?"

William Kronhorst might have had some such feeling himself. He was silent a moment, and then said:

"At least, I beg your permission to talk with him, Herr Bonsart."

"That I cannot refuse you. I consider frankness the best policy in everything, and, therefore, I do not conceal from you what I think of the matter and how I console myself. I have so long neglected my child and left her to the care of others, that I do not now feel as if I had a right to complain of her as I find her. She is mine again and I am very happy over it; she knows how happy, and so she has heroically resolved to go out into a strange world with her lonely father. She is mine again," he repeated, taking her hand and stroking it tenderly as he looked into her eyes, "but she has only given herself back to me as I found her. I found her with a heart that belonged to another, as she did not for a moment conceal from me. It was like receiving an estate with a mortgage upon it. The mortgage is in favor of Herr William Kronhorst, and I am obliged to recognize it; it cannot be discharged, can it, Irene? So you have my permission to talk with your father about it, and to expect as much from the conversation as your juvenile hopefulness will allow you to; and then we shall see what will come of it and what is to be done next."

While this conversation had been going on in the cabin, the noise on the deck had increased; there were sounds of hasty feet and cries of confused voices; the great ropes fell heavily on the deck, the wheels began to beat and toss the water, and with a shudder the boat started out into the channel.

William Kronhorst had not thought of leaving the boat; there was nothing that re-quired his return to his home. And Bonsart was probably glad of his company, as it gave him an opportunity to learn something of the character and disposition of the man, anxious to become so nearly connected with him.

Long after Irene had gone to her berth, the two men sat together in a quiet corner of the cabin. Bonsart first encouraged William to talk of his home, and describe the kind of life from which Irene had come. Then he gave detailed descriptions of his own changeful and adventurous life, talking so openly and frankly as to make William feel that he had made a favorable impression on Irene's father. He learned that Bonsart's efforts had at length given him a good position and a fair amount of property. He was a partner in a New York firm, and managed their business in Newcastle, where they had an iron foundry and machine-shop. He had accumulated a property which would replace at least one half of what Irene had lost. When they at length rose, Bonsart shook William's hand cordially.

"You are an honorable and solid man, I believe," he said, "and now that I know you, I am more resigned than I was before to the mortgage and the impossibility of discharging it. But, to speak plainly, it seems to me neither necessary nor best for you to accompany us any farther. You can understand that for a time now I would like to have my child to myself. So, if you please, we will part to-morrow in Dover; you can return, and write to us what the Iron Baron says about the matter."

William saw the reasonableness of the request and consented willingly. When they had landed the next day in Dover, he accompanied them to the dépôt, where they were to take the train for London. While they were waiting, Irene took him aside, and, with tears in her eyes, whispered:

"Isn't my father good, William—isn't he real good?"

"Yes, Irene," answered the young man; "he is a good, noble man, and deserves our perfect confidence; he has won mine as fully as he has a right to yours."

"Oh, William, how thankful I am to hear

you say that! It is so good of you, William; I love him so; he has had such a hard and lonely life! Think, William, how lonely! And now, William, there is one thing I want you to do—to go to all of them, to Aunt Elsie, to my adopted mother, and to Adele von Schott; don't forget to go to Adele, too. And tell them everything; we have no longer anything to conceal. Tell them how my father found me, and how I came with him; how I could not help coming with him; I couldn't help it, could I? Tell them that, and tell them how good and kind he is. But tell them, too, how much I love them, and that I will never forget them, never, in spite of all my father says about their doing wrong. They have been good to me as long as I can remember, and I owe everything I am to them; I shall never forget it. Will you tell them that, and ask them to forgive me and to have no anxiety about me? Will you promise me that you will?"

"Certainly, I will promise you, Irene; and do not weep; you will see them again; for some day I shall carry you back from this England; I shall, no matter what happens; I shall take you back to our home and to your father's rightful home."

As he said this, Philip Bonsart stepped up and separated them. He and Irene entered the train, which soon after started, and William went back to inquire when the next steamer would leave.

When he returned home, he made it his first business not to talk with the "Iron Baron," or to deliver Irene's messages to the ladies, but to look up Herr Groebler.

"Herr Groebler," he said, "I came to tell you that no one ever did me a greater favor than you did in making me your agent, as you called it. I found Irene and her father. My heart is freed from a heavy burden, and my great anxiety now is that I shall never be able to repay you for what you have done for me in confiding in me first. Will you promise always to think of me when you are in a position to need a friend?"

Herr Groebler took his offered hand and shook it heartily.

"Your gratitude proves your good heart,"

he said; "but it was in pure selfishness that I sent you—to spare myself a journey. But I will accept your promise, and as it's best to strike while the iron is hot, I will take advantage at once of your willingness to be sacrificed and ask for an exhaustive account of your experiences. Take a seat and tell me everything, exactly and minutely."

William gave an exact report. Groebler listened intently and then said:

"What strange turns men's destinies take, and how much more wonderful results fate can bring about than even the man that brings up a fox and a rabbit, or a hunting-dog and a partridge, peaceably in the same cage! Just imagine at your coming wedding the fraternal embrace of this state traitor, Bonsart, and the detective, Groebler, who, it is to be hoped, will be among the invited guests. It will make a fine closing effect for a strange drama!"

CHAPTER XXIV.

ADELE'S INTERFERENCE.

Several months had passed, bringing many changes. They had covered the trees with green and the fields with springing blades; they had filled the forests with song; had cheered the spirits of the rooks that had been cawing so sullenly from the roofs of the old minster, and sent them fluttering about in the sunny air; had given new courage to the despairing ducks, now splashing about in the half-dried pond before the old nunnery. The building itself still lay in the shadows thrown by the tall church. Shadows, too, lay on the life of the youngest member of the household, who, since Easter, had been obliged to go to school day after day, to the great detriment of the education of sundry squirrels and fishes, and a young kestrel, which, together with an obstinate silver watch, that still held regularly on its course, notwith-

11

standing the cuffs and thumps of many a small battle, were his own and his pride. But Carl bent to the command of duty and went regularly to school, for the dark shadows on the brow of his guardian inspired him with wholesome awe, and made him resigned to the inevitable must.

But the greatest change of all—a change, not from darkness and chill to sun and summer, had come to Castle Achsenstein. It had lost its master. Prince Gottlieb Anton had nearly recovered after his attack; he had felt so well and strong, that during the Easter holidays he wanted guests around him; they had come in only too great numbers; the prince had been too regardless of the physician's directions in regard to diet during these and the succeeding days. One evening he had another stroke, and lay unconscious till sundown the next day, when he died. His will gave nothing to his widow, except what had been secured to her by the marriage settlement, the use of an estate in the Wetterau, and a respectable annual income. Elsie was still living at Achsenstein, where Prince Waldemar, the oldest son of Gottleib Anton, had now taken up his residence. She was waiting for her estate to be put in order before moving there, and her sister was preparing to go with her.

After his return from Dover, William Kronhorst had talked with the princess and her sister, and told them everything Irene had asked him to. Elsie had listened, evidently with a lightened heart, to all he had to tell about Irene's present position and about Philip Bonsart. She did not conceal from him how heartily she sympathized with his love for Irene, or her hope to see Irene again—a hope that depended on his bringing her back sooner or later as his wife. She asked many questions about Philip Bonsart and listened attentively to all William had to tell about his changeful life. She expressed no blame for the sudden and unceremonious way in which he had carried off Irene.

He had a right to her and did not need to parlay long with any one about it, she said, in reply to her sister, who was extremely angry at Bonsart for his way of managing

the affair and giving [them both so much anxiety, causing her sleepless nights, and leading Elsie, in her excitement and grief, to suspect and accuse innocent persons.

William Kronhorst could have answered these complaints against Bonsart's way of proceeding. He could have explained to her what had induced Irene's father to take charge of her so suddenly. But he did not venture on that part of the subject; he naturally shrank from letting them know that he had been initiated into their secrets.

After this conversation, he collected his courage for a decisive interview with his father.

At twilight of the same day he stepped into the large room his father used as a study. It presented a striking contrast to the other and luxuriantly-furnished apartments of the villa. With a peculiar filial piety, Herr Kronhorst had collected here all the furniture his father had used in his room; the writing-desk, with its drawers and shelves; the old settees and chairs, and a little old piano that had belonged to his mother. He contented himself with these poor and faded relics of a half century before; they served to remind him of the narrow circumstances in which his father's life had passed, and on how small and modest a scale he himself had begun his successful career.

As William entered, his father was standing at the window, looking over some memoranda by the fading daylight. He laid down the book and motioned his son to take his grandfather's great old leather chair, while he himself went for a cigar.

"I would like to claim your attention for some time, father," William began; "have you leisure now?"

"If you have anything important to say, we will take the leisure. Is it business, or have you some travelling adventure to tell me about?"

"Not that, not either of them, although I shall have to speak about my journey; first, of the reason and real purpose of my journey."

"The real purpose—was it, then, some other than the one you gave me to understand?"

"Yes, quite a different one. I do not know whether you have heard that Irene was sent to the convent of Blumenthal."

"To be sure I have heard of it, and I think the reason why it was done is not hard to guess."

"Perhaps so; but I did not begin the subject to discuss that. I was going to tell you, father, that a few days ago, Frau Schott was surprised by the news that Irene had been abducted from the convent."

"Abducted? Irene? By whom?"

"That was the question, and to find an answer to it, I lost no time in putting myself on the road as soon as I heard of the matter."

"Ah, that was the cause of your sudden departure?"

"That was it. You must forgive me, father, for giving you a false reason; I was too anxious about Irene——"

"Well, well," interrupted Herr Kronhorst, blowing great clouds from his cigar, "did you succeed in clearing up the mystery?"

"Yes; I overtook Irene and the abductor, saw them, and talked with them."

"Indeed! And who was the abductor?"

"Her father, Philip Bonsart!"

"You talked with that man?"

"Yes, a whole night, on the passage from Ostend to Dover. We talked together very freely; he told me all about his circumstances and Irene's history. He has nothing against my suit for Irene's hand."

"Hasn't he?" said Herr Kronhorst, sarcastically. "But why," he continued, "did he take his daughter away from Blumenthal?"

"Because he wanted her with him; he was leading a lonely life; and because no one else had a right to her."

"No one?"

"No, no one; her mother died long, long ago."

"Are you so certain of that?"

"Yes, perfectly certain. Philip Bonsart told me who Irene's mother was—a poor, simple peasant girl, who died soon after Irene's birth."

"He told you that himself?"

"Yes. He told me the whole story of his life—how he grew up on the same estate with Princess Aschsentein; how he very early regarded her as his betrothed; how they quarrelled and he regarded his relation to her as broken off, and the girl who afterward——"

"It seems, in truth," interrupted Herr Kronhorst, "that this virtuous man, who once made himself very notorious here as a democrat—not exactly here in this part of the country, but there was a great deal in the newspapers about him—it seems that he was very frank and confidential with you?"

"Yes, father; his whole nature is perfectly frank and upright; if you only knew him, you would love him?"

"I have some doubt of that," answered his father, drily; "but even if it were so, I hardly think it would help us much. It would not alter the facts. Was there anything more you wanted to say?"

"I was going to say that I can, therefore, give you information now about Irene's origin—facts I had not the slightest suspicion of when I first asked your consent to my marriage with Irene——"

"And then you are going to ask my consent again?"

"Yes, certainly, father, and this time in the firm hope that you will not be so hard and cruel, for if you refuse me again now—but no, you cannot and will not."

"And if I should?"

William did not answer. He looked at his father with a pale and beseeching face.

The father took a few turns up and down the room. Then he said:

"You see, William, you are truthful and reliable; you know nothing, thank God, of trickery and lying, and, therefore, you do not believe in trickery and lies in others."

"Do you mean that I ought to see trickery and lies in what Irene's father told me?"

"Yes, my son, in spite of the fact that, as Irene's father, he seems to you worthy of all respect. In spite of that!"

"You will never convince me of that!"

"That may be; but just as little can you bring me to absolute faith in what this man has told you."

"Then I must get him to lay the proofs

in black and white before my incredulous father."

"If he can!"

"You will see that it will be easy for him. There must be baptismal records and public registers of everything."

"We shall see," said Kronhorst. "In the meantime, I do not want you to reproach me secretly with being less frank with you than this Herr Bonsart seemed to be. I will tell you, unreservedly, what led me to act as I did. You have a right to know it. I see, to my sorrow, that the affair has become so serious to you, that I should be doing wrong to leave you in the dark about anything relating to it, anything that can help bring you to reason. Perhaps I should have done better to talk freely with you before. But I could not without touching on a subject one approches with reluctance, especially an elderly man in conversation with his children."

"And yet, father," said William, "I would have been so grateful to you if you had told me openly why you were so strongly opposed to what involves my happiness, my future, all my hopes in life."

"A time will come when you will not take it so tragically."

"That time will never come," said William, firmly.

"Well, then, hear. You can imagine that when years had softened my sorrow at the loss of your mother, I began to wish to fill her place in my house. The place such a woman occupied in my heart could, I felt, never be filled. But it was possible that I might find a true, loving woman who would take her place at my side, share my duties with me, and give me a new domestic life."

"Certainly, certainly, father," said William, eagerly, "that was but natural; and we children were just as anxious to see some one to take the lead in the house, some one who would have loved us for your sake."

"Well, and so, when Frau Schott moved into our neighborhood, I thought of her. I found her amiable and womanly, without any tendency to that domineering spirit an elderly man has to fear in a second marriage; in short, I had made up my mind, and was about to offer her my hand when she told me that, in view of the confidence I had shown her, she felt it her duty to give me an account of all her circumstances. She told me Irene was not her daughter, but an adopted child of her sister, the princess; the daughter of the princess' former lover, Philip Bonsart, and a peasant-girl; when their engagement was broken, Philip had given the child into the care of the princess. As Frau Schott was better fitted to adopt the child than a young girl, she and her husband had decided to let the child pass as theirs."

"This statement, as you can understand, suprised and shocked me. If Irene was Philip Bonsart's daughter, and "adopted child" of his former betrothed, the princess, it seemed pretty certain that she was no other than the daughter of the princess; and Frau Schott had probably long ago sworn to her sister never to betray it; so that she could not confess it to me, but invented a nameless forgotten peasant-girl, whose actual existence seemed very doubtful to me."

"Oh, father, you did her a wrong, a great wrong!"

"You think so. Well, hear the rest. She confessed to me what pain and anguish of conscience she had felt when, in consequence of Irene having passed as her child, the large property of the banker Schott, had been assigned to her as the next heir, without any farther questions being asked. She could not refuse the property, because her sister had, in the meantime, become Princess of Achsenstein, and the prince was distrustful and suspicious, and if the matter were explained to him, he would believe—well, just what I believe without being a very distrustful or suspicious man either."

"And yet so wrongly and falsely, father," exclaimed William, "so wholly false!"

"It may be so," answered Herr Kronhorst, coolly. "But that was not all. What vexed and angered me most in the matter was to see how little conscience women can have about important business matters and legal rights. These women were in possession of a large property that did not belong to them, and yet they had no apprehensions of a time when the rightful heirs might come forward and expose them to all the world, and have them condemned as criminals! Can you comprehend that?"

"No; that I cannot."

"As you would suppose, I discontinued my attentions to Frau Schott, who would not take my advice to act in a straightforward way and listen only to the voice of her conscience. But the matter interested me so much, that I made inquiries about Irene's origin through a confidential business friend at H."

"Oh, father, was your incredulity as strong as that?"

"It was as strong as that; and, unfortunately, it was only made still stronger by the results of my inquiries."

William shook his head, and looked despondingly at the floor.

"Of course," continued his father, "I made sure that the inquiries were conducted with secrecy and care. The result was that, many years ago, it had come to the ears of many people at H. that there was a child, a daughter of Elsie von Melroth."

"Of course," said William. "Philip Bonsart told me that a few benevolent tea-table gossips in H. had made such a discovery——"

"That may be—that he said so. He may have said everything necessary to avoid compromising the princess. It is natural that he should desire not to expose her. But hear the rest. My inquiries also brought out the fact, that in the church register of the parish to which Asthof belonged, the village where Irene was said to have been born, there is absolutely no record of a daughter of Philip Bonsart, and none in the register of the neighboring parish."

"What does that prove?" said William, anxiously. "It is natural that Irene's mother should not have given Philip Bonsart's name."

"That may be," answered Herr Kronhorst. "But, William, you have understanding enough not to blame me if, under the circumstances I insist on my original idea of the matter. I cannot give my consent to your marriage with a girl of such origin, whether she is the daughter of the princess, as I think, or of a peasant-girl, as you think. She is no wife for my son and heir. It is not a trifling matter to be the heir of such a property, of such a name and position. I am not acting in an unfatherly way when I ask you to consider, that when we have the benefit of any good-fortune, we should be willing to bear the burdens and inconveniences connected with it; that we must fulfill the duties connected with any right. It is your duty not to bring into the house I have founded by my own efforts and which I hope to keep free from all dishonor, a wife who may bring into it the disgrace of a wretched scandal—a scandalous suit, as soon as the rightful heirs demand the inheritance they have been defrauded of and the interest they have been losing all these years."

"Can I not, then, give up the property, and pay the interest?"

Herr Kronhorst smiled.

"Good-natured fathers," he said, "sometimes pay little debts for their sons-in-law. But you can hardly expect me to welcome a daughter-in-law, with whom I should have to begin by paying a heavy sum; although I do not require that you should consider the question of property in choosing a wife. Let the one you choose have nothing, nothing whatever but an honorable family and an unsullied name—that I must insist upon! This is my final decision in the matter, William. Do not think that I do not sympathize with you and know how much you suffer. I wish most heartily that the case were otherwise, that it were not my duty to speak as I do. But as I believe it is, I cannot do otherwise. Bear it like a man and try to forget. Irene is separated from you now. You will, I hope, never see her again, and it is a great comfort to me to think so!"

William said nothing. He saw there was no hope of a more favorable decision now, and that any farther words from him would only make his father more hard and severe.

He rose and laid his cold, damp hand hastily in the one his father offered, and withdrew, avoiding his father's eyes.

His firm resolve to marry Irene was not shaken by what his father had said, neither was his faith in the truth of Bonsart's statements. At first he thought he would convince his father of their truth by going to

Asthof himself, and getting the proofs his father's agent in H. had failed to find. He went to Groebler to talk with him about it. But Groebler dissuaded him. "These parish registers," he said, "are often very carelessly kept by the clergymen. Sometimes they get the names entirely wrong, especially when they are as uncommon as Irene; so that it is very uncertain whether you would be any more successful than your father's agent was. But supposing you should be; what advantage would it be to you? What change would it make? It would not make Irene what your father would think a desirable daughter-in-law."

William could but acknowledge that Groebler was right; he, therefore, contented himself with reserving the journey for some future time, and went to seek consolation from Adele. He would talk to her freely; he had a presentiment that she would be the one to set everything right. It looked, too, as if Adele's influence over Herr Kronhorst was increasing every day; that he thought to find in her the one of whom he had talked with his son. He sought the society of her brother more and more, and a very lively intercourse had sprung up between the two families.

But this state of affairs placed Adele in a somewhat embarrassing position. She was suddenly called upon to listen to William's confidence. He seemed to regard her as his natural confidant, and poured all his sorrows into her ears. And as lovers always have very many, very exciting and never-before-experienced things to communicate, William, of course, came to her very often. His son's devotion to Adele could not escape Herr Kronhorst's notice; and so Adele's position became very embarrassing, while at the same time she could do nothing and say nothing that could help William. His father had repeated his refusal; and, notwithstanding all William's asseverations that he would be true to Irene, and would yet marry her and bring her home, it did not seem as if anything could be altered. She could not relieve him in the least from the sense of helplessness which oppressed him, notwithstanding all his brave talk. She could but expect that his father would have

suspicions that she was encouraging his son in opposition to his wishes. She would gladly have talked freely with Herr Kronhorst about the matter, as she had done once before. But her words were not taken in such a way the first time as to encourage her to make another attempt; and, moreover, she now felt too much under constraint in his presence to talk freely with him on the subject.

So there remained to her at last nothing but to be perfectly frank with William himself.

"You place me," she said, "in too painful a position; and you must not be angry with me for wanting to escape from it. My conscience will not allow me to do otherwise than say to you that your first duty is to trust your father and submit to the decision he has made, because it cannot be a mere arbitrary one; you yourself know that your father is not a self-willed despot, who thinks more of carrying his own point than of making his children happy. And if I tell you this, which your father's friendship for me makes it doubly my duty to do, then I make you impatient and angry, and you go away sullen. Would it not be better for us to avoid the unfortunate subject entirely, since I cannot give you the comfort you expect and desire?"

"That is very selfish of you, Fraülein Adele," answered William, hastily. "Must I, then, feel entirely forsaken in my sorrow? And even if you have not enough sympathy for me to listen to me, does it not concern Irene, too, who is so attached to you that you cannot possibly be indifferent to her happiness?"

"There is no indifference about it; that you know very well, my dear William. And is it selfish in me to express my sense of powerlessness to help you in any way, to say anything to comfort you or give you any hope? Or encourage you to wait patiently, and to withdraw from a position that gives me more pain than you think, and in which there seems to be no prospect of my doing any good?"

William sat silent for a while, with a gloomy face.

"You may be right, but it is none the

less painful for me to hear you talk so. What, in Heaven's name, will be left for me when I have not a single friend left to talk with and from whom I can expect sympathy? Nothing will be left for me but to carry out the plan I have long had in mind."

"What plan is that?"

"To tear myself entirely away from my position here; to make a fortune for myself, and independently gain a position where I can offer Irene a place worthy of her."

"It is a chimerical plan, my young friend. For, even if you could bring yourself to pain your father so—now, when he relies upon you as his help and his support, when his strength shall fail under his heavy burdens, after he has worked for you and when he depends upon you to carry on his great work—if you could bring yourself to give him so much pain and to desert him, you would not gain Irene by it. Do you think her father would look upon you in the same light, whether you were the eldest son and the heir of the privy councillor Kronhorst, or a clerk for some mercantile firm dependent on his own exertions, for that is the way you would have to begin?"

William had not much to say in answer to this. It pained Adele to express her opinion so bluntly, but she could not help it. Her finest feelings urged her to escape from the false position in which she found herself placed, and which she felt much more keenly than she had the similar position in which she had formerly been as Irene's confidant. Then she had only her sense of duty toward Frau Schott as Irene's mother, to trouble her conscience; and now her duty toward William's father seemed so much more solemn and sacred?

"It is true, I should have to begin with that," said William, after a pause. "But when once I had taken a decided step, my father would not be irreconcilable. And in this I counted a little on you."

"On me?"

"On the value my father places on your advice and your opinion, you need not make that deprecating motion; I know how much he respects your judgment, and what influence you might exert over him if you would. So I thought you would help me; that when

my father should see that I was inflexible in my determination, you would induce him to give me a small capital so that I could begin some business by which I could get on faster."

"If I could exert any influence over your father, William, it would be only so long as I might share his views and sentiments. When mine should be opposed to his, I am afraid we should find my influence very slight. And then, how could I have so little tact as to interfere in your relations to each other, which would then have taken on something of a hostile character?"

William threw a quick glance at her face.

"You are not honest with me," he said. "You know very well that——. But we will leave that, or you might charge me with want of tact. In one thing you are right. Before carrying out my plan, I must have an understanding with Irene's father."

William remained only a few minutes longer and Irene did not see him again for several days.

Adele had been left alone this afternoon. Her brother had gone soon after dinner to make arrangements for a new road which was to be laid through a ravine in the prince's forest. He was to meet the surveyor, and an officer of the prince at the place and make the arrangements there. The young prince, a pleasant and obliging man, who, quite in contrast to his departed father, willingly admitted that he understood nothing about such matters, and let his officer talk, took the landrath by the arm when the business was finished, and asked him to walk back to the city through the park. Ferdinand had no objection to offer; he walked along with the prince, listening to his lively talk; but his eyes wandered anxiously over the park; he dreaded seeing Elsie's form rise up before him. Since the day he had called and heard her explanation, the thought of meeting her again had been inexpressibly painful to him. But Elsie was not in the park. When they drew near the castle, the prince, to his dismay, invited him to take some refreshment with him on the veranda at the rear of the castle.

"You can, at the same time, remarked

the prince, take leave of the princess, who, I see, is on the veranda. She is going in a few days to her estate in the Wetterau, and will be glad to see you again before she goes. Come."

Ferdinand could not command his voice sufficiently to object; he was obliged to go with the prince. Else was sitting in an arm-chair on the veranda, leaning back and looking idly into the distance. She was dressed in deep mourning.

She grew very pale at sight of Ferdinand, but offered her hand with an air of perfect composure, saying:

"I ought to be very angry with you, Herr von Schott. Your conscience must tell you that you have neglected me cruelly in my affliction."

"And did you think I would have ventured——"

"To come and inquire after an old friend?" she put in, quickly, as if she observed his embarrassment and came to his help; "I believed that. You could not know whether I should be in need of a friend, or that Prince Waldemar had attended to my affairs with so much kindness, that without him I should have been very much in want of a friend's assistance."

"You must not scold Herr von Schott too much, my dear mother," said Prince Waldemar, smiling. "I hear he has the name of being something of a hermit, which is very virtuous, but not very pleasant for his neighbors, living lonely in the country as we do. And when you are gone, it will be still more lonely up here; I hope Herr von Schott will remember that no virtue should be carried to excess."

"I hardly believe," said Elsie, ' that this love of a hermit's life is natural to you, Herr von Schott. At least, it did not show itself when I knew you in my youth. So you must have acquired it in your life here. So, my dear Waldemar, you may expect that one of these fine days Herr von Schott will desert his dark office in the shadow of the old cathedral and return to the south, where I found him so happy more than a year ago, and where we spent some glorious days."

Ferdinand, who had avoided meeting El-

sie's eyes, thought he felt them resting questioningly on him as she said this.

"Who is not drawn toward the south again," he said, "when he has once lived there? But we have to learn to conquer such longings, when we have a duty to bind us to some other place. I have taken such a duty on myself, and so I shall probably stay in my dark office in the shadow of the old cathedral till the end."

As he said this, he met a peculiar glance from Elsie's eyes. Her countenance expressed something like terror.

"Will you really do that?" she asked eagerly.

"Why does that surprise you so?" asked Prince Waldemar. "Your words sound very much as if you would be gratified to see our circle deprived of Herr von Schott's society. Leave him here, and I will try every means for converting him from his devotion to a hermit-life."

They had seated themselves a a little round cast-iron table, and a waiter had brought wine and refreshments. The prince chatted pleasantly, until the officer who had been with them in the forest stepped up and asked directions from the prince about some other business. The prince rose and withdrew with him to the distance of a few steps, to discuss the matter. This left Ferdinand and Elsie alone for a few minutes.

"What does that mean, Herr von Schott? You declared you would stay here—here, in your office?"

"Certainly, princess; I shall stay [here in my office."

"In the office you took only reluctantly and from necessity, while all your preferences and hopes were with your former employment?"

"That employment, with all my hopes, lies behind me."

"But you gave it up only because you must; because you were too poor to stay in it; because you were too proud to accept help from a friend. But now, when the means are no longer lacking, now you will certainly resume it again?"

"No," answered Ferdinand, quietly; "I shall not resume it. The means you speak of will not make the slightest change in my life. I shall live as I did before, only on the avails of my position."

"But that is utterly foolish," said Elsie, redening and speaking angrily.

"Foolish to show you how little I cared for those means, when I was trying to find out whom they rightfully belonged to, how little I was troubled about my inheritance? It may be that it is foolish, but that is the way I shall act. The property may be of use to my sister. I shall take none of it."

Elsie looked at him a moment in speechless astonishment and indignation.

"But if I tell you," she whispered, eagerly, "that I desire you to return to your old life; that I cannot have a moment's rest till it is done; that I——"

Ferdinand shook his head, but they were just then interrupted. Prince Waldemar came back, and Elsie was obliged to leave the rest unsaid. The prince took up the conversation where he had dropped it, and in a few moments Ferdinand rose to go. The prince shook his hand, and Elsie returned his bow with a slight, proud nod.

She was evidently excited by what Ferdinand had said. Strange! Why should she be angry at that? What did it matter to her how he spent his future life? Did she hate him for his proceeding against her so that she could· not endure to have him do anything to show her that he was not so contemptible as her hatred would like to see him? Or was it due simply to her love of power, which took pleasure in determining his future, and could bear no opposition to the plans she had made? · Ferdinand could not understand it, but he felt an angry satisfaction because he could tell her. · Do not think I was anxious for this money I scorn to use, even though I humiliated myself enough to take it from you to give you back your peace of conscience and take away the burden that oppressed you!

In the evening he told his sister what Elsie had said and that she was soon going away. Adele was studying his features as he talked; they had a sort of rigid look, an expression she had noticed often during the last few weeks, since his last interview with Elsie.

"Then she is going?" said Adele, after a pause. "And I think it is well she is going. She separates from you in peace and in friendship with all, and I think you will feel relieved when she is gone."

Ferdinand did not answer. And, in fact, if he had assented to his sister's last remark, he would have lied. No; he did not feel relief at the thought that she was going. He had avoided meeting her, how long! And yet, the thought that she was going, that he was losing her forever, filled him with an icy despair it seemed he could hardly endure. There were moments when he felt that he could have given up himself, his will, his very soul; have thrown himself in the dust before her and begged her pardon and her pity.

But she could not pardon him; she could have no pity for the man he had shown himself to be, the man she must consider him. And he could not so bend his pride; nothing remained to him now but his pride and his defiance.

In this mood, it was hard for him to accept the invitation Herr Kronhorst sent, a few days afterward, to him and Adele, to take tea at the villa on Sunday afternoon, and which Adele wished to accept.

Sunday was a clear, warm, sunny day of early summer. Herr Kronhorst had tea served on the upper balcony, in front of the conservatory. There were but a few guests beside the von Schotts. From the balcony they had a fine view of the beautiful valley; looking off to Castle Achsenstein, whose position was less commanding than that of the villa, but which rose with more pleasant surroundings above its beautiful terraces, they could see its many windows glowing in the ruby light of the sinking sun. Ferdinand's eyes had long been resting upon it, when one of the guests called the attention of the company to the effect of the sunset light on the castle, and all eyes were turned toward it.

Adele had risen and gone forward alone to the balustrade of the balcony. She looked down at the rushing river, whose waters were a dark steel-blue in the shadow of the bank on the side toward the villa, but toward the other side were painted crimson by the sunset glow, while the young willows along the margin—which Prince Gottlieb Anton had seen glowing in the red torch-light on that evening so fatal to him—were now swaying idly in the evening wind. Attracted by the view, or absorbed in thought, Adele walked slowly along to the projection at the end of the balcony, and stood leaning on the parapet and looking down at the river.

"Why are you looking so thoughtfully into the river?" said a low voice at her side, and she looked up into Herr Kronhorst's eyes. "Is the river telling you its secret in this beautiful light?"

"Has it one?"

"I think it must have two, as it now has two colors, where it is going and what it hides in its depths."

"It is going with its restless flow where it will no longer be needed—to the sea. And what it hides in its depths? I think if you should draw it off, you would find nothing in its bed but sand and pebbles."

"You take a prosaic view of it, Fräulein Adele; but you may be right. I have no idea of drawing it off, merely to find in its bed what you find in most men, when you wait patiently for the stream of their talk to exhaust itself. But the river is still an emblem of human life; its irresistible impulse to press on to a greater stream in the distance, which will take it up and carry it to the boundless ocean, is an emblem of the impulse of the human soul. May I go on in this strain, or are you in too prosaic a mood to listen to it?"

"I have only to object that it flows because it must, while man does not obey a mere blind impulse, but considers where he will go, and determines for himself."

"So it is said. But, determines for himself! Some few privileged individuals, of a reflective disposition—as, for instance, a certain wise Fräulein not far away—they may afford confirmation to this dogma of free self-government in every crisis of life. But I must confess that my life has not always been determined by impulses far above the force of natural law, to which drives the unconscious river on to another stream, and finally to infinity."

"Ah," answered Adele, smiling, "do you say that—you, who from your youth have been holding steadily onward to a goal you had set for yourself, with the utmost strength and tenacity of will? But I will take you at your word and make a practical application. If you have not been able to resist the power of your heart and its inclinations, if your more reflective and stronger spirit cannot master them, how can you expect much younger and weaker souls to do it? Is it not tyrannical and in the highest degree unjust?"

"What do you mean?" asked Kronhorst, while his face darkened a little.

"You must understand. I am speaking for two poor young people whom you are making very unhappy, while the end will be that you will only have to acknowledge yourself conquered by the obstinacy of their attachment."

A proud smile played around Herr Kronhorst's lips, but Adele saw plainly some perplexity in the look he threw at her.

"You do not believe me?" she continued. "Well, then, I will tell you. Your incredulity puts you in danger of losing the heart of your child."

Kronhorst made no answer; but, after a pause, offered Adele his arm, saying:

"Let us take a few turns on the balcony. I would like a chance to tell you just how matters stand, without being disturbed.

When they reached the opposite end of the balcony, Kronhorst began speaking in a suppressed voice.

"It is impossible," said he, "for me to consent to William's marriage with a girl whose circumstances I do not understand, and of whom I am sure of one thing only—that she is in an entirely false position. She came here with her mother, Frau Schott; they lived in elegant style; she was said to be the heir of a rich relative. Frau Schott, however, afterwards confessed to me confidentially, that Irene was not her daughter; that she was a child the princess had in charge, and which she, Frau Schott, had adopted; that Irene's father was in America; that the inheritance she had received did not belong to her, and would be given up to the rightful heirs when she should be of age. Surprised at these disclosures, I urged Frau Schott to acknowledge the whole openly. But she excused herself on the ground that her sister would be compromised by it in the eyes of the prince; that he would put a wrong construction upon it. I could only shrug my shoulders, for I was convinced that he would not be far from the truth. Frau Schott did not, therefore, follow my advice, and I would not enter into any relation where I could not act with straight-forward honesty. Just as little could I consent to have William involved in such a position."

"But poor Irene was so guiltless!"

"Certainly; but yet, with her stolen inheritance she was no bride for my son."

"I must confess you are right there," answered Adele, sighing. "But now, Irene is in quite a different position,"

"William says so," said Kronhorst. "But is it really so? She has been reclaimed by her father, and is with him in England. But is there not the same mystery about her origin? Who is her mother? Can you convince me that it is not the"——

"Do not call any names, Herr Kronhorst, for you will be doing an injustice."

"Very well; I will not call any names; I have said enough, and you must admit that I am right; that I cannot consent to have William marry Irene for this reason alone, that I should fear to bring upon my family a most disgraceful, scandalous prosecution.'

"A scandalous prosecution? How can that be?" exclaimed Adele, in surprise.

"Why, that is very evident."

"I cannot see, for my life, how it could come about!"

"From the rightful heirs of that property, who, now that Bonsart has claimed his daughter, will draw their conclusions, and demand what belongs to them with the interest and damages."

"Oh," said Adele, smiling sadly, "has that been disturbing you? Your anxiety about that was needless."

"Are you so sure of that?"

"Yes; for the simple reason that my brother and I are the heirs."

"I thought of that, though I did not know that you were the only heirs. Are you?"

"We are the only ones. There is no one in the world more nearly related to our cousin than we."

"And you?"

"We have long since settled the matter quietly and satisfactorily with those ladies. The guardian who had charge of the property has given it into my brother's care, because my brother, as the nearest relative, asked the court to grant him the guardianship. Everything has been arranged, and there cannot possibly be any trouble. Irene's property is all in my brother's hands. Neither of us has the slightest idea of alluding to the affair again in the presence of either of those ladies, or of letting the world know anything about it."

"Well, that is perfectly satisfactory, as regards that part of the subject."

"And if you want to be satisfied with regard to your suspicion about the princess, I will refer you to my brother."

"And what has he learned about it?"

"Oh, he has spent only too many days, weeks, and months in searching into the past life of the princess."

"You say that with such a deep sigh!"

"I have reason to. My brother has been made most unhappy by the affair. May I trust you with it?"

"Do I not deserve your confidence a little?"

"Certainly. Well, through his relation to the princess, my brother has been placed in the strangest, and to him, most painful position; the position of a man passionately in love with the one he regards as his enemy, and who in his heart worships the one he accuses and pursues with suspicion, who all the time hates himself for what he is doing against the woman that has placed him in such an unhappy state of strife with himself. So at least it was for a long time; but now he considers the princess fully justified, and has forgiven her the wrong about the property; and now he is torn with sorrow and remorse."

"Can that really be true?" exclaimed Herr Kronhorst, in astonishment.

"It is a long, unhappy story," said Adele; "too long and sad to be told now. Let us return to our subject. Do you wish to be convinced by my brother of the perfect in nocence of the princess?"

"It is enough that you express your conviction of it."

"I do express it without the slightest hesitation ; I am ready, if you still doubt, and if you require it, to put my hand into the fire."

"I do not doubt the truth of what you say ; and since it is so, will you tell me candidly whether you believe in a deep, true attachment between these young people? do you believe it is a whole-hearted love that promises to be permanent, as so few of these ordinary juvenile love affairs are? Do you believe that of William, notwithstanding his youth?"

"Yes," answered Adele; "I have seen how deeply he suffers. It is possible that at first, his affection may not have differed much from that of what you call ordinary juvenile love affairs. But the opposition he has met with has strengthened it so that it cannot now be destroyed ; and you will have to be careful that it does not excite William to rebel against your authority."

"Do you then deem the matter so serious?"

"From all that William has told me in confidence, I judge that the matter is very serious. You have educated him to firmness and strength of will. You have shown him that a man ought to be strong and independent enough to make a position and fortune for himself."

"And with such ideas, you think, William might rebel against me?"

"If Irene's father should encourage him in them I think he might."

Kronhorst threw a troubled look at her face, and said, with a sigh :

"Well, Adele, I will do as you advise me. You know me and my circumstances, and it seems you know William better, unfortunately, than I do. You know, too, Irene's circumstances. Put yourself in my place and tell me what to do."

"I can understand," answered Adele, "that you may justly be ambitious to have your eldest son make a brilliant marriage. But you stand high enough to be independent of the consideration of property."

"Oh, that is not the question," interrupted Herr Kronhorst. "My opposition is based neither on ambition nor money considerations. I should not object, if William wanted to marry the daughter of an honest peasant."

"And you would prefer her to Irene? That would be very foolish in you ; for the daughter of an honest peasant would have neither Irene's grace nor her culture, and hardly her pure, true heart. And what other qualities have you to consider?"

"I see," said Kronhorst, with a sigh, "that I must yield before you threaten me with an instant revolt on William's part. It is always well to understand when the right moment has come for yielding of one's own accord. If that moment is passed, then, as the poet says :

'We meet the Must and lose the thanks.'"

Adele looked up with a face beaming with joy.

They returned to the company. Kronhorst looked for William, and was told that he had withdrawn a few minutes before. Going to William's room, he found him sitting with folded arms in the seat of the open window, looking fixedly at the golden clouds above the sinking sun. As Kronhorst looked into the gloomy face of his son, who sprang up, in surprise, and looked questioningly at him, he was glad that he had yielded so entirely to Adele, and let her decide for him. He felt that he could not have been so hard-hearted as to hold out forever against the dearest wish of the boy he so tenderly loved. He could not have relied on his firmness to carry him through.

He offered William his hand, and said, in a voice that betrayed his emotion:

"Give me your hand, William, I have come to make peace with you. And since I know you hold fast to your conditions with inflexible obstinacy, nothing remains for me but to accept them."

"Father," exclaimed William, grasping his father's hand in both his own, "Father, you really give your consent? Oh, how I thank you; how I shall thank you all my life!"

Give some of your thanks to Fraülein Adele; for, to tell the truth, it is she who has set the matter in a light that reconciles me to it."

"Adele? Oh, I knew she would be the angel that would make peace between us; I knew she is so good, and noble, and sensible. I knew she would make it right between us, father. But that does not in the least diminish the gratitude I feel, and which Irene and I will show you all our lives!"

CHAPTER XXV.

CONCLUSION.

Fraülein Adele's fortunate interference in the affairs of the two young people seemed to be but the beginning of her mission to help people out of their troubles, and bring them to the realization of their dearest hopes. Carl was the next one that came to her for help. Immediately after school one day he appeared before her and said, defiantly:

"The teacher told me I was a boy God had sent to his school as a judgment on him; that I ought to go and be a stable-boy. And I will do it! I will do that very thing! Help me, Fraulein!"

"To be a stable-boy? You? You are not in earnest, Carl?"

"But I am in earnest; the teacher thought he would shame me before the whole school; but I will do it in earnest! You know Herr Kronhorst; I want to help take care of his horses; he has such splendid horses! And it's so nice up there at the villa."

"Have you been there, then?"

"Of course I have. I go every half-holiday to fish in the river below the villa, with Herr Kronhorst's stable-boys; I have given them squirrels and they take me with them for that. And then we go to the stables, and evenings I help them fix the straw and sift the oats. Were you ever in the stables? It is as nice there as in a church. Speak for me, Fraülein Adele, and let me help in the stables. I understand all about horses, and I can ride—oh, you don't know how I can ride!"

"Do you really desire that? is it your whole ambition to be a stable-boy?"

"First stable-boy, then groom, then equerry!"

Carl spoke the last word with a peculiar emphasis, and his eyes sparkled. It seemed to represent to him the summit of human ambition.

Adele shook her head, but she thought to herself that possibly this might be Carl's true calling, as he seemed to have a passionate fondness for every living animal, large or small. So she promised him to talk with her brother about it; they agreed that it would be best to make no opposition to the boy's decided wish, since the consequences of compulsion on such an untractable nature could not be foreseen.

"His obstinate head may be the very one to make a wild colt tame and manageable," said Ferdinand; "I can ask the councillor to take him."

In a few days Adele made Carl more than happy by telling him of Herr Kronhorst's consent to give him a place among his grooms.

Adele felt very little of the pleasure she gave to those around her, so long as her brother remained in the unhappy mood he no longer tried to conceal. After considering and brooding for a long time about his mood and what might help him, she said to him, one day:

"If I were in your place, Ferdinand, I would resign my office. God knows, I should suffer to be obliged to live without you. But now I can live at my aunt's under quite different and pleasanter circumstances. Or perhaps William and Irene would give me a home with them; and I shall always have a good friend in Herr Kronhorst, if I should need protection. You need not, therefore, have any anxiety about me. And I am convinced that it would be better for you to throw off the burdens of your business, which affords you no satisfaction, to be free to return to your old profession that used to make you so happy, or to be entirely free and go into the world, and try change of scene, and enjoy the society of intellectual people, who would stimulate you and help you to enjoy life again. Take a long journey; go to Greece or the Orient; you are rich enough now to be independent anywhere."

"And do you think," said Ferdinand, with a forced laugh, "that I would use this money now to lead a free, merry life without care or anxiety?"

Adele looked at him in surprise.

"At least, I will not have it said of me that I chased like a hungry dog after the money for the money's sake," he continued, in a defiant tone.

"Ah!" she exclaimed; "you are, then, after all, too conscientious to regard the whole inheritance as yours?"

Ferdinand turned away without answering. Adele watched him in silence, as he walked slowly to the window, with his hands clasped behind him.

"Forever and eternally thinking of her!" she thought, with a sigh. "It will ruin him!"

In her powerlessness, Adele resolved to take her friend Kronhorst into her confidence, and ask his advice about what was to be done to bring Ferdinand to a different spirit. She did so at the next opportunity, explaining the matter more openly and fully than she had done before. He recommended a step that seemed to her to have every prospect of success.

"There is no hope," said he, "that by your persuasions alone you can induce Ferdinand to change his position entirely, and return to a world in whose fresher and more bracing air he may recover. The only thing that can plunge him into such a bath, under the foaming serf of the great world, is an impulse coming in some way from the princess—some consideration for her—since, as you say, she is the power that reigns sovereign over his life."

"But that proud woman," said Adele, "will she not feel mortally offended by his proceedings against her? Will she not hate him as the one who first discovered her secret, her fraud, and then compelled her to confess it? Could anything else be expected of her than that she would hate him intensely?"

"It is possible," answered Kronhorst. "Perhaps she hates him, and, perhaps—who knows—perhaps he is the first man she has ever met before whose will her own has had to bend. He may have inspired her with respect, and she may have a strong nand should not be merely in nominal possession of his inheritance. He wants to show her that he acted as he did from regard for her, not from a selfish desire to get possession of the property. The idea is rather high-flown than sensible or practical. But that is his will, and he has no very clear idea of what is to become of the property. You will hardly consent to please him by taking it all for yourself, and so encouraging him in his freak. So nothing remains but to explain to the princess, that so long as he does not enjoy the property and make himself independent with it, so long he is virtually deprived of it, and so long she remains the criminal who has deprived him of it. It is only the simple truth."

"That is true: it is the simple truth. And you think that the princess should be induced, when the subject is placed in this light, to demand directly of Ferdinand that he give up his resolution?"

"That is what I mean."

"But who is to do this? to go to her and speak so plainly of matters which——"

"Which concern you nearly enough—you who have been wronged and whose brother's welfare is concerned—to authorize you to speak openly and plainly. I think you should do it. I am ready to drive up to the castle with you and to stand by you bravely in the battle as a friend of your brother. For I shall have a reserve force in the background to bring the princess to terms. If she should be so filled with hatred and so haughty as to refuse to listen to your reasons, and bring her will to bear against Ferdinand's freak, I will give her to understand that I do not consider her a fit associate for my future daughter-in-law, and will take care that she shall never see her again!"

Adele felt deeply that such a step would be a double humiliation for her. She would not only be confessing her own powerlessness to influence her brother, but would also be showing the proud woman how great was her power over him; and she could bring herself to decide upon it only with the greatest reluctance. But her anxiety for Ferdinand's future overcame her reluc-

enough sense of justice to tell herself that he had a right to do everything he did. Let us suppose that she hates him too much to wish to do anything whatever, to exert any influence on him that would contribute to his happiness. It is still possible to appeal to her pride and her conscience, and compel her by them to do as you wish. Her pride and her conscience must require that Ferditance, and she consented to go to the castle the next day with Herr Kronhorst. They could not delay any longer, for it was understood that the princess would start before the end of the week.

She was, however, spared the humiliation. When Herr Kronhorst had gone, after appointing the hour at which he would come the next day, she took her usual seat at the window, wondering what would come of the next day's interview. She took up some fine embroidery and worked awhile, when a sudden darkness made her look up. It could not be the evening twilight, the days were now so long. Looking out, she saw that a heavy storm was gathering; the sky above the roofs and towers of the minster was covered with leaden clouds. A peculiar, tawny, spectral light, lay upon the old building, making it look still more decayed and gray with age. The frightened rooks fluttered hurriedly about and cawed louder than ever, as if to announce the coming storm, or as if angry that the old building stood so unmoved by the coming danger, and did not storm with all its bells to frighten it away.

Adele went to close the windows of an adjoining bed-room. As she did so, the first gust of wind, mingled with the first great drops of the rain, beat into her face. She returned to her place at the window, and glanced out at the dry, dusty grass-plat below. As she withdrew her eyes, they caught a glimpse of a lady's form just disappearing within the door below. She saw nothing distinctly but the folds of a black dress.

"It must be Frau Theresa Gröebler coming to make me a visit," she thought. "She has reached shelter just in time—she is so afraid of thunder-storms!"

It was, indeed, just in time; an instant after the storm broke forth in fury, whirled a cloud of dust high over the dry grass-plat, and threw it, with malicious force, on the panes of Adele's window, which rattled at the shock; then the rain-drops pattered on them so violently, that it was impossible for Adele to hear the lady's step, which must have ascended the stairs and approached her door. To her surprise, however, there was no knock. She went and opened the door, and looked up the long hall; not a human form was visible through its gloomy length; only a strong gust of wind and a furious howl of the storm came from its farther end.

Adele closed the door with an uneasy feeling.

"Have I seen a ghost, then?" she asked herself. "Perhaps it is a 'black lady' that haunts this old house. Maybe one of the convent sisters has left her grave behind the cathedral, and is gliding through these dark passages in the tempest. It would not be anything so very strange. How uncanny it is in this old building! If I were not afraid of disturbing Ferdinand, I would go to him."

She resumed her place at the window just as the first flash of lightning was reflected from the wet tiles of the cathedral roof.

The black lady she had seen, and who had disappeared so mysteriously, had, in the meantime, ascended the stairs and passed along the hall with a light, uncertain, and hesitating step, but quite in the manner of mortals still in the flesh. An instant before Adele opened the door she had stepped into Ferdinand's office, after a hasty knock. She stopped on the threshold. Ferdinand, who was bending over his work, raised his head slowly and turned toward her, then exclaimed:

"Elsie!—you!"

He sprang up and advanced a step toward her, exclaiming again:

"You, princess?"

"It is I," whispered Elsie, bringing out the words with difficulty. "You are frightened at the sight of me and you have a right to be. I do not come with any peaceful design. I come almost like that unhappy girl, who one night went into the hall in our house at H. to take vengeance on the one who was about to leave her and then destroy herself. Do you remember? I once said I had no key to such an act; I could not understand her; I should be incapable of acting so; I would not run after a faithless man. If he could desert me, I would quietly let him go. I said that years ago. I know now what an empty boast it was. The tortures of despair have taught me how presumptuous my pride was then and how broken it is now. That is what drives me here to-day. But do not be alarmed," she continued, with a bitter smile; "I am not going to seize any weapon to kill you. I only come to see you in this tempest and bring you the tempest in my soul; you must bear it, for you have caused it. You have treated me basely, strangely, detestably. You have been the demon of my whole life. If you had never come in my way, then——"

"For God's sake, princess!" exclaimed Ferdinand, in fearful emotion, "why do you come to tell me that? I know it well enough. It is the very thought that is killing me—the consciousness that I have sinned against you in a way you can never pardon. And if you do really come in the spirit of the unhappy girl in the old tradition you speak of, with the strong desire to take revenge, you might have spared yourself the journey—you are sufficiently avenged by the remorse that is gnawing at my life!"

"Remorse? By your remorse? Then, in heaven's name, why did not your remorse drive you to me? Why did you let day after day pass by, let me put off my journey under all sorts of lying pretexts, put it off again and again, while the days passed and neither brought you nor any message from you, until I submitted to the last humiliation, and came to you myself, to make this confession, to ask you, in my despair: How is it possible that you can forsake me, that you can let me go without a word or sign of sympathy, after I have long since told you everything, have laid my whole life open before you, after I have confessed to you how I have struggled and suffered on your account? Or do you think

it is so easy for a woman to play the hypocrite where she loves, to assume a freezing manner—so easy to make the last sacrifice, to renounce forever"——

"Elsie," exclaimed Ferdinand, with beating heart, "what does that mean? what are you saying? I do not understand!"

"You do not understand," she answered, in a tone through which something like contempt trembled; "you did not understand what it cost me when I played the hypocrite in Florence to gain the right to share with you the wealth I then had; when I tried to have you marry Irene in order to restore what I had defrauded you of! But it was well so, then; then, you ought not to have understood me! But now, now, when I have told you everything that has influenced my life—it should not be so now; you should not selfishly require me to come to you to tell you that I love you and have always loved you; that the power the thought of you had over me, consciously or unconsciously to myself, was all that saved me from that unhappy purpose of flying across the sea with a man whose real nature was strange to me"——

"Oh, Elsie, Elsie," interrupted Ferdinand, rushing toward her and grasping both her hands, "what are you saying? Do I really hear those words? Is it not a jest, a dream—oh, go on, go on!"

"Why need I go on? What else shall I say? What, but that nothing could be more stupid, more miserable than the pride that made you act as if I no longer existed for you, the pride that was in me till to-day, when I gained strength to tread it under foot and come to you to tell you all my heart. You know all now. I am free, and now decide what our life shall be!"

"Pride!" exclaimed Ferdinand; "oh, heavens, what a mistake! It was only the most terrible humility, that was destroying me—the thought that you had forever condemned me. Oh, Elsie," he continued, drawing her to his heart, "as you have told me all, tell me now how to bear this happiness; it seems as if I should die of so much happiness!"

She laid her head upon his shoulder, while the tears streamed down her face.

A sharp flash of lightning quivered through the dark room and played around them, but they did not see it.

The next day, when Herr Kronhorst called to take Adele to the castle, she received him with a face beaming with joy.

"We are spared the trouble of going to Achsenstein," she said, laughingly: "I have a great, an unlooked for announcement to make to you. They say man is a slender reed, moved by every breeze, now this way and now that. But my dear brother and his Elsie are stronger natures. It takes a storm like that of yesterday to move them. Only think, that storm whirled them together and into each other's arms."

"Ah!" cried Herr Kronhorst in surprise, "what does that mean?"

"It means that yesterday, becoming at length a little frightened by the fury of the storm, I went to Ferdinand's office to stay with him; and as I opened the door softly, what do you think I saw? Elsie in Ferdinand's arms—fire and flame together—and I had to turn my eyes away from the blinding glare. The glare, to tell the truth, was that of the lightning which was playing over them as if to unite them, and then the thunder rolled as if to add its blessing."

Kronhorst laughed in sympathy.

"Splendid!" he exclaimed. "But the thunder's blessing will not prevent you from adding yours in a quieter tone."

"Oh, certainly not; why should I not give it with all my heart, now that everything is made right?"

Adele's conviction that everything was made right, has not proved a mistake. William Kronhorst brought Irene home from England, and Philip Bonsart, who could not again be separated from his daughter, severed his connection with the trans-Atlantic firm, and accepted a position in Herr Kronhorst's great establishment in E. Ferdinand von Schott and his sister have left the dark house in the shadow of the minster. He has returned to his former profession, though not in the same city, with the princess Elsie at his side, for Elsie will always be a princess, though she no longer bears the title—she is at his side as security for the realization of the ambitious dreams he confessed to her with such frank naïveté on that spring evening years ago, when they walked down from the Michaelisberg to the city of H.

12

END.

STANDARD WORKS

SELECTED FROM THE STOCK OF

D. APPLETON & COMPANY.

PRICE

Adams, John. Works. 8vo. 10 vols. Cloth, 30 00................................Half calf, $50 00
Adams, Memoirs of John Quincy. 8vo. 12 vols. Per vol., cloth, 5 00
Addison's Works. 8vo. 3 vols. Cloth, 6 00; sheep, 7 50.....................Half calf, 12 75
12mo. 6 vols. Cl., 9 00; sheep, 12 00......Half calf, 19 50
Alford, Dean. Greek Testament. 8vo. 4 vols. Cloth, 30 00 ; sheep, 36 00.... ....Half calf, 42 00
New Testament. 8vo. 2 vols. in 4.....Cloth, 16 00
2 vols in 3.........................Half calf, 26 00
Alison's History of Europe. 21 vols. 12mo..Cl., 36 75
Half calf, 63 00
American edition. 8vo. 8 vols.........Cloth, 16 00
Allibone. Dictionary of Authors. Small 4to. 3 vols. Cloth. 22 50; sheep, 25 50; half mor., 28 50; half calf, 29 00; half mor., gilt, 31 50; French morocco, 45 00
Ancient Classics for English Readers. 16mo. 20 vols., 25 00 ; 20 vols. in 10, 15 00 ; 20 vols................................Half calf, 50 00
Anderson, Hans. Works. 12mo. 10 vols. Cloth, 18 75..................................Half calf, 36 25
Appletons' American Cyclopædia. Royal 8vo. 16 vols. Per vol., cloth, 5 00; sheep, 6 00; half mor., 7 00 ; half russ., 8 00 ; full russ., 10 00.
Published only by subscription....Morocco, 10 00
Audubon's Birds and Quadrupeds of North America. 4to. 11 vols. Half mor., 225 00 ; Full mor., 250 00
Austen, Jane. Novels. 12mo. 6 vols. Cloth, 18 00; half calf, 28 00; half morocco, 30 00; Tree calf, 32 00
Bacon, Francis. Works. 1825. 16 vols. Full calf, 55 00. English ed., edited by Basil Montagu. 15 vols. Cloth, 33 75. ....Half calf, 60 00
Baine's French Revolution. 8vo. 2 vols. Half calf, 10 00
Baird, Brewer, and Ridgway. N. A. Birds. 8vo. 3 vols. With black illustrations, 30 00; with colored illustrations, 60 00
Ballads, English and Scotch. By Childs. 8 vols. Cloth, 10 00
Bancroft, George. History U. S. 8vo. 10 vols. Cloth, 25 00; sh., 35 00 ; tr. cf., 45 00; f. calf, 55 00
History U. S. New edition. 12mo. 6 vols. Cloth, 13 50. Vols. 1 and 2 now ready.
Bancroft, H. Native Races Pacific States. 8vo. 5 vols. Cloth, 27 50: sheep, 32 50; half calf, 40 00; half roan, 40 00..........Full roan, 50 00
Becker, Prof. Charicles. Cloth, 3 00; half calf, 6 00
Gallus. Cloth, 3 00..................Half calf, 6 00
Behn, Mrs. Plays, etc. 12mo. 6 vols......Half morocco, 30 00
Bewick's Select Fables. Post 8vo....Half Roxb., 4 00
The same. Large-paper edition............. 10 00
Bible. Handy Volume Edition. 11 vols. Cloth, 9 00; imitation mor., 13 50.........Morocco, 40 00
Bigelow's Life of Franklin. 12mo. 3 vols..Cloth, 7 50
Half calf, 13 50
Birch, Samuel. Hist. Ancient Pottery, and Marryatt's Pottery and Porcelain. 2 vols. 8vo. Tree calf, 40 00
Blackwood's Tales. 6mo. 12 vols......Cloth, 9 00
Half Calf, 18 00
16mo. In 6 vols. Cl., 9 00; half Roxb., 12 00; Half morocco, 13 50
Black's General Atlas of the World. Ed. 1876. Folio.........................Half morocco, 22 50
Blaine. Encyclopædia of Rural Sport. 8vo..Cl., 10 50
Bohn's Various Libraries. The set in 640 vols., $1,057 80.
Standard Library.................161 vols....231 80
Historical................... 19 " 38 00
French Memoirs............... 6 " 8 40
Uniform with Standard.......... 47 " 71 60

PRICE

Bohn's Various Libraries :
Philological...................... 22 vols....$38 00
British Classics.................. 29 " 40 80
Ecclesiastical.................... 8 " ... 16 00
Antiquarian...................... 40 " ... 80 00
Cheap Series..................... 74 " ... 49 40
Illustrated..................,.... 79 " 162 80
Classical........................ 91 " 178 20
Scientific...:.................... 68 " 142 80
Extra............................ 8 " ... 11 20
Reference........................ 1 " 2 40
Boswell's Johnson. 16mo. 10 vols.....Half calf, 25 00
8vo. 3 vols. Cl., 18 00 ; half calf, 21 00 ; tree calf, 24 00
Bohn's Ed. 12mo. 5 vols. Cloth, 8 00 ; half calf, 18 00...................Full calf, 25 00
Botany, System of. By Emm. Le Maout and J. Desaisne. Translated by Mrs. Hooker. 4to. 5,500 illustrations...................Cloth, 25 00
Brande & Cox. Dictionary of Science, Literature, and Art. 8vo. 3 vols. Cloth. 20 00 ; Half Russia, 30 00
Bric-à-Brac Series. 12mo. 10 vols. Cloth, 15 00; half roan, 17 50...................Half calf, 20 00
Bridgewater' Treatises. (Original ed., 8vo., 12 vols...........................Calf, 60 00
12mo., 7 vols....................Half calf, 21 00
British Essayists. By A. Chalmers. 16mo. 38 vols. Cloth, 47 50; half calf, 95 00....Calf, 114 00
British Poets. 18mo. 130 vols........Cloth, 162 50
Half calf, 357 50
Brockedon, W. Passes of the Alps. 4to. 2 vols. Proofs.......................Half morocco, 60 00
Brontë (The) Novels. 8vo. 7 vols........Cloth, 21 00
Half calf, 35 00
12mo. 6 vols.......................Cloth, 9 00
Brougham's (Lord) Works. Crown 8vo. 11 vols. Cloth, 19 25; half calf, 38 50.......Half roan, 33 00
Statesmen and Men of Letters. 8vo. 5 vols. Tree calf, 48 00
Browning, Robert. Complete Works. 12mo. 11 vols. Cloth, 21 00.............Half calf, 42 00
Browning, Mrs. Elizabeth Barrett. Poems. Cr. 8vo. 2 vols. Cl., 5 00 ; half cf., 9 00...Mor., 12 00
Blue and Gold Edition. 5 vols. Cloth, 6 25; half calf, 12 50.............Calf or morocco, 17 50
12mo. 3 vols. Cl., 7 50 ; hf. cf., 13 50.Cf. or mor., 18 00
16mo. 5 vols. Cloth, 8 75.........Half calf, 15 00
8vo. Illustrated. Cloth, 5 00 ; sheep, 6 00 ; half calf, 7 50........................Morocco, 10 00
Household Edition. 12mo. 2 vols. Cl., 4 00; half calf, 8 00............Full calf or morocco, 10 00
Buckle, H. T. Miscellaneous and Posthumous Works. 8vo. 3 vols. Cloth, 22 50..Half calf, 28 00
Hist. of Civilization. 8vo. 2 vols. 4 00..Hf. cf. 8 00
Bulwer's Novels. Globe Edition. 16mo. 25 vols. Cloth, 37 00.................Half calf, gilt, 75 00
Lord Lytton Edition. 12mo. 25 vols. Cloth, 37 00......................Half calf, gilt, 75 00
Library Edition. 12mo. 46 vols,.......Cloth, 57 50
Half calf, gilt, 126 50
Knebworth Edition. 12mo. 35 vols 52 50
Half calf, 105 00
Bunsen, Baron. Egypt's Place in Universal History. 5 vols. 8vo........................ 87 50
Memoir of. 8vo. 2 vols..............Half calf, 14 00
Bunyan's Pilgrim's Progress. Cr. 8vo. Illust. 5 00
Burke, J. Bernard. The Patrician. 8vo. 6 vols. Cf, 30 00
Burke, Edmund. Complete Works. Crown 8vo. 12 vols. Cloth, 18 00...........Half calf, 36 00
Crown 8vo. 12 vols. Cloth, 30 00...Half calf, 48 00
Bohn's Ed. 12mo. 9 vols. Cl., 12 60. Half calf, 30 60
Large-paper Edition. 12 vols....Half mor., 100 00
Burns, Robert. Poems. 1809. 12mo. 4 vols. Half roan, 18 00
8vo Edina Ed. Cl., 6 00; half mor., 10 00..Mor., 12 00
8vo, sheep, 3 50......................Morocco, 10 00
The Land of. 4to. 2 vols. in one...Half mor., 25 00

PRICE

Burton, J. H.   History of Scotland. 12mo. 8 vols.
Cloth, 25 00; half calf, 44 00...Half morocco,$55 00
Byron, Lord. Works. 12mo. 16 vols. Cloth, 20 00
Half morocco, 50 00
8vo. 6 vols. Half calf, 36 00.....Full morocco, 54 00
12mo. 4 vols. Cloth, 9 00..............Half calf, 16 00
16mo. In a box. 8 vols..............Cloth, 10 50
Finden's Illustrations to. 1833. 8vo. 6 vols.
in 3........................Half morocco, 30 00
8vo edition. Sheep, 3 50............Morocco, 10 00
Cabinet Encyclopædia. 16mo. (Lardner's.) 130
vols..............................Half calf, 150 00
Campbell. Lives of the Chancellors. 10 vols.
8vo. Cloth, 35 00; sheep, 45 00...Half calf, 60 00
Crown 8vo. 10 vols. Cloth, 20 00...Half calf, 45 00
Half morocco, 40 00
Chief Justices, 8vo. 4 vols. Cloth, 14 00;
sheep, 18 00.....................Half calf, 24 00
Chief Justices. New ed. 4 vols........Cloth, ' 8 00
Canova's Works. 8vo. 3 vols.......Half roan, 20 00
8vo. 1 vol.........................Cloth, 12 60
Carleton's Traits and Stories of the Irish Peas-
antry. 8vo. 2 vols...............Half calf, 12 00
Carlyle's (Thomas) Works. 16mo. 38 vols. Cl.,
34 20............................Half calf, 95 00
16mo. 38 vols. Bound in 18 vols..Green cloth, 35 00
Essays. 12mo. 4 vols. Cloth, 9 00..Half calf, 16 00
Frederick the Great. 12mo. 6 vols. Cloth,
12 00; sheep, 14 40..............Half calf, 22 50
Carpenter's Readings. 12mo. 5 vols. Cloth,
10 00...........................Half calf, 20 00
Cassell's Natural History. Imp. 8vo. 2 vols.
Half calf, 25 00
Book of Birds. Imp. 8vo. 4 vols.in 2..Half calf, 25 00
Cathedrals of England (The). 12mo. 4 vols.
Half calf, 35 00................Full morocco, 50 00
Catlin's N. A. Indians. 8vo. 2 vols...Half calf, 16 00
Chambers's Book of Days. 8vo. 2 vols. Cloth,
8 00; sheep, 9 50.............Half c. g., 12 00
Encyclopædia of English Literature. 8vo. 2
vols. Cloth, 8 00; sheep, 9 50....Half c. g., 12 00
Information for the People. 8vo. 2 vols Cl.,
8 00; sheep, 9 50.............Half c. g., 12 00
Miscellany of Useful and Entertaining Tracts.
16mo. 10 vols. Cloth, 10 00.....Half c. g., 27 50
Chaucer's Canterbury Tales. 8vo. 3 vols..Hf. cf., 10 50
Chesterfield's Letters. 12mo. 2 vols. Cloth,
5 00; half calf, 7 50............Tree calf, 10 00
Churchill. Mount Lebanon. 8vo. 3 vols..Hf. cf., 13 00
Clarendon. Rebellion and Civil Wars in Eng-
land. Cr. 8vo. 7 vols. Hf. calf, 25 00..Calf, 30 00
Clark. Railway Machinery. Folio. 2 vols.
(1 vol. plates)..................Half morocco, 30 00
Coleridge's Complete Works. Crown 8vo. 7
vols...........................Cloth, 12 00
Coleridge (Sarah), Memoirs and Letters of. Cr.
8vo. 2 vols...................Half calf, 12 00
Collins, Wilkie. 15 vols....   ....Cloth, 22 50
Colton's General Atlas. Folio.............. 20 00
Commentary Wholly Biblical. 4to. 3 vols. Cl.,
20 00..........................Morocco, 40 00
Comte de Paris. History of the Civil War. 8vo.
Per vol., cloth, 3 50 ; sheep, 4 50 ; half mor., 6 00
Consecration and Coronation of Alexander II. of
Russia in 1856. Eleph. folio. 36 plates.....
Half morocco, 350 00
Conybeare and Howson. St. Paul. 4to. 2 vols.
Cloth, 30 00
Cooper's (J. F.) complete novels. 12mo. 32 vols.
Cloth, 48 00.....................Half calf, 110 00
Leather-Stocking Tales. 12mo. 5 vols. Cloth,
7 50...........................Half calf, 17 50
Sea Tales. 12mo. 5 vols. Cl., 7 50..Half calf, 17 50
Cresy's Encyclopædia of Civil Engineering. 8vo.
Cloth, 21 00...................Half Russia, 26 00
Crowe and Calvacaselle. Art in Italy. 8vo.
2 vols. Half calf, 20 00..........Tree calf, 30 00
Curtius. History of Greece. English Ed. 8vo.
5 vols..........................Half calf, 40 00
12mo. 5 vols. Cloth, 12 50 ....Half calf, 22 50
Cuvier. Animal Kingdom. 8vo...Half morocco, 12 00
Darwin's Works. 12mo. 7 vols. Cloth,
Half calf, 35 00
De Foe's Works. 12mo. 7 vols. Cloth, 9 80;
Half calf, ·18 00
Denny's Guide to China and Japan. 8vo. Cloth, 21 00
De Quincey's Works. 12mo. 11 vols. Cloth,
16 50...........................Half calf, 33 00
12mo. 22 vols. Half calf, 55 00 .....Full calf, 65 00
12mo. 16 vols. Cloth, 30 00 ; half morocco,
45 00.........................Tree calf, 90 00
Dibdin, Rev. T. F. Bibliographical Decameron.
Royal 8vo. 3 vols..........Olive morocco, 225 00

PRICE

Dibdin, Rev. T. F. Bibliogr. Antiq. and Pict.
Tour in France and Germany. Royal 8vo.
3 vols.......................Olive mor., $175 00
Bibliogr. Antiq. and Pict. Tour in Northern
Counties in England and Scotland. Royal
8vo..........................Olive morocco, 125 00
Dickens's (Charles) Works. 12mo. 30 vols. Half
calf, 112 50......................Tree calf, 150 00
Riverside edition. 12mo. 28 vols. Cloth,
56 00; half calf, 112 00 ....Tree calf, 140 00
Globe edition. 12mo. 15 vols. Cloth, 22 00;
Half calf, 48 00
Carleton's edition. 12mo. 15 vols. Cloth,
22 50...........................Half calf, 50 00
Illustrated Library Edition. · 12mo. 29 vols.
Cloth, 50 75.....................Half calf, 110 00
Standard edition. 8vo. Illustrated. Per
vol............................Cloth, 3 00
Gadshill edition. Crown 8vo. 15 vols...Cloth, 30 00
Dickens's edition. 12mo. 15 vols. Cloth,
22 50...........................Half calf, 45 00
15 vols. in 8. Cloth, 14 00... ....Half calf, 28 00
Appletons' edition. 12mo. 6 vols. Cloth,
10 50...........................Half calf, 21 00
Disraeli, Isaac. Curiosities of Literature. 12mo.
4 vols. Cloth, 7 00...............Half calf, 14 00
Amenities of Literature. Crown 8vo. 2 vols.
Cloth, 3 50.....................Half calf, 7 00
Calamities of Authors. Crown 8vo. 2 vols.
Cloth, 3 50.....................Half calf, 7 00
Literary Characters. Crown 8vo. 1 vol. Cloth,
2 25...........................Half calf, 4 00
Complete Works. Crown 8vo. 9 vols. Cloth,
15 00..........................Half calf, 30 00
Disraeli's (Benjamin) Novels and Tales. Small
8vo. 6 vols....................Half calf, 20 00
Another edition. 10 vols.............Cloth, 30 00
Doré, Gallery, The. Containing 250 drawings
by Gustave Doré. Small folio. 1 vol. com-
plete, 60 00 ; morocco, 80 00. 2 vols...Cloth, 65 00
Doré Bible. Small folio. 2 vols. Cloth, 64 00;
morocco, gold edge, 100 00 ; best morocco, 125 00
Bible, in French. Folio 2 vols. Cloth, 75 00 ;.
half morocco, 100 00 ; full morocco, 150 00 ;
Full extra morocco, 200 00
Doré's Milton's Paradise Lost. Crown fol. Cl.,
25 00.........................Morocco antique, 40 00
Dante's Inferno. Crown folio. Cloth, 25 00 ;
Morocco antique, 40 00
Dante's Purgatory and Paradise. Crown folio.
Cloth, 25 00...................Morocco antique, 40 00
Don Quixote. Royal 4to. Cloth. 15 00 ; half
morocco, 20 00.................Full morocco, 25 00
La Fontaine's Fables. Royal 4to. Cloth,
15 00 ; half morocco, 20 00.....Full morocco, 25 00
2 vols. Half crimson morocco...Large paper, 175 00
London. Folio................Half morocco, 35 00
Tour through the Pyrenees. By Taine. Sm.
4to. Cloth, 10 00 ; morocco, 20 00..Tree calf, 25 00
Dramatists and Poets (Old). Royal 8vo. 13 vols.
Cloth, 65 00 ; half calf, 90 00 ......Tree calf, 125 00
Dumas's (Alexandre) Novels. 16mo. 18 vols. in
10..............................Cloth, 15 00
Dyer's Pompeii. 8vo. Cloth, 6 00 ; half calf,
9 00...........................Tree calf, 12 00
Eastlake, Sir Charles L. History of the Gothic
Revival. Royal 8vo..........Half morocco, 16 00
Edgeworth's (Maria) Novels and Tales. 12mo.
10 vols. Cloth, 15 00 ; half calf, 30 00...Calf, 40 00
10 vols. in 5.....................Half calf, 25 00
Eliot's (Geor e) Novels. 12mo. 7 vols. Cloth,
8 50......g.....................Half calf, 18 25
Emerson's (R. W.) Works. 12mo. 10 vols.
Cloth, 20 00...................Half calf, 34 00
Prose Works. Crown 8vo. 2 vols. Cloth,
5 00...........................Half calf, 9 00
Encyclopædia Britannica. Ninth ed. (to be
completed in 22 vols.). Per vol., cloth, 9 00;
Half Russia, 11 00
Essayists, British. By Chalmers. 38 vols. Cl.,
47 50 ; cloth, gilt, 57 00...........Half calf, 95 00
Evans's Old Ballads. 8vo. 4 vols..Half morocco, 20 00
Evelyn's Diary. 12mo. 4 vols........Half calf, 14 00
Ewald. History of Israel. 8vo. 5 vols...Cloth, 31 50
Fairbairn. Crests of Families of Great Britain
and Ireland. 8vo. 2 vols.................. 21 00
Farrar, F. W. The Life of Christ. 8vo. 2 vols.
Cloth, 6 00.....................Half calf, 12 00
Without notes. One vol. 8vo. 2 50..Half calf, 5 00
Fielding's (Henry) Works. 8vo. 10 vols. Lon-
don, 1821......................Calf, 40 00
8vo. 11 vols. Half roan, 35 00 ; half calf,
50 00.........................Tree calf, 75 00

PRICE

Figuier's Works. Cr. 8vo. Cl., 17 50. Half calf, $25 00
Finden. Illustrations to Byron. 8vo. 3 vols.
  Half roan, 30 00
Forsyth's Cicero. 8vo. 2 vols. Large paper.
  Half morocco, 20 00
Froissart's Chronicles of England, France, Spain,
  etc. 2 vols. Royal 8vo.....Half Roxburgh, 12 00
Frothingham, R. History of the Siege of Bos-
  ton. 8vo. Cloth, 3 50........... ...Half calf, 5 50
  Rise of the Republic. 8vo. Cl., 3 50..Half calf, 5 50
Froude's History of England. 8vo. 12 vols.
  Half calf, 100 00....................Tree calf, 150 00
  12mo. 12 vols......................Tree calf, 65 00
  12mo. 12 vols. Cloth, 36 00 ; half calf, 50 00;
  Tree calf, 75 00
Popular ed. 12mo. 12 vols. Cloth, 15 00;
  Half calf, 36 00
Chelsea ed. 12mo. 12 vols........Half roan, 21 00
Gaskell's (Mrs.) Novels. 12mo. 7 vols. Half
  calf, 25 00.)....................Half Roxburgh, 27 50
Gazetteer of the World..............Sheep, 10 00
Gibbon's Decline and Fall of the Roman Em-
  pire. 8vo. 8 vols. Half cf., 40 00..Hf. mor., 45 00
  12mo. 6 vols. Cl., 6 00 ; sheep, 12 00 .Hf. cf., 19 50
  Bohn's ed. 12mo. 7 vols. Cloth, 9 80 ; half
  calf, 23 80....................Full calf, 35 00
  Chambers's Library. 3 vols............Cloth, 5 25
Gilfillan's British Poets. Complete set in 48
  vols.....................Half calf, 160 00
Gladstone, W. E. Studies on Homer. 8vo. 3
  vols.....................Full calf, 100 00
Globe edition of the Poets. 16mo. 16 vols.
  Cloth, 20 00 ; half calf, 48 00........Morocco, 64 00
Goethe's Works. 12mo. 7 vols. Cloth, 9 80;
  half calf, 23 80..................Tree calf, 35 00
Goethe and Schiller. 13 vols.....Half morocco, 40 00
Goldsmith's (Oliver) Works. 8vo. 4 vols. Cl.,
  15 ; half calf, 25 00.............Tree calf, 35 00
Grant's Novels. 12mo. 32 vols..Half Roxburgh, 40 00
Graphic, London. Folio. 9 vols. Per vol. Cloth, 9 00
Green, Mary A. E. Lives of the Princesses of
  England. 1849. 12mo. 6 vols.....Tree calf, 36 00
Grimm's Life of Michael Angelo. Crown 8vo. 2
  vols. Cloth, 5 00 ; half calf, 8 00........Calf, 10 00
Grote's History of Greece. 8vo. 12 vols. Cloth,
  21 00 ; half calf, 39 00.............Calf, 51 00
  8vo. 10 vols. Cloth, 40 00..........Half calf, 60 00
  12mo. 12 vols. Cl., 18: sheep, 22 80..Half calf, 39 00
Grote's Plato. 8vo. 3 vols.............Half calf, 22 50
Gwilt's Encyclopædia of Architecture. 4to. Cl.,
  20 00...... ....Half Russia, 26 00
Hall's Ireland. Original edition. 4to. 3 vols.
  Half morocco, 25 00..........Full morocco, 50 00
Hallam's Middle Ages. Cr. 8vo. 3 vols. Cloth,
  5 25............................Half calf, 10 50
  Introduction to Literature of Europe. Crown
  8vo. 4 vols. Cloth, 7 00........Half calf, 14 00
  Constitutional History of England. Cr. 8vo.
  3 vols. Cloth, 5 50...............Half calf, 10 50
  Complete Works. Cr. 8vo. 10 vols. Cloth,
  17 50..........................Half calf, 35 00
Hallam and May. Constitutional History of Eng-
  land. Cr. 8vo. 5 vols. Cl., 8 75....Hf. calf, 17 50
Hawthorne's (Nathaniel) Works. 16mo. 21 vols.
  Cloth, 42 00 ; half calf, 72 00............Calf, 95 00
  12mo. 9 vols. Cloth, 18 00..........Half calf, 36 00
  24mo. New ed. 21 vols. Per vol........ 1 25
Haydn's Dictionaries. Art—Science—Bible—Bi-
  ography—Dates—Popular Medicine. 6 vols.
  each. Cloth, 9,00....Half calf, 12 00
Haydon's Correspondence and Table-Talk. 8vo.
  2 vols............................ 13 50
Heeren's Historical Works. 8vo. 6 vols....... 15 00
Hildreth's History of the United States. 8vo.
  6 vols. Cloth, 18 00 ; sheep, 21 00..Hf. calf, 31 50
Hodge. System of Theology. 8vo. 3 vols...Cl., 12 00
Hogarth's Illustrations. 12mo. 3 vols. Cl., 9 00;
  Half calf, 15 00
Holland's (J. G.) Works. 12mo. 12 vols..Cloth, 20 25
Homer. Translation by Sotheby. 8vo. 4 vols.
  Calf, 45 00
  Translation by W. C. Bryant. 8vo. 2 vols. 4to.
  Cloth, 20 00....................Half calf, 40 00
  12mo. 4 vols. Cloth, 10 00..........Half calf, 18 00
  Translation by Earl of Derby. Cr. 8vo. 2 vols.
  Cl., 4 00 ; hf. cf., 8 00..Hf. morocco, gilt top, 8 00
Hone's Every-Day Book. 8vo. 4 vols...Hf. calf, 25 00
Hood's (Thomas) Works. 12mo. 10 vols. Hf.
  calf, 45 00. ....Tree calf, 60 00
  12mo. 7 vols. Cloth, 15 75..........Half calf, 28 00
Hood's Own. 8vo. 2 vols. Hf. cf., 10 50..Full cf., 12 50
Hopkins (S.) The Puritans and Queen Eliza-
  beth. 12mo. 3 vols. Cl., 7 50....Half calf, 15 00

PRICE

Horne's Introduction to the Holy Scriptures.
  4 vols. Cloth, 21 00 ....Half calf, $30 00
Humboldt's (Alexander von) Works. 12mo. 9
  vols........................Half calf, 36 00
  Cosmos. 12mo. 5 vols. Cloth, 6 25 ; sheep,
  8 25.......................Half calf, 15 00
Hume, David. History of England. 12mo. 6
  vols. Cloth, 9 00 ; sheep, 12 00....Half calf, 19 50
  8vo. 6 vols. Cl., 15 00 ; sheep, 21 00..Hf. cf., 27 00
Hunt, Leigh. 12mo. 4 vols. Cl., 6 00..Hf. calf, 13 00
India. By L. Rousselet. Folio. Illustrated.
  Cloth, gilt extra, 25 00 ....Full morocco, 35
Ireland, Joseph N. Records of the New York
  Stage. (1750-1860.) 4to. 2 vols..Half mor., 40
Irving's (Washington) Works. Sunnyside ed.
  28 vols. Cloth, 63 00............Half calf, 112 00
  Knickerbocker ed. 27 vols. Cl., 67 50..Hf. cf., 108 00
  Riverside ed. 26 vols. Cl., 45 50....Half calf, 84 50
  People's ed. 26 vols. Cl., 32 50....Half calf, 71 50
  Life of Washington. Mount Vernon Edition.
  8vo. 2 vols. Cloth, 7 00...........Half calf, 12 00
Jacquemart, Albert. History of Ceramic Art.
  8vo. Cloth, 18 00.............Half morocco, 22 50
James. Life of Richard Cœur de Lion. Lon-
  don. 8vo. 4 vols................Half calf, 12 00
Jameson's (Mrs.) Art Works. 8vo. 6 vols.
  Cloth, 40 00 ; half calf, 65 00 ; tree cf., 80 00;
  Morocco, 100 00
Jameson's (Mrs.) Works. 16mo. 10 vols. Cl.,
  15 00 ; half calf, 25 00 ....Morocco, 45 00
Jefferson's (Thomas) Works. 8vo........Cloth, 27 00
Jefferson, Life of. By Randall. 8vo. 3 vols.
  Cloth, 10 00
Jerrold's (Douglas) Works. 12mo. 5 vols. Cl.,
  10 50 ; half calf, 19 75.............Tree calf, 24 00
Jesse's London. 12mo. 2 vols........Half calf, 10 00
Jesse, G. A. The Dog. 8vo..........Half calf, 12 00
Jewell's (Bishop) Works. 8vo. 8 vols..Pol. cf., 60 00
Johnson's English Dictionary, by Latham. 4to.
  4 vols. ....Half Russia, 60 00
Johnson, Samuel. Lives of Eminent Poets.
  8vo. 3 vols...................Tree calf, 24 00
Johnson's General Atlas of the World. Folio... 20 00
Jonson's (Ben) Works. 8vo. 9 vols.....Cloth, 40 00
Josephus. Histories. Crown 8vo. 4 vols. Cl.,
  9 00 ; sheep, 10 00. ....Half calf, 18 00
Jowett's Plato. 8vo. 5 vols...........Cloth, 30 00
Junius (Woodfall's) Letters. (1814.) 8vo. 3 vols.
  Old calf, 12 00
  2 vols........................Half calf, 6 00
Kerl's Metallurgy. Edited by Crookes and Roh-
  rig. Royal 8vo. 3 vols..............Cloth, 30 00
Kitto's Pictorial Bible. 8vo. 4 vols...Half calf, 30 00
  Encyclopædia. 8vo. 3 vols. Half morocco,
  36 00..........................Half Russia, 45 00
Knight's (Charles) Gallery of Portraits. Imper.
  8vo. 7 vols....................... 45 00
  The Land we Live In. 4 vols. in 2. Imperial-
  8vo. ....Half morocco, 25 00
Knight's Pictorial History of London. Imperial
  8vo. 6 vols. in 3 ....Half calf, 25 00
Knight's History of England. Imperial 8vo.
  8 vols. Cloth, 25 00 ; hf. cf., 40 00...Tree cf., 60 00
Knight's Half-Hours with the Best Authors.
  Small 8vo. 4 vols. Cloth, 10 00 ; half calf,
  16 00 ; tree calf, 21 00.............Full calf, 20 00
Knight, Henry. Ecclesiastical Architecture of
  Italy. Folio. 2 vols.........Half morocco, 54 00
Knowles's (Sheridan) Dramatic Works. Small
  8vo. 3 vols....................Half calf, 12 00
Kugler's Hand-Books of Painting. Crown 8vo.
  4 vols. Cloth, 20 00 ; hf. cf., 80 00...Tree cf., 40 00
Lacroix, Paul. The Eighteenth Century. Imp.
  8vo. Cl. gilt, 15 00 ; hf. cf., 18 00 ; hf. mor.,
  20 00 ; French mor., 20 00 ; calf, 21 00 ; tree
  calf, 28 00.................Morocco extra, 28 00
  Arts in the Middle Ages. Imp. 8vo. Cloth,
  12 00 ; half calf, 15 00 ; half morocco, 15 00 ;
  French cf., 18 00 ; mor. ex., 21 00..Full mor., 25 00
  Manners, Customs, and Dress. Imperial 8vo.
  Cl., 12 00 ; hf. calf, 15 00 ; half mor., 15 00 ;
  French cf., 18 00 ; mor. ex., 21 00..Full mor., 25 00
  Military and Religious Life in the Middle
  Ages. Imp. 8vo. Cl., 12 00 ; hf. cf. or mor.,
  15 00 ; French calf, 18 00 ; morocco extra,
  21 00......................Full morocco, 25 00
Lamb's (Charles) Works. Moxon's Ed. 12mo.
  4 vols. Cl., 12 00 ; half calf, 16 00..Full calf, 20 00
  Crown 8vo. 5 vols. Cloth, 9 00........Calf, 18 00
Landor's (Walter Savage) Works. 8vo. (To be
  completed in 8 vols.) Per vol. 4 00
Lane's Thousand and One Nights. Royal 8vo.
  3 vols. Tree cf, 45 00..Crushed levant mor., 60 00

PRICE

Lane, E. W. Modern Egyptians. Post 8vo. 2
vols......................................Cloth, $5 00
Lange's Commentaries. 8vo. 18 vols. Per vol.,
cloth, 5 00 ; sheep, 6 50 .:.........Half calf, 7 50
Layard's Nineveh. (1849.) 3 vols..Hf. morocco, 20 00
Lever's (Charles) Novels. 12mo. 27 vols..Cloth, 35 00
Lewes. Life of Goethe. 8vo. 2 vols. Half cf.,
15 00...................................Full calf, 20 00
Lewin, T. Life and Epistles of St. Paul. Demy
4to. 2 vols. Cloth, 18 00.........Half calf, 28 00
Library of Wonders. 20 vols. 12mo. Cloth,
25 00 ; half roan, 30 00.............Half calf, 50 00
Lingard's History of England. 12mo. 10 vols.
Half calf, 18 00
Lippincott's Dictionary of Biography. Royal
8vo. 2 vols. Cl., 22 00 ; half
morocco, 27 00 ; half calf, 28 00 ; half Rus-
sia, 38 00..................French morocco, 36 00
In one vol., sheep, 15 00 ; hf. morocco, 17 00 ;
half calf, gilt, 18 00.............Half Russia, 18 00
Gazetteer. Royal 8vo. 1 vol..............Sheep, 10 00
Little Classics. 18mo. 16 vols. Cl., 16 00 ; hf.
calf, 40 00. 2 vols. bound in one...Tree calf, 36 00
Littré: Dictionnaire Français. Imp. 8vo. 4 vols.
Cloth, 36 00 ....Half morocco, 45 00
The same. Abridged. 8vo....Half morocco, 9 00
Lockhart's Life of Sir Walter Scott. 12mo. 3
vols. Cloth, 6 75......... .....Half calf, 13 50
Lodge's (Edmund) Portraits of Illustrious Person-
ages of Great Britain. 8vo. 12 vols..Hf. calf, 32 00
Longfellow's (H. W.) Poems. 12mo. 4 vols.
Cloth, 10 00 ; half calf, 18 00......Morocco, 24 00
Prose. 12mo. 3 vols. Cloth, 7 50 ; half calf,
13 50..................................Morocco, 18 00
Works. 12mo. 7 vols. Cloth, 17 50 ; half
calf, 31 50.............................Morocco, 42 00
Translation of Dante. 12mo. 3 vols. Cloth,
6 00 ; half calf, 12 00..............Morocco, 15 00
One vol. 12mo. Cloth, 3 00 ; half calf, 5 50;
Morocco, 7 00
Imperial 8vo. 3 vols. Cloth, 15 00 ; half calf,
30 00...................................Morocco, 40 00
Lossing. Field-Book of the Revolution. 2 vols.
Cloth, 14 00........................Half calf, 18 00
Lossing's History of the Civil War. 8vo. 3 vols.
Cloth, 15 00........................Half calf, 24 00
History of the United States. Cl., 5 00 ; sheep, 5 50
Loudon, J. C. Encyclopædia of Trees and
Shrubs. 8vo.....................Half roan, 12 50
Encyclopædia of Cottage, Farm, and Villa
Architecture, and Furniture. 8vo. Hf. roan, 12 50
Encyclopædia of Plants. 8vo................ 21 00
Encyclopædia of Agriculture. 8vo......... .... 10 50
Gardening. 8vo........................... 10 50
Lübcke. History of Sculpture. 8vo. 2 vols.
Cloth, 18 00 ; half calf, 25 00.....Tree calf, 33 00
Art. 8vo. 2 vols. Cloth, 18 00 ; half calf,
25 00.................................Tree calf, 33 00
Lundy, John T. Monumental Christianity. 4to.
Cl., 7 50 ; hf. mor., 10 00.....mor. or tree cf., 15 00
Luttrell's Diary. 8vo. 6 vols..........Tree calf, 36 00
Macaulay's Complete Works. 8vo. 8 vols. Cl.,
32 00..............Half morocco or half calf, 48 00
Crown 8vo. 4 vols. Cloth, 9 00 ; half calf,
16 00................................Tree calf, 24 00
Crown 8vo. 16 vols. Cloth, 32 00....Half calf, 64 00
12mo. 12 vols......................Tree calf, 65 00
Essays. 12mo. 7 vols. Cloth, 8 75 ; hf. calf,
24 00.................................Full calf, 31 50
History of England. 12mo. 5 vols. Cloth,
7 50 ; sheep, 8 75......... ....Half calf, 15 00
Macaulay's Life and Letters. By his Nephew,
G. Otto Trevelyan. 2 vols. 8vo......,.Cloth, 5 00
Macfarlane, Charles, and Thompson. Compreh.
Hist. of England. 8vo. 4 vols....Half mor., 40 00
Madison's (James) Works. 8vo. 4 vols..Cloth, 16 00
Mahon's History of England. Post 8vo. 7 vols.,
Cloth, 12 25.........................Half calf, 24 50
Marco Polo's Travels. Ed. by Yule. 8vo. 2
vols...................................Cloth, 21 00
Marcoy, Paul. Travels in South America. Sm.
fol. 2 vols. Cloth, 15 00..........Half calf, 25 00
Marryat's (Captain) Works. 12mo. 12 vols. Cl.,
15 00.................................Half calf, 36 00
McCulloch's Commercial Dictionary. 8vo. Cl.,
20 00...............................Half Russia, 25 00
McIntosh. History of England. 10 vols.Hf. cf., 30 00
Memoir of Norman Macleod, D. D. 2 vols. 8vo. 4 50
Memoirs of Courts of England. 8vo. 6 vols.
Half calf, 24 00
Merivale's History of Rome. 12mo. 7 vols.
Cloth, 14 00.......................Half calf, 28 00
12mo. 8 vols. Cloth, 17 00.....Half calf. 35 00

PRICE

Michaux and Nuttall. North American Sylva.
8vo. 5 vols.............................$70 00
Mill's (John Stuart) Wor s. Crown 8vo. 11
vols. Cloth, 27 50....k...........Half calf, 55 00
Miller's (Hugh) Works. 12mo. 13 vols. Half
roan, 26 00...........................Half calf, 40 00
Milman, H. H. History of the Jews. Cr. 8vo.
3 vols. Cloth, 5 25...................Half calf, 10 50
History of Christianity. Crown 8vo. 3 vols.
Cloth, 5 25...........................Half calf, 10 50
Latin Christianity. Cr. 8vo. 8 vols. Cloth,
14 00...............................Half calf, 28 00
Complete Works. Cr. 8vo. 14 vols. Cloth,
24 50..............................Half calf, 49 00
Milton, John. Poetical Works. 8vo. 8 vols.
1867.................................... 80 00
8vo. Edited by Masson. 3 vols........Cloth, 15 00
Sq. 8vo. Illustrated. 1 vol....Red morocco, 18 00
1 vol ....Antique morocco, 10 00
Mitchell's General Atlas of the World. Sm. fol., 11 00
Molesworth. History of England from 1830–1874.
12mo. 3 vols. Cloth, 5 25......Half calf, 12 00
Molière, Transl. by Henri Van Laun. 8vo. Per
vol., 7 50...........................3 vols. published.
Mommsen's History of Rome. 12mo. 4 vols.
Cloth, 8 00.........................Half calf, 16 00
Montalembert. Monks of the West. 8vo. 5 vols.
Half calf, 40 00
Moore's Poetical Works. 12mo. 6 vols....Half
calf, 16 50 ; sheep, 3 50..........Morocco, 10 00
8vo...........................Cloth, gilt top, 2 50
More, Hannah. Works. 12mo. 11 vols.
Half calf, 33 00
Motley's (J. L.) History of the Dutch Republic.
8vo. 3 vols. Cloth, 10 50 ; sheep, 12 00;
half calf, 17 25
United Netherlands. 8vo. 4 vols. Cloth,
14 00 ; sheep, 16 00...............Half calf, 23 00
John of Barneveld. 8vo. 2 vols. Cloth, 7 00 ;
sheep, 8 00.........................Half calf, 11 50
Complete Works. 8vo. 9 vols. Cloth, 31 50 ;
sheep, 36 00 ; half calf, 51 75 ; extra, 54 00;
full calf, 70 00
Müller, Max. Works. Cr. 8vo. 7 vols. Cloth,
18 00...............................Half calf, 28 75
Müller. Chips from a German Workshop. 8vo.
English edition. Cloth, 27 00..Half morocco, 45 00
Mulock, Miss. Works. 12mo. 19 vols......... 28 50
Muspratt's Chemistry. Imper. 8vo. 2 vols.
Half Russia, 28 00
Napier's Peninsular War. 8vo. 5 vols. Cloth,
12 50........................... .Half calf, 20 00
Napier's Florentine History. 12mo. 6 vols.
Half calf, 22 00
National Galleiy. Folio................Cloth, 16 00
Newton's Travels in the Levant. 8vo. 2 vols.
Half morocco, 12 00
Nursery Rhymes. 4to. 2 vols...Half morocco, 25 00
Ormond, Life of the Duke of. 8vo. 6 vols..Pol. c., 40 00
Ornament Polychromatic. 4to. Cloth, 63 00 ;
Half morocco, 75 00
Ornement Polychrome (L'). 4to. French edition.
Full morocco, 110 00
Oxford English Classics. 8vo. 44 vols. Half
morocco. Comprising Hume's History of Eng-
land (8) ; Smollett's History of England (5);
Gibbon's Roman Empire (8) ; Robertson's
Historic Works (8) ; Johnson's Works and
Life (15)...............................225 00
Palfrey, J. G. History of New England. 8vo.
4 vols. Cloth, 14 50.............Half calf, 22 50
Palliser, Mrs. A History of Lace. 8vo...Cloth, 10 50
Paradise of Dainty Devices. 1812. 4to...Mor., 50 00
Parker. Concise Glossary of Terms in Archi-
tecture. 16mo.......................... 3 75
Parkman's (Francis) Works. 8vo. 7 vols. Cloth,
17 50 ; half morocco, 27 00... .....Half calf, 31 50
Parsons. Rights of a Citizen of the United
States. 8vo.........................Sheep, 4 50
Pepys's Diary and Correspondence. 12mo. 4
vols................................Half calf, 14 00
Percy. Metallurgy. 8vo. 6 vols........each, 15 00
Percy Anecdotes. 12mo. 2 vols.....Half calf, 7 50
Reliques. 1 vol. 8vo. Cloth, 5 00....Sheep, 6 00
Petit. Mary Queen of Scots. 4to. 2 vols. Cloth,
25 00..............................Half morocco, 32 50
Plato's Works. Bohn's edition. 12mo. 6 vols.
Cloth, 12 00........................Half calf, 24 00
Plutarch's Lives by Clough. 8vo. 5 vols. Cloth,
15 00 ; half calf, 25 00...............Calf, 30 00
Morals. 8vo. 5 vols. Cloth, 15 00 ; half calf,
25 00..................................Calf, 30 00
Lives by Langhorn. 12mo. 4 vols .....Cloth, 5 00

PRICE

Poe, Edgar A. Works. Cr. 8vo. 4 vols. Cloth,
9 00 ; half calf, 16 00................Calf, $20 00
Prescott, W. H. Complete Works, with Life.
Cr. 8vo. 16 vols. Cloth, 36 00......Half calf, 72 00
New edition. 12mo. 15 vols. Cloth, 33 75.
Half calf, 67 50
Pugin. Gothic Architecture. 4to. 3 vols...... 37 50
Punch (London). 1841-1874. Original edition.
34 vols. Complete to 1874....Half morocco, 200 00
Another copy. 34 vols....Half crimson mor., 225 00
Raikes's Journal. 12mo. 4 vols.......Half calf, 15 00
Ramage, C. J. Beautiful Thoughts from Greek,
German, Spanish, French, Italian, and Latin
Authors. 12mo. 4 vols.........Half calf, 18 00
Ranke's History of England. 8vo. 6 vols...Cl., 24 00
History of the Popes of Rome, translated by
Sarah Austin. 3 vols. 8vo.......Half calf, 14 00
Rawlinson's Five Great Monarchies. 8vo. 3
vols................................Cloth, 15 00
Sixth Great Monarchy.............. ....Cloth, 6 00
8vo. 4 vols. Cloth, 21 00 ; half calf, 30 00 ;
Half morocco, 35 00
Seventh Monarchy. 8vo. 1 vol.........Cloth, 9 00
Rawlinson's Herodotus. 8vo. 4 vols. 10 00 ;
Half calf, 20 00
Reade's (Charles) Novels. 16mo. 11 vols. Cloth,
11 00...........................Half calf, 24 75
The same in 6 vols................Half calf, 18 00
Rebellion Record. Edited by Frank Moore.
8vo. 12 vols..................Half Russia, 90 00
Richardson, Samuel. Works. 12mo. 19 vols.
Comprising Clarissa Harlowe, Sir Charles
Grandison, Pamela, and Life. Half mor., 75 00
Richardson's Dictionary. 4to. 2 vols. Half
roan, 30 00...........Half morocco, 40 00
Ritter's Palestine. 8vo. 4 vols. Cloth, 14 00 ;
Half calf, 24 00
Robertson, J. C. History of the Christian
Church. 12mo. 8 vols.............Cloth, 18 00
Rollin's Ancient History. 8vo. 4 vols. Cloth,
10 00 ; sheep, 12 00...........Half Calf, 18 00
Romance of History. 12mo. 5 vols. Cloth,
12 50...........................Half calf, 20 00
Rule, William M. History of the Inquisition.
8vo. 2 vols....................Half calf, 15 00
Ruskin, J. Works. 12mo. 28 vols. Cloth, 40 00 ;
same with Plates, 48 00
12mo. 28 vols. in 17.............Half calf, 70 00
Modern Painters. 12mo. 5 vols. Cloth, 18 00 ;
Half calf, 27 00
Same without Plates. Cloth, 12 00...Half calf, 20 00
Stones of Venice. 12mo. 3 vols. Cloth, 7 00 ;
Half calf, 12 00
English edition. Royal 8vo. 3 vols......Half
morocco, 75 00
Russell's Naval Architecture. Folio. 3 vols.
Half levant mor., 150 00
Schiller's Works. 12mo. 6 vols. Cloth, 8 40 ;
half calf, 18 00....................Full calf, 24 00
Schlosser, F. C. History of the Nineteenth
Century. 8vo. 8 vols........Half morocco, 30 00
Scott, Sir Walter. Works. Complete : com-
prising Novels, 48 vols. Miscellaneous Es-
says, Life by Lockhart, Poetical Works,
History of Scotland, etc. 16mo. 100 vols.
Half calf, 250 00
Waverley Novels :
Abbotsford ed. 8vo. 12 vols........Calf, 250 00
The same. 8vo. 12 vols....Half red mor., 225 00
The same. 8vo. 12 vols.....Half mor., 175 00
Centenary edition. 12mo. 25 vols. Cloth, 31 25 ;
half calf, 68 75 ; calf, 80 00.....Tree calf, 100 00
Library edition. 8vo. 25 vols. Half calf,
100 00 ; half morocco, 125 00 ; tree calf,
175 00.............................. .....Morocco, 175 00
Standard edition. 12mo. 23 vols. 34 50 ;
Half calf, 69 00
Globe edition. 12mo. 23 vols. 28 75 ; hf. cl., 63 25
Osgood's. 12mo. 25 vols. Cloth, 37 50 ;
Half calf, 75 00
Appletons'. 12mo. 6 vols. Cloth, 10 50 ;
Half calf, 21 00
Melrose edition. Cr. 8vo. 13 vols.......... 26 00
Abbotsford edition. 12 vols. Cloth, 18 00 ;
sheep, 24 00......................Half calf, 39 00
Poetical Works. 1 vol. 8vo. Sheep, 3 50 ;
mor. ant., 10 00
Select Poetic Works. 12mo. 6 vols. Bound
in the Tartans of various Clans, in elegant
Tartan case, 25 00
Poetical Works. 18mo. 9 vols. Cloth, 11 25 ;
Half calf, 24 75
16mo. Half calf, 28 00.............Full calf, 32 00

PRICE

Shakespeare's Works :
Mary Cowden Clarke's edition. 8vo. 4 vols.
Cloth, 12 00 ; half calf, 20 00......Morocco, $25 00
8vo. 2 vols. Half calf, 18 00 ; half mor., 20 00 ;
Morocco, 25 00
8vo. 1 vol. Sheep, 3 50 ; half calf, 8 00..Mor., 10 00
8vo. 3 vols. Cloth, 17 50 ; half morocco, 25 00;
Morocco, 32 00
Stratford edition. 12mo. 6 vols. Cloth, 10 00;
sh., 13 50 ; imit. mor., 18 00 ; half calf, 20 00 ;
morocco, 25 00.....................Tree calf, 30 00
Bell's. 16mo. 6 vols. Cloth, 9 00........Mor., 18 00
Verplanck's. 8vo. 3 vols...........Half mor., 50 00
Chalmers's. 8vo. 8 vols. Calf, 40 00.Cf. ext., 45 00
Alex. Dyce. 8vo. 9 vols. 1866......... .Calf, 60 00
Boydell's Illust. ed. 8vo. 2 vols. Cloth, 20 00 ;
1 vol. ed...........................Cloth, 12 00
Knight, Dyce, Collier, Halliwell, and Richard-
son. 16mo. 8 vols. Cloth, 12 00 ; half calf,
24 00.............................Full calf, 28 00
Knight's original Illustrated edition. 8vo.
8 vols. 1839. Tree calf, red mor., 175 00 ;
mor. extra, crushed levant, 200 00
Knight's new ed. 8vo. 8 vols. Cloth, 40 00 ;
half calf, 60 00.......................Tree calf, 90 00
Bowdler's Family. 8vo. 8 vols. 1827....Calf, 40 00
Valpy's. 16mo. 15 vols. Half calf, 45 00 ;
Full calf, 50 00
Hudson's. 12mo. 11 vols...............Cloth, 22 00
Staunton's. 8vo. 3 vols. Cloth, 22 50 ; half
calf, 30 00 ; tree calf, 42 50........Morocco, 45 00
Reproduction of First Folio. 1623..Hf. mor., 40 00
Fac-simile Reprint of First Folio. 1623.
8vo.........................Half vellum, 20 00
A Reduced Fac-simile Reprint. Small 8vo.
Half roan, 4 20
Cornwall's. 8vo. 3 vols........Half morocco, 35 00
Pickering's. 12mo. 11 vols....Half morocco, 45 00
Variorum. 12mo. 21 vols.........Old calf, 60 00
Richard Grant White. Cr. 8vo. 12 vols. Cl., 24 00
Half calf, 36 00
16mo. 12 vols. Cloth, 18 00 ; half calf, 36 00 ;
calf, 48 00.......................Morocco, 54 00
Concordance to Shakespeare. By Mrs. H. H.
Furness. Poems.......................... 4 00
Shakespeare's Concordance. By M. C. Clarke.
8vo. Cloth, 9 00 ; half calf, 12 00..Full calf, 15 00
Shakespeare Society Papers. 8vo. 18 vols.
Tree calf, 175 00
Shelley, Percy Bysshe. Works. 16mo. 3 vols.
Cloth, 3 75 ; half calf, 7 50..........Full calf, 11 25
Sheridan's Works. 8vo. 2 vols. Hf. cf., 12 00 ;
Tree calf, 16 00
Shyp of Fooles (The). Cr. 4to. 2 vols. Cloth,
12 00 ; half mor., 24 00 ; half vellum, 30 00 ;
Morocco, 35 00
Simms, William Gilmore. Novels. 12mo. 17
vols. Cloth, 30 00..................Half calf, 50 00
Smiles. Lives of the Engineers. 8vo. 4 vols.
Half calf, 40 00.....................Full calf, 50 00
Cr. 8vo. 5 vols. Cloth, 12 50, half calf, 22 50 ;
Tree calf, 27 50
Smith, Rev. Sydney. Works. 8vo. 6 vols.
London.........................Tree calf, 40 00
3 vols. Cloth, $4 50................Half calf, 9 00
Smith, Philip. Ancient History. 8vo. Cloth,
10 50 ; sheep, 13 50 ; half morocco, 15 00 ;
Half calf, 18 00
Smith, William. Concise Bible Dictionary. 8vo.
Cloth, 4 50 ; sheep, 5 50...........Half calf, 6 50
Dic. of Biblical Antiquities and Biography.
8vo. 3 vols. Cloth, 18 00..........Half calf, 24 00
Dic. of Greek and Roman Biogr. and Mythol.
8vo. 3 vols......................Half calf, 24 00
Dic. of Greek and Roman Geogr. 8vo. 2 vols.
Half calf, 16 00
Dic. of Greek and Roman Antiquities. 8vo.
1 vol.............................Half calf, 8 00
Classic. Dic. of Biogr., Mythol., and Geog. 8vo.
1 vol.................................Sheep, 8 00
Ancient Atlas. Folio. 5 parts. 35 00 ; half
Morocco, 40 00
Smollett's Works. 8vo. 8 vols. Half roan,
28 00 ; half calf, 40 00............Tree calf, 60 00
Southey's Commonplace Book. 8vo. 4 vols.
Full calf, 25 00
The Doctor. 8vo....................Half calf, 8 50
Sparks. American Biography. 16mo. 10 vols.
Cloth, 12 50......................Half calf, 25 00
Spencer, Herbert. Philosophical Works. Cr.
8vo. 10 vols. Cloth, 21 25........Half calf, 44 00
Spenser, Edmund. Poetical Works. 8vo. 5 vols.
Half calf, 17 50....................Full calf, 25 00

PRICE

Spon's Dictionary of Engineering. 8vo. 8 vols.
Cloth, $40 00
Sterne, Laurence. Works. 8vo. 4 vols. Half
roan, 15 00; half mor., 21 00......Tree calf, 25 00
Strickland, Agnes. Lives of the Queens of Eng-
land. 12mo. 6 vols. Cloth, 12 00; half calf,
24 00; full calf, 30 00................Tree calf, 35 00
8vo. 8 vols. Cloth, 20 00; half calf. 40 00;
full calf, 45 00.....................Tree calf, 50 00
Strutt, J. Dress and Habits of People in Eng-
land. 4to. 2 vols............Half morocco, 75 00
Antiquities. 4to. 1 vol.........Half morocco, 75 00
Swift's Poetical Works. 12mo. 3 vols.Half calf, 15 00
Choice Works. Cr. 8vo..................Cloth, 3 00
Sybel, Heinr. v. History of French Revolution.
8vo. 4 vols......................Half calf, 30 00
Syntax's (Dr.) Tour. 12mo. Cloth, 3 00; half
calf, 5 00.........................Full calf, 6 50
Taine, Henri. Works. Cr. 8vo. 12 vols. Cl.,
30 00............................Half calf, 60 00
English Literature. 8vo. 4 vols. Cloth, 10 00;
half calf, 18 00; tree calf, 24 00 ..Extra calf, 35 00
8vo. 2 vols. Cloth, 7 50; half calf, 13 50;
Tree calf, 18 00
Cr. 8vo. 3 vols........................Cloth, 7 50
Taylor, Bayard. Works. Household edition.
12mo. 15 vols. Cloth, 30 00.......Half calf, 56 00
People's edition. 12mo. 15 vols.........Cloth, 22 50
Translation of Faust. 8vo. 2 vols. Cloth,
10 00; half calf, 20 00.............Morocco, 27 00
12mo. 2 vols. Cl., 5 00; half calf, 9 00..Mor., 12 00
Tennyson, Alfred. Works. 8vo. 6 vols. Cloth,
21 00; half calf, 33 00..........Half Russia, 36 00
Cabinet edition. 16mo. 10 vols. Cloth, 15 00;
French morcoco, 20 00
Fireside ed. 16mo. 10 vols. Cloth, 10 00; half
calf, 25 00........................Morocco, 35 00
Faringford edition. 16mo. 2 vols. Cloth,
5 00; half calf, 9 00..............Morocco, 12 00
Crown edition. 12mo. 2 vols. Cloth, 6 00;
half calf, 11 00.............Morocco antique, 14 00
Testament, New. 4to. Morocco, 50 00; cr. mor.,
60 00................Levant morocco, clasp, 70 00
4to. 2 vols. Cloth, 12 00; half calf, 16 00; full
calf, 18 00........................Morocco, 20 00
Thackeray, William M. Works. 8vo. 22 vols.
Cloth, 66 00; half calf, 100 00; tree calf,
125 00........................Tree calf, extra, 150 00
Cabinet edition. 8vo. 22 vols. Cloth, 44 00;
half calf, 75 00............Half red morocco, 84 00
Crown edition. 8vo. 11 vols..........Cloth, 33 75
Kensington edition. Cr. 8vo. 12 vols. Cloth,
24 00............................Half calf, 54 00
Osgood's ed. 12mo. 11 vols. Cloth, 13 75;
Half calf, 33 00
Thiers, Adolphe. French Revolution. 8vo. 4
vols. Cloth, 18 00................Half calf, 16 00
8vo. 2 vols. Cloth, 5 00...........Half calf, 10 00
History of the Consulate and the Empire. 8vo.
10 vols. Half calf, 60 00...........Full calf, 70 00
The same. 8vo. 5 vols...............Cloth, 12 50
Thirlwall's History of Greece. 8vo. 8 vols.
Half calf, 35 00
Thompson, W. M. The Land and the Book.
12mo. 2 vols.......................Cloth, 5 00
Thoms. Early English Prose Romances. 12mo.
3 vols.........................Half roan, 10 50
Ticknor (George). Life, Letters, and Journals.
8vo. 2 vols........................Cloth, 6 00
History of Spanish Literature. 8vo. 3 vols.
Cloth, 10 00 ....Half morocco, 25 00
Turbervile. Tragical Tales. 1 vol. 1585.
Old calf, 25 00
Turner's History of England. 8vo. 9 vols. 1825.
Full old calf, 36 00

PRICE

Tyndall, John. Works. 12mo. 6 vols. Cloth,
10 25......................Half calf, $22 50
Ueberweg's History of Philosophy. New ed.
2 vols ....Cloth, 5 00
Universal Songster. 8vo. 3 vols. Half mor.,
18 00..........................Half calf, 20 00
Ure's Dictionary. 8vo. 3 vols. Cloth, 15 00;
sheep, 18 00................Half morocco, 24 00
8vo. 3 vols. 6th ed. Cloth, 25 00.Half Russ., 30 00
Vasari's Lives of the Painters. 12mo. 5 vols.
Half calf, 15 00
Vaughan, Robert. Revolutions in English Hist.
8vo. 3 vols.....................Tree calf, 20 00
Voltaire, M. de. Complete Works. 12mo. 35
vols.........................Full calf, 60 00
Waagen, Dr. Treasures and Cabinets of Art.
8vo. 4 vols.....................Half calf, 25 00
Walpole, Horace. Works. 1840-'59. Best edition.
8vo. 25 vols....................Tree calf, 175 00
Walton's Angler. 8vo. 2 vols. 1836..Full mor., 75 00
War between Mexico and the United States.
Folio. Colored Plates........Half morocco, 50 00
Warburton, Eliot. Memoirs of Prince Rupert.
8vo. 3 vols....................Half calf, 15 00
Watt's Dictionary of Chemistry. 8vo. 7 vols.
Cloth, 77 00...................Half Russia, 100 00
Webster, Daniel. Works. 8vo. 6 vols. Cloth,
15 00...........................Half calf, 30 00
Webster's Unabridged Dictionary. 4to. Sheep,
12 00; half mor., 13 50; Russ., 16 00; calf,
18 00...........................Morocco, 20 00
Whittier, John G. Poems. Merriam edition.
12mo. 2 vols. Cloth, 5 00; half calf, 9 00;
Morocco, 12 00
Prose Works. 12mo. 2 vols. Cloth, 5 00;
half calf, 9 00...................Morocco, 12 00
Works. 4 vols. 12mo. Cloth, 10 00; half
calf, 18 00......................Morocco, 24 00
Wilkinson, Sir Gardner. Ancient Egyptians.
8vo. 5 vols......................Full calf, 110 00
Williams, S. W. Chinese Dictionary...... .. 30 00
Wilson and Bonaparte. American Ornithology.
4 vols. One volume of plates and three of text.
8vo. of text and folio Atlas of Plates. Cloth,
gilt top, 95 00.................Half morocco, 100 00
Wilson, Prof. Works. Small 8vo. 12 vols.
Half calf, 45 00
Wilson's Tales of the Border. 12mo. 12 vols.
Cloth, 15 00.....................Half roan, 24 00
Wilson, Prof. Noctes Ambrosianæ. Cr. 8vo.
6 vols. Cloth, 10 50..............Half calf, 21 00
Winkelmann, John. Ancient Art. 8vo. 4 vols.
Cloth, 20 00
Winkle's Cathedrals of England and Wales.
8vo. 3 vols...................Half morocco, 40 00
Woltmann (Dr. Alford). Holbein and his Time.
Sm. 4to. Cloth, 10 00.............Morocco, 15 00
Wood, J. G. Natural History. 8vo. 3 vols.
Cloth, 21 00; half calf, 28 50.....Tree calf, 40 00
Natural History of Man. 8vo. 2 vols. Cloth,
14 00; half calf, 19 00...........Tree calf, 27 00
New Illust. Natural History. 1 vol. 8vo. Cl.,
7 00; half calf, 10 00...........Tree calf, 15 00
Woodward and Cates. Encyclopædia of Chro-
nology. 8vo. Cloth, 15 00......Half Russia, 21 00
National Architect. 4to..........Half morocco, 12 00
Wordsworth, C. Greece, Pictorial, Descriptive,
and Historical. 8vo. 1840........Morocco, 25 00
Wordsworth, W. Poetical Works. 16mo. 6
vols...........................Cloth, 7 50
Wright's Womankind in Western Europe. Sm.
4to.............................Cloth, 8 00
Zoölogy. The Gardens and Menagerie of the
Zoölogical Society delineated. 8vo. 3 vols.
Half morocco, 12 00

LIBRARY OF CHOICE NOVELS.

IRE AND FLAME.

FROM THE GERMAN OF

LEVIN SCHÜCKING.

TRANSLATED BY

EVA M. JOHNSON.

NEW YORK·
D. APPLETON & COMPANY,
549 AND 551 BROADWAY.

A

MONTHLY MISCELLANY OF POPULAR LITERATURE.

NEW SERIES.

Twenty-five Cents per Number. Three Dollars per Annum.

APPLETONS' JOURNAL is now published monthly; it is devoted to popular literature and all matters of taste and general culture, and published at a price to bring it within the reach of all classes. It contains superior fiction, in the form of serials and short stories; papers graphically descriptive of picturesque places; articles upon men of note, and upon the habits of different peoples; essays upon household and social topics; articles of travel and adventure; scientific and industrial articles written in a graphic and popular style, etc. In brief, the aim is to be comprehensive, including in the plan all branches of literature and all themes of interest to intelligent readers.

WRITERS AND FEATURES.

Among the contributors and features are the following:

JULIAN HAWTHORNE.—Mr. Hawthorne, whose "Saxon Sketches" have been among the most brilliant and pungent essays of the time, will give a series of graphic delineations of London Suburban Life

ALBERT RHODES —This accomplished essayist will appear in papers on social life and foreign incidents.

CHRISTIAN REID.—Stories and sketches from this accomplished Southern writer will appear.

ALBERT F WEBSTER.—Stories, and descriptive sketches of Far-Western places, are expected from Mr. Webster's graphic pen

JUNIUS HENRI BROWNE.—Mr. Browne's brilliant society sketches will frequently appear.

M. E. W. S.—This accomplished writer will continue her sparkling papers on social topics, and her eminently picturesque stories

KAMBA THORPE —"Little Joanna," by this author, who is a Southern lady, was one of the most charming novels of 1875. Contributions from her pen will appear.

EDGAR FAWCETT.—Mr. Fawcett's poems are remarkable for their affluent beauty. He will contribute short stories as well as poems -

KATHARINE S MACQUOID (author of the famous novel, "Patty ") will send from abroad, specially for the JOURNAL, stories and descriptive sketches.

GEORGE M. TOWLE, whose treatment of biographic and historic subjects is well known.

ALFRED H. GUERNSEY (for many years editor of *Harper's Magazine*) will contribute papers on distinguished names in literature.

MAURICE THOMPSON.—This gentleman's papers of adventure in Florida have been greatly admired. Similar sketches are expected from his pen.

ART-LIFE IN ROME.—Mr. James Freeman, an American artist who has resided for thirty years in Rome, and during that time met many of the most distinguished men and women of the period, will give his reminiscences and experiences, which are of the most entertaining character.

HORACE E. SCUDDER.—Mr. Scudder's "Heirs of the Bodley Estate" is one of the best of recent short stories Similar productions may be looked for.

LUCY H. HOOPER.—Mrs. Hooper's articles from Paris are noted as among the most brilliant of current magazine papers

CONSTANCE FENIMORE WOOLSON.—Stories and poems will appear from this delightful writer.

JOHN ESTEN COOKE.—This well-known Southern writer will contribute.

WIRT SIKES —Mr. Sikes's papers are always graphic and eminently readable.

HOWARD GLYNDON.—Poems will appear from this gifted writer.

JOEL BENTON is among our regular contributors.

PAUL H. HAYNE, the best known of the Southern poets will also contribute.

These are names that appear in current numbers of the JOURNAL; but our plan necessarily opens the pages of the magazine to ALL WRITERS OF NOTE.

TERMS: Three dollars per annum, in advance, postage prepaid to all subscribers in the United States; or Twenty-five Cents per number. A Club of Four Yearly Subscriptions will entitle the sender to an extra subscription gratis; that is, five copies will be sent one year for twelve dollars. Subscriptions received for six months.

The JOURNAL and any of the other magazines will be sent one year, postage prepaid within the United States, at a discount of 10 per cent. from the regular subscription rates.

For $7.20, APPLETONS' JOURNAL and THE POPULAR SCIENCE MONTHLY (full price, eight dollars) postage prepaid to all subscribers in the United States.

D. APPLETON & CO., Publishers,

549 & 551 BROADWAY, NEW YORK.

NEW NOVELS FOR SUMMER READING.

THE LAND OF THE SKY;

Or, ADVENTURES IN MOUNTAIN BY-WAYS. By CHRISTIAN REID, author of "A Question of Honor," etc. 1 vol., paper covers, illustrated, 75 cents; cloth, $1.25.

The "Land of the Sky" is part story and part adventure, it relates the vicissitudes and experiences, humorous and otherwise, of a number of travelers in a summer jaunt amid the mountains of North Carolina. There is some good character-sketching, not a few amusing incidents, the thread of a love-story, and some capital descriptive passages.

II.

THE FORTUNES OF MISS FOLLEN.

By Mrs. GOODWIN-TALCOTT, author of "Madge," "Sherbrooke," etc. 1 vol., 12mo. Cloth, $1.50.

In the "Fortunes of Miss Follen" there are presented delightful views of the beautiful and picturesque in German country life and manners. Interwoven with these is a serial story of pure and devoted love, as manifested in the noblest characters. Written with fine taste by an accomplished pen, it forms a charming work that will interest and satisfy all readers.

III.

COMIN' THRO' THE RYE.

One vol., 8vo. Paper covers, 75 cents.

"A very amusing and well-written story. The history of the youth of the Adairs is extremely amusing, and told in a bright and witty manner. . . . One of the pleasantest novels of the season."—*Morning Post.*

"It is a clever novel, never dull, and the story never hangs fire."—*Standard.*

IV.

A CHEAP EDITION OF A POPULAR NOVEL.

BRESSANT.

A NOVEL. By JULIAN HAWTHORNE. 1 vol., 8vo. Paper, 75 cents.

"'Bressant' is a work that demonstrates the fitness of its author to bear the name of Hawthorne. More in praise need not be said; but, if the promise of the book shall not utterly fade and vanish, Julian Hawthorne, in the maturity of his power, will rank side by side with him who has hitherto been peerless, but whom we must hereafter call the 'Elder Hawthorne.'"—*New York Times.*

V.

GEIER-WALLY,

A TALE OF THE TYROL. By WILHELMINA VON HILLERN. Handy Volume Edition. 8vo. Paper covers, 50 cents; cloth, red edges, $1.25.

Auerbach, the great German novelist, in a recent letter to a lady in this country, pronounces this work "*the best short story in modern German literature.*"

"'Geier-Wally' is a wild and romantic story, highly descriptive of rustic life among the Tyrolese, and cannot fail to interest the reader."—*Fort Wayne Journal.*

"A very singular, but a very powerful story. It has great merit aside from its dramatic story."—*Liberal Christian.*

VI.

THE LITTLE JOANNA.

A NOVEL. By KAMBA THORPE. 1 vol., 8vo. Paper covers, 60 cents.

"Little Joanna" is a quiet but very charming novel, written in a delightful style, and marked by a great deal of excellent character-drawing. A distinguished Southern author writes to the publishers as follows: "Allow me to say how much I like 'Little Joanna'—I have enjoyed every page of it—and that it is the best story of Southern life *as it now is* with which I am acquainted.

D. APPLETON & CO., Publishers,

549 & 551 BROADWAY, N. Y.

Lightning Source UK Ltd.
Milton Keynes UK
UKHW010259231118
332756UK00012B/1824/P